PRAISE FOR

Chris Colfer

#1 New York Time
IndieBound Be
USA Today Be
Wall Street Journal Bestselling Author

"**Will please fans of the series** while offering
an entry for new readers as well."
—*Booklist*

"A **thoroughly satisfying** adventure."
—*Publishers Weekly*

"A **dynamic, engrossing fantasy** that will have readers
staying up late and dreaming big."
—*School Library Journal*

"In the Land of Stories, Colfer showcases his talent for
crafting **fancifully imaginative plots and
multidimensional characters**."
—*Los Angeles Times*

"There's **more in Colfer's magic kingdoms
than Disney** has dreamt of."
—*USA Today*

"It will hit big with its **combination of earnestness**

A TALE OF MAGIC...

BY CHRIS COLFER

The Land of Stories series:

The Wishing Spell

The Enchantress Returns

A Grimm Warning

Beyond the Kingdoms

An Author's Odyssey

Worlds Collide

The Ultimate Book Hugger's Guide

A Treasury of Classic Fairy Tales

The Mother Goose Diaries

Queen Red Riding Hood's Guide to Royalty

The Curvy Tree

Trollbella Throws a Party

A Tale of Magic ... series:

A Tale of Magic ...

A Tale of Witchcraft ...

CHRIS COLFER

ILLUSTRATED BY BRANDON DORMAN

LITTLE, BROWN BOOKS FOR YOUNG READERS

LITTLE, BROWN BOOKS FOR YOUNG READERS

First published in the US in 2019 by Little, Brown and Company
First published in Great Britain in 2019 by Hodder & Stoughton
This paperback edition published in 2020

5 7 9 10 8 6 4

A CIP catalogue record for this book
is available from the British Library.

ISBN 978 1 510 20212 2

Typeset in Bulmer MT by Initial Typesetting Services

Printed and bound in Great Britain by Clays Ltd, Elcograf S.p.A.

The paper and board used in this book
are made from wood from responsible sources.

MIX
Paper from
responsible sources
FSC
www.fsc.org   FSC® C104740

Little, Brown Books for Young Readers
An imprint of
Hachette Children's Group
Part of Hodder & Stoughton
Carmelite House
50 Victoria Embankment
London, EC4Y 0DZ

An Hachette UK Company
www.hachette.co.uk

www.hachettechildrens.co.uk

To all the brave people who dared to be themselves during a time that didn't accept them. Thanks to you, I get to be me.

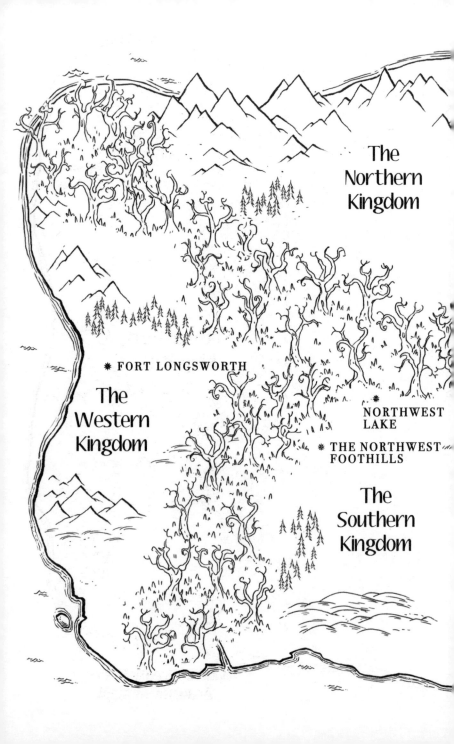

The
Northern
Kingdom

✳ FORT LONGSWORTH

The
Western
Kingdom

✳ NORTHWEST
LAKE

✳ THE NORTHWEST
FOOTHILLS

The
Southern
Kingdom

* TINZEL HEIGHTS

* APPLETON VILLAGE

* IRONHAND

The
In-Between

The Eastern
Kingdom

THE NORTHEAST *
PLAINS

CHARIOT HILLS

*

Madame Weatherberry's
Academy of Magic

AN UNEXPECTED AUDIENCE

Magic was outlawed in all four kingdoms—and that was putting it lightly. Legally, magic was the worst criminal act a person could commit, and socially, there was nothing considered more despicable. In most areas, just being *associated* with a convicted witch or warlock was an offense punishable by death.

In the Northern Kingdom, perpetrators and their families were put on trial and promptly burned at the stake. In the Eastern Kingdom, very little evidence was needed to sentence the accused and their loved ones to hang at the gallows. And in the Western Kingdom, suspected witches and warlocks were drowned without any trial whatsoever.

The executions were rarely committed by law enforcement or kingdom officials. Most commonly, the punishments were carried out by mobs of angry citizens who took the law into their own hands. Although frowned upon, the brutal sport was completely tolerated by the kingdoms' sovereigns. In truth, the leaders were delighted their people had something besides government to direct their anger toward. So the monarchs welcomed the distraction and even encouraged it during times of political unrest.

"He or she who chooses a path of magic has chosen a path of condemnation," King Nobleton of the North proclaimed. Meanwhile, *his* negligent choices were causing the worst famine in his kingdom's history.

"We must never show sympathy to people with such abominable priorities," Queen Endustria of the East declared, and then immediately raised taxes to finance a summer palace.

"Magic is an insult to God and nature, and a danger to morality as we know it," King Warworth of the West remarked. Luckily for him, the statement distracted his people from rumors about the eight illegitimate children he had fathered with eight different mistresses.

Once a witch or warlock was exposed, persecution was nearly impossible to escape. Many fled into the thick and dangerous forest known as the In-Between that grew between borders. Unfortunately, the In-Between was home to dwarfs, elves, goblins, trolls, ogres, and all the other species humankind had banished over the years. The witches and warlocks seeking asylum in the woods usually found a quick and violent demise at the hands of a barbaric creature.

The only mercy whatsoever for witch-and-warlock-kind (if it could even be considered *mercy*) was found in the Southern Kingdom.

As soon as King Champion XIV inherited the throne from his father, the late Champion XIII, his first royal decree was to abolish the death penalty for convicted practitioners of magic. Instead, the offenders were sentenced to life imprisonment with hard labor (and they were reminded every day how *grateful* they should be). The king didn't amend the law purely out of the goodness of his heart, but as an attempt to make peace with a traumatic memory.

When Champion was a child, his own mother was beheaded for a "suspected interest" in magic. The charge came from Champion XIII himself, so no one thought to question the accusation or investigate the queen's innocence, although Champion XIII's motives were questioned on the day following his wife's execution, when he married a much younger and prettier woman. Since the queen's untimely end, Champion XIV had counted down the days until he could avenge his mother by destroying his father's legacy. And as soon as the crown was placed on his head, Champion XIV devoted most of his reign to erasing Champion XIII from the Southern Kingdom's history.

Now in old age, King Champion XIV spent the majority of his time doing the least he possibly could. His royal decrees had been reduced to grunts and eye rolls. Instead of royal visitations, the king lazily waved to crowds from the safety of a speeding carriage. And the closest thing he made to royal statements anymore were complaints about his castle's halls being "too long" and the staircases "too steep."

Champion made a hobby of avoiding people—especially his self-righteous family. He ate his meals alone, went to bed early, slept in late, and cherished his lengthy afternoon naps (and God have mercy on the poor soul that woke him before he was ready).

Although on one particular afternoon, the king was prematurely woken, not by a careless grandchild or clumsy chambermaid, but by a sudden change in the weather. Champion awoke with fright to heavy raindrops thudding against his chamber windows and powerful winds whistling down his chimney. It had been such a sunny and clear day when he went to bed, so the storm was quite a surprise for the groggy sovereign.

"I've risen," Champion announced.

The king waited for the nearest servant to scurry in and help him down from his tall bed, but his call was unanswered.

Champion aggressively cleared his throat. "I said *I've risen*," he called again, but strangely, there was still no response.

The king's joints cracked as he begrudgingly climbed

out of bed, and he mumbled a series of curse words as he hobbled across the stone floor to retrieve his robe and slippers. Once he was dressed, Champion burst through his chamber doors, intending to scold the first servant he laid eyes on.

"Why is no one responding? What could possibly be more important than—"

Champion fell silent and looked around in disbelief. The drawing room outside his chambers was usually bustling with maids and butlers, but now it was completely empty. Even the soldiers who guarded the doors day and night had abandoned their posts.

The king peered into the hallway beyond the drawing room, but it was just as empty. Not only was it vacant of servants and soldiers, but all the *light* had disappeared, too. Every candle in the chandeliers and all the torches on the walls had been extinguished.

"Hello?" Champion called down the hall. "Is anyone there?" But all he heard was his own voice echoing back to him.

The king cautiously moved through the castle searching for another living soul, but he only found more and more darkness at every turn. It was incredibly unsettling—he had lived in the castle since he was a small boy and had never seen it so lifeless. Champion looked through every window he passed, but the rain and fog blocked his view of anything outside.

Eventually the king rounded the corner of a long hallway and spotted flickering lights coming from his private study. The door was wide open and someone was enjoying a fire inside. It would have been a very inviting sight if the circumstances weren't so eerie. With each step he took, the king's heart beat faster and faster, and he anxiously peered into the doorway to see who or what was waiting inside.

"Oh, look! The king is awake!"

"Finally."

"Now, now, girls. We must be respectful to His Majesty."

The king found two young girls and a beautiful woman sitting on the sofa in his study. Upon his entrance, they quickly rose from their seats and bowed in his direction.

"Your Majesty, what a pleasure to make your acquaintance," the woman said.

She wore an elegant purple gown that matched her large bright eyes, and curiously, only one glove, which covered her left arm. Her dark hair was tucked beneath an elaborate fascinator with flowers, feathers, and a short veil that fell over her face. The girls couldn't have been older than ten, and wore plain white robes and cloth headwraps.

"Who the heck are you?" Champion asked.

"Oh, forgive me," the woman said. "I'm Madame Weatherberry and these are my apprentices, Miss Tangerina Turkin and Miss Skylene Lavenders. I hope you don't mind that we made ourselves at home in your study. We've traveled an awfully long way to be here and couldn't resist a nice fire while we waited."

Madame Weatherberry seemed to be a very warm and charismatic woman. She was the last person the king had expected to find in the abandoned castle, which in many ways made the woman *and* the situation even stranger. Madame Weatherberry extended her right arm to shake Champion's hand, but he didn't accept the friendly gesture. Instead, the monarch looked his unexpected guests up and down and took a full step backward.

The girls giggled and eyed the paranoid king, as if they were looking into his soul and found it laughable.

"This is a private room in a royal residence!" Champion reprimanded them. "How dare you enter without permission! I could have you whipped for this!"

"Please pardon our intrusion," Madame Weatherberry said. "It's rather out of character for us to barge into someone's home unannounced, but I'm afraid I had no choice. You see, I've been writing to your secretary, Mr. Fellows, for quite some time. I was hoping to schedule an audience with you, but unfortunately, Mr. Fellows never responded to any of my letters—he's a rather inefficient man, if you don't mind me saying it. Perhaps it's time to replace him? Anyway, there's a very timely matter I'm eager to discuss with you, so here we are."

"How did this woman get inside?" the king shouted into the empty castle. "Where in God's name is everyone?!"

"I'm afraid all your subjects are indisposed at the moment," Madame Weatherberry informed him.

"What do you mean *indisposed*?" Champion barked.

"Oh, it's nothing to be concerned about—*just a little enchantment to secure our safety*. I promise, all your servants and soldiers will return once we've had time to talk. I find diplomacy is so much easier when there are no distractions, don't you?"

Madame Weatherberry spoke in a calm manner, but one word made Champion's eyes grow wide and his blood pressure soar.

"*Enchantment?*" The king gasped. "You're... you're...*you're a WITCH!*"

Champion pointed his finger at Madame Weatherberry in such a panic he pulled every muscle in his right shoulder. The king groaned as he clutched his arm, and his guests snickered at his dramatic display.

"No, Your Majesty, I am not a *witch*," she said.

"Don't you lie to me, woman!" the king shouted. "Only witches make enchantments!"

"No, Your Majesty, that is not true."

"You're a witch and you've cursed this castle with magic! You'll pay for this!"

"I see listening isn't your strong suit," Madame Weatherberry said. "Perhaps if I repeated myself three times my message would sink in? I find that's a helpful tool with slow learners. Here we go—*I am not a witch. I am not a witch. I am not a—*"

"IF YOU'RE NOT A WITCH, THEN WHAT ARE YOU?"

It didn't matter how loud the king yelled or how

8

agitated he became; Madame Weatherberry's polite demeanor never faded.

"Actually, Your Majesty, that's among the topics I would like to discuss with you this evening," she said. "Now, we don't wish to take any more of your time than necessary. Won't you please have a seat so we can begin?"

As if pulled by an invisible hand, the chair behind the king's desk moved on its own, and Madame Weatherberry gestured for him to sit. Champion wasn't certain he had a choice in the matter, so he took a seat and nervously glanced back and forth at the visitors. The girls sat on the sofa and folded their hands neatly in their laps. Madame Weatherberry sat between her apprentices and flipped her veil upward so she could look the sovereign directly in the eye.

"First, I wanted to thank you, Your Majesty," Madame Weatherberry began. "You're the only ruler in history to show the magical community any mercy— granted, some might say life imprisonment with hard labor is worse than death—but it's still a step in the right direction. And I'm confident we can turn these steps into strides if we just—Your Majesty, is something wrong? I don't seem to have your full attention."

Bizarre buzzing and swishing noises had captured the king's curiosity as she spoke. He looked around the study but couldn't find the source of the odd noises.

"Sorry, I thought I heard something," the king said. "You were saying?"

"I was professing my gratitude for the mercy you've

shown the magical community."

The king grunted with disgust. "Well, you're mistaken if you think I have any empathy for the *magical community*," he scoffed. "On the contrary, I believe magic is just as foul and unnatural as all the other sovereigns do. My concern is with the people who use magic to take advantage of the law."

"And that's commendable, sir," Madame Weatherberry said. "Your devotion to justice is what separates you from all the other monarchs. Now, I'd like to enlighten your perspective on magic, so you may continue making this kingdom a fairer and safer place for *all* your people. After all, justice cannot exist for one if it doesn't exist for everyone."

Their conversation had just begun and the king was already starting to resent it. "What do you mean *enlighten* my perspective?" he sneered.

"Your Majesty, the way magic is criminalized and stigmatized is the greatest injustice of our time. But with the proper modifications and amendments—*and some strategic publicity*—we can change all that. Together, we can create a society that encourages all walks of life and raises them to their greatest potential and—Your Majesty, are you listening? I seem to have lost you again."

Once more, the king was distracted by the mysterious buzzing and swishing sounds. His eyes searched the study more frantically than before and he only heard every other word Madame Weatherberry said.

"I must have misunderstood you," he said. "For a

moment, it sounded as if you were suggesting the *legalization of magic*."

"Oh, there was no misunderstanding," Madame Weatherberry said with a laugh. "The legalization of magic is *exactly* what I'm suggesting."

Champion suddenly sat up in his seat and clenched the armrests of his chair. Madame Weatherberry had his undivided attention now. She couldn't possibly be implying something so ludicrous.

"What is wrong with you, woman?" the king sneered. "Magic can *never* be legalized!"

"Actually, sir, it's very much in the realm of possibility," Madame Weatherberry said. "All that's required is a simple decree that decriminalizes the act and then, in good time, the stigma surrounding it will diminish."

"I would sooner decriminalize murder and thievery!" the king declared. "The Lord clearly states in the Book of Faith that magic is a horrendous sin, and therefore a *crime* in this kingdom! And if crimes didn't have consequences, we would live in utter chaos!"

"That's where you're mistaken, Your Majesty," she said. "You see, magic is *not* the crime the world thinks it is."

"*Of course it is!*" he objected. "I have witnessed magic being used to trick and torment innocent people! I have seen the bodies of children who were slaughtered for potions and spells! I have been to villages plagued by curses and hexes! So don't you dare defend magic to me, Madame! The magical community will never receive an ounce of sympathy or understanding from *this* sovereign!"

Champion couldn't have made his opposition any clearer, but Madame Weatherberry moved to the edge of her seat and smiled as if they had found common ground.

"This may surprise you, sir, but I completely agree," she said.

"You do?" he asked with a suspicious gaze.

"Oh yes, *completely*," she repeated. "I believe those who torment innocent people *should* be punished for their actions—*and harshly*, I might add. There's just one minor flaw in your reasoning. The situations you've witnessed aren't caused by magic but by *witchcraft*."

The king tensed his brow and glanced at Madame Weatherberry as if she were speaking a foreign language. *"Witchcraft?"* he said mockingly. "I've never heard of such a thing."

"Then allow me to explain," Madame Weatherberry said. "Witchcraft is a ghastly and destructive practice. It stems from a dark desire to *deceive* and *disrupt*. Only people with wicked hearts are capable of witchcraft, and believe me, they deserve whatever fate they bring upon themselves. But *magic* is something else entirely. At its core, magic is a pure and positive art form. It's meant to *help* and *heal* those in need and can only come from those with goodness in their hearts."

The king sank back into his chair and held his head, dizzy with confusion.

"Oh dear, I've overwhelmed you," Madame

Weatherberry said. "Let me simplify it for you, then. *Magic is good, magic is good, magic is good. Witchcraft is bad, witchcraft is bad, witchcraft is—*"

"Don't patronize me, woman—I heard you!" the king griped. "Give me a moment to wrap my head around it!"

Champion let out a long sigh and massaged his temples. It was usually difficult for him to process information so shortly after a nap, but this was an entirely different beast. The king covered his eyes and concentrated, as if he were reading a book behind his eyelids.

"You're saying magic is not the same as witchcraft?"

"Correct," Madame Weatherberry said with an encouraging nod. "Apples and oranges."

"And the two are different in nature?"

"Polar opposites, sir."

"So, if not *witches*, what do you call people who practice magic?"

Madame Weatherberry held her head high with pride. "We call ourselves *fairies*, sir."

"Fairies?" the king asked.

"Yes, *fairies*," she repeated. "Now do you understand my desire to enlighten your perspective? The world's concern isn't with fairies who practice magic, it's with witches who commit witchcraft. But tragically, we've been grouped together and condemned as one and the same for centuries. Fortunately, with my guidance and your influence, we are more than capable of rectifying this."

"I'm afraid I disagree," the king said.

13

"I beg your pardon?" Madame Weatherberry replied.

"One man may steal because of greed, and another may steal for survival, but they're both thieves—it doesn't matter if one has *goodness* in his heart."

"But, sir, I thought I made it perfectly clear that witchcraft is the crime, not magic."

"Yes, but *both* have been considered sinful since the beginning of time," Champion went on. "Do you know how difficult it is to redefine something for society? It took me *decades* to convince my kingdom that potatoes aren't poisonous—and people still avoid them in the markets!"

Madame Weatherberry shook her head in disbelief. "Are you comparing an innocent race of people to potatoes, sir?"

"I understand your objective, Madame, but the world isn't ready for it—heck, *I'm* not ready for it! If you want to save the fairies from unfair punishment, then I suggest you teach them to keep quiet and resist the urge to use magic! That would be far easier than convincing a stubborn world to change its ways."

"Resist the *urge*? Sir, you can't be serious!"

"Why not? Normal people live above temptation every day."

"Because you're implying magic comes with an off switch—like it's some sort of *choice*."

"Of course magic is a choice!"

"NO! IT! IS! NOOOOT!"

For the first time since their interaction had begun,

14

Madame Weatherberry's pleasant temperament changed. A shard of deep-seated anger pierced through her cheery disposition and her face fell into a stony, intimidating glare. It was as if Champion were facing a different woman altogether—a woman who should be feared.

"Magic is *not* a choice," Madame Weatherberry said sharply. "*Ignorance* is a choice. *Hatred* is a choice. *Violence* is a choice. But someone's *existence* is never a choice, or a fault, and it's certainly not a crime. You would be wise to educate yourself."

Champion was too afraid to say another word. It may have been his imagination, but the king could have sworn the storm outside was intensifying as Madame Weatherberry's temper rose. It was obviously a state she rarely surrendered to because her apprentices seemed as uneasy as the king. The fairy closed her eyes, took a deep breath, and calmed herself before continuing their discussion.

"Perhaps we should give His Majesty a demonstration," Madame Weatherberry suggested. "Tangerina? Skylene? Will you please show King Champion why magic isn't a choice?"

The apprentices exchanged an eager grin—they had been waiting for this. They hopped to their feet, removed their robes, and unwound their headwraps. Tangerina revealed a dress made from dripping patches of honeycomb and a beehive of bright orange hair that was the home of a live swarm of bumblebees. Skylene uncovered a sapphire bathing suit, and instead of hair, she had a continuous stream of water that flowed down her body, evaporating as it reached her feet.

Champion's mouth dropped open as he laid eyes on what the girls had been concealing. In all his years on the throne, he had never seen magic so materialized in a person's appearance. The mystery of the strange buzzing and swishing noises was solved.

"My God," the king said breathlessly. "Are all fairies like this?"

"Magic affects each of us differently," Madame Weatherberry said. "Some people lead completely normal lives until their magic presents itself, while others show physical traits from the moment they're born."

"That can't be true," the king argued. "If people were born with magical features, the prisons would be filled with infants! And our courts have never imprisoned a baby."

Madame Weatherberry lowered her head and looked to the floor with a sad gaze.

"That's because most fairies are killed or abandoned at birth. Their parents fear the consequences of bringing a magical child into the world, so they do what is necessary to avoid punishment. It was a miracle I found Tangerina and Skylene before they were harmed, but many aren't so lucky. Your Majesty, I understand your reservation, but what's happening to these children is cruel and primitive. Decriminalizing magic is about much more than injustice, it's about *saving innocents*! Surely, you can find sympathy and understanding in your heart for that."

Champion knew he lived in a harsh world, but he had been oblivious to such horrors. He rocked back and forth in his chair as his reluctance waged war with his empathy. Madame Weatherberry could tell she was making progress with the king, so she used a sentiment she had been saving for just the right moment.

"Think how different the world would be if it had a little more compassion for the magical community. Think how different *your* life would be, Your Majesty."

Suddenly, Champion's mind was flooded with memories of his mother. He remembered her face, her smile, her laugh, but most prominently of all, he remembered the tight embrace they had shared just before she was dragged to an untimely death. Despite how rusty his memory had become with age, those images were forever branded in his brain.

"I would like to help you, but decriminalizing magic may be more problematic than productive. Forcing the public to accept what they hate and fear could cause a rebellion! Witch hunts as we know them could escalate into full-fledged genocide!"

"Believe me, I'm no stranger to human nature," Madame Weatherberry said. "The legalization of magic can't be rushed. On the contrary, it must be handled gently, with patience and persistence. If we want to change the world's opinion it must be encouraged, not forced—and nothing encourages people like a good spectacle."

A nervous tension spread over the king's face.

"Spectacle?" he asked fearfully. "What sort of *spectacle* are you planning?"

Madame Weatherberry smiled and her bright eyes grew even brighter—this was the part she had been waiting for.

"When I first met Tangerina and Skylene, they were captives of their own magic," she told him. "No one could get near Tangerina without being attacked by her bees, and poor Skylene was living in a lake because she soaked everything she stepped on. So I took the girls under my wing and taught them to control their magic, and now they're both perfectly functioning young adults. It breaks my heart to think of all the other children out there who are struggling with who or what they are, so I've decided to open my doors and give them a proper education."

"You're going to start a *school*?" the king asked.

"Precisely," she said. "I call it Madame Weatherberry's Academy for Young Practitioners of Magic— although it's still a working title."

"And where will this academy be?" he asked.

"I've recently secured a few acres in the southeast In-Between."

"The *In-Between*?" the king protested. "Woman, are you mad? The In-Between is much too dangerous for children! You can't start a school there!"

"Oh, I won't argue that," Madame Weatherberry said. "The In-Between is exceptionally dangerous for people unfamiliar with its territories. However, there are many members of the magical community, including myself, who have lived quite comfortably in the In-Between for decades. The land I've acquired is very remote and private. I've installed all the proper protections to guarantee my students' safety."

"But how is an academy going to help achieve the legalization of magic?"

"Once I've trained my pupils to master their abilities, we'll slowly introduce ourselves to the world. We'll use our magic to heal the sick and help those in need. After some time, word of our compassion will have spread through the kingdoms. Fairies will become examples of generosity and we'll win people's affection. The world will see all the good that magic has to offer, their opinions on magic will change, and the magical community will finally be embraced."

Champion scratched his chin as he contemplated Madame Weatherberry's lavish plan. Of all the details she had given him, she was forgetting the most important of all—*his* involvement.

"You seem very capable of doing this on your own. What do you want from me?"

"Naturally, I want your consent," she said. "Fairies want to be trusted, and the only way we'll earn trust is by doing things the right way. So I would like your official permission to travel openly through the Southern Kingdom as I recruit students. I would also like your promise that the children and families I encounter will be spared from prosecution. My mission is to offer these youngsters a better life; I don't want to put anyone in legal jeopardy. It'll be very difficult convincing parents to let their children attend a school for magic, but having their sovereign's blessing will make it much easier—especially if that blessing is in writing."

Madame Weatherberry waved a hand over the king's desk and a golden piece of parchment appeared before him. Everything she had requested was already written out—all she needed was the king's signature. Champion anxiously rubbed his legs as he read the document over and over again.

"This could go wrong in so many ways," the king said. "If my subjects found out I gave a witch—excuse me—a *fairy* permission to take their children to a magical school, there would be rioting in the streets! My people would want my head on a platter!"

"In that case, tell your people you ordered me to *cleanse* your kingdom of the magical children," she suggested. "Say that in an effort to create a future without magic, you had the young rounded up and taken away. I've found that the more vulgar a declaration, the more humankind embraces it."

"Still, this is a gamble for both of us! Having my permission doesn't guarantee your protection. Aren't you worried about your safety?"

"Your Majesty, I'll remind you that I made the staff of an entire castle disappear into thin air, Tangerina controls a swarm of bees, and Skylene has enough water flowing through her body to flood a canyon. We can protect ourselves."

Despite her testimony, the king appeared more fearful than convinced. Madame Weatherberry was so close to getting what she wanted—she had to extinguish Champion's doubt before it overpowered him. Luckily, she still had one more weapon in her arsenal to gain his approval.

"Tangerina? Skylene? Would you please give the king and me a moment alone?" she asked.

It was evident Tangerina and Skylene didn't want to miss any part of Madame Weatherberry's conversation with the king, but they respected their chaperone's wishes and waited in the hall. Once the door was shut behind them, Madame Weatherberry leaned toward Champion and looked deep into his eyes with a grave expression.

"Sir, are you aware of the *Northern Conflict*?" she asked.

If the king's bulging eyes were any indication, Champion was much more than *aware*. Just the mention of the Northern Conflict had a paralyzing effect on him and he struggled to respond.

"How—how—how on earth do you know about that?" he inquired. "That is a classified matter!"

"The magical community may be small and divided, but word spreads quickly when one of us is…well, *causing a scene*."

"*Causing a scene*? That's what you people call it?!"

"Your Majesty, please keep your voice down," she

said, and then nodded to the door. "Bad news has an easy way of finding young ears. My girls would worry themselves sick if they knew about what we're discussing."

Champion could relate because he was starting to feel sick himself. Being reminded of the subject was like being reacquainted with a ghost—a ghost he thought had been put to rest.

"Why are you even mentioning such a horrible thing?" he asked.

"Because right now there is no guarantee the Northern Conflict won't cross the border and arrive at your front door," Madame Weatherberry warned him.

The king shook his head. "That won't happen. King Nobleton assured me he took care of the situation. He gave us his word."

"King Nobleton lied to you! He told the other sovereigns he has the conflict under control because he's humiliated by how severe the situation has become! Over half the Northern Kingdom has perished! Three-quarters of his army are gone and what's left shrinks daily! The king blames the loss on *famine* because he's terrified he'd lose the throne if his people knew the truth!"

All the color faded from Champion's face and he trembled in his seat. "Well? Can anything be done? Or am I just supposed to sit and wait to perish, myself?"

"Recently, there's been hope," Madame Weatherberry said. "Nobleton has appointed a new commander,

General White, to lead the remaining defenses. So far, the general has sequestered the situation more successfully than his predecessors."

"Well, that's something," the king said.

"I pray General White will resolve the matter, but you must be prepared if he fails," she said. "And should the conflict cross into the Southern Kingdom, having an academy of trained fairies in your corner could be *very* beneficial to you."

"You believe your *students* could stop the conflict?" he asked with desperate eyes.

"Yes, Your Majesty," she said with complete confidence. "I believe my future students will accomplish many things the world considers impossible today. But first, they'll need a place to learn and a teacher to guide them."

Champion went very still as he thought the proposition over.

"Yes...yes, they could be *extremely* beneficial," he said to himself. "Naturally, I'll have to consult my Advisory Council of High Justices before giving you an answer."

"Actually, sir," Madame Weatherberry said, "I believe this is a matter we can settle without consulting the High Justices. They tend to be a rather old-fashioned group and I would hate for their stubborn tendencies to get in our way. Besides, there have been *discussions* circulating the country that you should be aware of. Many of your people are convinced the High Justices are the true rulers of the Southern Kingdom, and you are nothing but their puppet."

"Why, that's outrageous!" the king exclaimed. "I'm the sovereign—my will is law!"

"Indeed," she said. "Any able-minded person knows that. However, the rumors remain. If I were you, I would start disproving those nasty theories by defying the High Justices every so often. And I can't think of a better way to practice that than by signing the document before you."

Champion nodded as he considered her warning, and eventually, her persuasion guided him to a decision.

"Very well," the king said. "You may recruit *two students* from the Southern Kingdom for your school of magic—one boy and one girl—but that is all. And you must receive written permission from your pupils' guardians or they are not allowed to attend your school."

"I confess I was hoping for a better arrangement, but I will take what I can get," Madame Weatherberry said. "You have a deal."

The king retrieved a quill and ink from inside his desk and made his amendments to the golden document. Once he was finished with his corrections, Champion signed the agreement and authenticated it with a wax seal of his family's royal crest. Madame Weatherberry jumped to her feet and clapped in celebration.

"Oh, what a wonderful moment this is! Tangerina? Skylene? Come in! The king has granted our request!"

The apprentices hurried into the study and became giddy at the sight of the king's signature. Tangerina rolled up the document and Skylene tied it with a silver ribbon.

"Thank you so much, Your Majesty," Madame Weatherberry said, lowering her fascinator's veil over her face. "I promise you won't regret this!"

The king snorted skeptically and rubbed his tired eyes. "I pray you know what you're doing, because if you don't, I'll tell the kingdom I was bewitched and bribed by a—"

Champion gasped when he looked up. Madame Weatherberry and her apprentices had vanished into thin air. The king hurried to the doorway to see if they had dashed into the hallway, but it was just as empty as before. Within moments of their departure, all the candles and all the torches throughout the castle were magically relit. Footsteps echoed down the halls as the servants and soldiers returned to their duties. The king went to a window and noticed that even the storm had disappeared, but Champion found little comfort in the clearing weather.

On the contrary, it was impossible for the king to feel anything but dread as he skimmed the northern skies, knowing that somewhere on the horizon, the true storm awaited....

CHAPTER ONE

BOOKS AND BREAKFAST

It was no mystery why all the monks in the Southern Kingdom's capital were hard of hearing. Every morning at dawn, the city of Chariot Hills was subjected to ten minutes of uninterrupted, ear-piercing cathedral bells. Like the tremors of an earthquake, the clanking tones rattled the town square, then pulsated through the city streets and shook the surrounding villages. The monks purposely rang the bells in a manic and irregular manner to ensure every citizen was awake and participating in the Lord's day, and once they finished waking all the sinners, the monks hurried back to bed.

Although not everyone in the area was affected by the cathedral bells. The monks would have been furious to learn a young woman in the countryside managed to sleep through their obnoxious ringing.

Fourteen-year-old Brystal Evergreen awoke the same way she did every morning—to the sound of banging on her bedroom door.

"Brystal, are you awake? Brystal?"

Her blue eyes fluttered open somewhere between the seventh and eighth time her mother pounded on the door. Brystal wasn't a heavy sleeper, but mornings were a challenge because she was usually *exhausted* from staying up late the night before.

"Brystal? Answer me, child!"

Brystal sat up in bed as the cathedral bells played their final toll in the distance. She found an open copy of *The Tales of Tidbit Twitch* by Tomfree Taylor lying on her stomach and a pair of glasses dangling from the tip of her nose. Once again, Brystal had fallen asleep reading, and she quickly disposed of the evidence before she was caught. She stashed the book under her pillow, tucked her reading glasses into the pocket of her nightgown, and extinguished a candle on her nightstand that had been burning the whole night.

"Young lady, it's ten past six! I'm coming in!"

Mrs. Evergreen pushed the door open and charged into her daughter's bedroom like a bull released from a pen. She was a thin woman with a pale face and dark circles under her eyes. Her hair was pulled into a tight bun on top of her head, and like the reins of a horse, it kept her alert and motivated throughout her daily chores.

"So you *are* awake," she said with one eyebrow raised. "Is a simple acknowledgment too much to ask for?"

"Good morning, Mother," Brystal said cheerfully. "I hope you slept well."

"Not as well as you, apparently," Mrs. Evergreen said. "Honestly, child, how do you sleep through those dreadful bells every morning? They're loud enough to wake the dead."

"Just lucky, I suppose," she said through a large yawn.

Mrs. Evergreen laid a white dress at the foot of Brystal's bed and shot her daughter a scornful look.

"You left your uniform on the clothesline again," she said. "How many times do I have to remind you to pick up after yourself? I can barely manage the laundry for your father and brothers—I don't have time to clean up after you, too."

"I'm sorry, Mother," Brystal apologized. "I was going to get it after I finished the dishes last night, but I guess I forgot."

"You've got to stop being so careless! Daydreaming is the last quality men look for in a wife," her mother warned. "Now hurry up and get dressed so you can help me with breakfast. It's a big day for your brother so we're making his favorite."

Mrs. Evergreen headed for the door but paused when she noticed a strange scent lingering in the air.

"Do I smell *smoke*?" she asked.

"I just blew out my candle," Brystal explained.

"And *why* was your candle burning so early in the morning?" Mrs. Evergreen said.

"I—I accidentally left it on during the night," she confessed.

Mrs. Evergreen crossed her arms and glared at her daughter. "Brystal, you better not be doing what I *think* you're doing," she warned. "Because I worry what your father might do if he finds out you've been *reading* again."

"No, I promise!" Brystal lied. "I just like sleeping with a lit candle. Sometimes I get scared in the dark."

Unfortunately, Brystal was a terrible liar. Mrs. Evergreen saw through her daughter's dishonesty like a window she had recently cleaned.

"The *world* is dark, Brystal," she said. "You're a fool if you let anything tell you otherwise. Now hand it over."

"But, Mother, please! I only have a few pages left!"

"Brystal Evergreen, this is not up for discussion!" Mrs. Evergreen said. "You're breaking the rules of this house *and* the laws of this kingdom! Now hand it over immediately or I will fetch your father!"

Brystal sighed and surrendered her copy of *The Tales of Tidbit Twitch* from under her pillow.

"And the others?" Mrs. Evergreen asked with an open palm.

"That's the only one I have—"

"Young lady, I will not tolerate any more of your lies! Books in your bedroom are like mice in the garden—there's never just *one*. Now give me the others or I will fetch your father."

Brystal's posture sank with her spirits. She stepped out of bed and led her mother to a loose floorboard in the corner of the bedroom where she kept a hidden collection. Mrs. Evergreen gasped when her daughter revealed over a dozen books in the floor. There were texts on history, religion, law, and economics, as well as fictional titles of adventure, mystery, and romance. And judging by the distressed covers and pages, Brystal had read each book multiple times.

"Oh, Brystal," Mrs. Evergreen said with a heavy heart. "Of all the things for a girl your age to be interested in, why does it have to be *books*?"

Mrs. Evergreen said the word like she was describing a foul and dangerous substance. Brystal knew it was wrong to have books in her possession—the Southern Kingdom's laws clearly stated that books were for *male eyes only*—but since nothing made Brystal happier than reading, she repeatedly risked the consequences.

One by one, Brystal kissed each book's spine like she was saying good-bye to a small pet, then passed it to her mother. The books piled over Mrs. Evergreen's head, but she was used to having her hands full and had no trouble finding her way to the door.

"I don't know who is supplying you with these, but you

need to cut ties with them immediately," Mrs. Evergreen said. "Do you know what the punishment is for girls who get caught reading in public? *Three months in a workhouse!* And that's *with* your father's connections!"

"But, Mother," Brystal asked, "*why* aren't women allowed to read in this kingdom? The law says our minds are too delicate to be educated, but it isn't true. So what's the *real* reason they keep books from us?'"

Mrs. Evergreen paused in the doorway and went silent. Brystal figured her mother was thinking about it, because she rarely paused for anything. Mrs. Evergreen looked back at her daughter with a long face, and for a brief moment, Brystal could have sworn she saw a rare spark of sympathy in her mother's eyes—like she had been asking herself the same question all her life and still didn't have an answer.

"If you ask me, women have enough to do as it is," she said to bury the subject. "Now get dressed. Breakfast isn't going to make itself."

Mrs. Evergreen turned on her heel and left the room. Tears came to Brystal's eyes as she watched her mother depart with her books. To Brystal, they weren't just stacks of parchment bound by leather; her books were *friends* that offered her the only escape from the suppressive Southern Kingdom. She dried the corners of her eyes with the edge of her nightgown but her tears didn't last very long. Brystal knew it was only a matter of time before she would rebuild her collection—her *supplier* was much closer than her mother realized.

She stood in front of her mirror as she applied all the layers and accessories of her ridiculous school uniform: the white dress, white leggings, lacy white gloves, a fuzzy white shoulder wrap, and white buckled heels, and to complete the transformation, Brystal tied a white ribbon in her long brown hair.

Brystal looked at her reflection and let out a prolonged sigh that came from the bottom of her soul. Like all the young women in her kingdom, Brystal was expected to resemble a living doll anytime she left her home—and Brystal *hated* dolls. In fact, anything that remotely influenced girls to want *motherhood* or *marriage* was instantly added to her list of things to resent—and given the Southern Kingdom's stubborn views of women, Brystal had acquired a long list over time.

For as long as she could remember, Brystal had known she was destined for a life beyond the confinements of her kingdom. *Her* accomplishments would surpass acquiring a husband and children, *she* was going to have adventures and experiences that exceeded cooking and cleaning, and *she* was going to find undeniable happiness, like the characters in her books. Brystal couldn't explain why she felt this way or how it would happen, but she felt it with her whole heart. But until the day arrived that proved her right, Brystal had no choice but to play the role society had assigned her.

In the meantime, Brystal found subtle and creative ways of coping. To make her school uniform bearable, Brystal put her reading glasses on the end of a gold chain, like a locket, and then tucked them into the top of her dress. It was doubtful she would get to read anything worthwhile at school—young women were only taught to read basic recipes and street signs—but knowing she was *prepared to read* made Brystal feel like she was armed with a secret weapon. And knowing she was rebelling, however slightly, gave her the energetic boost she needed to get through each day.

"Brystal! I meant breakfast TODAY! Get down here!"

"I'm coming!" she replied.

· • ★ • ·

The Evergreen family lived in a spacious country home just a few miles east of the Chariot Hills town square. Brystal's father was a well-known Justice in the Southern Kingdom court system, which granted the Evergreen family more wealth and respect than most families. Unfortunately, because their livelihood came from taxpayers, it was considered distasteful for the Evergreens to enjoy any "extravagances." And since the Justice valued nothing more than his good reputation, he deprived his family of "extravagances" whenever and wherever possible.

All the Evergreens' belongings, from their clothes to their furniture, were hand-me-downs from friends and neighbors. None of their drapes had the same pattern, their dishes and silverware came from different sets, and every chair had been made by a different carpenter. Even the wallpaper had been peeled off the walls of other houses and was a chaotic mix of different designs. Their property was large enough to employ a staff of twenty, but Justice Evergreen believed servants and farmhands were "the most extravagant of extravagances," so Brystal and her mother were forced to complete all the yard work and household chores by themselves.

"Stir the porridge while I make the eggs," Mrs. Evergreen ordered Brystal when she finally arrived in the kitchen. "But don't overstir them this time—your father hates soggy oats!"

Brystal tied an apron over her school uniform and took the wooden spoon from her mother. She was at the stove for less than a minute when a panicked voice called to them from the next room.

"Moooother! Come quick! It's an emergency!"

"What's the matter, Barrie?"

"One of my buttons has popped off my robe!"

"Oh, for the king's sake," Mrs. Evergreen muttered under her breath. "Brystal, go help your brother with his button. And make it fast."

Brystal retrieved a sewing kit and hurried into the sitting room beside the kitchen. To her surprise, she found her seventeen-year-old brother seated on the floor. His eyes were closed and he rocked back and forth while clutching a stack of notecards. Barrie Evergreen was a thin young man with messy brown hair and had been wide-eyed and nervous since the day he was born—but today, he was *exceptionally* nervous.

"Barrie?" Brystal addressed him softly. "Mother sent

me to fix your button. Can you take a break from study-ing or should I come back later?"

"No, now is fine," Barrie said. "I can practice while you sew."

He got to his feet and handed his sister the detached button. Like all students at the Chariot Hills University of Law, Barrie wore a long gray robe and a square black hat. As Brystal threaded a needle and stitched the button back onto his collar, Barrie glanced down at the prompt on his first notecard. He fiddled with the other but-tons of his uniform while he concentrated, and Brystal slapped his hand away before he caused more damage.

"The Purification Act of 342 . . . the Purification Act of 342 . . . ," Barrie read to himself. "That was when King Champion VIII charged the troll community with vulgarity and banished their species from the Southern Kingdom."

Satisfied with his answer, Barrie flipped the first notecard over and read the correct answer written on the back. Unfortunately, he was wrong, and reacted with a long, defeated moan. Brystal couldn't help but smile at her brother's frustration—he reminded her of a puppy chasing its own tail.

"This isn't funny, Brystal!" Barrie said. "I'm going to fail my examination!"

"Oh, Barrie, calm down." She laughed. "You're not going to fail. You've been studying the law your entire life!"

"That's why it'll be so humiliating! If I don't pass

the examination today, then I won't graduate from the university! If I don't graduate from the university, then I won't become a Deputy Justice! If I don't become a Deputy Justice, then I won't become a Justice like Father! And if I don't become a Justice, I'll *never* become a High Justice!"

Like all the men in the Evergreen family before him, Barrie was studying to become a Justice in the Southern Kingdom's court system. He had attended the Chariot Hills University of Law since he was six years old, and at ten o'clock that morning, he would take the grueling examination that would determine whether he would become a Deputy Justice. If he was accepted, Barrie would spend the next decade prosecuting and defending criminals on trial. Once his time as a Deputy Justice was over, Barrie would become an official Justice and preside over trials, like his father. And should his career as a Justice please the king, Barrie would be the very first Evergreen to become a High Justice on the King's Advisory Council, where he would help the sovereign *create* the law.

Becoming a High Justice had been Barrie's dream since he was a child, but his path to the King's Advisory Council would end today if he didn't pass the examination. So for the last six months, Barrie had studied his kingdom's law and history every possible moment he could, to ensure a victory.

"How will I ever look Father in the eye again if I don't pass?" Barrie worried. "I should just give up now and spare myself the embarrassment!"

"Stop catastrophizing," Brystal said. "You know all this stuff. You're just letting your nerves get to you."

"I'm not nervous—I'm a *wreck*! I was up all night making these cards and I can barely read my own handwriting! Whatever the Purification Act of 342 was, it's definitely not what I said!"

"Your answer was really close," Brystal said. "But you're thinking of the Declawing Act of 339—that was when Champion VIII banished trolls from the Southern Kingdom. Unfortunately, his army mistook the elves for trolls and kicked out the wrong species! So to validate the mix-up, Champion VIII introduced the Purification Act of 342 and banished *all* talking creatures besides humans from the kingdom! The trolls, elves, goblins, and ogres were rounded up and forced into the In-Between! Soon, it inspired the other kingdoms to do the same thing and led to the Great Cleansing of 345! Isn't that terrible? And to think, the most violent period of history could have been avoided if Champion VIII had just apologized to the elves!"

Brystal could tell her brother was half thankful for the reminder and half embarrassed it came from his little sister.

"Oh, right . . . ," Barrie said. "Thanks, Brystal."

"My pleasure," she said. "It's a real shame, too. Can you imagine how exciting it would be to see one of those creatures *in person*?"

Her brother did a double take. "Wait, how do *you* know all of this?"

Brystal glanced over her shoulder to make sure they were still alone. *"It was in one of the history books you gave me,"* she whispered. *"It was such a fascinating read! I must have read it four or five times! Do you want me to stay and help you study?"*

"I wish you could," Barrie said. "Mother will be suspicious if you don't return to the kitchen. And she'll be furious if she catches you helping me."

Brystal's eyes twinkled as a mischievous idea popped into her head. In one swift move, she yanked *all* the buttons off Barrie's robe. Before he could react, Mrs. Evergreen charged into the sitting room, as if she sensed her daughter's mischief in the air.

"How long does it take to sew *one button?*" she reprimanded. "I've got porridge in the pot, eggs in the pan, and rolls in the oven!"

Brystal shrugged innocently and showed her mother the handful of buttons she had plucked.

"Sorry, Mother," she said. "It's worse than we thought. He's *really* nervous."

Mrs. Evergreen threw her hands into the air and moaned at the ceiling.

"Barrie Evergreen, this house is not your personal tailor shop!" she scolded. "Keep your twitchy hands off your robe or I'll tie your hands behind your back like when you were a child! Brystal, when you're finished, go set the table in the dining room. We're eating in ten minutes—*buttons or not!*"

Mrs. Evergreen stomped back into the kitchen,

muttering slurs under her breath. Brystal and Barrie covered each other's mouths as they laughed at their mother's dramatics. It was the first time Brystal had seen her brother smile in weeks.

"I can't believe you did that," he said.

"Your examination is more important than breakfast," Brystal said, and began sewing the rest of the buttons. "And you don't need your cards—I've practically memorized all the old schoolbooks you've given me. Now, I'll name a historical act and you tell me the history behind it. All right?"

"All right," he agreed.

"Good. Let's start with the Border Act of 274."

"The Border Act of 274 . . . the Border Act of 274 . . . ," Barrie thought out loud. "Oh, I know! That was the decree that established the Protected Paths through the In-Between so the kingdoms could participate in safe trade."

Brystal winced at his answer. "Almost, but no," she said gently. "The Protected Paths were established with the Protected Paths Act of 296."

Barrie groaned and pulled away from Brystal while she was in the middle of sewing. He paced around the sitting room and rubbed his face with his hands.

"This is pointless!" he grumbled. "I don't know any of this! Why do there have to be so many numbers in history?!"

"Oh, that's a really interesting story, actually!" Brystal happily informed him. "The Southern Kingdom developed a calendar system when the very first King Champion was crowned! It was so efficient that the other kingdoms began using the same—*Oh, I'm sorry, Barrie!* That was a rhetorical question, wasn't it?"

Her brother had dropped his arms and was staring at her in disbelief. He had meant it as a rhetorical question, but after hearing his sister's explanation, he realized he was wrong about the invention of the calendar, too.

"I give up!" Barrie declared. "I'm going to quit the university and become a shopkeeper! I'm going to sell rocks and sticks to small children! I won't make much money, but at least I'll never run out of materials!"

Brystal was losing patience with her brother's attitude. She grabbed his chin and held his head still so she could look him in the eye.

"Barrie, you need to snap out of it!" she said. "All your answers are coming from the right place, but you keep putting the cart before the horse. Remember, the law is history, and history is just another *story*. Each of these events had a prequel and a sequel—a cause and an effect. Before you answer, put all the facts you know on an imaginary timeline. Find the contradictions, focus on what's missing, and then fill in the blanks the best you can."

Barrie went quiet as he thought about his sister's advice. Slowly but surely, the seed of positivity she had planted in him began to grow. Barrie gave Brystal a determined nod and took a deep breath like he was about to dive off a high cliff.

"You're right," he said. "I just need to relax and focus."

Brystal released Barrie's chin so she could continue repairing his wardrobe while she also repaired his self-confidence.

"Now, the Border Act of 274," she said. "Give it another try."

Barrie concentrated and didn't make a sound until he was certain he had the right answer.

"After the Four Corners World War of 250, all four kingdoms agreed to stop fighting over land and their leaders signed the Border Act of 274. The treaty finalized the borders of each kingdom and established the In-Between zone between nations."

"Very good!" Brystal cheered. "What about the In-Between Neutralization Act of 283?"

Barrie thought very carefully, and his eyes lit up when the answer came to him.

"The In-Between Neutralization Act of 283 was an international agreement to neutralize the In-Between zone so none of the kingdoms could claim it as their territory! As a result, the In-Between was left with no authority and became a very dangerous place. Which then led to the Protected Paths Act of 296—OUCH!"

Brystal was so proud of her brother she had accidentally poked him with her sewing needle.

"That's correct!" she said. "See, you have all the information you need to pass the examination! You just have to believe in yourself as much as I do."

Barrie blushed and color finally returned to his face.

"Thank you, Brystal," he said. "I'd be lost in my own head if it weren't for you. It's really a shame you're... well, you know... *a girl*. You would have made an incredible Justice."

Brystal lowered her head and pretended she was still sewing the final button so he didn't see the sadness in her eyes.

"Oh?" she said. "I've never really thought about it."

On the contrary, it was something Brystal wanted more than her brother could ever imagine. Being a Justice would allow her to redeem and elevate people, it would provide a platform to spread hope and understanding, and it would give her the resources to make the world a better place for other girls like her. Sadly, it was highly unlikely a woman would have any role but wife and mother in the Southern Kingdom, so Brystal extinguished her ideas before they turned into hopes.

"Maybe when you're a High Justice, you could convince the king to let women read," she told her brother. "That would be a great start."

"Maybe...," Barrie said with a weak smile. "For now, at least you have my old books to keep you entertained. That reminds me, did you finish *The Tales of Tidbit Twitch* yet? I'm dying to talk to you about the ending but I don't want to give anything away."

"I only had seven pages left! But then Mother caught me this morning and confiscated all my books. Could you stop by the library and see if there are any old books they're getting rid of? I've already thought of a new hiding spot to keep them in."

"Certainly. The examination will last until late this afternoon, but I'll stop by the library tomorrow and..." Barrie's voice trailed off before he finished his thought. "Actually, I suppose it'll be more difficult than it used to be. The library is next to my university, but if I get accepted into the Deputy Justice program, I'll be working at the courthouse. It may be a week or two before I can sneak away."

Until this moment, Brystal had never realized how much her brother's pending graduation was going to affect *her*. Barrie would no doubt pass his examination with flying colors and be put to work as a Deputy Justice right away. For years to come, all his time and energy would be spent prosecuting or defending criminals at the courthouse. Supplying his little sister with books would be his last priority.

"That's all right," Brystal said through a forced smile. "I'll find something to do in the meantime. Well, all your buttons are attached. I better set the table before Mother gets upset."

Brystal hurried into the dining room before her brother noticed the anguish in her voice. When he said *weeks*, she knew it might be months or even a year before she had another book in her hands. So much time without a distraction from her mundane life would be torturous. If she wanted to keep her sanity, she would have to find something to read outside their home, and given the kingdom's harsh punishments for female readers, Brystal would have to be clever—*very* clever—if she didn't want to get caught.

"Breakfast is ready!" Mrs. Evergreen announced. "Come and eat! Your father's carriage will be here in fifteen minutes!"

Brystal quickly set the dining room table before her family members arrived. Barrie brought his notecards to the table and flipped through them while they waited for the meal to begin. Brystal couldn't tell if it was his freshly sewn buttons or his restored confidence, but Barrie was sitting much taller than when she found him on the floor. She took great pride in the physical and mental alterations she had provided.

Their older brother, Brooks, was the first to join Brystal and Barrie in the dining room. He was tall, muscular, had perfectly straight hair, and always looked like he had somewhere better to be—especially when he was with his family. Brooks had graduated from the university and gone into the Deputy Justice program two years earlier, and like all the other Deputies, he wore a gray-and-black-checkered robe and a slightly taller black hat than Barrie's.

Instead of greeting his siblings, Brooks grunted and rolled his eyes when he saw Barrie flipping through his notecards.

"Are you *still* studying?" he sneered.

"Is there something wrong with studying?" Barrie shot back.

"Only the way you do it," Brooks ridiculed him. "Really, brother, if it takes *this long* for information to sink in, perhaps you should pursue another profession? I hear the Fortworths are in the market for a new stable boy."

Brooks took a seat across from his brother and put his feet on the table, inches away from Barrie's notecards.

"How interesting. I heard the Fortworths are also in the market for a new *son-in-law* since their daughter declined your proposal," Barrie replied. "*Twice*, the rumor goes."

Brystal couldn't stop a laugh from surfacing. Brooks mocked his sister's laughter with a crude imitation and then squinted at Barrie while he plotted his next insult.

"In all honesty, I hope you pass your examination today," he said.

"You do?" Brystal asked with suspicious eyes. "Well, *that's* out of character."

"Yes, I do," Brooks snapped. "I look forward to going head-to-head with Barrie in a courtroom—I'm bored with humiliating him at home."

Brooks and Barrie glared at each other with the complicated hatred only brothers could have. Fortunately, their exchange was interrupted before it became more heated.

Justice Evergreen entered the dining room with a stack of parchment under his arm and a quill between his fingers. He was an imposing man with a thick white beard. After a long career of judging others, several deep lines had formed across his forehead. Like all the

Justices in the Southern Kingdom, Justice Evergreen wore a black robe that flowed from his shoulders to his toes and a tall black hat that forced him to duck through doorways. His eyes were the exact shade of blue as his daughter's, and they even shared the same astigmatism—which was greatly beneficial to Brystal. Unbeknownst to her father, whenever the Justice discarded an old pair of reading glasses, his daughter got a new pair.

Upon his arrival, the Evergreen children rose and respectfully stood by their chairs. It was custom to rise for a Justice while attending the courthouse, but Justice Evergreen expected it from his family at all times.

"Good morning, Father," the Evergreens said together.

"You may be seated," Justice Evergreen permitted, without looking any of his children in the eye. He took his seat at the head of the table and immediately buried his nose in his paperwork, as if nothing else in the world existed.

Mrs. Evergreen appeared with a pot of porridge, a large bowl of scrambled eggs, and a hot tray of rolls. Brystal helped her mother serve breakfast, and once the men's plates were full, the women filled their own and sat down.

"What's this rubbish?" Brooks asked, and poked the food with a fork.

"Eggs and oats," Mrs. Evergreen said. "It's Barrie's favorite."

Brooks moaned as if he found the meal offensive. "I should have known," he scoffed. "Barrie has the same taste as a sow."

"Sorry it isn't *your* favorite, Brooks," Barrie said. "Perhaps Mother can make *cream of kitten* and *infant tears* for you tomorrow."

"Dear Lord, these boys will be the death of me!" Mrs. Evergreen said, and looked to the ceiling in distress. "Would it kill either of you to take a day off from this nonsense? Especially on a morning as important as this? Once Barrie passes his examination, the two of you are going to be working together for a very long time. It would do you both some good if you learned to be civil."

In many ways, Brystal was thankful she didn't have the opportunity to become a Justice; it spared her from the nightmare of working with Brooks at the courthouse. He was very popular among the other Deputy Justices, and Brystal worried how Brooks would use his connections to sabotage Barrie. Ever since his younger brother was born, Brooks had seen Barrie as a threat of some kind, as if only one Evergreen son was allowed to succeed.

"I apologize, Mother," Brooks said with a phony smile. "And you're right—I should be helping Barrie get ready for his examination. Let me share some of the questions that nearly stumped me during *my* examination—questions I guarantee he won't see coming. For example, what is the difference between the punishment for trespassing on private property and the punishment for trespassing on royal property?"

Barrie beamed with confidence. Clearly, he was much more prepared for his examination than Brooks had been for his own.

"The punishment for trespassing on private property is three years in prison and the punishment for trespassing on royal property is fifty," Barrie said. "And the serving Justice decides whether hard labor should be added."

"I'm afraid that's *wrong*," Brooks said. "It's *five* years for private property and *sixty* years for royal property."

For a moment Brystal thought she had misheard Brooks. She knew for a fact that Barrie's answer was correct—she could even visualize the exact page of the law book where she had read it. Barrie looked just as confused as his sister. He turned to Justice Evergreen, hoping his father would correct his brother's claim, but the Justice never glanced up from his paperwork.

"I'll give you another one," Brooks said. "In what year was the death penalty changed from drawing-and-quartering to beheading?"

"Good heavens, Brooks! Some of us are eating!" Mrs. Evergreen scolded.

"That was...that was...," Barrie mumbled as he tried to recall. "That was the year 567!"

"Wroooong again," Brooks sang. "The first public beheading wasn't until 568. Oh dear, you're not very good at this game."

Barrie started second-guessing himself, and his confidence faded with his posture. Brystal cleared her throat to get Barrie's attention, hoping to expose Brooks's charade with a telling look, but Barrie didn't hear her.

"Let's try something simple," Brooks said. "Can you name the four pieces of evidence a prosecutor needs to charge a suspect with murder?"

"That's easy!" Barrie replied. "A body, a motive, a witness, and...and..."

Brooks was enjoying watching his brother struggle. "You're already *way* off, so let's try another one," he said. "How many Justices does it take to appeal the ruling of another Justice?"

"What are you talking about?" Barrie asked. "Justices can't appeal!"

"Once again, *wrong.*" Brooks screeched like a crow. "I can't believe how unprepared you are—especially given the amount of time you've been studying. If I were you, I would pray the examiner is out sick."

All the color drained from Barrie's face, his eyes grew large, and he gripped his notecards so firmly they started to bend. He looked as hopeless and scared as he had when Brystal found him in the sitting room. Every brick of self-esteem she had laid was now being demolished for Brooks's amusement. She couldn't take another moment of his cruel game.

"Don't listen to him, Barrie!" she shouted, and the room went silent. "Brooks is asking you trick questions on purpose! First, the punishment for trespassing on private property *is* three years in prison and the punishment for trespassing on royal property *is* fifty—it's only five and sixty years if the property is damaged! Second, the first public beheading was in 568, but the law changed in 567, like you said! Third, there aren't *four* elements needed to charge a suspect with murder, there are only *three*—and you named them all! And fourth, Justices *can't* appeal the ruling of another Justice, only a High Justice can overturn a—"

"BRYSTAL LYNN EVERGREEN!"

For the first time all morning, Justice Evergreen found a reason to look up from his paperwork. His face turned bright red, veins bulged out of his neck, and he roared so loudly all the dishes on the table rattled.

"How dare you reprimand your brother! Who do you think you are?"

It took Brystal a few seconds to find her voice. "B-b-but, Father, Brooks isn't telling the truth!" she stuttered. "I—I—I just don't want Barrie to fail his—"

"I don't care if Brooks said the sky was purple, it is not a young woman's place to correct a man! If Barrie isn't smart enough to know he's being fooled, then he has no business being a Deputy Justice!"

Tears came to Brystal's eyes and she trembled in her seat. She looked to her brothers for support, but they were just as frightened as she was.

"I'm—I'm sorry, Father—"

"You have no right knowing any *of the information*

you just recited! If I find out you've been reading *again, so help me God, I will throw you out on the street!"*

Brystal turned to her mother, praying she wouldn't mention the books she'd found in her bedroom earlier. Just like her sons, Mrs. Evergreen stayed silent and still, like a mouse in the presence of a hawk.

"N-n-no, I haven't been reading—"

"Then where did you learn all that?"

"I—I—I suppose I just picked it up from Barrie and Brooks. They're always talking about laws and the courthouse at the table—"

"Then perhaps you should eat outside until you learn to tune it out! No daughter of mine is going to defy the laws of this kingdom by being precocious!*"*

The Justice continued to shout about his disappointment in and disgust for his daughter. Brystal wasn't a stranger to her father's temper—in fact, she rarely communicated with him unless he was screaming at her—but nothing was worse than being on the receiving end of his fury. With every heartbeat, Brystal sank a little more into her chair, and she counted down the seconds until it was over. Usually if he didn't stop yelling by the count of fifty, her father's wrath would escalate into something physical.

"Is that the carriage I hear?" Mrs. Evergreen asked.

The family went silent as they tried to hear whatever Mrs. Evergreen heard. A few moments later the faint sounds of bells and galloping filled the house as the carriage approached outside. Brystal wondered if her mother had actually heard it, or if her interruption was just lucky timing.

"The three of you better hurry before it gets too late."

Justice Evergreen and his sons gathered their things and met the carriage outside. Barrie took his time as he shut the front door behind him so he could wave good-bye to his sister.

"Thank you," he mouthed to her.

"Good luck today," she mouthed back.

Brystal stayed in her seat until she was certain her father and brothers were a good distance down the road. By the time she regained her senses, Mrs. Evergreen had already cleared the dining room table. Brystal went into the kitchen to see if her mother needed help with the dishes, but her mother wasn't cleaning. Instead, Brystal found Mrs. Evergreen leaning on the sink, staring down at the dirty dishes with a heavy gaze, as if she were in a trance.

"Thank you for not mentioning the books to Father," Brystal said.

"You shouldn't have corrected your brother like that," Mrs. Evergreen said quietly.

"I know," Brystal said.

"I mean it, Brystal," her mother said, and turned to her daughter with wide, fearful eyes. "Brooks is very well-liked in town. You don't want to make him your enemy. If he starts saying bad things about you to his friends—"

"Mother, I don't care what Brooks says about me."

"Well, you *should*," Mrs. Evergreen said sternly. "In two years, you'll be sixteen and men will start courting you for marriage. You can't risk a reputation that scares all the good ones away. You don't want to spend your life with someone mean and ungrateful. . . . *Trust me.*"

Her mother's remarks left Brystal speechless. She couldn't tell if she was just imagining it, but the dark circles under her mother's eyes seemed a shade darker than they were before breakfast.

"Now go to school," Mrs. Evergreen said. "I'll take care of the dishes."

Brystal was compelled to stay and argue with her mother. She wanted to list all the reasons why *her* life would be different than other girls', she wanted to explain why *she* was destined for greater things than marriage and motherhood, but then she remembered she had no evidence to support her beliefs.

Perhaps her mother was right. Maybe Brystal was a fool for thinking the world was anything but dark.

With nothing more to say, Brystal left her home and headed for school. As she walked along the path into town, the image of her mother leaning at the sink stayed prominently on her mind. Brystal worried it was as much a glimpse into her own future as it was a memory of her mother.

"*No,*" she whispered to herself. "That is *not* going to be my life. . . . That is *not* going to be my life. . . . That is *not* going to be my life. . . ." Brystal repeated the statement as she walked, hoping if she said it enough times, it might extinguish her fears. "It may seem impossible right now, but I know *something* is going to happen.... *Something* is going to change.... *Something* is going to make my life different...."

Brystal was right to be worried; escaping the confinements of the Southern Kingdom was impossible for a girl her age. But in a few short weeks, Brystal's definition of *impossible* would change forever.

Chapter Two

A Sign

That day at the Chariot Hills School for Future Wives and Mothers, Brystal learned the proper amount of tea to serve to an unexpected visitor, the type of appetizers to cook for a formal gathering, and how to fold a napkin into the shape of a dove—among other *riveting* subjects. Toward the end of class Brystal had rolled her eyes so many times her eye sockets were sore. Usually she was better at hiding her annoyance during school hours, but without the comfort of a good book waiting for her at home, it was much more difficult to conceal her irritation.

To soothe her aggravation, Brystal thought about the last page she had read in *The Tales of Tidbit Twitch* before falling asleep the night before. The story's hero, a field mouse named Tidbit, was hanging off a cliff while battling a ferocious dragon. His tiny claws were getting tired as he swung from ledge to ledge to dodge the monster's scorching breath. With his last bit of strength, he threw his small sword at the dragon, hoping it would wound the beast and give him a chance to climb to safety.

"Miss Evergreen?"

By some miracle, Tidbit's sword flew through the air and pierced the dragon's eye. The creature jerked its head toward the heavens and howled in pain, sending fiery geysers through the night sky. As Tidbit crawled down the side of the cliff, the dragon whipped its pointed tail and knocked the mouse off the boulder he clung to. Tidbit fell toward the rocky earth below, limbs flailing all around as he reached for something—*anything*—to grab on to.

"Miss Evergreen!"

Brystal sat straight up in her seat like she had been pricked with an invisible pin. All her classmates turned toward her desk in the back row and stared at her with matching frowns. Their teacher, Mrs. Plume, glared at her from the front of the classroom with pursed lips and one of her penciled eyebrows raised.

"Um . . . yes?" Brystal asked with large innocent eyes.

"Miss Evergreen, are you paying attention or are you daydreaming again?" Mrs. Plume asked.

"I'm paying attention, of course," she lied.

"Then what is the appropriate way to handle the situation I just described?" the teacher challenged.

Obviously, Brystal didn't have a clue what the class was discussing. The other girls giggled in anticipation of a good chastising. Fortunately, Brystal knew an answer that solved *all* of Mrs. Plume's questions, no matter what the topic was.

"I suppose I would *ask my future husband what to do*?" she replied.

Mrs. Plume stared at Brystal for a few moments without blinking.

"That's...*correct*," the teacher was surprised to admit.

Brystal sighed with relief and her classmates sighed with disappointment. They always looked forward to moments when Brystal was reprimanded for her infamous daydreaming. Even Mrs. Plume seemed disappointed at a missed opportunity to scold her. The teacher would have slumped if her tight corset allowed it.

"Moving on," Mrs. Plume instructed. "We'll now review the difference between tying hair ribbons and shoelaces, and the *dangers* of mixing them up."

The students cheered for their next lesson, and their enthusiasm made Brystal die a little inside. She knew she couldn't be the *only* girl at school who wanted a more exciting life than what they were being prepared for, but as she watched her classmates strain their necks to see ribbons and shoelaces, she couldn't tell if they were all phenomenal actors or just phenomenally brainwashed.

Brystal knew better than to mention her dreams or frustrations to anyone, but she didn't have to say anything for people to know she was different. Like wolves from an opposing pack, the whole school could practically smell it on her. And since the Southern Kingdom was a scary place for people who thought differently, Brystal's classmates kept their distance from her, as if *difference* was a contagious disease.

Don't worry, one day they'll regret this..., Brystal thought. *One day they'll wish they were nicer to me.... One day I'll be celebrated for my differences.... One day they'll be the unhappy ones, not me....*

To avoid any more unwanted attention, Brystal remained as quiet and alert as possible until the end of class. The only time she moved a muscle was to lightly caress the reading glasses hidden in her dress.

· • ★ • ·

That afternoon, Brystal walked home from school at a slower pace than usual. With nothing but chores waiting for her, she decided to stroll through the Chariot Hills town square, hoping the change of scenery would take her mind off her troubles.

The Champion Castle, the cathedral, the courthouse, and the University of Law each towered over the four sides of the town square. Busy shops and markets filled the corners and spaces between the authoritative structures. In the center of the town square was a grassy patch where a statue of King Champion I stood above a shallow fountain. The statue depicted the sovereign on horseback as he pointed a sword into a seemingly prosperous future, but the tribute received more attention from pigeons than from the citizens wandering through town.

As Brystal walked past the University of Law, she gazed up at its stone walls and impressive glass domes with envy. At that very moment, she knew Barrie was somewhere inside agonizing over his examination. Brystal could have sworn she felt her brother's anxiety radiating through the walls, but still, she would have given anything to trade places with him. She stopped to say a prayer for him before moving on.

Brystal had no choice but to pass the courthouse as she continued through the town square. It was an ominous building with tall pillars and a triangular roof. Each pillar had the image of a High Justice carved into it, and the carvings scowled down at the citizens on the ground like disapproving parents—an expression Brystal knew well. She couldn't stop a wave of anger from flooding her stomach as she eyed the intimidating faces above her. Men like them—men like her *father*— were the reason she had such little happiness.

In a corner of the town square, between the university and courthouse, was the Chariot Hills Library. It was a small and modest structure compared to the buildings surrounding it, but to Brystal, the library could have been a palace. A black plaque with a red triangle was displayed above its double doors—a common symbol in the Southern Kingdom that reminded women they weren't allowed to enter—but the law did nothing to diminish Brystal's desire to go in.

Being so close to so many books and being forbidden to enjoy them gave Brystal a terrible feeling whenever she laid eyes on the library, but today the sensation was unbearable. The helplessness she felt triggered an avalanche of emotions, and all the fear, doubt, and heartbreak she had been suppressing trampled over her like a stampede. The scenic route home was creating the opposite effect of what she had intended, and the town square suddenly felt like a cage closing in on her.

Brystal was so overwhelmed she could barely breathe. She shooed a cluster of pigeons away from the Champion statue and had a seat on the edge of the fountain to catch her breath.

"I can't do this anymore...," she panted. "I keep telling myself that things will get better, but they only get worse and worse.... If life is just a series of disappointments, then I wish I had never been born.... I wish I could turn into a cloud and float far, far away from here...."

Tears spilled down her face before she knew they were coming. A few townspeople noticed the emotional scene and paused to gawk at her, but Brystal couldn't care less. She buried her face in the palms of her hands and wept in front of everyone.

"Please, God, I need more than just faith to keep going...," she cried. "I need proof that I'm not as foolish as I feel. . . . I need a message that life won't always be so miserable. . . . Please, I need a sign. . . ."

Ironically, after Brystal finished crying and had dried her tears, *a sign* was the first thing she saw. An old and rickety librarian emerged from the library with a bright yellow board under his arm. With shaky hands, he pinned the board on the library's entranceway. Brystal had never seen a sign posted outside the library before and was very curious. Once the librarian returned inside, she hurried to the front steps to read the words painted across the board:

MAID WANTED

Suddenly, an idea came to Brystal that sent tingles through her entire body. Before she could second-guess herself—and before she was even fully aware of what she was doing—Brystal pushed through the front doors and entered the Chariot Hills Library.

Her first glimpse of the library was so overstimulating it took a few moments for Brystal's mind to catch up with her eyes. In all the years she had spent wondering what the library looked like inside, she never imagined it could be so magnificent. It was an enormous circular room with an emerald carpet, the walls were covered in wooden paneling, and natural light flowed in from a glass ceiling. A massive silver globe stood in the center of the first floor, and dozens of law students were spread out at antique tables and armchairs around it. But most amazing of all, the library was surrounded by *three stories of bookshelves* that stretched into the upper floors like a multilevel maze.

The sight of thousands and thousands of books made Brystal light-headed, like she had just stepped into a dream. She never knew so many books existed in the whole world, let alone in her local library.

Brystal spotted the elderly librarian standing behind a counter at the front of the room. Her impromptu plan would end in disaster if she didn't play her cards right. She closed her eyes, took a deep breath, wished herself luck, and approached him.

"Excuse me, sir?" Brystal asked.

The librarian was busy applying labels to a fresh stack of books and didn't notice her right away. Brystal instantly felt a spark of jealousy toward the old man— she could only imagine how many books he had touched and read over the years.

"Excuse me, Mr. Woolsore?" she asked after reading the nameplate on the countertop.

The librarian squinted at her and reached for a pair of thick spectacles nearby. Once his glasses were on, the old man's jaw dropped. He pointed at Brystal like a wild animal was loose in the building.

"Young lady, what are you doing in here?" Mr. Woolsore exclaimed. *"Women aren't allowed in the library! Now, get out before I call the authorities!"*

"Actually, it's perfectly legal for me to be inside," Brystal explained, hoping her tranquil tone would mellow his. "You see, according to the Hired Help Act of 417, women are allowed to enter male-only premises to seek employment. By posting the sign outside, you've given me the legal right to enter the building and apply for the position."

Brystal knew the Hired Help Act of 417 only applied to women older than twenty, but she was hoping the librarian wasn't as familiar with the law as she was. Mr. Woolsore scrunched his fuzzy eyebrows and watched her like a hawk.

"*You* want to be a maid?" he asked.

"Yes," Brystal said with a shrug. "It's honest work, is it not?"

"But shouldn't a girl your age be busy learning how to curtsy and flirt with boys?" Mr. Woolsore asked.

Brystal was compelled to argue, but she swallowed her pride and kept her eye on the prize.

"To be honest, Mr. Woolsore," she said, "a boy is *exactly* why I want the position. You see, there's this Deputy Justice I'm *just smitten with*. I desperately want him to propose to me one day, but I don't think he sees me as wife material. My family has servants—*many, many servants*—so he has no reason to believe I'm even capable of household chores. But when he finds out I've been cleaning the library all by myself—*to perfection*, I might add—he'll know I'll make him a better wife than all the other girls in town."

Brystal even twirled her hair and blinked her eyes helplessly like a deer to sell the performance.

"I sympathize, but you aren't a practical candidate for the position," the librarian said. "I can't have you in the library while law students are studying. A young girl would be too much of a distraction for young men."

"Then perhaps I could clean in the evening after the library closes," Brystal suggested. "Most establishments have their maids clean after hours. I could start as soon as you leave and it would be spotless when you return the next morning."

Mr. Woolsore crossed his arms and eyed her suspiciously. She was almost too convincing to be trusted.

"This isn't some scheme, is it?" he inquired. "You aren't applying for the job so you can be around *books*, are you?"

Brystal felt her heart plunge into her gut. The librarian was seeing through her dishonesty as easily as her mother would. But instead of letting the panic surface on her face, Brystal laughed the idea off and tried using his ignorance against him.

"Mr. Woolsore, I'm *a fourteen-year-old girl*. What interest would I have in *books*?"

According to the librarian's body language, reverse psychology did the trick. Mr. Woolsore chuckled to himself, as if he was foolish for thinking it in the first place. Brystal knew she was close to persuading him— she just needed to offer him one more perk to sweeten the deal.

"How much does the position pay, sir?" she asked.

"Six gold coins a week," he said. "The position is

five days a week. Employees don't work weekends or the royal holidays Kingsgiving and Champions Eve."

"I'll tell you what, Mr. Woolsore, since you'll be doing *me* a favor, I'll do *you* a favor, too. If you hire me to clean the library, I'll do it for three gold coins a week."

Her offer was music to Mr. Woolsore's ears. He scratched his chin and nodded as it became more and more appealing to him.

"What's your name, young lady?" he asked.

"It's Brystal Ev—"

Luckily, Brystal stopped herself before revealing her family name. If the librarian knew she was an Evergreen, her father might find out she had applied for the job—and that was a risk she couldn't take. So Brystal gave him the first name that came to mind, and her alias was born.

"My name is *Bailey*—Brystal Eve Bailey."

"Well, all right then, Miss Bailey," Mr. Woolsore said. "If you can start tomorrow evening, you're hired."

Brystal couldn't contain her excitement. Her whole body began to vibrate like she was being tickled from the inside out. She reached across the counter and vigorously shook the librarian's frail hand.

"Thank you, Mr. Woolsore—thank you so much! I promise I won't let you down! *Oh, pardon my grip—hope that didn't hurt!* See you tomorrow!"

Brystal practically floated out of the library and down the road to the eastern countryside. Her plan was more successful than she could ever have predicted. In just one day, she would have access to thousands and thousands of books. And with no one in the library to supervise her, Brystal could easily sneak a few home each night after she was finished cleaning.

The prospect was exhilarating and Brystal couldn't remember the last time she had felt so much happiness coursing through her veins. However, Brystal's euphoria came to a screeching halt as soon as the Evergreen house appeared on the horizon. For the first time, she realized just how impractical the situation was. There wasn't a feasible way she could work evenings at the library without her family noticing her absence—she would need to give them a reason for why she was leaving the house at night and staying out so late.

If she wanted to work at the library, Brystal would have to create a spectacular lie that not only gained her family's approval, but also avoided any suspicion whatsoever. If she was caught, the consequences would be catastrophic.

Brystal clenched her jaw as she thought about the daunting challenge ahead. Apparently getting a job at the library was only her *first* impossible task of the day.

Later that night, the Evergreen house was buzzing with celebration. A messenger had arrived from the University of Law with the news that Barrie had passed his examination with the highest marks in his class. Brystal and Mrs. Evergreen cooked up a feast to commemorate Barrie's victory, including a chocolate cake Brystal made from scratch. By the time the Evergreens sat down to eat, Barrie was already wearing his new Deputy Justice robes.

"How do I look?" he asked everyone at the table.

"Like a child wearing a man's clothes," Brooks quipped.

"No, you look perfect," Brystal said. "Like you were born for it."

Brystal was so proud of her brother, but also especially grateful for an excuse to look so cheerful. Whenever she thought of her new job at the library, no one questioned the smile that beamed across her face. Everyone in her family shared the same excitement— even Brooks's bitterness softened after a few glasses of sparkling cider.

"I can't believe my little boy is going to be a *Deputy Justice*," Mrs. Evergreen said through happy tears. "It feels like only yesterday you were wearing my long shirts and sentencing your toys to hard labor in the backyard. My, how time flies!"

"I am so proud of you, son," Justice Evergreen said. "You're keeping the family legacy alive and well."

"Thank you, Father," Barrie said. "Do you have any advice for my first week at the courthouse?"

"You'll only be observing cases for your first month, but pay attention to every detail of the proceedings," the Justice advised. "After that, you'll be assigned your first prosecution. No matter what the charges are, you *must* recommend the maximum penalty, otherwise the sitting Justice will think you're weak and will likely side with the defense. Now, when you're assigned your first defense, the secret to—"

Justice Evergreen went quiet as his eyes fell on Brystal. He had almost forgotten she was in the room.

"On second thought, perhaps we should continue this at a later time," he said. "I would hate for our conversation to be absorbed by *prying* ears."

The Justice's comments made Brystal go tense, but not because her father's words offended her. After a long afternoon of plotting, Brystal was waiting for the perfect moment to secure her future at the library, and this might be her only chance.

"Father? May I say something?" she asked.

Justice Evergreen grunted like it was a chore to give his daughter any attention. The other Evergreens looked back and forth at Brystal and the Justice with nervous eyes, fearing dinner would end on the same note as breakfast had.

"Yes, what is it?" the Justice asked.

"Well, I've been thinking a lot about what you said this morning," Brystal began. "I don't want to be disrespectful to the law, so perhaps you were right when you suggested I eat meals elsewhere."

"Oh?" her father said.

"Yes, and I believe I've found the perfect solution," Brystal continued. "Today after school, I stopped by the Chariot Hills Home for the Hopeless. They're desperately understaffed, so with your blessing, I would like to start volunteering there evenings after school."

"You want to catch fleas at a *poorhouse*?" Brooks asked in disbelief.

Mrs. Evergreen held out a hand to silence her eldest son. "Thank you, Brooks, but your father and I will handle this," she said. "Brystal, it's very kind that you want to help the less fortunate, but *I* need your help in this house. I can't manage all the chores and cooking dinner on my own."

Brystal lowered her head and looked at her hands so Mrs. Evergreen wouldn't detect any dishonesty in her eyes.

"But I'm not abandoning you, Mother," she explained. "After school, I'll come home and help you cook and clean—*just like always*. And when it's time for dinner, I'll simply slip away for a few hours to volunteer at the Home for the Hopeless. At night, I'll return home and do the dishes before bed—*just like always*. I may lose an hour or two of sleep, but it shouldn't affect anything else."

The dining room went quiet as Justice Evergreen considered his daughter's request. Brystal felt like an invisible weight was tied around her stomach, and with every passing moment, it became heavier and heavier. The thirty seconds it took to get an answer seemed like hours.

"I agree, a change is needed to prevent other *incidents* like the one this morning," her father said. "You may volunteer evenings at the Home for the Hopeless, but *only* if it doesn't create extra work for your mother."

Justice Evergreen banged the table with his fork like it was a gavel, cementing his final ruling of the day. Brystal couldn't believe she had pulled it off—*working at the library was now a reality*! The weight around her stomach was suddenly released, and Brystal knew she had to get out of her family's sight before she started bouncing off the walls.

"Thank you so much, Father," she said. "Now, if you'll excuse me, I'll give you and Barrie some privacy so you can speak freely about the courthouse. I'll come back to clear the table when you've finished dessert."

Brystal was excused from the dinner table and hurried upstairs to her bedroom. Once the door was closed behind her, Brystal danced around her room as energetically as she could without making a sound. As she twirled past her mirror, Brystal saw something she hadn't seen since she was a small child. Instead of a depressed and defeated girl in a silly school uniform, she was facing a happy and vibrant young woman with hopeful eyes and rosy cheeks. It was like she was looking at a different person altogether.

"You're a *bad girl*, Brystal Eve Bailey," she whispered to her reflection. "A very, very *bad girl*."

CHAPTER THREE

JUSTICES ONLY

B rystal read more books in just two weeks of cleaning the library than she had in her entire life. By the end of her first month, she had devoured every title on the ground floor and was working her way through the second level.

Her quick consumption rate was thanks to an efficient schedule she developed early on: Each evening, Brystal dusted the shelves, mopped the floors, polished the silver globe, and wiped the surfaces as fast as she possibly could. When the cleaning was finished, Brystal selected a book—or a few books if it was the weekend—and snuck them back to her house. Once she finished washing the dishes from her family's dinner, Brystal would lock herself in her bedroom and spend the rest of the night reading. The following evening, Brystal would return what she had borrowed and her secret routine would start all over again.

Brystal couldn't believe how quickly her life had changed. In just one month, she went from having an emotional breakdown in public to the most exciting and stimulating time she had ever experienced. Working at the library gave her access to biographies, encyclopedias, dictionaries, anthologies, and textbooks that expanded her grasp of reality, and it introduced her to works of fiction, poetry, and prose that expanded her imagination beyond her wildest dreams. But perhaps most gratifying of all, Brystal found the library's copy of *The Tales of Tidbit Twitch* and finally learned how the story ended:

> *Tidbit reached in all directions as he fell off the side of the cliff, but there was nothing to grab hold of. He feared his fall would come to a brutal end against the rocky earth, but by some miracle, the mouse plunged into a rushing river instead. The dragon swooped down the cliff and flew over Tidbit as he floated in the river. The monster tried to swipe the mouse from the powerful stream, but the water was moving too fast for the dragon to get a steady grip.*

Tidbit thrashed around the river as it swept him toward a towering waterfall. As he rolled over the edge, the dragon dived after him with wide-open jaws. The mouse was convinced these were his last moments alive— he would either be consumed by the monster above him, or collide with the boulders at the base of the waterfall. As he fell farther and farther, the dragon dived closer and closer, and soon the creature's sharp teeth encompassed him in midair.

Just before the monster sank its teeth into the falling mouse, Tidbit fell through a small crack between the boulders at the bottom of the waterfall, and he safely dropped into the lake at the river's end. When Tidbit surfaced in the water, he saw the dragon was spread out across the rocks behind him, lying lifeless with a broken neck.

Tidbit washed ashore and took his first deep breath in years. With the dragon finally defeated, the Kingdom of Mice was free from the reign of terror at last. The world welcomed a new era of much-needed peace, and it was all thanks to a tiny mouse who braved a big monster.

Naturally, Brystal's new routine was exhausting. She only managed to sleep for an hour or two each night, but the excitement of getting to read more the next day energized her like a drug. However, Brystal found clever ways of resting so she wasn't *entirely* sleep deprived.

During Mrs. Plume's lessons at school, Brystal tied a quill to her fingers and lowered her gaze so she appeared to be taking notes, but was actually taking a much-needed nap instead. On one occasion, while her classmates learned how to apply makeup, Brystal used the supplies to draw pupils on her eyelids so no one noticed she was sleeping through the demonstrations. At lunch, while the other girls went to the bakery in the town square, Brystal visited the furniture store and "tested the products" until the owners caught on.

On the weekends, Brystal snoozed in between her chores at the Evergreen house. At church, she spent the majority of the service with her eyes closed, pretending to pray. Luckily, her brothers did the same thing, so her parents never noticed.

Aside from the fatigue, Brystal thought her scheme was going very smoothly and she didn't face anywhere near as much suspicion as she had feared. She only saw her family for a few minutes each morning, so there wasn't much time for them to question her about her daily activities. Everyone was so focused on Barrie's inaugural weeks as a Deputy Justice that they never even asked about her volunteering for the Home for the Hopeless. Still, Brystal had developed stories about feeding the hungry and bathing the sick in case she needed them.

The only hitch happened at the beginning of her second month of employment. One evening Brystal entered the library to find Mr. Woolsore on his hands and knees searching under the furniture.

"Mr. Woolsore? Can I help you with something?" she asked.

"I'm looking for *Champions of the Champions, Volume 3*," Mr. Woolsore explained. "A student requested it this afternoon and it's vanished from the shelves."

Unbeknownst to the librarian, Brystal had borrowed *Champions of the Champions, Volume 3* the night before. She pulled her coat a little tighter around her shoulders so the librarian wouldn't see that the book was tucked under her arm.

"I'm sure it's here somewhere," she said. "Would you like me to help you look?"

"No, no, no," he grumped, and got to his feet. "The assistant librarian probably filed it incorrectly—*idiot man*! Just leave it on the counter if it shows up while you're cleaning."

Once Mr. Woolsore was gone, Brystal left *Champions of the Champions, Volume 3* on the counter. It was a simple remedy to a simple situation, but Brystal didn't want to experience a *closer* call to getting caught. To avoid any future risk, Brystal decided it would be wise if she stopped sneaking books home altogether. From then on, after she finished cleaning, Brystal stayed at the library to read. Sometimes she didn't return home until the early hours of the morning and had to sneak back into the house through a window.

At first, Brystal welcomed the change to her schedule. The empty library was very peaceful at night and the perfect place to get lost in a good book. Sometimes the moon shone so brightly through the glass ceiling she didn't even need a lantern to see the pages. Unfortunately, it wasn't long before Brystal became *too comfortable* with the new setup.

One morning Brystal was awoken by the cathedral bells—but they were different this morning. Instead of the distant ringing that gradually stirred her awake, a thunderous clanging caused her to jump to her feet. The noise was so sudden and alarming it was discombobulating. When she finally gained consciousness of her whereabouts, Brystal received her second shock of the morning—she wasn't standing in her bedroom. *She was still at the library!*

"Oh no!" she gasped. "I fell asleep reading! Father will be furious if he realizes I've been gone all night! I've got to get home before Mother notices my bed is empty!"

Brystal tucked her reading glasses into the top of her dress, stashed the books she had been reading on the nearest shelf, and ran out of the library as fast as she could. Outside, the cathedral bells were causing a hurricane of noise in the town square. Brystal covered her ears and had trouble staying upright as she was hit by wave after wave of sound. She dashed down the path toward the eastern countryside and reached the Evergreen home just as the final bell tolled. When she arrived, Mrs. Evergreen was standing on the front porch, frantically looking in every direction for her daughter. Her shoulders sank almost an entire foot when she saw Brystal approaching.

"Where on God's green earth have you been?" she

yelled. "You had me worried half to death! I almost sent for the King's Royal Guard!"

"I'm so sorry, Mother!" Brystal panted. "I—I—I can explain—"

"There better be a good reason why you weren't in your bed this morning!"

"It—it—it was an accident!" Brystal said, and quickly fabricated an excuse. "I was up late making beds at the Home for the Hopeless.... The beds looked so comfortable I couldn't resist lying down.... The next thing I heard were the bells this morning! Oh, please forgive me! I'll go inside and do the dishes from dinner right away!"

Brystal tried to go inside the house, but Mrs. Evergreen blocked the front door.

"This isn't about the dishes!" her mother said. "You can't imagine the fright you gave me! I convinced myself you were lying dead in an alley somewhere! Don't ever do that to me again! *Ever!*"

"I won't, I promise," Brystal said. "Honestly, it was just a silly accident. I didn't mean to worry you. Please don't tell Father about this. If he finds out I was gone all night, he'll never let me volunteer at the Home for the Hopeless again."

Brystal was in such a panic she couldn't tell if her performance was convincing or not. The look behind her mother's eyes was difficult to decipher, too. Mrs. Evergreen seemed convinced *and* unconvinced at the same time—like she knew her daughter wasn't telling the truth but was *choosing* to believe her lies.

"This *volunteering*...," Mrs. Evergreen said. "Whatever it entails, you must be more careful if you don't want to lose it. Your father will have no problem taking it away if he thinks it's making you irresponsible."

"I know," Brystal said. "And it'll never happen again. I swear."

Mrs. Evergreen nodded and softened her stern glare. "Good. I may only see you for a few minutes each morning, but I can tell volunteering is making you happy," she said. "You've been a different person since you started. It's nice to see you so content. I would hate for anything to change that."

"It makes me *very* happy, Mother," Brystal said. "Actually, I didn't realize I could *be* so happy."

Despite her daughter's excitement, something about Brystal's enthusiasm made Mrs. Evergreen noticeably sad.

"Well, that's wonderful, dear," she said with an unconvincing smile. "I'm pleased to hear it."

"You don't seem very pleased," Brystal said. "What's the matter, Mother? Am I not supposed to be happy?"

"What? No, of course not. Everyone deserves a little happiness now and then. *Everyone*. And nothing makes me happier than knowing you're happy, it's just... it's just..."

"What?"

Mrs. Evergreen smiled at her daughter again, but this time Brystal knew it was genuine.

"I just miss having you around, that's all," she

admitted. "Now get upstairs before your father or brothers see you. I'll do the dishes while you wash up. When you're finished you can help me in the kitchen. Happiness or no happiness, breakfast doesn't cook itself."

· • ★ • ·

The following week Brystal took her mother's advice to heart. To prevent herself from falling asleep in the library again, Brystal limited her nightly reading to just one hour after she finished her evening duties (two hours at the most if she found something *really* good) before packing up and heading home. She didn't get to read nearly as much as she wanted, but any time at the library was better than none.

Late one night, while searching for something to read, Brystal strolled down a long, winding hall on the second floor. Of all the sections in the library, she figured this was the least popular because it always needed the most dusting. The shelves were filled with collections of old public records and outdated ordinances—so it was no mystery why the hall was virtually forgotten.

As Brystal browsed the shelves at the end of the hall, a book on the very top shelf caught her attention. Unlike all the leather-bound records surrounding it, this book had a wooden cover and practically blended into the wooden shelf.

Brystal had never noticed the strange book before, and as she marveled at its peculiar camouflage, she began wondering if *anyone* had ever noticed it.

"Could there be books in this library that have never been read before?" she wondered aloud. "What if *I'm* the first person to read something?"

The notion was very exciting. Brystal rolled a ladder to the end of the hall and climbed to the top shelf. She tried to retrieve the wooden book, but it didn't budge.

"It's probably been sitting here for centuries," she speculated.

Brystal pulled on the book again, with all her strength, but it didn't move. Her feet rose off the ladder as she used all her weight to try to pry it loose, but even that didn't help. No matter how hard she tried, the wooden book wouldn't part from the shelf.

"It must be nailed down! What kind of sick person would nail a book to—*AAAAAAH!*"

Without warning, Brystal and the ladder were knocked to the floor by something large and heavy. When she looked up, Brystal discovered that the entire bookcase had swung away from the wall to reveal a long and dark hallway hidden behind it. She quickly realized the wooden book wasn't a book at all—*it was a lever to a secret door!*

"Hello?" Brystal nervously called into the hallway. "Is someone there?"

The only thing she heard was her own voice echoing back to her.

"If anyone can hear me, I'm sorry about this," she said. "I was just cleaning the shelf and it opened. I wasn't expecting to find a door to...to...*wherever this creepy hall leads.*"

Once again, there was no reply. Brystal assumed the hidden corridor was just as empty as the rest of the library and didn't see any harm in inspecting it. She retrieved a lantern and slowly walked down the hall to see where it led. At the end of the hallway, Brystal found a wide metal door with a plaque bolted on it:

JUSTICES ONLY

"'Justices Only'?" Brystal read aloud. "That's strange. Why would the Justices need a secret room in the library?"

She reached for the doorknob and her heart fluttered when she felt it was unlocked. The metal door creaked open and the sound echoed into the empty library behind her. Curiosity overpowered her judgment, and before Brystal could stop herself, she disregarded the sign and stepped through the door.

"Hello? Is anyone in here?" she asked. "Innocent maid coming through."

Brystal found a small room with a low ceiling on the other side of the door. Luckily, it was just as vacant as she had predicted. The walls had no windows or artwork but were lined with black bookcases. The only furniture was a small table and a single chair in the center of the room. An empty candlestick adorned the table, and a coatrack stood beside it with only two hooks: for one hat and one coat. Based on the minimal furnishings, Brystal figured the room was meant for only *one* Justice at a time.

She put on her reading glasses and raised her lantern toward a bookcase to see what kind of books were kept in the secret library. To her surprise, the Justices' collection was sparse. Each shelf contained less than a dozen titles, and every book was next to a file of paperwork. Brystal selected the thickest book from the nearest shelf and read the cover:

HISTORY & OTHER LIES
BY ROBBETH FLAGWORTH

The title was difficult to read because the book was coated in ash. Brystal moved her lantern closer and saw that the front cover had been branded with a word in large lettering:

"'Banned'?" Brystal read aloud. "Well, that seems silly. Why would anyone need to ban a book?"

She flipped the book open and read the first page it turned to. After skimming a few paragraphs, Brystal had her answer:

> *One of the greatest deceptions in recorded "history"*
> *was the reasoning for the Declawing Act of 339. For*
> *hundreds of years, the people of the Southern Kingdom*

have been told that King Champion VIII banished the trolls for acts of vulgarity, but this was nothing but propaganda to disguise a macabre plot against an innocent species.

Prior to the Declawing Act of 339, the trolls were respected participants in Southern Kingdom society. They were gifted craftsmen and built many of the structures that still stand in the Chariot Hills town square today. They lived quietly in the caves of the Southwest region and were regarded as a peaceful and private minority.

In 336, while expanding their caves in the Southwest, the trolls uncovered a large amount of gold. At the time, the Southern Kingdom was still crippled with debt from the Four Corners World War. Upon learning of the trolls' newfound wealth, Champion VIII claimed the gold was government property and ordered the trolls to turn it over at once.

Legally, the trolls had every right to keep their discovery, and they refused the king's demands. In retaliation, Champion VIII and his High Justices orchestrated a sinister ploy to tarnish the trolls' reputation. They spread nasty falsehoods about the trolls' lifestyle and behavior, and after time, the residents of the Southern Kingdom started believing the rumors. The king banished the trolls to the In-Between, seized their gold, and successfully brought the Southern Kingdom out of debt.

Sadly, the leaders of neighboring kingdoms were inspired by the Declawing Act of 339 and used the

*same method to erase their own debts. Soon the trolls
were unjustly ransacked and exiled from all four
kingdoms. Other intelligent species came to the trolls'
defense, but their efforts only caused them to suffer
a similar fate. Together, world leaders instituted the
Great Cleansing Act of 345, which expelled all talking
creatures other than humans from their kingdoms.*

*The troll, elf, ogre, and goblin populations lost
their homes and their possessions, and were forced into
the harsh environments of the In-Between. With limited
resources, the species had no choice but to resort to
the barbaric and primitive survival measures they're
resented and feared for today.*

*The so-called "monsters" of the In-Between are not
humankind's enemy, but humankind's creation.*

Brystal had to read the excerpt twice before she fully
understood what it was saying. Was Robbeth Flagworth
exaggerating, or was the Declawing Act of 339 as dishonest as he implied? And judging by the size of his book,
if the author was correct, then the Southern Kingdom's
history was jam-packed with other fabrications.

At first, the idea of history being dishonest was difficult for Brystal to comprehend. She didn't want to
believe a topic she knew so much about was filled with
lies, but the more she thought it over, the more plausible
it seemed. After all, the Southern Kingdom was a blatantly flawed and oppressive country—why should she
believe it was an *honest* place?

Brystal continued looking through the bookcases and selected another title that caught her eye:

THE WAR ON WOMEN
BY DAISY PEPPERNICKEL

Just like the previous book, *The War on Women* was covered in ash and branded with the word BANNED. With one quick glance at the pages inside, Brystal was instantly captivated by the subject matter:

> The female mind is not the fragile flowerpot we're made to believe. According to many studies on human anatomy, there is no evidence to suggest a woman's brain is any weaker, slower, or less capable than a man's. So the question remains: Why are we kept from education and positions of power? *Because the Justices use the oppression of women as an instrument to maintain their grip on the Southern Kingdom!*
>
> By nature, women are more maternal than men. If we ruled the Southern Kingdom, we would govern on principles of enlightenment, empathy, and nourishment. But the Justices and the current court system can only function in a society operated by fear, scrutiny, and punishment. If the country began valuing compassion over control, the Justices and their governing techniques would be rendered obsolete. That is why they take every step necessary to prevent women from rising above them.
>
> From the moment we're born, women are brainwashed to prioritize motherhood and marriage over intellect and personal

fulfillment. We're handed baby dolls and aprons and told our greatest contributions are accomplished in the nursery and the kitchen. But that lie is as damaging as it is degrading, because *a kingdom is only as strong as its weakest citizen*! And a society with unjust limitations is less likely to prevail than a country of equal opportunity.

When a nation segregates any percentage of its population, it only segregates a percentage of its potential! So for the sake of the kingdom, it is time for women to stand together and demand a new government that values every citizen's thoughts, ideas, and morals. Then and only then will our country journey into realms of prosperity it has never seen before.

Brystal's mouth dropped open—it was like she was reading a book of her own thoughts. She had never heard anyone else *speak* about the things she believed, let alone seen them printed in a book. She stacked *The War on Women* and *History & Other Lies* on the table, eager to finish them later, but first she wanted to see what other books were in the secret library. Another enticing title she found was called:

LOSING FAITH IN FAITH
By QUINT CUPPAMULE

Like the previous books, it too had BANNED branded into its cover. Brystal opened the book to a random page to get a sense of what it was about:

If the Book of Faith was as pure as the monks claim it is, there would be no need to amend it or publish *versions* over time. However, if you compared a current Book of Faith to one from a hundred years ago, you would discover vast differences between the religion of today and the religion of yesterday.

So what does this mean? Has the Lord simply changed His mind over the years? Has the Great Almighty corrected His mistakes after being convinced he was wrong? But wouldn't the very notion of being "wrong" contradict the "all-knowing" qualities the Lord is supposed to possess?

The truth is, what started as a joyful and loving faith is now a politically motivated ruse to control the people of the Southern Kingdom. Whenever the fear of incarceration is not enough to make people obey the law, the Justices alter the principles of religion and use the fear of eternal damnation to enforce their agenda.

The law and the Lord should be separate entities, but the Southern Kingdom has strategically made them the same. Therefore, any activity or opinion that questions the government is considered a sin. And every lifestyle or preference that doesn't help expand the population is considered demonic.

The Book of Faith no longer reflects the Lord's will, but the will of men who use the Lord as a tool to manipulate their people.

Brystal was absolutely fascinated by Quint Cuppamule's writing. In all her years attending church, she had never questioned the monk's sermons denouncing murder and theft, but she had always wondered why the monks preached just as passionately about the importance of paying taxes. Now it appeared Brystal had her answer.

She put *Losing Faith in Faith* in her stack and continued searching through the bookcases. The next BANNED title that gained her interest was called:

THE INJUSTICE OF THE JUSTICES:
How the King Is Only a Pawn to a Monarchy in Disguise

By Sherple Hinderback

As she moved the book off the shelf, Brystal accidentally knocked over the file of paperwork placed next to it. The documents spilled onto the floor, and Brystal knelt as she picked up the mess. Until this moment, Brystal hadn't had much interest in the files throughout the bookcases, but now she couldn't help reading the papers as she restacked them.

Among the paperwork was a detailed profile of the author Sherple Hinderback. It was followed by a log on Hinderback's whereabouts over a period of years. The addresses became more and more obscure with time—what started as houses and inns became bridges and caverns. The dates of the entries also became closer and closer together—as if Hinderback had changed his location more and more frequently. The log ended with a warrant for the author's arrest, and finally, the paperwork concluded with his death certificate. The cause of death was *EXECUTED FOR CONSPIRACY AGAINST THE KINGDOM.*

Brystal got to her feet and inspected the files beside the books of Robbeth Flagworth, Daisy Peppernickel, and Quint Cuppamule. Similar to the documents in the previous file, she found profiles of the authors, records of their residences, warrants for their arrests, and eventually, their death certificates. And just like Sherple Hinderback, each author's cause of death was *EXECUTED FOR CONSPIRACY AGAINST THE KINGDOM.*

As if struck by a cold breeze, Brystal had chills, and her body went tense. She felt sick to her stomach as she looked around and recognized the small room for what it truly was. This wasn't a private library—it was a graveyard for truth and an archive of people the Justices had silenced.

"They killed them," Brystal said in shock. "They killed them *all.*"

In time, the books throughout the secret room would introduce Brystal to an assortment of troubling ideas. Her perspective of the world would change forever, but most troubling of all, one of these books was going to change Brystal's view of *herself.* And once she read it she would never look into a mirror the same way again. . . .

CHAPTER FOUR

THE TRUTH ABOUT MAGIC

Every evening after cleaning the library, Brystal returned to the Justices' private room on the second floor to devour another BANNED title. The nightly ritual was by far the most dangerous exercise she had ever embarked on. Brystal knew she was playing with fire every time she passed the JUSTICES ONLY sign, but she also knew she had struck intellectual gold. This was the opportunity of a lifetime—it could be her only exposure to such a treasure trove of truth and ideas. If she didn't risk the consequences now,

Brystal was sure she would spend the rest of her lifetime regretting it.

With the completion of each BANNED book, Brystal felt like another veil had been lifted from her eyes. Everything she thought she knew about the Southern Kingdom—the laws, the economy, the history, how the army was run, what the class system was—it was all shrouded with conspiracies the Justices used to preserve their influence and control. The very foundation she was raised on crumbled beneath her feet more and more with every page she turned.

The most uncomfortable part for Brystal was wondering what her father's involvement was in the malicious schemes she read about. Was he even aware of the information Brystal was uncovering, or was he a leader in the corruption? Were some Justices kept in the dark, or did they *all* play a part in the deception? And if so, did that mean her brothers would eventually become as dishonest and power-hungry as the other Justices seemed to be?

Her world was turned virtually upside down, but the BANNED titles also proved something that Brystal found profoundly comforting: *she wasn't nearly as alone as she had feared.*

All the books in the secret room were written by people who felt and thought exactly like she did, by people who questioned information, who criticized social restrictions, who challenged the systems set in place, and who weren't afraid to make their ideas known. And for every person the Justices had successfully hunted down, there must be dozens who were still at large. Brystal just hoped the day would come when she would get to meet them.

Despite the lucky discovery, Brystal was prepared for it all to end in disaster. Should she get caught in the act, Brystal thought continuing her role as a frivolous and innocent maid was her best chance at avoiding any trouble. She spent a great deal of time imagining what the interaction might sound like:

"What are you doing in here?"

"Me, sir? Well, I'm the maid, of course. I'm here to clean."

"You are not allowed in this room! The sign on the door clearly states this room is for Justices only!"

"I'm sorry, sir, but my employer's instructions were to clean *every* part of the library. He never mentioned certain rooms were off-limits. Even private rooms get dusty."

Fortunately, the library remained as empty and quiet as always, allowing Brystal to read in safety.

· • ★ • ·

By the end of Brystal's second month of employment, she had read every BANNED title in the Justices' private library except for one. As she retrieved the final book, on the bottom shelf of the last bookcase, Brystal was consumed by a bittersweet sensation. For weeks, the secret room had been a private classroom where she got to study the most fascinating subjects imaginable, and now she was taking her final lesson:

The Truth About Magic
By Celeste Weatherberry

Curiously, unlike all the other books in the room, *The Truth About Magic* didn't have a file beside it. The cover was a pale violet and practically glowed in the dark chamber. The title was surrounded by an elaborate silver crest with a unicorn and a gryphon on opposite sides, and the space between the creatures was filled with winged pixies, stars, and a crescent moon.

It was by far the most beautiful book Brystal had ever come across. Of all the topics she had read about in the private library, she was the least familiar with magic. She knew it was considered a demonic practice and a heinous crime, but other than the *reactions* to it, Brystal knew very little about magic itself. She sat at the table and excitedly opened the book to the very first page, eager to learn more:

Dear Friend,

If this book has found a way into your hands, I hope you are reading it in a safe place. As I'm sure you're aware, magic is a rather *sensitive* subject around the world. In most areas, possessing anything remotely related to magic is just as punishable as the act of magic. However, by the end of this book, you will learn that magic is as pure as existence itself, and why it's worthy of the world's admiration and respect.

To get a proper perspective on what I'm saying, we must first take a look at history. Thousands of years ago, humanity and other intelligent species lived in harmony with members of the magical community. We were one another's neighbors, friends, and family. We helped one another, looked out for one another, and all worked together toward the same goals of peace and prosperity. Unfortunately, that all changed when humankind began its bloody quest for world domination.

Before King Champion I was crowned, the young sovereign-in-waiting had a wonderful relationship with the magical community. He pledged his loyalty to us, and in return, we aided his ascension to the throne. After Champion I's coronation, the king's first royal act was to establish his Advisory Council of High Justices, and history was changed forever.

The High Justices saw magical people and their abilities as a threat. They filled Champion I's head with lies about our intentions to overthrow him and seize control of the kingdom. They rewrote the Book of Faith and convinced the entire kingdom that our spells, charms, and enchantments were demonic practices, and that our very existence was an abomination. So Champion I declared all members of the magical community to be "witches," and criminalized magic to the same caliber as treason and murder. Eventually the other kingdoms followed Champion I's example, and the first witch hunt in recorded history began.

Across the world, all alleged witches were arrested and executed, all the unicorns, dragons, gryphons, pixies, and other animals deemed "magical" were slaughtered into extinction, and all the good that the magical community had done for humankind was erased from history. The High Justices' plan was so efficient that it became the template for how they dealt with all conflicts in the future.

Hundreds of years have passed since Champion I's reign, but the stigma against people with magical blood is stronger than ever. In recent decades, King Champion XIV changed the punishment for conjuring magic in the Southern Kingdom from death to imprisonment with hard labor, but this does nothing to salvage all the innocent lives being lost throughout the world. To this day, many people abandon their children or flee into dangerous territories just to avoid being associated with magic. But the very notion that magic is wrong or something to be ashamed of is the greatest misconception of our time.

Magic is the beautiful and rare gift to manifest and modify the elements. It's a pure and positive art form used to create something from nothing. It's the ability to help those in need, heal those in pain, and improve the world around us. Magic can only be accomplished by those with goodness in their hearts, and they aren't the witches that popular belief suggests, but rather are known as fairies. And their talents should be celebrated, not suppressed.

While witches do exist, they represent a very small fraction of the remaining magical community. The wickedness in their hearts prevents witches from doing magic, so instead, they practice a foul and destructive art called *witchcraft*. Those who commit witchcraft usually do it with disruptive intentions. They deserve the harsh punishments they receive, but their vile ways should *never* be mistaken for the goodness that magic offers.

It may seem complicated to differentiate a fairy from a witch, but there is a simple test that members of the magical community have used for centuries. By reading a passage of ancient text aloud, a questioning fairy or witch can easily determine where they stand:

Ahkune awknoon ahkelle–enama, telmune talmoon ahktelle–awknamon.

Brystal found the phrase so amusing she read it out loud just to hear what it sounded like. *"'Ahkune awknoon ahkelle-enama, telmune talmoon ahktelle-awknamon,'"* she pronounced with a laugh.

Did something macabre manifest nearby?
Were you unexpectedly hit by a storm of locusts or
a plague of fleas? Was your skin suddenly covered
in blistering blemishes? If there are no visible
changes to your body or immediate surroundings,
then congratulations, you are not a witch!

Now, by reading the next passage aloud, you
can determine whether you are a fairy:

*Elsune elknoon ahkelle–enama, delmune dalmoon
ahktelle–awknamon.*

Brystal knew reading the second passage would have
as little effect on her as the first, but she enjoyed playing
along with the author. It wasn't every day she took a test
to determine whether she had magical capabilities.

"*'Elsune elknoon ahkelle-enama, delmune dalmoon
ahktelle-awknamon,'*" she read aloud.

Did something beautiful appear? Are rubies
and diamonds raining from the sky? Has your
clothing changed into something much more stylish
than before? If so, then congratulations, you're a
fairy! If reading that text resulted in no physical
changes to you or your surroundings, then it is safe
to assume you do not have magic coursing through
your veins.

Although you are not part of the magical
community, I hope you will still support our efforts
to find acceptance and—

Suddenly, Brystal was distracted by an unexpected smell. As if someone had lit a scented candle, the small room was consumed with the pleasant aromas of lavender, jasmine, and roses, among other fragrances. Out of the corner of her eye, she saw something moving and jerked her head in its direction.

To her absolute amazement, hundreds upon hundreds of flowers had begun growing out of the walls around her. Once the walls were covered, the blossoms sprouted across the ceiling, the floor, and through the bookcases. Brystal screamed as the phenomenon spread across the table in front of her and she jumped out of her seat when she felt flowers grow out from under the chair.

"What... what... *what just happened?*" she asked in disbelief.

Brystal knew exactly what had happened; she just didn't want to admit it. After reading a passage from a book about magic, she had unintentionally transformed the dull and windowless room into a vibrant and colorful floral wonderland. There was no other explanation for the change, but she rejected the implications with her entire being.

"No, no, no—this isn't real!" Brystal told herself. "This is just a hallucination caused by sleep deprivation. In a few seconds it'll all disappear."

No matter how many deep breaths she took or how hard she rubbed her eyes, the flowers did not vanish. Brystal became dizzy and her hands trembled as the inconvenient reality began to sink in.

"I...I...*I can't be*!" she thought aloud. "Of all the people in the world, this can't be happening to *me*.... This can't be who I am....I have enough working against me as it is. I can't be *magic* on top of it all!"

Brystal was desperate to destroy all the evidence that proved otherwise. She hurried to the ground level of the library and returned with the largest wastebaskets she could find. She frantically pulled all the flowers out of the walls and floor and furniture, and didn't pause until every petal and leaf had been tossed away and the Justices' room was back to normal. Brystal placed *The Truth About Magic* on its shelf and dragged the wastebaskets out of the private library. She closed the wide metal door behind her with the intention of never returning, as if she could keep the truth locked inside.

· • ★ • ·

For several days, Brystal pretended as if she had never found the secret room on the second floor. She told herself *The Truth About Magic* and the other BANNED books didn't exist, and that she had never read the spell that manifested the flowers. In fact, Brystal was in such denial about the ordeal that she went straight home every night after cleaning without reading anything at all, afraid the very sight of another book would remind her of what she wanted to forget.

Unfortunately, the more effort she put into erasing the event from her mind, the more she thought about it.

And soon it was no longer an issue of *if* it had happened, but of *why* it had happened.

"This all has to be a big misunderstanding," she said to herself. "If I was magical—or a *fairy*, as the author put it—there would have been signs! A *fairy* would know they were different. . . . A *fairy* would have trouble blending in. . . . A *fairy* would spend their whole life feeling like they didn't belong. *Oh, shut up, Brystal! You've just described yourself!*"

In many ways, having magic in her blood made sense. Brystal had always been so different from everyone she knew—perhaps magic was the source of her uniqueness? Perhaps she had always wanted more out of life because, deep down inside, she knew there *was* more to her life.

"But why did it take me so long to find out?" she asked herself. "Was I completely oblivious, or has a part of me known all along? Then again, I live in a kingdom that keeps *all* forms of knowledge from young women. Maybe this just proves how efficiently the Justices are oppressing their people. And if I wasn't a menace to society before, I certainly am now."

And now that she knew the truth, would it be easy for others to figure it out, too? Would her classmates smell it on her as easily as her other differences? Was it possible to hide magic, or would it inevitably resurface and expose her? And if it did, would it finally give her father the right to disown her and send her away for good? The dangers were endless.

· • ★ • ·

"Is everything okay, Brystal?" Barrie asked one morning before breakfast.

"Yes, everything is fine," Brystal was quick to respond. "Why—why do you ask?"

"No reason," he said with a smile. "You've just seemed a little tense lately. And I've noticed you haven't been spending as much time at the Home for the Hopeless as usual. Is there anything you need to talk about?"

"Oh, I've just decided to take a little break," she said. "Something happened—nothing serious, of course—but I thought a little distance would be helpful. It would give me a chance to think about things and figure out what to do next."

"Figure out what to do next?" Barrie asked with concern. "All right, now you *have* to tell me what's going on so my imagination doesn't fill in the blanks."

Brystal was so exhausted from worrying that she didn't have the energy to put on a show. So she told her brother a story that was as close to the truth as possible without giving anything away.

"I recently discovered something about myself that's a little hard to live with," she said.

Barrie's eyes went large. "And that is?"

"Well, I . . . I . . . I'm not sure *I like charity anymore*."

Barrie did a double take at his sister's odd response.

"You've been tense because you *don't like charity anymore*?" he asked.

"Um . . . *yes*," Brystal said with a shrug. "And quite

frankly, I'm not certain how much longer I'll be able to hide it. Now that I know, I'm afraid other people are going to find out, too. I'm terrified about what might happen to me if I'm ever exposed."

"*Exposed?* But, Brystal, disliking charity isn't illegal. It's just a preference."

"I know, but it's *practically* a crime," she exclaimed. "The world is very cruel to *people who don't like charity*—but that's just because they're misunderstood. Society thinks that *disliking charity* is the same as *disliking kindness*, when in reality, *disliking charity* and *disliking kindness* are very, very different! Oh, Barrie—I wish I could tell you just how different they are, because it's fascinating! One of the greatest misconceptions of our time!"

According to the expression on her brother's face, he might have been less concerned if she had just told him the truth. Barrie was looking at his sister like she was on the verge of a mental breakdown, and to be fair, she was.

"How long have you *disliked charity*?" he asked.

"Almost a week," she said.

"And do you remember the incident that changed your mind?"

"Yes, it all started when I accidentally covered a room in flowers," she said, forgetting to alter her story. "Um—I mean, there was a homeless woman who was feeling ill, so I filled her room with flowers to cheer her up. But it was the wrong room—a room I honestly had no business being in. So I had to throw all the flowers away before someone caught me."

"Right...," Barrie said. "But prior to that moment, you had never disliked charity before, had you?"

"Not at all," she said. "Before that, I didn't think I was capable of disliking charity."

"Then that settles it," he said. "You just had a bad day. And you should never let one day change who you are. We can never be certain about anything in life— especially if we only experience it once."

"We can't?" Brystal asked with hopeful eyes.

"Of course not," Barrie said. "If I were you, I would go back to the Home for the Hopeless and give charity another try to make sure you genuinely dislike it. Then, and only then, would I worry about being *exposed* for it."

Although her brother had no idea what was really bothering her, Brystal thought he had given her excellent advice. After all, it took more than one trip on a boat to turn someone into a sailor—maybe magic was similar? Perhaps it would take years of practice before she had to worry about it putting her life in danger. And like Barrie suggested, there was always the chance the whole ordeal had been a fluke and would never happen again. Right or wrong, for her own sanity, Brystal had to find out.

The following night after she finished cleaning the library, Brystal returned to the Justices' private library on the second floor. She put her reading glasses on, retrieved *The Truth About Magic* by Celeste

Weatherberry from the shelf, and turned to the page with the ancient text. After a deep breath and a silent prayer, she read the incantation aloud to prove whether she was a fairy, once and for all.

"*'Elsune elknoon ahkelle-enama, delmune dalmoon ahktelle-awknamon.'*"

Brystal was afraid to look and covered her eyes. At first, she didn't feel or hear anything, so she peeked at the room through her fingers. Nothing appeared to have changed in the slightest, and Brystal's spirits began to soar. She watched the walls with bated breath, waiting for the flowers to materialize again, but they never came. Tears filled her eyes and she let out a sigh of relief that turned into a long, thankful laugh.

"Barrie was right," she said. "We should never let *one day* change who we—"

Suddenly, the pages of *The Truth About Magic* started to glow. Bright orbs of white light slowly rose from the book and filled the dark room. As the orbs spread out, they became smaller and smaller, creating the illusion of depth in every direction, and soon the private library resembled a limitless galaxy.

Brystal got to her feet and looked around the room in amazement. Not only had she confirmed the magic in her veins, but she never imagined she was capable of creating such a beautiful sight. The magic was transcendent, and Brystal forgot where she was. It didn't feel like she was standing in the private library anymore, but floating through her very own starry universe.

"MISS BAILEY! WHAT IN THE NAME OF CHAMPION ARE YOU DOING?!"

The voice startled Brystal, and all the orbs throughout the room instantly vanished. When her eyes adjusted, Brystal saw the metal door had swung open without her noticing. Mr. Woolsore was standing in the doorway with two armed guards, and all three men were staring at her like she was the foulest creature they had ever seen.

"That's the girl I've been warning you about!" Mr. Woolsore shouted, and he pointed a shaky finger at her. "I've been telling you for months that she was up to something! But none of you believed me! You said I was mad for believing a young girl was capable of such things! Now look—*we've caught a witch in the act!*"

"Mr. Woolsore!" Brystal said. "Wait, I can explain! This isn't what it looks like!"

"Save your lies for the Justice, witch! You've been caught red-handed!" the librarian yelled, and then turned to the guards. "Don't just stand there, seize her before she casts another spell!"

Brystal had imagined many scenarios where she was caught in the Justices' private library, but she never imagined it would happen while she was *conjuring magic*. Before she had the chance to defend herself further, the guards charged toward her and forcefully grabbed her by the arms.

"No! You don't understand!" she pleaded. "I'm not a witch! Please, I'm begging you! Let me prove it!"

As the guards dragged Brystal out of the room, Mr. Woolsore snatched the reading glasses off her face and snapped them in two.

"You won't be needing these where you're going," he said. *"Take her away!"*

CHAPTER FIVE

TRIAL BY FAMILY

For the first time Brystal understood what it was like to be scared senseless. There were heavy shackles around her wrists, but she didn't feel them. The smell of decaying rats and mildew filled the air, but it didn't bother her. Bloodcurdling screams of prisoners getting whipped echoed through the halls, but she hardly noticed them. Her eyes were fixated on the steel bars surrounding her, but she didn't understand what she was looking at.

She was sitting straight up on the edge of the stone

bench in her prison cell and hadn't moved a muscle since she was placed there. Everything happened so fast the night before, she couldn't remember where she was or how she got there. Then again, she was in such a state of shock, she could barely think at all.

At dawn, the ear-piercing cathedral bells didn't even make Brystal flinch. It was now the morning after the worst night of her life, but she had no concept of time. Her mind was completely blank, her body was completely still, and as far as she was concerned, the world had stopped spinning.

Her cell door swung open and a prison guard stepped inside, but his arrival didn't break her petrified trance.

"Your Defense Deputy Justice has arrived," the guard said.

After hearing this, Brystal was finally able to make sense of where she was and what had happened. She, *Brystal Evergreen*, had been imprisoned for a crime. She was sitting in the prison deep below the Chariot Hills Courthouse, and the Deputy Justice assigned to defend her had come to speak with her about the pending trial.

The guard stepped aside and a tall young man in a black hat and a gray-and-black-checkered robe entered the cell. When Brystal gazed up at the Deputy Justice, she thought her mind was playing tricks on her.

"Brooks?" she said.

Her eldest brother froze after taking his first step into the prison cell. His eyes went wide and his face grew pale at the sight of his sister in chains.

"Brystal?" he gasped.

The Evergreen siblings stared at each other for a full minute without saying a single word. It was the only time in Brystal's life that she had been genuinely pleased to see her brother, but the pleasure quickly faded as she realized why he was there: *Brooks was going to defend her in court!*

"Brooks, I—I—" Brystal tried to break the silence, but she was at a loss for words.

"Do you two *know* each other?" the guard asked suspiciously.

As Brooks stared at his sister, the disbelief in his eyes changed into a very serious and urgent expression. He raised his index finger to his mouth, imploring her to be quiet. Brystal didn't understand why the silence was necessary, but she obliged.

"We're acquainted," Brooks told the guard behind him. "She's just one of the many schoolgirls who admire me. But who can blame her?"

Her brother's charade was confusing—she knew it was perfectly legal for Deputy Justices to defend family members on trial—so why was he pretending they weren't related? Brooks opened his briefcase and retrieved a quill and a piece of parchment. He scribbled a quick note on the paper, folded it, and handed it to the guard.

"I need you to deliver this message to Justice Evergreen's office on the fourth floor," Brooks instructed. "I was just reminded of something involving another case that needs to be addressed immediately."

"Sir, I can't leave you alone with the prisoner," the guard replied.

"Don't insult me—this *girl* is hardly a physical threat. The note, however, regards a very serious and timely matter. Justice Evergreen will want this message right away, and if your reluctance jeopardizes his case, I'll make sure he knows *you* caused the delay."

Obviously, the guard didn't appreciate being ordered around. He glared at Brooks and then begrudgingly headed to the fourth floor with the note in hand, slamming the cell door behind him. Brooks turned to Brystal and the disbelief returned to his face.

"My God, Brystal! What the hell have you gotten yourself into?" he exclaimed. "One count of trespassing! One count of female literacy! And one count of *committing magic*! Do you have any idea how serious this is?"

Brystal looked to the floor and shook her head. "I don't know what to say," she said softly. "It all feels like a bad dream."

"When you weren't at breakfast this morning, Mother assumed you had gone to the Home for the Hopeless to volunteer before school!" Brooks said. "When I got to the courthouse, all the Deputy Justices were talking about the witch they caught in the library last night—but I didn't put the two together! I never imagined in a million years the witch would be *my own sister*!"

"But I'm not a witch!" Brystal exclaimed. "The banned book I was reading explains everything! Please, you have to find it and show it to—"

"Are you mad?" Brooks asked. "I can't use a *banned book* as evidence!"

"Then what are we going to use for my defense?" Brystal asked.

"Defense?" Brooks said, as if he was appalled by her choice of words. "Brystal, you were caught by three witnesses—*there's no defense*! You're facing life imprisonment with hard labor for *committing magic* alone, but with *trespassing* and *female literacy* on top of it, you'll be lucky to make it out of here alive!"

"You mean . . . they might *execute* me?"

Brystal felt like a cold hand had suddenly reached into her body and ripped out her stomach. She had willingly gone down a long path of mistakes, but she had never thought it would lead to this. She started hyperventilating.

"No, this can't be happening!" she cried. "You can't let them execute me! Please, Brooks, you have to help me! *I'm your sister!*"

Brooks rolled his eyes at the remark. "Oh yes, and what a *joy* you are!" he said spitefully. "I'm afraid even with my superb defense skills, my hands are tied."

"There has to be *something* we can do!"

Her brother went quiet and he bit his nails as he thought about it.

"There's only one thing I can think of that could possibly help you now."

"What?"

"Father."

111

Brooks said it like it was good news, but it only made Brystal feel more hopeless than before. Her father was the last person on the planet she expected to save her.

"Father isn't going to help me," she said. "When he finds out what I've done, he'll want to kill me himself!"

"Well, you're right about that," Brooks scoffed. "Father may not value your life, but he thinks very highly of his own. He would do anything to preserve his reputation. And nothing is going to tarnish his name more than one of his children getting arrested and sentenced to death. Luckily for him, I'm the only one who knows you're in here."

"How?"

"As far as anyone knows, this is the case of *Bailey vs. the Southern Kingdom*—the charges have been filed under the alias you gave the library! When Father gets my note and realizes *you're* the one on trial, he's going to do whatever he can to sweep this case under the rug before his colleagues find out!"

"But what if he doesn't?" Brystal asked. "Father can't be my *only* chance of survival."

"Then it all depends on your trial," Brooks explained. "First, the Prosecution Deputy will present your charges to the sitting Justice and recommend a penalty. If they recommend the *minimum penalty*, the Justice will most likely sentence you to life imprisonment with hard labor, but if the Deputy recommends the *maximum penalty*, I guarantee the Justice will sentence you to capital punishment."

"But the sitting Justice doesn't have to take the recommendation, it's just a suggestion," Brystal recalled from what she had read. "Even if the Prosecution Deputy recommends the maximum penalty, the Justice could still be merciful."

Brooks's face fell flat and Brystal knew there was something he wasn't telling her.

"There won't be any mercy this time," he said. "Your trial is being overseen by Justice Oldragaid."

"Who?"

"Justice Oldragaid is the most despised Justice in the court system. He has a God complex and is notorious for condemning people to death whenever possible. Even when Prosecution Deputies recommend the minimum penalty, Oldragaid likes to bully them into recommending the maximum penalty just so he can enforce it."

"Oh my gosh!" Brystal gasped.

"It gets worse," Brooks went on. "Oldragaid has hated Father since their days at the University of Law. During their time as Deputy Justices, Father never lost a case against Oldragaid and would humiliate him during the trials. That's the reason he assigned me to your defense—it's impossible for a Defense Deputy to win a case like this and he wanted to watch an Evergreen lose! And Oldragaid would be thrilled to sentence you to death if he had the chance."

Brystal couldn't believe her misfortune. She was getting punished not only by the laws of the Southern Kingdom, but also, apparently, by the universe itself.

"Then I'm doomed," she said quietly. "There's no way around it."

"There's still one thing in our favor that you're forgetting," Brooks reminded her. "Like I said, as far as anyone knows, this is the case of *Bailey vs. the Southern Kingdom*. Justice Oldragaid doesn't know who you are. Trials usually don't begin until a day or two after incarceration, so hopefully that'll give Father enough time to help you before Oldragaid finds out."

"So *that's* why you pretended we weren't related in front of the guard. You didn't want anyone to realize who I am."

"Exactly."

Brystal never thought a day would come when she was thankful for having a brother like Brooks, but here it was. All the calculating and mischievous qualities she resented about him were now the tools he was using to save her life.

"I'm so scared, Brooks," she said.

"Well, you should be," he said. "Even if Father finds a way to help you, you aren't going to walk out of here freely. Best-case scenario, you'll probably spend the rest of your life in a prison far away from Chariot Hills."

"I suppose you think I deserve it for being so stupid . . . ," she said through tears. "I didn't mean for any of this to happen. . . . I just wanted life to be *different*. . . ."

"Then I guess you got what you asked for."

The door swung open as the guard returned to the

cell. He was wheezing and sweating profusely from his journey to and from the fourth floor.

"I delivered your message to the Justice, sir," the guard grumbled.

"Just in time, too. I'm all finished here."

Brooks picked up his briefcase and headed for the door, but Brystal stopped him as he stepped into the hall.

"Deputy Justice Evergreen?" she asked. "If you happen to see them, will you please give my love to my mother and my brother? And tell them I am so, so sorry for all this?"

Her brother gave the slightest nod possible without attracting the guard's attention. "I am not your messenger, *criminal*," he said dramatically. "See you in court."

Brooks continued down the hall and the guard followed, locking the cell door behind him. As the sound of their footsteps faded, Brystal was consumed by the most extreme sorrow she had ever experienced. She lay on the stone bench and wept until there wasn't a teardrop left inside her.

As far as she knew, her brother was the last piece of home she'd ever see again.

That night, Brystal was jolted awake when her cell door suddenly burst open. Two prison guards charged inside, grabbed her by the arms, and forced her onto her feet. Without saying a word, the guards rushed Brystal out of the cell, raced her across the prison, and then hurried her up a spiral staircase. They moved at such a frantic pace Brystal had trouble keeping up and had to be dragged a majority of the way. She had no idea what was happening or where they were taking her, and she was too afraid to ask.

They reached the top of the staircase and entered the main corridor of the courthouse. The corridor, usually bustling with Deputy Justices and Justices alike, was dark and completely empty. Brystal figured it must have been past midnight, which made the whole situation even more frightening. What could be so important that it required her to be transported in the middle of the night?

At the end of the dark corridor, Brystal spotted Brooks pacing in front of a pair of tall double doors. His face was bright red and he angrily muttered to himself as he moved.

"Brooks!" she called out. "What's going on? Why are we in the courthouse so late?"

"Justice Oldragaid found out who you are!" he said. "The guard must have read my note and tipped him off—*that bastard*! Oldragaid moved up your trial— he's trying to sentence you before Father has time to intervene!"

"Wait, I don't understand," Brystal said. "When's the trial happening?"

"*Now,*" he said.

The guards pushed open the double doors and

pulled Brystal into the courtroom. Her brother followed closely behind.

They were the first to arrive and Brystal was overwhelmed by her first glimpse—it was easily the biggest room she had ever been in. It was surrounded by massive marble pillars that stretched into the darkness of a seemingly endless ceiling. Wooden risers wrapped around the courtroom with enough seats for a thousand witnesses. The only source of light came from two torches burning, one on either side of the Justice's chair, which was raised on a tall platform at the front of the room. An enormous portrait of King Champion XIV was hung on the wall behind the platform, and the sovereign scowled down at the courtroom like a judgmental giant.

The guards locked Brystal in a tall iron cage that stood in the very center of the room. The bars were so wide she could barely see through them. Brooks took a seat at an empty table to the left of the cage, and Brystal assumed the empty table to her right was reserved for the Prosecution Deputy.

"Try to stay calm," her brother whispered. *"And whatever you do, don't say anything. It'll only make things worse."*

A small door behind the platform opened and Justice Oldragaid entered the courtroom from his private chambers. Even if he wasn't the Justice overseeing her trial, the sight of Oldragaid would have been chilling. He was a skeletal man with a pitch-black beard and large sunken eyes that had pupils the size of pinpricks. His skin was the color of pea soup, and his long fingernails made his hands look like claws.

Oldragaid was followed by four guards, and to Brystal's horror, an executioner also emerged from the Justice's private chambers, carrying a large silver axe. Brystal turned to her brother, hoping to find reassurance in his eyes, but Brooks was as alarmed as she was. The trial hadn't even started and her fate seemed to be sealed.

The Justice climbed up the steps of the platform and took his seat. He glared down at Brystal with a twisted grin, like a cat gawking at a mouse in a trap. With three loud bangs of his gavel, the proceedings began.

"The case of *Bailey vs. the Southern Kingdom* shall commence," he announced.

"Your Honor, I'd like to remind you that it is illegal to begin a trial without a Prosecution Deputy," Brooks said. "And furthermore, it is *completely* unethical to have an executioner present in court before a defendant has been sentenced."

"I am aware of the law, Defense Deputy," the Justice sneered. "The Prosecution Deputy will be here momentarily. However, *you* of all people should not be lecturing *me* about ethics. It's recently come to my attention that you have made deliberate attempts to conceal information from the court. That is a direct violation of your moral duties as a Deputy Justice, and violators must be reprimanded."

Justice Oldragaid gave the guards a signal and they

covered Brystal's cage with a sheet. Her limited view of the courtroom was now entirely obstructed.

"Your Honor, what is the purpose of this?" Brooks objected.

"As I'm sure you're aware, Defense Deputy, whenever a Deputy Justice is caught committing a violation in court, it is up to the presiding Justice to apply an appropriate punishment," Oldragaid explained. "I've decided to teach you a lesson about the *importance of transparency.* Since you attempted to conceal the defendant's identity from me, her identity will be concealed for the rest of this trial. You are not to speak a word about who she is until *after* the Prosecution Deputy has recommended penalties. Let one word slip, and I'll charge you with *conspiracy to assist a criminal.* Is that understood?"

Brystal didn't have to see the hatred beaming from her brother's eyes to know it was there.

"Yes, Your Honor," Brooks said. "I understand."

"Good," Oldragaid said. *"Bring in the Prosecution Deputy!"*

The double doors creaked open and Brystal heard a new pair of footsteps enter the courtroom. Strangely, the Prosecution Deputy only made it halfway through the room before he stopped in his tracks.

"Brooks?" a familiar voice asked.

"Barrie?" he gasped. "You're the Prosecution Deputy?"

Brystal felt light-headed and went weak in the knees. She had to grab the bars of her cage to prevent herself from sliding to the floor. Justice Oldragaid was using her trial to get revenge on the Evergreen family, and it was more malicious and cruel than she could ever have imagined.

"This is my first assignment," Barrie said happily. "Why didn't you tell me you were the Defense Deputy on *Bailey vs. the Southern Kingdom*?"

"I—I—I was trying to keep it quiet," Brooks said.

"Why is the defendant covered up?" Barrie asked.

"I'm not allowed to discuss it," Brooks said. "Barrie, listen to me, this trial isn't what it seems—"

"That's quite enough, Defense Deputy!" Justice Oldragaid commanded. "Thank you for joining us on such short notice, Prosecution Deputy. Now please step forward and present the charges against the defendant."

Barrie took his place behind the table to Brystal's right. She heard him remove papers from his briefcase. He cleared his throat before reading them aloud.

"Your Honor, three men witnessed the defendant conjuring a spell from an open book in a private section of the Chariot Hills Library," he said. "The first witness was the librarian, Mr. Patwise Woolsore, the other two are officers in the King's Royal Guard, and all three have signed sworn statements of what they encountered. Given the credibility of the observers, the defendant has been charged with one count of trespassing, one count of female literacy, and one count of committing magic. I'll now relinquish the floor to the Defense Deputy."

"Given the substantial evidence, and the nature of

the crimes, we will not waste any time with the defense," Justice Oldragaid said.

"*Your Honor, I object!*" Brooks shouted.

"*Overruled!* And watch your tone, Defense Deputy!" the Justice warned. "Now, moving on. What penalty does the prosecution recommend?"

This was the moment Brystal had been dreading. With just two words, her own brother would either save her life or cement her demise. Her heart was pounding out of her chest and she forgot to breathe as she waited to hear his answer.

"Your Honor, due to the number of felonies that were committed in such a short period of time, I believe the defendant may commit more crimes if given the chance. We must remove all likelihood of it happening again, and furthermore, we must prevent all possibility of the defendant harming innocent lives in the process. That is why I must recommend you sentence them with a—"

"Barrie, you've got to stop!" Brooks shouted.

"DEFENSE DEPUTY, CONTROL YOURSELF!" Oldragaid ordered.

"*I know you think you're doing the right thing, but you're not!*"

"GUARDS! RESTRAIN AND SILENCE HIM IMMEDIATELY!"

"*Oldragaid is hiding the defendant from you on purpose! Don't recommend a maximum punishment! Trust me, you're going to regret it for the rest of your life!*"

Brystal could hear Brooks fighting off the guards

as he tried to convince their brother. He grunted and choked as they pinned him down and stuffed a cloth into his mouth.

"God, you're pathetic," Barrie told his brother. "Your desire to sabotage me is so great you're willing to make a complete fool of yourself in court! But I'm not as daft as you think and I won't let you jeopardize my career! Father said I needed to show strength if I wanted the court to take me seriously, and that's exactly what I'm going to do! *Your Honor, the prosecution recommends the maximum penalty!*"

After hearing her brother's recommendation, Brystal lost all feeling and collapsed on the floor of the cage like a marionette with severed strings. Brooks screamed at the top of his lungs, but the cloth muffled his words.

"Then without further notice, I hereby sentence the defendant to death," Justice Oldragaid ruled. "The execution shall take place immediately. Guards, please remove the defendant from the cage and position her for the executioner. But first, please restrain the Prosecution Deputy—this may be unpleasant for him to watch."

The guards seized Barrie and tied his hands behind his back. He tried to resist them, but they were too strong.

"What's the meaning of this?" he asked. "Why am *I* being restrained? Unhand me at once! I've done nothing wrong!"

The sheet was removed from the cage, and with one glance at the blue eyes peeking out from inside, Barrie realized who the defendant was.

"Brystal?" he said in shock. "But—but—but what are you doing *in there*? You're supposed to be volunteering at the Home for the Hopeless!"

The executioner placed a thick wooden block on the floor below the Justice's platform. The guards dragged Brystal out from the cage and positioned her head on the block. As the executioner hovered over her, the reality of what Barrie had just done began to sink in. He became manic and struggled against the restraints with all his might.

"Noooooo!" he screamed. "I didn't know what I was doing! I didn't know it was her!"

Justice Oldragaid smiled and cackled at the trauma he was causing the Evergreen family. The executioner raised his axe above Brystal's neck and practiced swinging it. From the floor, Brystal could see both her brothers frantically trying to fight off the guards holding them back. In that moment, she was almost grateful for Oldragaid's vengeful tactics—if she was going to die, at least this way she would die looking at the people she loved.

"Brystal, I'm sorry!" Barrie sobbed. "Forgive me! *Forgive meeeeee!!"*

"It's going to be all right, Barrie...," she whispered. *"This isn't your fault.... This isn't your fault.... This isn't your fault...."*

WHAM! The double doors suddenly swung open, causing everyone to jump and turn to the back of the courtroom. Justice Evergreen stormed inside with the rage of a hundred men.

"OLDRAGAID, STOP THIS BLASPHEMY AT ONCE!" he demanded.

"How dare you interrupt a trial in progress, Evergreen!" Oldragaid shouted. "Leave the courtroom this instant or I'll have you removed!"

"THIS ISN'T A TRIAL, IT'S AN ATROCITY!" Justice Evergreen declared.

The executioner glanced back and forth at the sparring Justices, uncertain of who to take orders from.

"Carry on, man!" Oldragaid yelled. "This is my courtroom! Justice Evergreen has no authority here!"

"As a matter of fact, I do!" Justice Evergreen said, and raised a scroll of parchment high into the air. "I have just returned from High Justice Mounteclair's home in the Western Countryside. He has granted me the power to commandeer this trial and overrule your sentencing!"

The Justice unrolled the scroll so everyone in the courtroom could see it. The document was an official order from High Justice Mounteclair, and his large signature was featured at the bottom.

"This is outrageous!" Oldragaid exclaimed. "Your daughter is a *witch*, Evergreen! She must be punished for her crimes!"

"And punishment she shall receive, but it won't be from you," Justice Evergreen said. "Mounteclair has sentenced her to live at a facility in the Northeast Plains of the Southern Kingdom until further notice. The facility, as I'm told, specializes in treating young women with my daughter's *condition*. There is a carriage outside, waiting to transport her as we speak. In the meantime, the High Justice has ordered you to erase any mention of this trial from all records in court."

Justice Oldragaid went silent as he contemplated his next move. When he realized how limited his options were, Oldragaid became furious and banged his gavel until it broke into two pieces.

"Well, it appears Justice Evergreen has used his connections to manipulate the law," he told the room. "At the moment, I have no other choice but to follow the High Justice's orders. Guards, please take the Evergreen witch to the carriage outside."

Before she had the chance to say good-bye to her brothers, the guards raised Brystal off the executioner's block and began dragging her out of the courtroom.

"But, Father, where am I going?" she cried. "What facility are they taking me to? Father!"

Despite her desperate pleas, Justice Evergreen refused to answer his daughter's questions. He didn't even look her in the eye as the guards pulled her past him.

"Don't you dare address me as *Father*," he said. "You're no daughter of mine."

CHAPTER SIX

THE BOOTSTRAP CORRECTIONAL FACILITY FOR TROUBLED YOUNG WOMEN

By sunrise, Brystal was already so far from Chariot Hills she couldn't hear the morning cathedral bells. She was shackled in the back of a small carriage that traveled down a long and bumpy road through the Northeast Plains of the Southern Kingdom. True to its name, there was absolutely nothing to see in the plains but the same flat earth that stretched for miles around them. With every passing hour the grassy land became drier and drier and the sky became grayer and grayer, until land and sky blended into one dismal color.

The driver stopped only rarely to feed the horses, and occasionally the guards let Brystal out of the carriage to relieve herself on the side of the road. The only food they gave her was a piece of stale bread, and Brystal was afraid to eat it because she didn't know how long she was supposed to ration it. The drivers said nothing about an estimated time of arrival, so as their second day of travel began, she started worrying their destination didn't exist. She convinced herself that the carriage would eventually pull over and the drivers would abandon her in the middle of nowhere—perhaps *that* was what her Father and the High Justice's plan had been all along.

In the late afternoon of their second day, Brystal finally spotted something in the distance that suggested there was civilization nearby. As the carriage moved closer to the object, she saw it was a wooden sign that pointed down a new path:

THE BOOTSTRAP CORRECTIONAL FACILITY
FOR TROUBLED YOUNG WOMEN

The carriage turned onto a dirt road, heading in the direction the sign pointed to. Brystal was relieved to see their destination existed, but as the facility appeared on the horizon, she realized being abandoned might have been a better option. Brystal had never laid eyes on such a miserable place, and just the sight of it sucked all the remaining hope and happiness from her body.

The Bootstrap Correctional Facility for Troubled Young Women sat on top of the only hill Brystal had seen in the Northeast Plains. It was a wide five-story building made from crumbling bricks. The walls were severely weathered and cracked, and all the windows were tiny, covered in bars, and the glass was mostly shattered. There were gaping holes in the thatched roof, and a crooked chimney in the center made the whole facility look like an enormous rotting pumpkin.

The building was surrounded by a few acres of parched land, and the property was bordered by a stone wall with sharp spikes along the top. Brystal's carriage stopped at the facility's gate and the driver whistled for a hunchbacked gatekeeper, who limped out from his small post and removed the barriers.

Once the gate was open, the carriage continued down a path that snaked through the facility's grounds. Everywhere she looked, Brystal saw dozens of young women between the ages of about eight and seventeen sprinkled across the property. Each girl wore a faded gray-and-black-striped dress, a bandanna to keep the hair out of her face, and a pair of oversize work boots. All the young women were pale and emaciated and shared the same expression of utter exhaustion, as if they hadn't had a decent meal or a good night's rest in years. It was a haunting sight, and Brystal wondered how long it would be until she, like the other girls, resembled a ghost of her former self.

The young women were separated into groups performing various chores. Some fed chickens in an overcrowded coop, some milked malnourished cows in a small pen, and some pulled wilted vegetables from a withering garden. However, Brystal didn't understand the point of the other activities she saw the girls performing. Some dug large holes in the ground with shovels, some moved heavy stones back and forth from one pile to another, and some carried heavy buckets of water around in circles.

The girls showed no objections to the pointless exercises and completed their tasks almost mechanically. Brystal assumed they were trying to avoid attention from the wardens who were patrolling them. The wardens wore dark uniforms and kept a hand on the whips dangling from their belts as they supervised the young women.

As if the facility wasn't grim enough, a peculiar contraption in the middle of the property gave Brystal an uneasy feeling in the pit of her stomach. It appeared to be a large stone well, but instead of a water bucket hanging from its roof, there was a thick wooden board with three holes—the perfect sizes to fit around someone's wrists and neck. Whatever it was, Brystal hoped she would avoid the mechanism during her time at the facility.

The carriage stopped at the building's entrance. The driver and guards pulled Brystal out of the back and she shrieked because the air was much colder than she'd anticipated. The front doors slowly opened from inside, the rusty hinges screeching like an animal in pain, and a man and woman stepped outside to greet the newcomers.

The man was short and shaped like an upside-down pear: he had an incredibly wide head, a very thick neck, and a torso that narrowed as it lowered into his tiny waist. He was a sharp dresser and wore a red bow tie with a blue suit that was perfectly tailored to his awkward measurements. His mouth was curled into a devious grin that never faded. The woman beside him was shaped like a cucumber: she was almost twice as tall as him, and she was the exact same width from head to toe. She looked more conservative than the man and wore a black dress with a high lacy collar. A permanent frown was frozen on her face, like she had never laughed in her entire life.

"May we help you?" the man asked in a deep, raspy voice.

"Are you Mr. and Mrs. Edgar? The administrators of this facility?" the driver asked.

"Yes, that's us," the woman said in a sharp, nasally voice.

"By order of the High Justice Mounteclair of Chariot Hills, Miss Brystal Lynn Evergreen has been sentenced to live at your facility until further notice," one of the guards informed them.

He handed the man a scroll with the official order in writing. Mr. Edgar read over the document and then eyed Brystal like he had won a prize.

"My, my," he said. "Miss Evergreen must have done something *very* naughty for a High Justice to sentence her personally. Of course we would be delighted to have her join us."

"Then she's all yours," the driver said.

The guards unlocked Brystal's shackles and shoved her toward the administrators. Without missing a beat, the guards and the driver returned to the carriage and raced away from the facility. Mr. and Mrs. Edgar looked Brystal up and down like two dogs inspecting a steak.

"Let me be the first to warn you, *deary*, that this is a house of the Lord," Mrs. Edgar said in a spiteful tone. "If you know what's good for you, you'll leave your debauchery at the door."

"You must be tired and hungry from your journey," Mr. Edgar said in a friendly manner that Brystal didn't trust. "You're just in luck—it's nearly dinnertime. Come inside and we'll get you changed into something more *appropriate*."

Mr. Edgar placed a hand on the back of Brystal's neck and the couple escorted her inside. The interior of the Bootstrap Correctional Facility was just as cold and battered as the outside. The floor was made of rotting wooden planks, the ceiling was stained from leaks, and the walls were covered in dents and scrapes. The administrators moved Brystal down a corridor and through a large archway into a spacious dining hall.

The dining hall had three long tables that stretched the entire length of the room and a small table at the front for faculty members. More young women in faded gray-and-black-striped dresses were seated at the long tables, hard at work sewing pieces of leather boots together. Just like the girls outside, the young women in the dining hall were gaunt and looked fatigued. Their fingertips were bruised and bleeding from being forced to work with dull needles. Additional wardens paced the hall as they inspected the girls' work, and they back-handed some of the young women who weren't sewing fast enough to their satisfaction.

At the front of the room, hanging above the smaller table, was an enormous banner with a message that made Brystal's blood boil:

GOOD GIRLS DO WHAT THEY'RE TOLD.
THEY NEVER ASK QUESTIONS.

GOOD GIRLS FINISH THEIR WORK.
THEY NEVER TAKE BREAKS.

GOOD GIRLS KEEP THEIR HEADS DOWN.
THEY NEVER LOOK FOR TROUBLE.

GOOD GIRLS ARE ALWAYS TRUTHFUL.
THEY NEVER TELL LIES.

GOOD GIRLS KNOW THEIR PLACE.
THEY NEVER SHOW DISRESPECT.

GOOD GIRLS ARE GRATEFUL.
THEY NEVER WANT MORE.

Before Brystal could comment on the infuriating message, the administrators pushed her up a rickety staircase at the back of the dining hall. Mrs. Edgar unlocked a heavy barred door and the couple moved Brystal into their office at the top of the stairs.

Unlike the rest of the facility, the Edgars' office was very elegant. It had carpeted floors and a crystal chandelier, and the walls were painted with murals of beautiful landscapes. The office had large windows that peered into the dining hall and the facility's grounds. It was the perfect place to spy on the young women as they worked.

Mr. Edgar took a seat in a leather chair behind a cherrywood desk. Mrs. Edgar pulled Brystal behind a privacy screen in a corner of the office and had her remove the clothes and shoes she had arrived in. She tossed Brystal's things into a wastebasket and crossed to a bulky wardrobe on the other side of the room. The woman opened the drawers and selected a faded gray-and-black-striped dress, a bandanna, and a pair of work boots.

"Here," she said, and handed the items to Brystal. "Get dressed."

Brystal had nothing on but her undergarments and was freezing, so she put the new clothes on as fast as she could. Unfortunately, the uniform wasn't nearly as warm as her old clothes and Brystal shivered in the cold room.

"Ma'am? May I please have a sweater?" she asked.

"Does this look like a boutique?" Mrs. Edgar snapped. "The cold is good for you. It makes you seek the warmth of the Lord."

She sat Brystal in the chair across from her husband. His devilish grin grew as he watched Brystal shiver, and his double chin turned into four.

"Miss Evergreen, allow me to officially welcome you to the Bootstrap Correctional Facility for Troubled Young Women," Mr. Edgar said. "Do you know *why* the High Justice has placed you under our care?"

"They say you're supposed to *cure* me," Brystal said.

"Indeed," he said. "You see, there's something inside of you that shouldn't be there. What may seem like a talent or a gift is actually an *illness* that must be remedied immediately. My wife and I created this facility so we could help girls with your *condition*. With some hard work and prayer, we'll root out all the unnatural qualities you possess, and nothing will prevent you from becoming a respectable wife and mother one day."

"I don't understand how manual labor and prayer cures anyone," she said.

Mr. Edgar let out a low, rattling laugh and shook his head.

"Our methods may seem tedious and grueling, but they are the most effective tools for treatment," he explained. "You are infected with a horrible disease—it's a *sickness of the spirit* that the Lord himself opposes— and it's going to take time and effort to destroy it. However, with dedication and discipline, we can crush the very source of your symptoms. Our facility will *starve* the evil from your soul, *pump* the darkness out of your heart, and *drain* the wickedness from your mind."

Brystal knew it was in her best interest to just stay silent and nod, but every word out of Mr. Edgar's mouth infuriated her more than the last.

"Mr. Edgar, you agree the Lord is all-knowing, all-powerful, and the sole creator of all existence, correct?" she asked.

"Without question," Mr. Edgar replied.

"Then why would the Lord create magic if he hates it so much?" she asked. "It's a little counterproductive, don't you think?"

Mr. Edgar went quiet and it took him a few moments to answer her.

"To test the loyalty of your soul, of course," he declared. "The Lord wants to separate the people who seek salvation from the people who surrender to sin. By willingly making sacrifices to overcome your condition, you are proving your devotion to the Lord, and to his beloved Southern Kingdom."

"But if the Lord wants to identify those who *willingly* overcome magic, aren't you interfering by *forcing* young girls to overcome it?"

Her second question was even more befuddling than the first. Mr. Edgar became flustered and his cheeks turned the same color as his bow tie. His eyes darted between Brystal and his wife as he composed a response.

"Of course not!" he said. "Magic is an unholy manipulation of nature! And *no one* should manipulate the Lord's beautiful world but the Lord himself! He smiles upon the people who try to stop such abominations!"

"But *you're* trying to manipulate *me*—isn't that *also* an abomination?" Brystal asked.

Mr. and Mrs. Edgar gasped—they had never been accused of such a thing. Brystal knew she should stop while she was ahead, but she couldn't stomach any more hypocrisy. She was going to speak her mind whether the administrators liked it or not.

"How dare you!" Mr. Edgar exclaimed. "My wife and I have devoted our lives to the Lord's work!"

"But what if you're wrong about the Lord?" she argued. "What if the Lord is much kinder and loving than you're giving Him credit for? What if the Lord invented magic so people could help each other and enrich their own lives? What if the Lord thinks *you're* the unholy ones for abusing people and making them believe their existence is a—"

WHACK! Mrs. Edgar slapped Brystal so hard her whole head jerked in a different direction.

"You disrespectful little beast," Mrs. Edgar said. "You will bite your tongue or *I will have it removed*! Is that understood?"

Brystal nodded as blood dripped from the corner of her mouth. Mr. Edgar leaned back in his chair and stared at Brystal like she was a wild animal he was excited to tame.

"You have a long road ahead of you, Miss Evergreen," he said. "I'm looking forward to watching your *progress*."

A loud gong sounded through the facility.

"Ah, time for dinner," Mr. Edgar said. "You may join the

other girls in the dining hall. Try to get some rest tonight—tomorrow is going to be a very, very long day for you."

Mrs. Edgar raised Brystal onto her feet, walked her to the door, and gave her a shove on her way down the rickety staircase.

At the announcement of dinner, the young women sewing boots in the dining hall put away their work. The girls filed in from outside and joined the others at the tables. Brystal didn't know where to sit so she took the first empty seat she could find. None of the girls noticed the newcomer in their presence; in fact, none of the girls said a word or shifted their focus from whatever was directly ahead of them. Despite Brystal's attempts to introduce herself, the young women remained silent and still as statues.

Mr. and Mrs. Edgar sat in throne-like chairs at the faculty table and were joined by the wardens and the hunchbacked gatekeeper. Once they were seated, a group of young women with aprons over their gray-and-black-striped dresses entered from the kitchen and served the faculty members roasted chicken, mashed potatoes, and baked vegetables. The delicious aroma reminded Brystal of how hungry she was and her stomach growled like a neglected pet.

After the faculty's plates were full, the young women were sent table by table to line up at a serving cart for their own supper. Brystal was handed a crusty bowl of a chunky brown stew that bubbled and smelled like skunk. It took every ounce of willpower not to gag at the revolting food. She followed the line back to her table, where the young women stood at their seats until all the girls in the hall were served.

While they waited, Brystal's eyes fell on a girl a few seats down from her. She was the smallest girl in the dining hall and couldn't have been older than six or seven years old. She had big brown eyes, a tiny button nose, and a very short choppy haircut. Unlike the others, the little girl sensed Brystal's gaze and turned to her. At first, Brystal was taken aback by the acknowledgment and didn't know what to do.

"Hello," she whispered with a smile. "What's your name?"

The little girl didn't respond and just stared at Brystal with blank eyes, as if her body was deprived of a soul.

"My name is Brystal," Brystal said. "Today's my first day. How long have you—"

Their one-sided conversation was interrupted when Mr. Edgar pounded his fist on the faculty table. All the young women had finally returned to their seats and the administrator rose from his chair to address the room.

"It's time for the evening prayer," he instructed. *"Begin!"*

Brystal didn't know the young women *could* speak, but to her surprise, they followed Mr. Edgar's command and recited a prayer in perfect unison:

> *"To our Lord in heaven, we send our daily*
> *thanks for the meal we're about to receive.*
> *May it nourish our bodies, so we may*

*continue the work of our hands and the
work of our hearts. May you bless us with
the wisdom to recognize our faults, the
strength to fix what's broken inside us, and
the guidance to stray from our unnatural
temptations. In the name of the Southern
Kingdom, we pray. Amen."*

When the prayer was finished, the girls took their seats and devoured the brown stew like they had never eaten before. Brystal couldn't remember the last time she was so hungry, but she couldn't even touch the food; the daily blessing had made her too angry to eat. Even in her worst nightmares, she had never imagined a place as terrible as this, and as far as she knew, she would be stuck there for a very, very long time.

Brystal's room at the Bootstrap Correctional Facility was the size of a closet, but that was the least of her worries. Shortly after dinner, two wardens escorted her to the small chamber on the fifth floor and locked her behind its sliding barred door. As the temperature dropped overnight, Brystal had nothing but a thin and raggedy blanket to keep warm. She had never been so cold in her entire life and shivered so hard her cot was practically vibrating. Her jaw rattled with such intensity her teeth sounded like a horse's hooves against pavement.

Around midnight, Brystal was distracted from the

cold by the strange sensation of being watched. When she looked up, she was startled to see the little girl with short choppy hair standing behind the bars of her door. The girl stared at her just as blankly as she had at dinner and carried a folded wool blanket.

"Um ... *hello*," Brystal said, wondering how long the little girl had been standing there. "Can I help you?"

"Pip," she said.

Brystal was confused and sat up to get a better look at the odd little girl.

"Excuse me?" she asked.

"It's *Pip*," the little girl repeated.

"I'm sorry, I don't understand what you're saying," Brystal apologized. "Does that mean something in another language?"

"At dinner you asked me what my name was," the little girl said. "It's Pip."

"Oh, that's right," Brystal recalled. "Well, it's a pleasure to meet you, Pip. Is there a reason you're giving me your name so late?"

Pip shrugged. "Not really," she said. "I just finally remembered it."

The little girl's distant gaze never changed, but there was an innocence about her that Brystal found charming.

"Do you have a last name, Pip?"

The little girl looked at the floor and her shoulders sank. Remembering her first name was such a challenge she hadn't prepared for any more questions.

"Wait, I *do*," she said. "It's Squeak—*Pip Squeak*."

"Pip *Squeak*?" Brystal was surprised to hear. "Is that your real name?"

"It's the only name I remember being called," Pip said with a shrug. "Then again, I don't have many memories from before I lived here."

"How long have you been here?" Brystal asked.

"About six years, I think."

"You've been here *that* long?"

"I was just a toddler when I arrived," Pip said. "My parents brought me here as soon as they realized I was different. I started showing signs pretty early."

"You mean signs of *magic*?" Brystal asked. "You were doing magic when you were just a toddler?"

"Mhmmm," Pip said. "Still can, too. Want me to show you?"

"Please," Brystal said without hesitating.

The little girl looked up and down the hallway to make sure they were alone. When she'd seen the coast was clear, Pip stretched out her neck and limbs, and then pressed her head against the barred door. Brystal watched in amazement as, slowly but surely, the little girl squeezed through the bars like her body was made of clay. Once she was on the other side, Pip's body snapped back to its original shape.

"That's unbelievable!" Brystal exclaimed, forgetting to keep her voice down. "You've been doing that since you were a baby?"

"I used to squeeze through the railing of my crib."

Brystal laughed. "I guess that explains how you got out of your room tonight."

"I sneak out all the time," Pip said. "Oh, that reminds me, I came to bring you this. I could hear you shivering from my room, so I snuck into the Edgars' linen closet to get you an extra blanket."

She wrapped the blanket around Brystal's shoulders. Brystal was extremely touched by Pip's gesture—but she was also extremely cold and had no trouble accepting it.

"That was so kind of you," she said. "Are you sure you don't need it?"

"No, I'm used to the cold," Pip said. "Although it's been getting a lot colder lately. It usually starts warming up this time of year, but I overheard Mr. Edgar saying there's a really bad blizzard in the Northern Kingdom. We're not too far from the border, so let's hope the storm doesn't get any closer."

"Yes, let's hope," Brystal said. "I don't think I could manage anything colder than this. It rarely snows in Chariot Hills."

"What's Chariot Hills?" Pip asked.

Brystal was shocked she had never heard of the city before, but then reminded herself that Pip didn't even know her own real name.

"It's the city where I'm from," she explained.

"Oh," Pip said. "I'm sorry, I don't get out much— well, *never*, actually. What's Chariot Hills like?"

"It's big and busy." Brystal described it: "There's a town square with a courthouse, a cathedral, and a law university. It's also the capital of the Southern Kingdom and where the king lives with the royal family."

"You're from the same place as the *royal family*?" Pip asked. "How did a girl like you end up here?"

"Same as you. I got caught doing magic," Brystal said. "I didn't even know I was capable of magic until a week ago. I found a book called *The Truth About Magic* in the library I worked at. There was an ancient incantation in the book to test whether someone has magic in their blood. I was stupid enough to read it aloud, and now here I am."

"What happened when you read it?"

"The first time, I covered a room in flowers. The second time, I filled the room with thousands of lights and made it look like the universe."

Pip's large eyes grew even larger. "That's amazing!" she said. "I've never met someone who could do anything like *that* before. Most of the girls here just have little tricks like mine. A girl down the hall from my room can grow her hair at will, a girl on the second floor can stand on water without sinking, and I've seen one girl talk to the cows outside—but that might not be magic, she might just be *weird*. You must be really powerful if you covered a whole room in flowers and lights!"

Brystal had never thought about it before. "You think so?" she asked. "I've never had anything to compare it to. Your magic is the only magic I've seen besides my own. I'm glad Mr. and Mrs. Edgar haven't drained it out of you yet."

"Don't worry, their treatments don't actually *cure magic*," Pip said. "This facility is just a front for the Edgars' family business. It was a regular boot factory before Mr. Edgar inherited it—hence the name *Bootstrap*. The only reason he and his wife turned it into a correctional facility was to get free labor out of young girls. At least, that's what I heard the gatekeeper say—he's also an aspiring poet, but that's a different story. It's funny how much you learn when no one thinks you're listening."

"The Edgars are such terrible people!" Brystal said. "And they have the nerve to say *we're* the sinful ones!"

Suddenly, both girls jumped at the sound of footsteps echoing from a few floors below.

"Who is that?" Brystal asked.

"The wardens are making their nightly rounds," Pip said. "I should get back to my room before they reach our floor."

"Wait, don't forget this." Brystal removed the blanket from her shoulders and tried to hand it back, but Pip wouldn't take it.

"You can keep it for the night," she said. "But I'll have to collect it early in the morning and return it to the closet before Mrs. Edgar wakes up. She caught me sneaking out of my room last week and chopped off all my hair as punishment—if it happens again they'll put me in the *dunker* for sure."

"What's the dunker?" Brystal asked.

"When girls misbehave—I mean *really* misbehave—they're strapped to the well outside and dunked in the cold water until Mr. Edgar thinks they've learned their lesson. Sometimes it takes hours!"

Brystal couldn't believe her ears. "This place gets more dreadful by the minute!" she said. "How have you survived it for so long?"

"I guess it could be worse," Pip said.

"How?"

"Oh, I don't actually know how it could be worse," she said. "I haven't been many places to compare it to—well, *none*, actually."

"It's certainly the worst place I've ever been to," Brystal said. "But I'm grateful I met someone as kind as you. Let's break out of here one day and move someplace warm where we can see the ocean. What do you say?"

Brystal knew the thought intrigued Pip because the corners of her mouth began to twitch and slowly curved into a smile—possibly the first smile she had ever had.

"It's a nice thought to fall asleep to," she said. "Good night, Brystal."

Pip squeezed through the bars and quietly snuck back to her room before the wardens reached the fifth floor. Brystal lay back down on her cot and tried her best to sleep. She was still cold even with a second blanket, but she shivered a lot less thanks to the warmth of her new friend.

Brystal thought working at the library was strenuous, but it was nothing compared to her first days at the Bootstrap Correctional Facility. Every morning at dawn, the wardens unlocked the young women from their rooms, rushed them through a grotesque breakfast in the dining hall, and then forced them to complete chores until dinner. The tasks were brutal on Brystal's body, and with every passing hour, she didn't know how she would get through the next—but she didn't have a choice. By the end of her first week, her faded gray-and-black-striped dress was much looser than it had been the day she first put it on.

The most challenging part of all was keeping the frustration from surfacing on her face; otherwise she would meet the wrath of the wardens. Occasionally, Brystal would get the eerie sense that she was being watched by more than just the wardens. She'd look up and see Mr. Edgar glaring down at her from his office, delighted to see how much she was struggling.

By the end of each day, Brystal's body ached so much she didn't even notice the freezing temperature. Pip was kind enough to sneak her a blanket each night after the Edgars went to bed and then she promptly returned the blanket the next morning before they woke. Brystal hated that Pip was risking getting caught for her sake, but their nightly visits were all she had to look forward to. Their daydreams about escaping the facility and moving to the coast were the only thing that kept her going—she didn't know how she would survive without them.

· • ★ • ·

One night, Pip didn't show up and Brystal became

concerned. Her friend had spent the day digging holes in the yard, so Brystal hoped she was just too tired to sneak out of her room. The following morning, while she waited for breakfast to be served, Brystal's concerns skyrocketed because she didn't see Pip anywhere in the dining hall. She strained her neck trying to spot her friend's choppy hair among the bandannas, but Pip was gone.

Just then, Mr. and Mrs. Edgar emerged from their office, slamming the heavy door behind them. They marched down the rickety steps in a huff, causing the staircase to sway beneath them, and then proceeded to the front of the hall.

"Breakfast has been canceled this morning," Mr. Edgar announced.

Brystal sighed and slumped in her seat—she had become dependent on the nauseating meals—but she was the only girl at her table who was affected by the news. The others remained as motionless and expressionless as always.

"Something very troubling occurred late last night," Mr. Edgar went on. "While my wife and I slept, the wardens caught a young lady *stealing* our private property. As you know, *thievery* is an unforgivable sin in the eyes of the Lord, and it will not be tolerated under this roof! We must make an example out of this thief so the Lord does not think we've deserted Him! *Bring her in!*"

At his signal, Brystal watched in horror as the wardens pushed Pip into the dining hall. Her hands were tied behind her back and her large eyes were more distant than normal, like her mind had abandoned her body out of fear. The wardens moved her to the front of the room beside Mr. Edgar, and the administrator walked in circles around Pip as he questioned the small girl.

"Tell the other girls what you did," he ordered.

"I . . . I . . . I took a blanket from the linen closet," Pip confessed.

"And *why* would you do such a wicked thing?" Mr. Edgar asked.

"I . . . I . . . I was cold," she said.

Pip looked up and her eyes immediately found Brystal in the crowd. Watching her friend lie on her behalf made Brystal sick to her stomach—she had to do something to save Pip, but she didn't know how to help her.

"And what do we say about the cold?" Mr. Edgar asked.

"You . . . you . . . you say the cold is good for us," Pip recited. "It makes us seek the warmth of the Lord."

"Precisely," Mr. Edgar said. "But you weren't interested in the warmth of the Lord last night. All you cared about was *yourself*, so you abandoned the Lord and resorted to sin to satisfy your physical desires. And what do we do with sinners at this facility?"

"We . . . we . . . we *cleanse* them," Pip said.

"Exactly," he replied, and turned to the rest of the room. "To ensure none of you follows in her footsteps, you will join us outside and watch the thief be punished for her shameful actions! *Take her to the dunker!*"

The name of the horrible device sparked a wave of fear through the young women in the dining hall—it was the only reaction Brystal had seen the girls have since she had arrived. Their mouths dropped open and they looked to one another with wide, frightful eyes. The wardens grabbed Pip by the arms and headed out of the hall, but Brystal jumped in front of them and blocked their path.

"Wait!" she screamed. "This is my fault! Pip did nothing wrong!"

"Stand aside, you reckless little worm!" Mrs. Edgar yelled. "This girl was caught red-handed while you were in your room!"

"No, it was me!" Brystal declared. "I put her under a spell! I *bewitched* her into stealing the blanket! Punish me and let her go!"

"Liar!" Mr. Edgar shouted. "No one in this facility has *that* kind of power! Now stand aside or you'll—"

"I can prove it!" Brystal yelled. *"Elsune elknoon ahkelle-enama, delmune dalmoon ahktelle-awknamon!"*

The ancient incantation echoed through the dining hall. For a few tense moments, the administrators looked around in terror, but nothing appeared. Brystal wondered if she had mispronounced the text, because the spell was taking longer than it had in the library. Mr. and Mrs. Edgar began to laugh at her attempt to sidetrack them.

"You foolish, girl!" Mr. Edgar sneered. "We will deal with you later! Now, wardens, *take the little one outside and strap her to the—*"

Suddenly, Mr. Edgar was distracted by screeching.

The noise grew louder and louder, like the thunder of an approaching storm. To everyone's astonishment, a flock of colorful birds burst through the windows and soared into the dining hall, causing the room to erupt in panic. The birds circled Brystal like a tornado and then lunged at the faculty members, knocking the wardens and the administrators off their feet.

Next, the flock flew to the front of the room and attacked the banner hanging above the faculty table, ripping it apart with their claws and beaks. By the time they finished, the banner was almost completely shredded and only five words of the oppressive message remained:

Once they had finished with the banner, the birds flew out the windows, vanishing as quickly as they had appeared. The dining hall froze for an entire minute of uninterrupted shock. Finally the silence was broken when Mr. Edgar let out a mortified scream and pointed to Brystal.

"TAKE THAT HEATHEN TO THE DUNKER!" he commanded.

Before she could fully comprehend what was happening, the wardens seized Brystal and dragged her outside. The entire facility followed them to the dunker and gathered around it. The wardens fastened the contraption's wooden board around Brystal's neck and wrists, then hoisted her above the deep well, her feet dangling over the icy water. The suspension was incredibly painful and Brystal could barely breathe.

"Drop her in on my signal!" Mr. Edgar ordered. "One...two..."

Brystal braced herself to meet the freezing water below, but oddly, Mr. Edgar never gave the wardens his signal. For a second, Brystal thought the flock of birds had returned, because Mr. and Mrs. Edgar went stiff and stared into the horizon in bewilderment. Soon the property was filled with the sounds of galloping hooves, and all the spectators around the well turned to see what the Edgars were gawking at.

On the outer road, a golden carriage raced toward the facility at an unprecedented speed. It was pulled by four large horses with long magenta manes, but there was no driver steering the magnificent steeds. As the carriage approached, Brystal realized the creatures weren't horses at all, but *unicorns* with silver horns.

The carriage reached the facility and the gate unlocked and swung open on its own without the help of the gatekeeper. The unicorns slowed down as they trotted through the property and came to a stop directly in front of the dunker. The carriage door opened and its sole passenger stepped out. She was a beautiful woman with dark hair and bright eyes, and she wore a vibrant purple gown, a stylish fascinator, and one glove, on her left arm. The woman observed the facility with a judgmental gaze.

"So *this* is where gloom comes from," she said.

No one said a word to the woman. All the faculty members and young women remained very still, staring at the unicorns in disbelief, like they were all experiencing the same hallucination.

"Well, you're a talkative bunch," the woman said. "Then again, there isn't much to talk about around these parts, is there? Am I right to assume this is the Bootstrap Correctional Facility?"

"And *who* might you be?" Mr. Edgar exclaimed.

"Oh, forgive my manners," the woman said with a cheerful smile. "I'm Madame Weatherberry. I'm looking for *Brystal Evergreen*."

CHAPTER SEVEN

PERMISSION

P erhaps I wasn't clear," Madame Weatherberry said
to the crowd of bewildered faces. "I'm looking for
a young woman named *Brystal Evergreen*. Would
one of you be kind enough to point her out?"

Without saying a word, the Edgars, the wardens, and
all the young women from the facility turned in Brystal's
direction. Madame Weatherberry hadn't noticed her
dangling above the well until now, and she gasped.

"Is that *Miss Evergreen* hanging up there?" she asked

in disbelief. "What on earth are you doing to her? Bring her down this instant!"

"We do *not* take orders from outsiders," Mr. Edgar shouted.

The woman raised an eyebrow at the administrator. "Very well," she said. "I'll do it myself."

Madame Weatherberry clapped her hands, and suddenly, Brystal's wrists and neck were released from the dunker's wooden board. But instead of dropping into the freezing water below, Brystal's body floated out of the well and descended gently to the ground. Mr. and Mrs. Edgar shrieked at Madame Weatherberry's magic.

"You demon girl!" Mrs. Edgar yelled at Brystal. "First you conjure a flock of wicked birds and now you've summoned a witch! You've plagued this facility with sin!"

"Excuse me, but I'm *not* a witch," Madame Weatherberry corrected her. "And I don't mean to be rude, but it looks like this place has been plagued with worse things than sin. A fresh coat of paint would do wonders—*wait a moment*. Did you just say Miss Evergreen conjured *a flock of birds?*"

The woman was clearly impressed and turned to Brystal with a wide grin. Brystal didn't respond—she was still trying to process all the events from *before* Madame Weatherberry had arrived. Although she could see and hear the woman, Brystal wasn't present enough to accept that Madame Weatherberry, the unicorns, and the golden carriage were actually in front of her.

"You listen to me, *Madame*!" Mr. Edgar barked. "I don't care *who* or *what* you are; we do not accept your kind here! Leave this facility at once!"

"I think that's a splendid idea," Madame Weatherberry said. "But Miss Evergreen will be coming with me."

No one was more shocked to hear this than Brystal herself. She couldn't imagine what Madame Weatherberry wanted with *her*, but it was just one of many things that were confusing her in the moment. But before she could ask any questions, Mr. and Mrs. Edgar stepped in front of Brystal and blocked her from going anywhere near the woman.

"You will do *no* such thing!" Mr. Edgar roared. "This girl has been sentenced to the Bootstrap Correctional Facility by High Justice Mounteclair of Chariot Hills! She will remain in our care until the High Justice notifies us otherwise!"

Madame Weatherberry seemed amused by his theatrical protest. She raised an open hand and a golden scroll with a silver ribbon appeared out of thin air. Madame Weatherberry unrolled the document and presented it to the administrators. The Edgars' eyes grew large at the sight of King Champion XIV's curvy signature and official royal seal at the bottom of the scroll.

"I've been given the king's permission to collect Miss Evergreen, and as any law-abiding citizen knows, His Majesty's wishes outrank the High Justice," she said. "But if you have any objections you would like to share with the king, please, be my guest."

Mr. and Mrs. Edgar exchanged nervous glances and then took a defeated step aside—even *they* weren't self-righteous enough to challenge the king. Brystal didn't think she could be more puzzled than she already was, but learning that King Champion was somehow involved made her dizzy. Madame Weatherberry sensed her perplexity and knelt in front of Brystal to look her in the eye.

"Are you all right, my dear?" she asked.

"Sorry," Brystal said. "I'm a bit fuzzy."

"I'm sure this is quite a shock for you," the woman said. "If I were in your shoes, I'd be terrified of a strange lady with unicorns, but you have absolutely nothing to fear. I've come to take you away for a wonderful opportunity, and I promise you'll be perfectly safe with me."

Madame Weatherberry removed a handkerchief from the pocket of her gown and wiped the dirt off Brystal's face. There was something so warm and comforting about the woman; she practically glowed with kindness. Even in her confused state, Brystal knew she could trust her.

"Now, Miss Evergreen, would you like to gather your things and join me in the carriage?"

"I ... I ... I don't have any *things*," Brystal said.

"Oh?" Madame Weatherberry said. "Well, there's nothing wrong with being a minimalist. The unicorns appreciate light travelers."

"But where are we going?" Brystal asked.

Instead of answering her, Madame Weatherberry

eyed Mr. and Mrs. Edgar, who were shamelessly eaves-dropping on her and Brystal's conversation.

"I'm afraid I can't discuss that here," she said. "But I'll answer all your questions and explain everything on the way. Now, shall we?"

"Can I bring my friend, Pip?" Brystal asked. "She's small and won't take up much room."

"I'm sorry, sweetheart, but the king has only given me permission to collect *one girl*," Madame Weatherberry said. "Your friend will have to stay here with the others."

Brystal shook her head and slowly backed away from the woman. Being whisked away from the facility was a dream come true, but she would never forgive herself if she left Pip behind.

"I can't do it," she said. "I'm sorry, but I can't leave her here."

Madame Weatherberry caressed Brystal's cheek. "My dear, I wish you didn't have to," she said. "I'm not going to force you to come with me, but I believe you're going to be very happy where we're headed. Please reconsider."

"I want to," Brystal said. "I just couldn't live with myself if I left her—"

"Brystal, are you nuts?"

Brystal turned to the crowd of young women behind her and saw Pip pushing her way to the front.

"What are you waiting for?" her friend said. "Get out of here while you can!"

"No, Pip," Brystal said. "I can't leave you alone in this place!"

"But I'm used to being alone in this place," Pip said. "This facility has been my home since I was a toddler, remember? And technically, I've been getting into more trouble with you around, so maybe you'll be doing me a favor by leaving."

"I don't even know where I'm going," Brystal said. "What if I never see you again?"

"Then at least *one* of us got out of here," she said. "And if you waste your only chance on me, I'll never speak to you again. So there, now you *have* to go."

Pip gave Brystal no choice, but she didn't make leaving any easier. With a heavy heart and tearful eyes, Brystal gave her small friend a hug good-bye.

"We've wasted enough time for one day!" Mr. Edgar yelled at the young women. "Everyone go inside at once! Get ready for your chores!"

Like roaches, all the young women scrambled into the facility, and Pip slipped away from Brystal's embrace.

Madame Weatherberry offered Brystal her hand and escorted her to the golden carriage. The inside of the carriage had tufted silk seats and velvet curtains— quite a contrast to the facility's decor—and as she sat on the seat across from Madame Weatherberry, Brystal was reminded of how comfortable a *cushion* was. The carriage's ceiling was covered in leafy vines that grew berries in every color of the rainbow.

"Are those real?" Brystal asked.

"Yes," Madame Weatherberry said. "You must be famished. Please, help yourself."

Brystal didn't have to be told twice. She plucked the fruit from the ceiling and devoured it whole. It was the most delicious food she had ever tasted, and every time she pulled a handful of berries from the vines, a new bunch magically appeared in its place.

The carriage door shut on its own and the unicorns raced down the path through the property. By the time Brystal had finished eating, the Bootstrap Correctional Facility had already disappeared in the bleak distance behind them.

"It was very considerate of you to think of your friend," Madame Weatherberry said. "Not many people would have done that."

"She doesn't deserve to be there," Brystal said. "None of the girls do."

Madame Weatherberry nodded and let out a prolonged sigh. "This may be difficult to hear, but the girls at the facility are *lucky* compared to others I've seen," she said. "What the world does to people like you and me is a downright tragedy, and humanity's understanding of magic is one of the greatest misconceptions of our time."

Brystal did a double take. Madame Weatherberry's choice of words reminded her of something she had read a couple of weeks earlier.

"Wait a second," she said. "Are you *Celeste Weatherberry*? The author of *The Truth About Magic*?"

Madame Weatherberry was shocked to hear Brystal mention the title of her book.

"Why, *yes*," she said in disbelief. "But how did you know that?"

"*The Truth About Magic* is the reason I was sent to the Bootstrap Correctional Facility," Brystal explained. "I found a copy in a secret section of the library I worked at—it was with all the other books that have been banned in the Southern Kingdom."

"Well, I can't imagine a greater compliment for an author than making the *banned book section*." Madame Weatherberry laughed. "Did you read my book?"

"As much as I could," Brystal said. "I read all about the history of magic, the difference between fairies and witches, and how the world mistakes magic for witchcraft. Eventually, I got to the part with the ancient incantations and I foolishly read them aloud. The librarian caught me conjuring magic and the High Justice sent me to the facility to get cured of it."

"How absurd!" she said. "Magic isn't an illness—it can't be *cured*. What kind of magic did you conjure when you read the text?"

"It's been different each time," Brystal explained. "The first time I covered a room in flowers, the second time I made thousands of lights appear, and this morning, a flock of birds showed up—that's why I was hanging in the well."

Madame Weatherberry moved to the edge of her seat.

"Had you experienced anything magical prior to reading the text in my book?"

"No," Brystal said with a shrug. "I never even suspected I was capable until then. Is that a bad thing?"

"On the contrary," she said. "Magic presents itself differently to each of us. Some fairies have magical traits and abilities from birth, and some develop them later in life. Usually, beginners can only *alter* the elements around them—but a talent for *manifestation* is rarely found in novices. With practice and proper instruction, you could develop your abilities into something quite extraordinary."

Madame Weatherberry became lost in thought and rubbed her chin as she thought of Brystal's potential. The woman's curiosity made Brystal uneasy—she still had so many questions, and they only seemed to multiply in Madame Weatherberry's presence.

"Madame Weatherberry, can you please tell me what's going on?" Brystal asked. "Why did the king give you permission to take me out of the facility?"

"Oh, I apologize for leaving you in suspense," Madame Weatherberry said. "As you may have gathered from reading *The Truth About Magic*, I'm on a mission to change the world's perception of magic. And if everything goes according to my plan, we can create a new world that finally accepts and respects people like us."

"But *how*?" she asked. "Where do you even begin?"

Madame Weatherberry's eyes twinkled with excitement. "With a *school* for magic."

"A school?"

"Right now, I'm calling it Madame Weatherberry's Academy of Magical Comprehension, but it's still a working title," she said. "With compassion and guidance,

I'm going to teach young fairies to harness and develop their abilities. Once their training is complete, my students and I will use magic to help and heal people around the world. With time, our acts of kindness will change people's opinions, and they'll realize magic isn't the vile practice they fear. The magical community will be embraced, and all the senseless violence and hatred toward us will become a thing of the past."

"And you want *me* to join your academy?" Brystal asked in shock.

"Of course I do," Madame Weatherberry said. "Why else would I have made the trip to collect you?"

Brystal tried to make sense of it all, but her day had been so overwhelming it was impossible to think clearly.

"But the facility was filled with girls who have been doing magic their entire lives," she said. "Why choose *me*?"

"Because you were the brightest star on my map," Madame Weatherberry said.

Before Brystal could ask what she meant, Madame Weatherberry moved up the armrest of her seat to reveal a secret compartment. She removed a large scroll and carefully unrolled it across her lap. As soon as the document was opened, the carriage was filled with shimmering light. It was a regular map of the world, showing the borders of the four kingdoms and the In-Between, but it was sprinkled with hundreds of twinkling stars.

"What is this?" Brystal asked, wide-eyed.

"It's a Map of Magic," Madame Weatherberry said.

"Every speck of light represents a different fairy or witch who's living in the world today. The brighter the light, the more powerful their magic. King Champion only permitted me to recruit two students from the Southern Kingdom, so I've decided to recruit the *brightest* students I can find."

"And *I* was one of the brightest lights?" Brystal asked.

Madame Weatherberry nodded and pointed to the northeast corner of the Southern Kingdom on the map.

"Do you see this cluster of small lights here? Those are the girls at the Bootstrap Correctional Facility. But these *larger* lights, slowly moving away from the others, represent you and me."

Madame Weatherberry touched the smaller of the two, and as if written by an invisible quill, the name *Brystal Evergreen* appeared beside it. Then she tapped the bigger star and the name *Celeste Weatherberry* appeared next. Brystal was awestruck as she looked over the map—she hadn't known so many fairies and witches existed in the world. Now that Madame Weatherberry's point had been made, she rolled up the map and placed it back in the compartment under the armrest.

"Do you have to follow the king's instructions?" Brystal asked. "Surely he wouldn't notice if you recruited one or two extra students along the way."

"Unfortunately, it's best if I do," Madame Weatherberry said. "I've been down this road many times before. If we want acceptance in this world, then we must be very careful about how we *seek* acceptance. No one is going to respect us if we cut corners or cause problems. I could have snapped my fingers and transported all the girls out of the facility, but it would only have caused people to resent us more. Hatred is like fire, and no one can extinguish fire by giving it fuel."

"I wish hatred was fire," Brystal said. "People like the Edgars and the Justices deserve to be burned for how they treat people."

"Without question," Madame Weatherberry said. "However, we cannot let *vengeance* motivate us and distract us from doing what's right. It may seem like justice, but revenge is a double-edged sword—the longer you hold it, the deeper you cut yourself."

Brystal sighed. "I just feel so bad for those girls at the facility," she said. "Every time I close my eyes I see their faces in my mind. I wish there was a way we could help them."

"But we *are* helping them. We may not save your friends today or tomorrow, but with patience and diplomacy, we can make a *lasting difference*, so girls like Pip are never sent to places like the Bootstrap facility ever again."

Brystal understood what Madame Weatherberry was saying, but her plan seemed too ambitious to work. The world would require a tremendous change of heart to accept magic, and she couldn't picture the world changing *that* much.

"I'm sorry, but it feels like an unrealistic goal," she

said. "I'd like to imagine a world where fairies can live openly and honestly, where they can live happily without fear or persecution, but I can't."

"Every accomplishment in history started as an unrealistic goal," Madame Weatherberry said. "A prosperous future is built by the persistence of its past—and we can't let doubt hold our persistence hostage. What I'm suggesting isn't certain, and it isn't going to be easy, but we have to at least *try*. Even if we fail, every step *we* take forward will be a step our successors won't have to take."

Although she still felt a bit cynical, Brystal was inspired by Madame Weatherberry's passion. She had never imagined a future for herself that involved a school for magic, but in many ways, Madame Weatherberry was offering her the purpose and future she had always dreamed about. Whether they successfully changed the world or not, a life devoted to helping people and developing her magical abilities was infinitely better than living in the Bootstrap Correctional Facility.

"It sounds like an adventure," she said. "I would love to join your academy of magic."

"I'm delighted to hear it," Madame Weatherberry said. "Delighted and relieved—unicorns *hate* changing direction mid-journey."

"Where is your school?" Brystal asked.

"It sits in the southeast In-Between, between the Southern and Eastern Kingdoms," Madame Weatherberry said. "Don't let the location worry you; the academy is very well protected. I spared no expense to keep it safe. But first we'll have to make a brief stop so I can get your parents' permission to take you."

"What?" Brystal exclaimed. "But why do we need their permission?"

"The king was adamant that I get approval from my pupils' guardians," she said. "And as I explained, it's important we follow his wishes."

Brystal had suspected Madame Weatherberry's plan was too good to be true—and now she had proof. Just as she had started looking forward to a new life at the academy of magic, the rug was pulled out from under her and her high hopes came crashing down.

"We should turn around," Brystal said. "My father is a very well-known Justice in the Southern Kingdom. He had me sent to the Bootstrap Correctional Facility as a personal *favor*, so no one would ever find out I was arrested for magic! He'll *never* let me attend your school!"

Madame Weatherberry waved her hand like Brystal's concern was a harmless fly.

"Don't worry, dear, I'm very persuasive," she said. "I managed to get the king's blessing—how hard could a Justice be? We'll have a nice chat when we see him this evening."

"This evening?" Brystal asked. "But my family lives in Chariot Hills. It's a two-day journey."

Madame Weatherberry was charmed by Brystal's obliviousness and a coy smile grew on her face.

"Actually, unicorns make better time than average horses," she said, and gestured to the window. "Take a look for yourself."

Brystal had been so wrapped up in their conversation she hadn't taken a glimpse out the window since they left, but when she finally did, her mouth dropped open. The golden carriage was moving through the Northeast Plains at lightning speed. The dismal land zipped past her window so quickly it was all a blur.

"I think I'm going to like magic," she said.

By dusk, the unicorns reached the outskirts of Chariot Hills and slowed to a normal pace. They pulled the golden carriage through the busy town square and all the pedestrians froze as Brystal and Madame Weatherberry drove past them. Brystal saw a cluster of her former classmates among the gawking crowd. As she rolled by, the girls went as white as their uniforms and their eyes doubled in size. Brystal gave them a friendly wave, but quickly realized this was a mistake because it caused one of the girls to faint.

The golden carriage took the path into the eastern countryside and soon the Evergreen home appeared in the distance. Although Brystal hadn't been gone very long, it felt like years had passed since she was home. The unicorns stopped in front of the house and Madame Weatherberry climbed out of the carriage, but Brystal lingered behind.

"Don't worry, I'll handle this," Madame Weatherberry said. "Trust me."

She offered Brystal her hand and helped her to the ground. They approached the front door and Madame Weatherberry gave it a cheerful knock with her gloved left hand. A few moments later, Brystal heard her mother's footsteps in the entryway behind the door.

"I'm coming! I'm coming!" she grumbled. "What can I do for—"

As soon as the door opened, Mrs. Evergreen shrieked and covered her mouth like she was seeing a ghost. Brystal was taken aback by her mother's appearance, too. She noticed that the circles under Mrs. Evergreen's eyes had grown darker and her bun was pulled even tighter. Clearly, doing all the household chores without help had taken a toll on her.

"Hello, Mother," Brystal said sheepishly. "Surprise."

"Brystal!" her mother cried. "What in the Lord's blue skies are you doing here?"

"It's a long story," she said.

Before Brystal had a chance to explain, Mrs. Evergreen threw her arms around her daughter and hugged her so tight she couldn't breathe.

"I didn't think I would ever see you again," she said with tears in her eyes. "Your father said you were caught conjuring magic at the library! I didn't believe it—I told him there had to be a mistake! My beautiful girl couldn't be capable of such a thing! Then your brothers told me about that awful trial! I swear, if I ever see that Justice Oldragaid I will strangle him until he's a normal color! They said the High Justice sent you to a facility in the Northeast to be cured. Have they cured you already? Is that why you've come back?"

Brystal winced at her mother's wishful thinking—it wasn't going to be easy for her to hear the truth. Mrs. Evergreen was so pleased to see her daughter that she hadn't noticed Madame Weatherberry or the golden carriage until now.

"Um...who are you?" she asked.

"Hello, Mrs. Evergreen, my name is Madame Weatherberry," she said. "Forgive me for showing up unannounced. I was given permission by His Majesty to remove Brystal from the Bootstrap Correctional Facility for a special project I'm developing. May I have a word with you and your husband to discuss it?"

"Oh?" Mrs. Evergreen was surprised to hear this. "My husband only had one trial this afternoon, so he should be home momentarily. Please, come in and I'll make some tea while you wait."

Mrs. Evergreen escorted Brystal and Madame Weatherberry to the sitting room and then stepped into the kitchen to make tea. As Madame Weatherberry looked around, she was tickled by the Evergreens' mismatched furniture and wallpaper.

"Your house is so *thrifty*," she said.

"My father isn't a fan of extravagance," Brystal said.

"It shows."

Mrs. Evergreen returned to the sitting room with a tray of tea.

"Please, have a seat," she said while she served them. "I imagine you're both very tired from your journey. Your father said the facility is all the way at the tip of the Northeast Plains."

"Actually, the trip flew by," Brystal said with a nervous laugh.

"How long are you staying?" Mrs. Evergreen asked. "Your brothers usually don't get home from the courthouse until late. They'll be sorry if they miss you."

"I can't imagine our conversation with Father will last very long," Brystal said. "We'll probably be on our way shortly after he arrives. Please give Brooks and Barrie my love."

"I will," Mrs. Evergreen said, and then looked her daughter up and down with concern. "Oh, Brystal, what have they done to you in that facility? You're practically skin and bones! I hope they're helping you at least—you know—with your *condition*."

"Ah . . . not exactly," Brystal said.

Before she elaborated, their conversation was interrupted by the sounds of her father's carriage pulling up to the house. Brystal took a deep breath to mentally prepare herself for what was to come. A few moments later, Justice Evergreen entered the house and charged down the hall—he hadn't even seen his daughter yet and was already in a temper.

"Why is there a ridiculous carriage and four

flamboyant horses outside our house?" he shouted. "What will the neighbors think if they see the—"

As the Justice barged into the sitting room, Madame Weatherberry and Brystal rose from their chairs to greet him. It took a few seconds for Justice Evergreen to recognize his daughter, and once he did, his face turned bright red, his nostrils flared, and he growled like a defensive animal.

"What is she doing in my house?" he barked.

Mrs. Evergreen jumped in front of her husband and waved like a clown distracting a bull.

"Please don't get upset just yet," she pleaded. "This woman has removed Brystal from the facility with permission from the king."

"The king? What could he possibly want with her?"

"I don't know, they just arrived," Mrs. Evergreen said. "Give them a chance to explain."

A few deep breaths later, Justice Evergreen had taken a reluctant seat on the sofa across from his daughter. Madame Weatherberry extended her arm to shake the Justice's hand, but he didn't accept the gesture.

"Justice Evergreen, it's a pleasure to make your acquaintance," she said. "My name is Madame Weatherberry. Thank you for taking the time to speak with us."

"Get to the point," he ordered.

"Ah, I see you're a man who appreciates a good summary," Madame Weatherberry said. "Very well, I'll make this short. I'm here because King Champion has given me permission to open an academy. I'm traveling through the Southern Kingdom to recruit students. But my academy isn't your typical school; it's an academy for very *special* children with very *unique* abilities."

Mrs. Evergreen clapped her hands in celebration. "Why, that's wonderful! His Majesty wants our daughter to join a special school!"

"What do you mean *unique abilities*," the Justice asked suspiciously. "I sincerely doubt you're recruiting academics or athletes from correctional houses."

"Well, if I may be completely transparent with you," Madame Weatherberry said with hesitation, "it's a school for *magic*."

Brystal could practically hear her father's heartbeat as his blood pressure soared.

"Excuse me?" he roared.

"I'm calling it Madame Weatherberry's Academy of Magical Endeavors and Philosophy, but don't get attached to the name, it's still a work in progress," she explained. "I promised His Majesty that I would get permission from my students' parents before recruiting them. So if you don't have any objections, I'll ask you to sign Brystal's permission form."

Madame Weatherberry pointed at the tea table and a golden document appeared with a long-feathered quill beside it. The Justice and Mrs. Evergreen both jumped at the sight of magic in their own house.

"All the details are spelled out on the form if you'd like to take a moment to read it," Madame Weatherberry said.

Brystal knew her father was already upset, but seeing the permission form infuriated him so much he turned the color of a tomato. He seized the form from the table and ripped it into shreds.

"How dare you disrespect me with such a request!" he yelled.

"Actually, Justice Evergreen, it would be more disrespectful if we *didn't* seek your approval," Madame Weatherberry said. "You see, I want everything about my academy to be handled tastefully and properly, and that starts with how I acquire my students. Our objective is to show the world that the magical community is much more decent than—"

The Justice was enraged by her words and knocked over the table with one angry swipe of his arm. The teacups hit the floor and shattered into pieces.

"I would rather see my daughter rot in jail than turn her over to the likes of you!" he shouted.

"There's no need to make a mess," Mrs. Evergreen said. "Let's all take a deep breath and I'll get us some more tea."

Mrs. Evergreen scooped up the broken teacups and the shredded permission form into her apron and hurried into the kitchen. Brystal closed her eyes and pretended she was somewhere else. It didn't matter how many deep breaths her father took; she knew he would never change his mind. But Madame Weatherberry wasn't ready to give up.

"Sir, I understand your *passionate* opposition," she

said. "You think I'm trying to take your daughter to a despicable place and teach her despicable things, but you're only imagining this because your perception of magic is flawed."

"I am a Justice of the Southern Kingdom, Madame! There is nothing flawed about my perception!"

"And in your impressive career, I'm sure you've presided over many cases that were caused by an unfortunate misunderstanding. I assure you, magic is like one of these misunderstandings. In fact, it's the single greatest misconception of our—"

"Magic is an abomination in the eyes of the law and in the eyes of the Lord! Do not insult my intelligence by pretending otherwise!"

"Justice Evergreen, you of all people know that the laws and religion of the Southern Kingdom have altered over time to reflect the opinions of those in power. Magic is a victim to that tradition. What the world thinks is a dreadful and wicked sin is actually a beautiful and nurturing gift. Your daughter is blessed with a very rare and powerful talent. In recent weeks, she has shown *remarkable* potential, and I believe my academy would be a wonderful opportunity for her to develop—"

"I will not have my daughter tarnish my good name by practicing magic!"

"But the king himself has approved my academy. It may cause some awkwardness at first, but in time, your daughter's magic will be a source of great pride for you. One day, the whole world may know her name and look up to her as a symbol of kindness and compassion. Her reputation may very well exceed your own and she could become the most admired Evergreen to ever—"

"ENOUGH!" the Justice yelled, and jumped to his feet. "I will not hear another word of this nonsense! You will take my daughter back to the Bootstrap Correctional Facility where she belongs at once! NOW GET OUT OF MY HOUSE!"

Justice Evergreen stormed out of the room, but before he entered the hall, he turned back to Brystal to give her one final, scornful glare.

"I should have let them execute you," he said.

Her father's words shattered Brystal into more pieces than all the teacups he had knocked to the floor. Once Justice Evergreen was out of her sight, it took Brystal a few moments to regain her senses. Madame Weatherberry shook her head, appalled by the Justice's cruel remarks.

"Well, *that* could have gone better," she said. "Don't lose hope just yet, Brystal. We'll find a way around this."

Brystal appreciated Madame Weatherberry's optimism, but she knew there was nothing she could do that wouldn't break her promise to the king. Without her father's permission, her only option was to return to the facility.

"It was a mistake to come here," Brystal said. "We should leave."

Brystal and Madame Weatherberry showed themselves to the front door. As they stepped outside and headed for the golden carriage, Brystal's spirits were so low she was afraid she might sink into the ground. Just as she was about to climb into the carriage, Mrs. Evergreen emerged from the house and ran after her daughter.

"Brystal?" she called.

"Mother, I'm sorry I didn't say good-bye," Brystal said. "I didn't want to see your face when I told you I—"

"Here," Mrs. Evergreen said. "Take this."

Her mother discreetly slid a folded piece of paper into her daughter's hand. Brystal opened it and couldn't believe what she was looking at. Mrs. Evergreen had sewn together the permission form and *signed the bottom of it*!

"Mother!" she gasped. "What have you done?"

Mrs. Evergreen pulled Brystal into a tight embrace so she could whisper directly into her daughter's ear.

"Keep your voice down in case your father is listening from inside," her mother said. "The form says it only requires the signature of *one* parent. I don't care what your father thinks; you're *my* daughter, too, and I will not stand the thought of you getting worked to death in that awful facility. Now, you go to that school and make a life that *you* can be proud of. Get as far away from here as you can and find the happiness you deserve. And please, for your own sake, don't come back to this miserable house again."

Before Brystal had the chance to respond, Mrs. Evergreen released her daughter and hurried back inside the house. Brystal was left speechless by her mother's

176

actions. She couldn't think, she couldn't breathe, and she couldn't move—she just stayed perfectly still and stared at the house in shock.

"Brystal, are you all right?" Madame Weatherberry asked. "What happened?"

"My mother just handed me a new life," she said.

CHAPTER EIGHT

THE BOY OF FIRE AND THE GIRL OF EMERALDS

As the unicorns drew the golden carriage away from Chariot Hills, Brystal couldn't help but smile from ear to ear. Life had been a living nightmare in recent weeks, but by some miraculous twist of fate, the day had turned into a dream come true. Not only was it the most confusing and surprising day of her life, but thanks to her mother, it was the first day of an entirely *new* life. Signing the form was the most profound thing anyone had ever done for her and Brystal hoped she could return the favor and help her mother escape the Southern Kingdom someday.

Mrs. Evergreen had asked her daughter to leave and never come back, but Brystal couldn't wrap her head around it. She didn't have many fond memories of her family's home, so it would be easy to keep her distance, but until this moment, Brystal had never been able to *choose* her whereabouts. The Evergreen house, the School for Future Wives and Mothers, the courthouse, and the Bootstrap Correctional Facility were all places she had been *forced* to go—and now that Brystal was officially under Madame Weatherberry's supervision, she never had to return to those terrible places again. The newfound freedom was an exhilarating sensation and made Brystal's big smile grow even wider.

"Has anyone ever told you what a lovely smile you have?" Madame Weatherberry asked.

"Not that I recall," Brystal said. "Then again, I haven't had many things to smile about."

"I hope that changes once we get to the academy," Madame Weatherberry said.

"I can't wait to see it," Brystal said. "How much longer until we get there?"

"We still have one student to pick up in the Southern Kingdom, and then another in the In-Between after that," Madame Weatherberry said. "With any luck, they'll be easy recruits, and we'll arrive by tomorrow evening. I can't imagine how exhausted you must be after a day like today, so please, feel free to get some rest."

An enormous yawn escaped Brystal's mouth and confirmed Madame Weatherberry's hunch. Brystal stretched out across the satin cushions and became so comfortable she was asleep within seconds. Overnight, the golden carriage traveled into the Northwest Foothills of the Southern Kingdom. Brystal awoke the following morning more rejuvenated than she had felt in months. Instead of colorful fruit, the vines on the carriage's ceiling grew muffins, bagels, and other breakfast pastries.

"Good morning, Madame Weatherberry," Brystal said, and helped herself to a muffin. "Did you sleep well?"

It appeared Madame Weatherberry hadn't moved since Brystal went to sleep. She was looking over the Map of Magic and was so captivated by it she didn't respond.

"Madame? Is everything all right?" Brystal asked.

Still Madame Weatherberry didn't look up from the map. "How peculiar," she said.

"What's peculiar?" Brystal asked.

"Oh, forgive my concentration, dear," Madame Weatherberry said. "I'm a little concerned about the potential student we're traveling to. He's changed locations twice since last night and seems to be heading to a third."

Madame Weatherberry turned the Map of Magic around so Brystal could see what she was referring to. In the northwest corner of the Southern Kingdom was a bright star moving ever so slightly toward the border of the In-Between. The name beside the star was *Xanthous Hayfield*.

"What do you think that means?" Brystal asked.

"Well, it simply means he's on the move," Madame Weatherberry said. "But I'm worried about what he's moving *from*. We should try to reach him before he crosses the border."

Madame Weatherberry snapped her fingers and the unicorns started galloping even faster. The rolling land and oak trees of the Northwest Foothills zoomed past Brystal's window so quickly she couldn't even see them. Madame Weatherberry kept a close eye on the Map of Magic as her and Brystal's stars approached the young man's star.

Suddenly, the air outside was hazy and the carriage filled with the smell of smoke. Madame Weatherberry snapped her fingers again and the unicorns slowed to a normal pace. She and Brystal looked out their windows and saw that the land was scorched for acres around them. Many of the trees and bushes were still ablaze, like the area had been hit by a recent wildfire.

The debris continued for miles down the path, and then, strangely, the damage ended at a large wooden barn. The barn was a blazing inferno with flames stretching well above its crumbling roof. It was as if the wildfire had paused to take a rest inside before moving on.

"Now we know what he was running away from," Brystal said. "Do you think he escaped the fire?"

Madame Weatherberry squinted as she inspected the burning barn.

"No, I think he *is* the fire," she said. "Brystal, stay in the carriage. Things may get heated if we overwhelm him."

"*May* get heated?" Brystal asked.

The golden carriage stopped a safe distance away from the burning barn. Madame Weatherberry climbed out and approached the barn while Brystal watched from the carriage. The fairy moved her hands in big circles through the air, summoning a sudden rainstorm that extinguished all the flames. Once the fire was out, all that remained of the structure was its charred framing and support beams.

To Brystal's amazement, a boy about eleven years old was sleeping on the ashy ground inside the barn. He had golden hair and fair skin, and his clothes had been significantly singed in the fire. Although his clothing was damaged, there wasn't a single burn mark or scratch on his entire body.

"Hello, Xanthous," Madame Weatherberry called to him.

The boy awoke with a fright. He was startled to see Madame Weatherberry walking toward him and quickly hid behind a burned beam. Brystal gasped when flames appeared on his head and shoulders. Madame Weatherberry was right—Xanthous wasn't *running* from the fire; he was *creating* it.

"Stay where you are!" he said. "Don't come any closer!"

Madame Weatherberry gave the boy a warm smile but didn't stop her approach.

"Don't worry, sweetheart," she said. "I'm not going to hurt you."

"No, but I might hurt *you*!" Xanthous warned. "Stay away from me or you'll get burned!"

With every step Madame Weatherberry took, Xanthous became more and more anxious. The fire on his head and shoulders flickered with more intensity, and the flames traveled down his arms and torso.

"Lady, I mean it!" he yelled. "I can't control it! You're putting yourself in danger!"

"Xanthous, you have nothing to fear," she said. "My name is Madame Weatherberry and I promise you aren't going to hurt me—I'm just like *you*."

"Just like *me*?" he asked in disbelief. "Look, I don't know what you're doing here, but there's no way you're like me! Please, turn around before you get burned!"

To prove him wrong, Madame Weatherberry raised her arms above her head and her body was suddenly engulfed in bright violet flames. Brystal and Xanthous couldn't believe their eyes and both their mouths dropped open. The boy's state of shock temporarily extinguished the fire on his own body. Once Madame Weatherberry thought her point was achieved, she lowered her arms and the violet flames vanished without leaving a blemish on her skin or clothing.

"I told you," she said. "I'm magical just like you, and we can do all sorts of things that other people can't. Your fire is just the beginning."

"I'm . . . I'm . . . I'm *magical*?" he asked.

"Of course you are," Madame Weatherberry said. "Why else would you be able to produce fire from your skin?"

"I thought I was cursed," he said.

"It's perfectly natural to feel scared and confused," Madame Weatherberry said. "Magic is a very misunderstood concept in our world. I'm sure you've been told it's a loathsome and demonic practice, but that isn't true. It may not seem like it now, but you're actually blessed with a very powerful gift."

Xanthous shook his head and backed away from her. "You must be mistaken," he said. "I'm not *blessed* with anything—I'm a walking disaster! I have to be stopped!"

"And you think crossing the border is going to help?" Madame Weatherberry asked.

"What are you talking about?" Xanthous said. "I'm not headed to the border."

"Then where are you headed?" she asked.

"I'm going to the Northwest Lake!" he said. *"I'm going to strap boulders around my feet and drown myself before I cause any more damage!"*

After he confessed his plans, the boy fell to his knees and began to weep, but instead of crying tears, glowing embers sparked out of his eyes. Madame Weatherberry and Brystal were heartbroken to hear about Xanthous's intentions. The fairy knelt beside him and placed a comforting hand on his shoulder.

"My dear boy," she said. "That's a bit extreme, don't you think?"

"But it's the only way to stop it!" he cried. "And I don't want to hurt anyone else!"

"What do you mean *hurt anyone else*?" Madame Weatherberry asked. "Did something happen that made you run away from home?"

"I don't have a home to run away from anymore," the boy cried.

"Why is that?" Madame Weatherberry asked.

Xanthous shook his head. "I can't tell you," he said. "You'll think I'm a monster."

"My dear, I have a very long history with magic," she said. "I know how complicated an introduction can be. Even though magic comes from a good place within us, if we don't have control over our abilities, sometimes they cause unfortunate things to happen. So unless you intentionally caused harm, whatever happened was *not your fault*. Now, please, start from the beginning and tell me what's brought you here."

Just like Brystal's first interaction with her, it didn't take long for Xanthous to sense Madame Weatherberry's kindness and realize she could be trusted. After he took a deep breath, the embers stopped sparking from his eyes, and he sat up to tell her what was causing him so much grief.

"I suppose I always knew this day was coming," Xanthous said. "My mother died while giving birth to me. The doctor told my family it was due to burns she

185

received during the delivery, but he couldn't explain what caused them. My father must have known it was my fault because he refused to hold me or give me a name. Eventually, the midwife called me *Xanthous* because of a warm yellow glow I was born with, but it faded after a couple days."

"Many of us are born with signs," Madame Weatherberry said. "I'm sorry yours came at such a tragic cost."

"Me too," he said. "As I got older there were more signs. I always had a fever, I never needed a coat in the winter, and things would melt in my hands if I squeezed them too hard. About a year ago, everything got worse. There were sparks whenever I coughed or sneezed, there were flares when I was surprised or scared, and sometimes I'd have a nightmare and set my sheets on fire. But a few days ago, my father came home from the pub, and he started beating me...."

"Because he discovered your magic?" Madame Weatherberry said.

"No, it wasn't because of that," Xanthous said. "My father has always hated me since my mother died.... But a few nights ago, he caught me with something, something I shouldn't have had, something he had warned me to stay away from...."

The memory was clearly painful for Xanthous to relive. More embers sparked out of his eyes and the flames returned to his head and shoulders.

"You can spare any details you're not ready to share,"

Madame Weatherberry said. "What happened *after* your father caught you?"

"As he was hitting me, I became angry—*really* angry," Xanthous recalled. "I felt all this heat building up inside me, like I was a volcano. I knew something bad was about to happen, so I begged my father to stop and run away, but he wouldn't! The next thing I knew, there was fire everywhere! It came out like an explosion! Our house burned to the ground and my father...my father...*my father*..."

"Your father perished in the fire," Madame Weatherberry said without having to ask.

Xanthous rolled onto his side and sobbed so hard his embers turned into two fiery streams. His entire body was consumed in powerful flames and Brystal could feel the heat even from inside the carriage. Madame Weatherberry raised her hand and created a shield around the boy so his fire didn't spread. Once all his pent-up emotion was released, the flames died down, and Xanthous returned to normal.

"I want you to listen to me very carefully," Madame Weatherberry said. "What you've experienced is nothing short of tragic—but a tragic beginning doesn't mean you have to have a tragic ending. I know it feels like the end of the world right now, but you are not as alone as you think you are. There is an entire community of people *just like you* who can help you through this trying time and teach you to control your abilities."

"I don't deserve to be helped," Xanthous said. "I hurt everyone who gets too close."

Madame Weatherberry reached toward the golden carriage, and the armrest across from Brystal opened on its own. A crystal medal with a red ribbon rose out of the compartment, floated out the window, and flew into Madame Weatherberry's hand.

"Here," she said, and placed the ribbon around his neck.

"What is this?" Xanthous asked.

"I call it a *Muter Medal*," Madame Weatherberry said. "It stops the magical abilities of whoever wears it. I invented the medal myself just in case I encountered a child like you. It doesn't matter how upset you get—as long as that medal is around your neck, your fire won't return."

Xanthous didn't believe her. He scrunched his forehead as he tried to think the most troubling thoughts possible—but his skin remained perfectly normal. The boy even slapped himself across the face a couple of times, looking happier with every smack, because the flames never appeared.

"It works!" Xanthous said.

"Of course it does," Madame Weatherberry said. "Sometimes the biggest problems in life have the simplest answers. I hope this will save you a trip to the lake."

"Can I keep the Muter Medal?" he asked with hopeful eyes.

"You won't need it forever," Madame Weatherberry

said. "One day you'll learn to control your abilities on your own."

"How will I learn to *control* them?" he asked.

"Because I'm going to teach you," she said. "I'm starting my own school for children like you. I'm calling it Madame Weatherberry's Institution of Magical Arts—but the name is a bit of a mouthful, so I'll probably shorten it. King Champion has given me permission to recruit young fairies in the Southern Kingdom so I can teach them to develop their magical abilities."

"Fairies?" Xanthous asked.

"Yes, that's the appropriate term for people like us," Madame Weatherberry explained. "Once my students are properly trained, we're going to travel the world and use our magic to help and heal people in need. Hopefully with time, our selfless acts will be recognized, and the world will learn to accept us. Would you like to join our quest?"

"You want *me* to join your school?" Xanthous asked. "But I just scorched a thousand acres of land! Are you sure you want someone like me on your campus?"

"You're exactly the kind of student I'm looking for," she said. "After what you've been through, you know how important it is to spread acceptance and awareness of magic, so no one has to repeat your experience. And together, we can create a world where little boys never think *jumping into lakes* is the only way to fix their problems."

Xanthous went quiet as he considered Madame

Weatherberry's proposal. Brystal crossed her fingers in the carriage, hoping the boy would accept the offer.

"Well, since I'm not sinking to the bottom of a lake anymore, my schedule is pretty open," he said. "If you're sure I won't be a problem, then I would love to join your school!"

Madame Weatherberry clapped in celebration. "That's wonderful, dear!" she said. "I know you're going to be very happy there. Now let's get you something a little more comfortable to wear for our journey."

Madame Weatherberry twirled a finger, and thread by thread, Xanthous's burned clothes grew back into the brown pants and patchy vest he'd worn before his fire started. She escorted the boy to the golden carriage and helped him climb aboard. Xanthous was surprised to see Brystal waiting inside and became shy.

"Xanthous, I'd like you to meet your new classmate Brystal Evergreen," Madame Weatherberry said. "She's very powerful, just like you."

"Hello, Xanthous," she said. "It's nice to meet you!"

Brystal tried to shake his hand, but Xanthous quickly dodged the gesture.

"I'm sorry," he said. "It's nothing personal, I'm just used to burning things."

After a moment, Xanthous cautiously shook Brystal's hand and was relieved when he didn't hurt her. Even though the Muter Medal suppressed his powers, Xanthous had a very warm touch.

"It's nice to meet you, too, Brystal," he said.

Madame Weatherberry and Xanthous took their seats and the carriage door closed behind them. The fairy retrieved the Map of Magic from the compartment under the armrest and double-checked the whereabouts of her third and final recruit, in the In-Between. Once she confirmed the location, she snapped her fingers and the unicorns lunged forward, pulling the golden carriage in a new direction. Xanthous's eyes went wide as the Northwest Foothills raced past his window.

"This is unbelievable!" he exclaimed. "We must be going a hundred miles an hour!"

"Isn't it amazing?" Brystal said. "I've traveled across the kingdom with Madame Weatherberry and my heart still flutters when I look out the window."

"How long have you known you were magic?" he asked.

"It was a recent discovery," she said. "But if it's any consolation, I understand what you're feeling. The second time I did magic, I was arrested and then locked away in a correctional facility. It's difficult to imagine *good things* can come from magic, too, but I look forward to Madame Weatherberry convincing us."

Xanthous nodded sadly. "It'll be a miracle if anything good comes out of my magic."

"I bet you'll be surprised," Brystal said. "You may think it's a curse now, but I know a few places that would be lucky to have a boy like you."

"Like where?" he asked.

"The correctional facility I was sent to, for example,"

she explained. "It was so cold at night my friend would sneak me an extra blanket so I didn't freeze to death. I would have given anything to be near one of your fires then! And I'm sure you would be a big help with all the trouble they've been having in the Northern Kingdom lately."

Suddenly, Madame Weatherberry looked up from the Map of Magic and glared at Brystal like she had said something controversial.

"*What did you just say about the Northern Kingdom?*" she asked.

Madame Weatherberry's intense reaction surprised Brystal—it was the first time she had seen the fairy without her trademark charm.

"I just said the Northern Kingdom could use a boy like Xanthous," Brystal said.

"Yes, but *why*?" Madame Weatherberry pressed. "What have you heard?"

"Just that they've had blizzards," Brystal said. "That's all."

Once the subject was clarified, Madame Weatherberry's cheerful manner slowly returned, but a hint of aggression remained in her eyes.

"Oh, yes—the *blizzards*," she said. "I heard about those, too. Poor people, let's hope the weather changes for them soon. Forgive me, Brystal, I misunderstood what you were saying."

"Madame Weatherberry, is anything *else* happening in the Northern Kingdom that we should be worried about?" Brystal asked.

"Nothing to trouble you with, my dear," she said. "Just politics as usual—it's all quite dull, actually. Forget I mentioned it."

Out of respect, Brystal didn't inquire any further, but Madame Weatherberry's suspicious behavior made one thing abundantly clear: there was something about the Northern Kingdom she wasn't telling them.

· • ★ • ·

The golden carriage was quiet as it traveled south from the Northwest Foothills. Although she didn't say anything, Brystal's mind was racing with exciting thoughts about her future at the school for magic. Xanthous was still in awe over how fast the carriage was moving and whipped his head from side to side to try to catch a glimpse of the blurry landscape outside. Madame Weatherberry mostly kept to herself, studying the Map of Magic in silence. At one point, something strange seemed to catch her attention and she stared at the map even more intently for a few minutes without looking up.

"Madame?" Brystal asked. "Is something wrong?"

"Nothing's *wrong*," Madame Weatherberry said. "However, there is something very *curious* about our next recruit's location."

"Are they moving, too?" Brystal asked.

"On the contrary," Madame Weatherberry said. "Her whereabouts have remained exactly the same for as long as I've been aware of her. That should make her easy to find, but I'm interested in why she hasn't moved at all."

"What's her name?" Brystal asked.

"Emerelda Stone," Madame Weatherberry said. "Pretty, isn't it?"

"I can't wait to meet her," Brystal said. "It'll be nice to know a girl I have something in common with."

An hour or so into their journey from the Northwest Foothills, the unicorns made an abrupt right turn and began traveling west. Brystal wasn't expecting the change in direction and glanced down at the map in Madame Weatherberry's lap.

"Are we going the right way?" Xanthous asked. "We're getting awfully close to the western border."

"That's exactly where we're headed," Madame Weatherberry said. "Miss Stone lives a few miles west of the Southern Kingdom in the coal mines of the In-Between."

The mention of the infamous territory between the kingdoms caught Xanthous's attention. He sat straight up in his seat and glanced at his companions with big, fearful eyes.

"We're going into the *In-Between*?" Xanthous gasped. "But isn't it dangerous?"

"Oh, it's more than dangerous," Madame Weatherberry said. "There are creatures living in the forests of the In-Between that humankind has only seen in nightmares. Food and water are limited, so the inhabitants are constantly fighting over resources. People are wise to keep their distance. That's why it's the perfect location for the academy."

Xanthous's anxiety doubled. "The academy is in the In-Between, too?" he asked.

"Yes," Madame Weatherberry said with a shrug. "Did I not mention it?"

"I'm afraid you left out *that* detail," he said.

"Well, fear not, you have me to protect you," Madame Weatherberry said with a prideful nod. "My academy is in a very secure area of the southeast In-Between, and the property is protected by powerful magic."

"What about the coal mines?" he asked. "Are they safe?"

"We should be perfectly fine," Madame Weatherberry said. "The coal mines are only a few minutes' walk past the western border."

Xanthous shook his head like his ears were deceiving him. "Did you say *a few minutes' walk*?" he asked in a panic. "We're getting *out* of the carriage?"

"Of course we're walking," Madame Weatherberry said with a laugh. "Four unicorns and a golden carriage would only bring attention to ourselves. As long as we stay quiet and calm, everything will be fine."

Xanthous gulped, unconvinced by the fairy's assessment. Brystal trusted Madame Weatherberry slightly more than he did, but her stomach tightened at the idea of entering the dangerous forest. Young women in the Southern Kingdom were rarely taught about worldly matters, but even *they* knew to avoid the In-Between.

The unicorns slowed down as they approached the western border. As Brystal and Xanthous anxiously looked out the window, there was no argument about where the Southern Kingdom ended and where the In-Between began. The horizon was consumed by a thick and monstrous forest. All the trees were gigantic, their trunks were crooked, and their mangled branches stretched into the sky like the arms of prisoners reaching for freedom.

As they moved closer, the carriage passed a sign that gave Brystal and Xanthous chills:

WARNING
YOU ARE NOW ENTERING
THE IN-BETWEEN ZONE
BEWARE OF MONSTERS

"Did they have to paint the sign with such a creepy font?" Xanthous asked. "I mean, was that really necessary?"

The golden carriage pulled off the road and stopped at the edge of the forest. Madame Weatherberry happily hopped down from the carriage without a care in the world and then helped—*forced*, rather—Brystal and Xanthous out as well. Once all three passengers were outside, Madame Weatherberry snapped her fingers and the large unicorns began to shrink. The majestic steeds were transformed into small field mice with horns and bushy magenta tails. The fairy snapped her fingers again and the golden carriage shrunk to the size of a brooch, which Madame Weatherberry pinned to her gown. With a third and final snap, a large piece of cheese appeared on the ground for the mice to snack on.

"We should be back in an hour or so," Madame Weatherberry told the mice. "Have a nice break and enjoy the cheese—oh, and please watch out for owls. You remember what happened to Prancy."

Brystal and Xanthous followed the fairy back to the road and they continued into the In-Between on foot. The path was so bumpy and narrow a carriage wouldn't have managed. The tree branches filled the sky above them and blocked most of the sunlight, making it impossible to tell the time. The deeper they walked, the more jittery Brystal and Xanthous became. Madame Weatherberry was amused by their paranoia.

They were halfway to the mine when two enormous creatures lunged at them from the dark forest. Brystal and Xanthous screamed and grabbed each other in terror. As the figures stepped into the light, the travelers realized they had crossed paths with two ogres. The first ogre had brown skin and his face was covered in bone piercings. The second ogre was green and covered in warts. Both creatures had an underbite with sharp teeth, their clothes were made from the fur of several dead animals, and they each carried a club carved from a log.

"Well, look what's wandered into the woods," the brown ogre sneered.

"You must have gotten lost if you're all the way out here," the green ogre growled.

The ogres circled the travelers like wolves circling prey. Brystal and Xanthous were so scared they closed their eyes, but Madame Weatherberry never even flinched.

"Actually, we're perfectly content, thank you," she said. "It's very kind of you to check on us, though."

Brystal, Xanthous, and the ogres were equally surprised by Madame Weatherberry's cheerful response. She proceeded down the road and pulled her students with her, but the ogres sprinted ahead and blocked the path with their clubs.

"You don't think you're getting away *that* easily, do you?" the brown ogre asked.

"Fresh meat is hard to find around here," the green ogre said, and licked his lips.

Madame Weatherberry eyed the creatures like they were disobedient children.

"Just so we're clear, you've interrupted our journey with the intention of *eating us*, is that correct? And your obscene gestures and suggestive language are not meant to be interpreted as sarcasm, is that right?"

The ogres shared a puzzled glance—they didn't understand all the words Madame Weatherberry was using.

"Of course we're going to eat you!" the brown ogre roared.

"How wonderful!" Madame Weatherberry cheered.

"Wonderful?" Brystal exclaimed. "Madame, how is this wonderful?"

"We're about to be their lunch!" Xanthous cried.

"The ogres have just given me the perfect opportunity to teach a valuable lesson," Madame Weatherberry explained. "As I've said before, magic comes from a place of love and joy within us. Its purpose is to stabilize, improve, and nourish. However, on the rare occasion when it can be justified, magic can also be used for *self-defense*. By admitting their intentions to harm us, these ogres have given us permission to—"

"MADAME WEATHERBERRY, LOOK OUT!" Brystal screamed.

The brown ogre raised his club high above his head and swung it in their direction. Without looking, Madame Weatherberry snapped her fingers and the club crumbled to the ground before it struck them. She whipped around and pointed both hands at the creatures. The ogres rose into the air and spun like cyclones, and the dead leaves covering the forest floor twirled around them. Madame Weatherberry dropped her hands and the spinning stopped, but instead of ogres, two small turtles fell to the ground.

"As I was saying," she continued, "by admitting their intentions to harm us, these ogres have given us permission to use our magic to stop them. And now that they've been transformed into smaller animals, they'll learn a much-needed lesson in humility. It's a win-win for everyone. Any questions?"

Brystal and Xanthous were flabbergasted by what they had just witnessed. When the feeling finally returned to their bodies, Xanthous raised his hand.

"Yes, Xanthous?" Madame Weatherberry asked.

"Will you teach us how to do *that*?" he asked eagerly.

"In time," she said with a smile. "Now let's move on."

Madame Weatherberry led Brystal and Xanthous a few more miles into the In-Between and the road finally came to the entrance of an enormous coal mine at the base of a mountain. Brystal and Xanthous were amazed to see that the mine was operated entirely by dwarfs. The small miners pushed carts of coal out of the mountain and dumped the dark substance into a huge pile outside. Once the carts were emptied, the miners returned to the mine to fetch more, and the pile of coal was separated and boxed by packers.

The workers were used to seeing ferocious animals and dangerous creatures emerge from the forest around them, but as Madame Weatherberry, Brystal, and Xanthous walked out from the trees, they all froze and stared at their visitors in disbelief. The dwarfs guarding the entrance were so surprised they didn't even question the strange visitors as they strolled past them.

"Good afternoon, gentlemen," Madame Weatherberry said with a friendly wave. "Keep up the good work."

They entered a dark tunnel and it took a few seconds for their eyes to adjust. The clanking of pickaxes grew louder the farther they walked. Eventually, the tunnel brought them to a massive cavern where miners chiseled coal on multiple levels around them. In the center of the cavern, built on a cluster of stalagmites, was an observation deck, where an older dwarf sat behind a miniature desk. He wore a suit and tie and squinted through a monocle as he studied blueprints of the mountain.

"Excuse me, sir?" Madame Weatherberry called to him. "Will you please point me in the direction of whoever is in charge?"

The old dwarf looked up from the blueprints and was stunned to see that a woman and children had wandered into the mine. One by one, the miners throughout the cavern noticed their visitors and dropped their pickaxes to watch them.

"That would be me, ma'am," the old dwarf said. "I'm Mr. Slate, the Miner Superior."

"Pleased to meet you, Mr. Slate," she said. "My name is Madame Weatherberry and these are my students, Brystal Evergreen and Xanthous Hayfield."

"What brings you to the mine?" Mr. Slate asked.

"I'm looking for a young woman named Emerelda Stone," Madame Weatherberry said. "Can you please tell me where she is?"

All the dwarfs went quiet and the cavern became very tense. Mr. Slate exchanged an uneasy glance with the miners around him.

"I'm sorry, but there's no one here by that name," the dwarf said.

"Are you certain?" Madame Weatherberry said.

"Because according to my map, Miss Stone is some-where within the mine. Perhaps she goes by another name?"

"Your map must have misled you, then, because I assure you, there are no young women here," Mr. Slate said. "I'm sorry you came all this way for nothing. However, I'd be happy to offer you a discount on our coal so you don't leave empty-handed."

Madame Weatherberry eyed the Miner Superior sus-piciously.

"Mr. Slate, my map doesn't lie," she said. "I know there is a girl with magical abilities nearby, and if I dis-cover you are harboring Miss Stone against her will, I will use force to liberate her."

Beads of sweat appeared on Mr. Slate's forehead. "I just told you, there is no young woman in this mine," he said. "Now please leave before I have you removed. We don't want any trouble here."

Madame Weatherberry turned to Brystal and Xanthous with an enthusiastic smile they weren't expecting to see.

"Our luck continues!" she said happily. "Mr. Slate has given me another opportunity to teach a valuable lesson. You see, when we have reason to believe some-one is in danger or being held hostage, magic can be used to rescue them. Watch this."

With one flick of her wrist, all the miners throughout the cavern suddenly hit the floor like dominoes and fell into a deep sleep. Mr. Slate dived under his desk to avoid the spell, but Madame Weatherberry spared him.

"You horrible witch!" Mr. Slate screamed. *"What have you done to them?"*

"I've halted your production and given your miners a rest," she explained. "You will get your employees back as soon as you show us the girl."

"No!" the dwarf yelled. "I won't let you take her from us!"

"Mr. Slate, please don't make this any more difficult than it needs to be," Madame Weatherberry said. "I wouldn't enjoy turning your coal mine into a fertilizer plant, but I'm certainly not above it."

She gave the dwarf no choice. Mr. Slate climbed down from the observation deck and begrudgingly guided his visitors to the back of the cavern. They followed him into a long tunnel that snaked even deeper into the mountain and ended at a small cave. Unlike the other parts of the mine, the sequestered cave sparkled like the night sky because the floor was covered in piles of diamonds, rubies, sapphires, and every other gem imaginable.

In the back of the small cave was a girl of about twelve, with bright green eyes, beautiful brown skin, and black curly hair. She wore a dress made from a burlap sack and sandals made from wood and rope. The girl stood behind a workbench that was illuminated by a jar of fireflies.

Piece by piece, the girl selected coal from a cart beside her bench, closed her eyes, and concentrated as she squeezed it. When she opened her hand, the piece of coal had transformed into a colorful gem, and she tossed it into the pile it belonged to. Brystal and Xanthous were mesmerized by her process and they watched her for several moments before she noticed she had company.

"Who are you?" she asked, wary of her unexpected guests.

"Hello, Emerelda, my name is Madame Weatherberry," the fairy said. "It's so great to finally meet you."

Madame Weatherberry approached the workbench to greet Emerelda with a handshake, but the girl didn't accept it. Instead, Emerelda folded her arms and looked Madame Weatherberry up and down with a dirty scowl.

"What are you doing in my cave?" she asked.

"They're witches and they demanded to see you," Mr. Slate said. "I'm sorry, Em, they gave me no choice."

"Actually, we're not witches," Madame Weatherberry corrected him. "We're *fairies* and we're here to save you."

"*Save* me?" Emerelda was offended by the notion. "Papa, what's this woman talking about? What does she think she's saving me from?"

"Papa?" Madame Weatherberry was surprised to hear. "Why does she call you *Papa*?"

"Because I raised her," Mr. Slate said. "We're not holding her hostage—this is her home! Her parents abandoned her when she was just an infant and I found her crying in the woods. Of course, I didn't realize she was *magical* until I brought her back to the mine. My plan was to find her a nice human home, but then every-thing she got her hands on turned into jewels."

"So you decided to keep her and profit from her magic," Madame Weatherberry accused.

"No, to *protect* her!" Mr. Slate exclaimed. "Can you imagine what would happen if humankind found out she existed? Their greed has no bounds! Kings would go to war to get their hands on a child who can turn coal into diamonds! She'd never have a moment of peace until the day she died! Yes, we make a nice living off of Emerelda's creations, but at least she's safe with us!"

Brystal could tell Madame Weatherberry was embar-rassed for misjudging the situation, because she paused for a few moments before saying another word.

"Mr. Slate, I apologize for the misunderstanding," she said. "But the mine isn't the only place she can be protected. In fact, there's only one place I know of that can guarantee her safety, that is, until she learns to pro-tect herself."

Madame Weatherberry leaned down so she could look into Emerelda's eyes.

"I'm starting an academy of magic," she explained. "I'm going to teach young fairies like you to control and expand their abilities. I've traveled all this way because I'm hoping you'll want to join us."

Emerelda raised an eyebrow at Madame Weatherberry, like it was the dumbest idea she had ever heard.

"Why would you start a school of magic?" she asked. "The world hates magic!"

"That's exactly why I'm starting it," Madame Weatherberry said. "After my students are properly trained, our plan is to travel around the world and use our magic to help people. Hopefully, humankind will recognize our good deeds and learn to accept us, so little girls like you will never have to hide in caves again."

Brystal and Xanthous watched Emerelda closely, hoping she would be intrigued by Madame Weatherberry's offer, but she remained just as defensive as before.

"I'm not interested," she said.

"Are you sure?" Madame Weatherberry asked. "This is a very big opportunity. Would you like some time to consider it?"

"I don't need to consider anything," Emerelda snapped. "Why would I want to use my magic to help humankind? Like my papa just said, humankind is awful! All they do is make life difficult for other species!"

"Well, I won't argue with that," Madame Weatherberry said. "Humankind is a flawed race, but unfortunately, as long as they have the numbers and resources to stay in power, their acceptance of us is the key to our survival. If the magical community doesn't do *something* to improve our relationship with humanity, we risk extinction. Showing them kindness is the first step in changing their perception of us."

"Humans don't deserve kindness!" Emerelda said. "My parents were human and they left me to die when I was just a baby! What kind of monsters would do that to their own child?"

"We all have our scars, Emerelda, but that doesn't mean we should give up."

Madame Weatherberry slowly removed the glove covering her left arm and everyone in the cave gasped. Brystal had never questioned why the fairy wore only one glove, but now it was obvious. Madame Weatherberry's left arm was skeletal and her skin was pitch-black from the tips of her fingers to the bottom of her shoulder, like it had been burned to the bone. It looked less like a human limb and more like the branch of a withering tree.

"My family was human, too, and when they discovered my magical abilities, they tried to burn me at the stake," she told them. "Luckily, there was a terrible storm that night and the fire didn't last long—but I'll never forget the pain as long as I live, because my family's betrayal hurt far worse than the flames burning my skin."

After the gruesome memory was shared, Madame Weatherberry slipped her charred arm back into her glove.

"Why would you want to help the people who did *that* to you?" Emerelda asked.

"Because if we want a better world, we have to be better *than* the world," Madame Weatherberry said. "If we let one experience destroy our faith in an entire species, then we're no better than the people who hurt us. Just like in the magical community, there is good and evil in humanity, and now more than ever, they need to be reminded of the goodness in their hearts. Our pursuit of acceptance could be the example humankind needs to change its ways—it could inspire them to finally value their compassion over their hatred. We could create a new era where the world respects not just *us*, but those from *all* walks of life."

Madame Weatherberry's passionate plea poked a few holes in Emerelda's resistance, but it didn't tear it down.

"I guess I'm still valuing my hatred over my compassion, too," Emerelda said. "I'm sorry you came all this way, Madame Weatherberry, but I won't be attending your school. Now, if you'll excuse me, I have a lot of work to do."

Emerelda returned to her workbench and continued transforming the coal into gems. Madame Weatherberry seemed extremely saddened by the girl's decision but didn't press the issue any further. She headed out of the cave, gesturing for Brystal and Xanthous to follow her.

"We should get going, children," she said. "I'm sure the unicorns are anxious for us to return."

Although Madame Weatherberry had accepted Emerelda's choice, Brystal thought the girl was making a horrible mistake and wasn't ready to give up on her. She went back to the workbench and stood in front of Emerelda until the girl acknowledged her.

Emerelda rolled her eyes. "Yes?" she asked.

"I'm just curious: How do you decide which jewel to turn the coal into?" she asked.

Emerelda sighed, like her method was too complex for Brystal to understand.

"I don't *decide*," she said. "Each piece of coal is unique and has its own energy. All I do is find the jewel inside and bring it to the surface."

"Interesting," Brystal said. "So you're doing to the coal exactly what Madame Weatherberry wants to do to us."

Emerelda scrunched her forehead. "What are you talking about?" she asked.

"Even if you disagree with Madame Weatherberry's reasons for opening the school, she's still offering us a chance to become the best versions of ourselves. I understand how you feel about humankind, but you aren't going to let *them* keep you from reaching your full potential, are you? Haven't they taken enough already?"

Clearly, Brystal's words resonated with Emerelda more than Madame Weatherberry's had, because the girl dropped the coal and went deep into thought. Brystal turned to Madame Weatherberry and the fairy beamed with gratitude for her assistance. The entire cave waited with bated breath for Emerelda to make her decision.

"I appreciate what you're trying to do, but I can't leave the mine," Emerelda said. "The dwarfs need me and I belong with my—"

"Em, pack your things," Mr. Slate said. "You're going to that school."

Everyone in the cave turned to the dwarf—it was the last thing they expected to hear coming out of his mouth.

"What did you just say, Papa?" Emerelda asked in shock.

"I said you're going to that school," Mr. Slate said. "I'll admit, I'm not convinced Madame Weatherberry's plan will work, either, but the girl is right. This is an opportunity for you to become a better version of yourself, and I won't let you turn it down."

"No!" Emerelda exclaimed. "The mine is my home! I'm happy here!"

"Yes, but that won't always be the case," Mr. Slate said. "Eventually, you're going to grow up and want more out of life. You'll want to make friends and start a family, you'll want to have fun and fall in love, and you won't be able to do that in a mine surrounded by dwarfs."

"But you need me!" she said. "You just said you profit off my magic!"

"We've benefited from you long enough," Mr. Slate said. "But you're like a jewel yourself, Em—you won't do any good hiding out in a dark cave. It's time you shared your beauty with the world."

Emerelda tried to argue with her papa, but he wouldn't hear another word from her. Tears came to her eyes as she reluctantly put her belongings into a small bag. Once Emerelda finished packing, Mr. Slate kissed his adopted daughter on the forehead and gave her a hug.

"I'm not happy about this," Emerelda said. "And I'm not saying good-bye—because this isn't good-bye. Right, Papa?"

"No, my child," her papa said. "This is just the beginning."

Although they didn't live in the Southern Kingdom, Madame Weatherberry had Mr. Slate sign a permission form just to be safe. The Miner Superior escorted everyone back to the main cavern and Madame Weatherberry awoke the miners from their sleep. Emerelda said farewell to the dwarfs and each of them was more dismayed to see her go than the last, like they were *all* losing a child. Mr. Slate walked his adopted daughter and their guests to the entrance of the mine and waved them on their way.

"All right, children," Madame Weatherberry said. "Let's go home."

CHAPTER NINE

MADAME WEATHERBERRY'S
ACADEMY OF MAGIC

After leaving the mine, Emerelda tried her best to remain as unimpressed by Madame Weatherberry's magic as possible. When the fairy transformed four field mice into unicorns, Emerelda's eyes grew very large, but she didn't make a sound. When Madame Weatherberry removed the brooch from her gown and turned it into a golden carriage, Emerelda's breathing increased, but she didn't say a word. However, as the unicorns transported them across the Southern

Kingdom at extraordinary speed, Emerelda was having a difficult time concealing her amazement.

"Isn't this spectacular!" Xanthous said. "If you whip your head around really fast like this, you can catch a glimpse of the land."

The boy gave Emerelda an example, and she almost tried it herself, but then she remembered to keep her appearance unenthusiastic. Brystal giggled at Emerelda's failing facade.

"You know, it's okay to be a *little* excited," Brystal said. "No matter what we see or do, nothing will ever make the mine any less special to you."

Emerelda pursed her lips to suppress a smile, but it surfaced anyway.

"All right, I admit this is pretty amazing," she said. "For fun, the dwarfs and I used to race runaway carts through the mine, but they never went as fast as this. How are the unicorns doing it?"

"They're compelled by magic," Madame Weatherberry explained. "Not only are unicorns the fastest animals on the planet, but they also always know their passengers' exact destination and the quickest route to get there."

"Are we close to the academy?" Emerelda asked.

"It'll take a couple of hours to reach the Southern Kingdom's eastern border, then it's just a short distance through the east In-Between," Madame Weatherberry said. "We should arrive just before sunset."

"We aren't getting out of the carriage again, are we?" Xanthous asked.

"Unfortunately not," Madame Weatherberry said. "As much as I would love to teach you another lesson at the expense of a hostile creature, there's a special path in the forest the unicorns know to take."

"Madame Weatherberry? I keep forgetting to ask, but what *is* the academy?" Brystal inquired. "Is it a house? A cabin? A cave?"

Madame Weatherberry smiled playfully as she thought about her academy. "You'll see," the fairy said. "Some things in life are better *seen* than described."

A couple of hours later, the golden carriage approached the eastern border of the Southern Kingdom. Just like the western border, the thick forest of the In-Between grew along the eastern border like a gigantic, twisted fence. The trees were so close together there was barely room for a person to walk between them, but the unicorns charged ahead. They found an opening Brystal would never have spotted on her own and the steeds pulled the golden carriage onto a narrow road.

As they traveled through the In-Between, the unicorns slowed down to guide the carriage safely down the winding path. Brystal was unsettled by the eerie sights of the dark forest outside her window. She expected a ferocious animal or monstrous creature to jump out from the darkness and attack their carriage at any moment. Brystal figured Xanthous and Emerelda were feeling the same way, because both her companions had covered their eyes and sunk in their seats.

Unsurprisingly, Madame Weatherberry wasn't affected by their frightening surroundings at all. The fairy kept a confident and watchful eye on the trees passing by, like she was prepared for whoever or whatever might cross their path.

Time seemed to move much slower in the In-Between than it had in the Southern Kingdom, but eventually the golden carriage came to an abrupt stop. Brystal, Emerelda, and Xanthous looked out the window and saw that the unicorns had stopped because the road was blocked by a massive hedge wall. The strange plant was taller than the trees and stretched for miles in both directions. The leaves and branches were so thick the hedge was practically solid.

"We're here," Madame Weatherberry said cheerfully.

Her students had no idea what the fairy was talking about. The longer the unicorns stayed put at the dead end, the more they felt like sitting ducks in the dangerous forest.

Suddenly, the hedge started to shake and snap. The leaves and branches slowly parted to form an arch that was wide enough for the carriage to fit through. The unicorns moved under the arch and entered a long leafy tunnel that cut through the thick hedge. The passageway went on for several hundred feet and the children were amazed by how dense the hedge was. It was so dark in the tunnel Brystal couldn't see her hands in front of her face.

"Madame Weatherberry, what is this?" Brystal asked.

"Just a little barrier I planted around the property to protect the academy," Madame Weatherberry said.

"A *little* barrier?" Xanthous asked. "This shrub is enormous!"

"It may seem like overgrown shrubbery, but the hedge is actually equipped with a very powerful spell," Madame Weatherberry said. "It only opens for people and animals with magic in their blood. It'll keep us safe from all the restless creatures wandering the In-Between."

The unicorns reached the end of the tunnel and stopped at another leafy wall. Beams of bright light shone into the dark tunnel as a second arch opened and granted the carriage access to Madame Weatherberry's property. The unicorns exited the hedge barrier and their young passengers realized they weren't in the creepy woods anymore.

The golden carriage proceeded down the path into a rolling field of the most vibrant wildflowers the children had ever seen. The land was sprinkled with trees that were covered in colorful maple leaves, blushing cherry blossoms, and blooming magnolias. A crystal-clear lake was lined with weeping willows and it spilled into streams and ponds with vivid water lilies. The picturesque estate stretched toward a cliff overlooking a sparkling blue ocean, where the sun was setting in a horizon of rosy clouds.

"I don't believe it," Brystal said. "It's like we're inside a painting!"

"I've never seen so much color in my whole life!" Emerelda exclaimed.

"We must be dead," Xanthous said. "Our carriage crashed in the forest and now we're in paradise. It's the only explanation."

Madame Weatherberry was incredibly touched by the excitement in her student's faces.

"I've waited a long time to see smiles like those," she said. "Many years of hard work have been put into developing this place. I hope it becomes as much your home as it is mine."

The carriage continued down the path, and there were more surprises at every turn. Brystal was mesmerized when she saw there were herds of unicorns grazing and frolicking throughout the fields around them. She looked up and noticed the sky was filled with huge colorful butterflies and enormous birds with long auburn feathers.

"Look at all the unicorns in the field!" she said. "And up there! Have you ever seen such big birds and butterflies before?"

"I've seen some pretty nasty bugs and bats in the mine, but nothing like *those*!" Emerelda said.

Madame Weatherberry chuckled. "Actually, those aren't butterflies or birds," she said. "You might want to take a closer look."

Brystal, Emerelda, and Xanthous pressed their faces against the window for a better view. After a thorough inspection, the children realized the butterflies had tiny humanlike bodies and they wore clothing made from leaves and flower petals. The tiny creatures flew in and out of miniature mushroom homes along the path. The birds in question had heads and wings like eagles, front claws like reptiles, and hind legs and tails like lions. They soared through the sky like hawks and brought squirrels, mice, fish, and other prey to the hungry hatchlings waiting in their nests.

"What the heck are those things?" Xanthous asked.

"They're *pixies* and *gryphons*," Madame Weatherberry said. "And they're both easily offended, so make sure you never call them bugs and birds to their faces."

"So they still exist?" Brystal asked. "In *The Truth About Magic* you wrote that humankind had hunted all the magical animals into extinction."

"And they nearly did," Madame Weatherberry said. "Fortunately, I was able to find survivors and save a few species before they were lost forever. It was safer to let humanity go on believing they had all been annihilated. Sadly, I wasn't able to rescue all the magical animals that used to roam the earth. This property is as much a sanctuary for the pixies, the gryphons, and the unicorns as it is for us."

Emerelda gasped and pointed out the window.

"Is that what I *think* it is?" she asked.

Brystal and Xanthous looked in the direction Emerelda was referring to and had the same reaction.

In the distance, perched on the edge of the cliff overlooking the ocean, was a golden castle. The castle had tall pointed towers and hundreds of wide windows, and the entire structure sparkled in the sunlight. The carriage continued on the path through the property and stopped at the castle's front steps. Madame Weatherberry escorted the children outside and gestured excitedly to the castle before them.

"Welcome to Madame Weatherberry's Academy of Magic!" the fairy said. "What do you think of the new name? I decided less was more."

Brystal, Xanthous, and Emerelda didn't respond because they were completely overwhelmed by the dazzling structure in front of them. Madame Weatherberry was right—some things in life *were* better seen than described. Even after all the incredible books she had read in the library, Brystal doubted words could ever explain the castle's magnificent appearance or the exhilarating feeling it gave her. It was difficult to believe something so beautiful existed in the world, but the castle never faded from her view.

Madame Weatherberry clapped her hands and the unicorns were released from their reins. The steeds galloped into the nearby field and joined their grazing herd. She snapped her fingers to shrink the golden carriage to a brooch again, and pinned it to her gown. The castle's giant front doors opened and two little girls and an old woman came outside to greet the new arrivals.

The first little girl was about ten years old and wore a dress made from dripping patches of honeycomb. Her bright orange hair was styled into a beehive and it was home to a live swarm of bumblebees. The second little girl also looked ten years old, and she wore a navy robe over a sapphire bathing suit. Instead of hair, a continuous stream of water flowed down her body and evaporated as it reached her feet, like she was a walking waterfall. The old woman was dressed much more simply than the girls and wore a plum dress with a matching apron. She had grayish-violet hair in a messy bun, but other than the unusual hair color, her appearance wasn't as magical as the others'.

"Children, I'd like you to meet Miss Tangerina Turkin, Miss Skylene Lavenders, and the academy's housekeeper, Mrs. Vee," Madame Weatherberry said. "Girls, these are our new students Brystal Evergreen, Emerelda Stone, and Xanthous Hayfield."

Mrs. Vee was ecstatic to see the newcomers. She hurried down the front steps and gave each of them a huge bear hug, rocking them back and forth.

"I don't mean to invade your personal space—but I'm just so happy I could burst!" Mrs. Vee said with tearful eyes. "Madame Weatherberry has been dreaming of opening an academy for so long and the day is finally here! I hope you've all brought an appetite because I am cooking up a *feast* in the kitchen! Does anyone have any allergies or dietary restrictions I should know about?"

Brystal, Emerelda, and Xanthous all shrugged and shook their heads.

"Well, that's a big relief," Mrs. Vee said. "Tonight I'm

serving one of my specialties; gryphon potpie. *HA-HA!*
I'm just kidding! Oh, you should have seen the looks
on your faces! I would never cook something like that.
Besides, gryphons are way too fast to catch. *HA-HA!*
Got you again! But in all seriousness, I couldn't be more
thrilled to have you. Now if you'll excuse me, I better
get back to the kitchen before dinner grows legs and
runs away. *HA-HA!* Actually, that one is based on a true
story. I'll see you inside!"

Mrs. Vee hurried back up the front steps and dashed
into the castle. Brystal, Xanthous, and Emerelda were
slightly terrified after meeting the animated housekeeper
and looked to Madame Weatherberry for reassurance.

"Don't worry, Mrs. Vee's cooking is much better than
her comedy," she said.

Although the housekeeper seemed eccentric and
goofy, Brystal, Xanthous, and Emerelda appreciated
her attempt to welcome them to the academy. Tangerina
and Skylene, however, stayed on the castle's front steps
and eyed the newcomers like they were competition of
some kind. Brystal sensed the tension and tried to break
the ice.

"I love what you both are wearing," she said. "Are
you students, too?"

Tangerina and Skylene both grunted, insulted by
Brystal's comment.

"We're *apprentices*," Tangerina said in a conde-
scending tone.

"What's the difference?" Brystal asked.

"We *apprentice* things," Skylene said, like it was obvious.

Brystal, Xanthous, and Emerelda looked to one another to see if Skylene made sense to anyone else, but no one knew what the girl was talking about. Tangerina was embarrassed by her friend's remark and quickly pulled her aside.

"Skylene, I told you to let me do all the talking when the newbies showed up," she whispered.

"Oh, I thought you said new bees," Skylene whispered back. *"I thought you were finally doing something different with your hair."*

"You never listen!" Tangerina said. *"You've got too much water in your ears!"*

Skylene tilted her head to the left and the right, and sure enough, over a gallon of water poured out from both ears. Tangerina rolled her eyes at her friend and turned back to the newcomers.

"As I was saying, apprentices are much more *advanced* than students," she explained. "We're going to assist Madame Weatherberry as she teaches the three of you to use your magic. And now that you're here, I can see she's going to need all the help she can get."

"Tangerina, be nice to the new students," Madame Weatherberry said. "We'll all be learning and growing together, no matter how advanced some of us might be. But we can discuss all of that during our first lesson tomorrow. In the meantime, let's give our new recruits a tour of the castle while Mrs. Vee finishes preparing dinner."

The fairy escorted her students and apprentices up the front steps and through the castle's front doors. Brystal's mouth dropped open at her first glimpse of the castle's interior because it was just as breathtaking as the exterior. The entrance hall had shimmering white walls, sparkling silver floors, and golden pillars that stretched into a towering ceiling above them. In the center of the hall was a gigantic tree that grew crystal leaves and blossoms. An elegant staircase curled around the tree and the steps floated in midair as the stairs spiraled toward the upper levels of the castle.

"This castle is one of the last magical residences left," Madame Weatherberry said. "The majority of them were destroyed when King Champion I declared that magic was a crime. I inherited the estate from my family and I've kept it hidden and protected ever since. It's very important that none of you leave the property without me. As you know, the In-Between is full of people and creatures who would like to harm us."

Something about Madame Weatherberry's warning didn't sit well with Brystal.

"Madame Weatherberry?" she asked. "I thought you said your family was human?"

The fairy was pleasantly surprised by Brystal's attention to detail.

"Oh, I forgot I mentioned that," Madame Weatherberry said. "While my *birth family* were human, I was referring to the fairies who adopted me and taught me to develop my magic. You see, the magical community is lucky because we get to create new families if our relatives forsake us. The six of us may not be related by blood, but with time, I hope we'll regard each other as a *chosen family*."

Since they had all just met, it was hard for Brystal to picture becoming *that* close with the other students. Still, it was nice to imagine someone could fill the void created by leaving her mother and brothers behind.

"Now, if you'll follow me, I'll show you to the sitting room," Madame Weatherberry said.

The fairy led them down a corridor to the right of the entrance hall and they entered a spacious room with silk sofas and tufted lounge chairs. The walls were covered in floral wallpaper and decorated with the heads of horned animals. Once they stepped inside the sitting room, the flowers and vines in the wallpaper became three-dimensional and a flowery aroma filled the air. The deer and elk heads mounted on the walls also came to life and snacked on the plants growing around them.

"Be careful around the decorative heads—they like to bite," Madame Weatherberry warned. "Moving on, the dining room is just around the corner."

Down the hall from the sitting room was another large room with a table made from a wide, flat rock. The dining room was illuminated by a cluster of glowing moonstones that hovered over the table like a chandelier. The walls were dark and decorated with twinkling lights so the room looked like a starry night sky. As Brystal examined the lights, she screamed when a shooting star suddenly shot across the ceiling.

"Breakfast is served every morning at seven o'clock sharp, lunch starts at noon, and dinner begins at six o'clock," Madame Weatherberry informed them. "Please be on time for meals—Mrs. Vee is a perfectionist when it comes to her food and she hates serving her dishes cold. The kitchen is through the swinging door at the end of the dining room, and Mrs. Vee's chambers are just beyond that. Well, that's everything on the first floor. Now, if you'll please follow me back to the entrance hall, I'll show you to my office on the second floor."

"But, Madame Weatherberry?" Xanthous asked. "You said this was a school. So where are all the classrooms?"

"There aren't any classrooms in the castle," the fairy said. "I'll be teaching the majority of my lessons outside on the academy grounds. I've always thought fresh ideas are easier to retain with fresh air."

The tour returned to the entrance hall and they carefully climbed the floating staircase to the second level of the castle. Madame Weatherberry's office was through a pair of wooden doors. Just like the cover of *The Truth About Magic*, they were engraved with the images of a unicorn and a gryphon.

The office was a circular chamber with incredible views of the ocean and the academy property. All the furniture was made of glass, including a bulky desk that sat at the far end of the room. The chamber was lined with shelves of spell books and cabinets of potions and elixirs. The high ceiling was filled with white fluffy clouds that changed into the shapes of different animals as they bobbed up and down. Instead of fire, a stream of bubbles emitted from a grand fireplace and floated through the air. The entire wall above the fireplace was covered in a massive replica of the Map of Magic. To the students' amusement, a rack of elaborate fascinators was placed by Madame Weatherberry's desk, and the fairy owned a hat in every color.

"If you ever need something, please don't hesitate to find me in here," Madame Weatherberry said. "However, on the rare occasion I'm called away from the academy, my office is off-limits to students. Well, if there aren't any questions, I'll show you to your bedrooms on the third floor."

"We have our own rooms?" Xanthous asked.

"Oh yes," Madame Weatherberry said. "The castle has seven bedrooms and counting."

"What do you mean *and counting*?" Emerelda asked.

"It's one of the many perks of living in a magical residence," Madame Weatherberry explained. "The castle *grows* extra bedrooms based on the number of residents, and it usually designs the chambers around the occupants' specific needs. There were only bedrooms for Tangerina and Skylene on the third floor when I left the castle to recruit you, but there should be one for each of you now. Shall we take a look?"

The students eagerly followed Madame Weatherberry up the stairs to a long corridor on the third floor. Just as she predicted, the corridor had five doors, and the latter three looked much newer than the first two, like the corridor had recently been renovated.

As they passed the first door, the students peered inside Tangerina's bedroom and instantly understood what Madame Weatherberry meant about the rooms being designed for the resident's needs. All the walls and furniture in Tangerina's bedroom were made of honeycomb and everything was drenched in honey. Just like her hair, the chamber was the home of a thousand buzzing bumblebees and the floor was covered with live daisies to provide the swarm with nectar.

The room across the corridor from Tangerina's bedroom belonged to Skylene. The chamber had no floor, and instead dropped straight into an indoor pool. Every inch of the room was tiled with blue porcelain, and the only piece of furniture was a gondola-bed floating on the pool's surface.

The third room in the corridor had a heavy steel door and Madame Weatherberry grunted as she heaved it open.

"Xanthous, I'm assuming this one belongs to you," she said.

Inside, the entire room was made out of the same industrial steel as the door. There were no windows in the chamber and absolutely nothing was flammable—even Xanthous's metal bed had foil sheets. Instead of carpet or tile, the floor was finished with metal grates, and instead of a ceiling, a brick chimney was built over the room.

"It's like a giant oven!" Xanthous said enthusiastically. "Even if I took off my medal, I wouldn't hurt anyone in here!"

"It's the perfect place to blow off some steam," Madame Weatherberry said. "Now, Emerelda, I believe your room is next."

Behind the fourth door in the corridor was a dark room with dirt walls. There was a four-poster bed made from stalagmites, a wardrobe constructed out of a mine cart, and a workbench that held stacks of coal. Emerelda stepped inside her room and had a dizzying moment of déjà vu.

"It's just like my cave at the mine," she said. "It even smells like dwarfs in here."

"Hopefully it'll keep you from getting too homesick," Madame Weatherberry said. "Last but not least, we have Brystal's room."

The fifth and final door in the corridor led to the base of a tower. There was a bed identical to the bed she had had in the Evergreen house and a big comfy armchair exactly like the ones she enjoyed at the Chariot Hills Library. But most amazing of all, the walls were covered with shelves of books from the floor to the ceiling. A display case in the corner of the room held over two dozen pairs of reading glasses, and like Madame Weatherberry's collection of fascinators, there was a pair in every color.

As Brystal looked around her new bedroom, her eyes filled with happy tears, and her heart fluttered in her chest. She scanned the titles on the shelves and caressed the books' spines like she was saying hello to long-lost friends.

"*The Tales of Tidbit Twitch*, volumes two through ten!" She was shocked to find them. "I didn't even know there was *one* sequel, let alone *nine*!"

"Oh, and look at this," Madame Weatherberry said, and pointed to another book on one of the shelves. "You even have a copy of *The Truth About Magic*. Perhaps you'll be inspired to finish it one of these days—no pressure, of course. Well, children, that completes our tour of the castle. You're more than welcome to inspect the other rooms and towers, but I'm afraid you'll only find a century's worth of storage and cobwebs."

Suddenly, a chime rang through the castle to announce the start of dinner. Unlike the gong at the Bootstrap Correctional Facility, the chimes were pleasant and inviting, like they were announcing the start of a grand performance.

"Sounds like Mrs. Vee is finally ready for us," Madame Weatherberry said. "Let's not keep her waiting."

The students followed Madame Weatherberry down the corridor, but Brystal stayed in her room for a few moments before joining them. Of all the astonishing things she had seen today, nothing was more beautiful than the sight of her very own library.

At dinner, the students were served a three-course meal

of tomato soup, grilled chicken with roasted carrots, and blueberry pie. Other than the colorful berries and muffin Brystal ate in the golden carriage, it was the most delicious food she had ever tasted. She couldn't believe she would be treated to three meals like *this* every day—it was quite a contrast to the food at the Bootstrap Correctional Facility.

Over the meal, Madame Weatherberry told the new students stories about the obstacles she faced while starting their academy. She recalled how she met with the sovereigns of all four kingdoms, and despite her persuasive requests, was only granted permission by King Champion XIV, to recruit students in the Southern Kingdom. Brystal, Xanthous, and Emerelda were on the edge of their seats as they listened to her exciting tales.

"May I have some more water?" Xanthous asked, after stuffing his face with a third helping of blueberry pie.

"I can help you with that," Skylene said.

She leaned over the table and stuck her hand in the boy's glass. A stream of water poured out of her index finger and filled his glass to the brim. Brystal and Emerelda were impressed by Skylene's trick but Xanthous was disturbed by the liquid coming out of her body.

"Is there any *other* water?" he asked.

Of all seven people around the table, Tangerina seemed to be enjoying herself the least. She grunted at everything the newcomers said and rolled her eyes at every question they asked. She found their curiosity about magic to be incredibly irritating, like they should have been more prepared before arriving.

"So what do you *do*?" she asked.

"Sorry?" Brystal said.

"Well, I know you're all here because you can do magic, but what are your specialties?" Tangerina asked.

"What's a specialty?" Brystal asked.

Tangerina and Skylene were shocked by her ignorance.

"A specialty is your strongest magical talent," Tangerina explained. "It's usually the trait that reveals your magic and separates you from the rest of the world. Bees are my specialty, water is Skylene's, and based on his room upstairs, I'm guessing Xanthous's specialty has something to do with fire."

"Ooooooh, *that's* why his room is made of metal," Skylene said. "I was hoping it had something to do with *barbecue*. How disappointing."

Tangerina ignored her friend. "As I was saying," she went on. "Xanthous's was easy to figure out, but I'm still not sure about *you two*."

Emerelda was a little annoyed by Tangerina's need to categorize them. She closed her eyes, placed an open palm on the stone table, and transformed the whole thing into a giant amethyst.

"*That's* what I do," she said blankly.

Despite their best attempts to conceal it, Tangerina and Skylene were awestruck by Emerelda's demonstration.

"What about you, Brystal?" Skylene asked. "What's your specialty?"

"Oh, I'm not sure that I have one of those," she said. "I've never done magic without the help of a spell."

"All fairies have specialties," Tangerina said, and crossed her arms. "Unless your specialty is that *you're not special at all.*"

"Tangerina, please keep your stinger to yourself," Madame Weatherberry reprimanded. "So far, Brystal has shown a talent for manifestation, and she had one of the brightest stars on my Map of Magic. Just because her specialty hasn't revealed itself yet doesn't mean it won't do so very soon."

Madame Weatherberry gave Brystal an encouraging wink, but it didn't make Tangerina's comments any less hurtful. Without an obvious specialty, Brystal felt inferior to the other students and she started wondering if she even belonged at the academy. The embarrassment made her blush and she counted down the seconds until dinner was over.

"Well, I know one thing for sure," Mrs. Vee said. "My specialty has always been food, and if anyone disagrees after *that* meal, they can go catch a gryphon! *HA-HA!*"

After dinner, Madame Weatherberry excused the students from the table and they went to their rooms to get ready for bed. Brystal was still feeling crummy from Tangerina's remarks, but fortunately, she knew the perfect remedy to take her mind off it. She selected *The Tales of Tidbit Twitch, Volume Two* from her shelf, chose a fresh pair of reading glasses, and crawled into her soft bed.

While Brystal read the sequel to her favorite book, an abrupt storm blew in from the ocean and soaked the academy grounds. Brystal was startled by the booming thunder and the flashes of lightning outside her window, but she wasn't going to let the *weather* disturb her first night at the castle. Her floormates, however, weren't so brave.

A few minutes into the storm there was a soft knock on Brystal's door.

"Come in," she called.

The door swung open and Emerelda peeked inside with large, fearful eyes.

"Sorry to bother you, Brystal," Emerelda said.

"Is everything all right with your room?" Brystal asked.

"No, everything is fine," she said. "I'm just not used to *thunder*. That's one of the best parts about living in an underground mine—you don't have to worry about the weather. If you wouldn't mind, I was wondering… well, I was wondering…"

"You're more than welcome to sleep here if the thunder is scaring you," Brystal said.

Emerelda sighed with relief. "Gee, thanks!" she said. "What are you reading?"

"*The Tales of Tidbit Twitch, Volume Two*," Brystal said. "It's the sequel to my favorite book of all time. Have you heard of it?"

Emerelda thought about it and shook her head. "Papa used to read me stories before bed, but I don't remember that one."

"Would you sleep better if I read the first one to you?" Brystal asked.

"Really?" Emerelda said. "Are you sure you wouldn't mind?"

"Not at all," she said. "It's on the shelf to your left."

Emerelda retrieved *The Tales of Tidbit Twitch* and joined Brystal in bed. Brystal opened the book to the very first page, but before she started reading, both girls jumped at the growling thunder outside. It was followed by the sound of feet frantically running down the corridor. Xanthous appeared in the doorway, just as startled by the weather as Emerelda had been.

"Hi, girls," Xanthous peeped. "Crazy storm, huh?"

"It's wild," Brystal said. "How are you holding up?"

"Me? Oh, I'm doing great," Xanthous said, but his panicked face told otherwise. "I just came to check on you two."

"We're fine," Brystal said. "Actually, Emerelda and I were just about to start a book, if you're interested in hearing a story."

Another crack of thunder influenced Xanthous's decision and he leaped into the bed with the girls. Brystal and Emerelda were tickled by his reaction and they made room. Brystal cleared her throat in preparation for reading aloud, but just as she started the first sentence, Tangerina and Skylene burst into her room and shut the door behind them, as if the terrible storm had been chasing them.

"Hello, ladies," Brystal said. "What seems to be the problem?"

Tangerina and Skylene were too embarrassed to admit they were scared. They looked to each other, hoping the other would come up with a good excuse.

"Umm . . . *I wet the bed?*" Skylene said.

Tangerina rolled her eyes. *"Skylene, your bed is always wet,"* she whispered.

"Oh yeah," she mumbled back.

"We just heard noises coming from your room and wanted to make sure the three of you weren't causing any trouble," Tangerina said.

"Well, as you can see, we're very well-behaved," Brystal said. "We're just about to read a book to calm our nerves."

"Good, I'm glad you're not up to any mischief," Tangerina said. "Now that we've seen you're acting appropriately, we'll head back to our rooms."

Although she said they were leaving, neither Tangerina nor Skylene moved a muscle.

"You know, just because apprentices are more *advanced* than students doesn't mean they enjoy stories any less," Brystal said. "You're both welcome to stay with us if the storm is making you uneasy."

Before Tangerina or Skylene could respond, the thunder roared louder than before. The girls shrieked and dived into bed with the others.

"I suppose we could stick around for a few minutes," Tangerina said. "What are you reading?"

"*The Tales of Tidbit Twitch* by Tomfree Taylor," Brystal said.

"What's it about?" Skylene asked.

Emerelda grunted and eyed the others threateningly.

"If everyone would just shut up and stop interrupting her, we might find out," she scolded.

All the classmates went quiet so Brystal could start the book.

" 'Once upon a time, there was a kingdom of mice,' " she read. " 'And of all the mice in the kingdom, none was braver than a young mouse named Tidbit Twitch....' "

Brystal read the book for hours and she was delighted by what a captivated audience her floormates were. Eventually, all the students and apprentices began to fall asleep, and she marked their last page so they could continue the story later.

They all slept in a pile on Brystal's bed while they waited for the weather to die down. It was only their first night at the castle, but thanks to a thunderstorm and a good story, the children at Madame Weatherberry's Academy of Magic were already acting like the *chosen family* their instructor hoped they'd become.

CHAPTER TEN

THE MUSICIANS' DAUGHTER

The following morning, the students and apprentices gathered around the dining room table and laughed about their impromptu sleepover while they enjoyed breakfast. Even Tangerina admitted she had fun listening to Brystal read *The Tales of Tidbit Twitch*. Madame Weatherberry was delighted her pupils were getting along so well, but naturally, she reminded them how important it was to get rest on nights before their lessons, and asked them to save future sleepovers for special occasions.

Halfway through breakfast, Mrs. Vee entered the

dining room and presented Madame Weatherberry with a black envelope.

"This just arrived for you, Madame," Mrs. Vee said.

The envelope immediately caught Brystal's attention because it was scaled like a reptile's skin and sealed with wax the color of dried blood. Madame Weatherberry went pale the minute she noticed the envelope's strange texture. She opened it with a butter knife and quickly unfolded the message written inside.

"The post delivers all the way out here?" Xanthous asked.

Tangerina rolled her eyes. "It's not from the human post, it's from the magic post," she explained. "When you place your envelope in a magic mailbox, and close the lid behind it, the letter is instantly transported to the mailbox it's addressed to."

"It works with other small objects, too," Skylene said, and slumped in her chair. "I'm still waiting for my gerbil to be sent back."

"Wow, *instant mail*," Xanthous said. "What a concept."

While the others talked about the magic post, Brystal's eyes never left Madame Weatherberry. She assumed the black envelope contained bad news because the fairy's posture became stiff as she read it. Once she finished reading the note, Madame Weatherberry folded it and put it back into the envelope. Her eyes filled with concern and she stared off into space.

"Madame Weatherberry, is something wrong?" Brystal asked.

"Oh, not at all," Madame Weatherberry said, but she didn't elaborate further.

"Who wrote to you?" Brystal asked.

"Just an old friend," she said. "Unfortunately, our mutual acquaintance has been battling a terrible illness, and my friend was writing to update me on her progress. Now, if you'll excuse me, I'm going to write her back before we begin today's lessons. I'll meet you outside in just a few minutes."

Madame Weatherberry held the black envelope by the corner and a burst of violet flames incinerated the message. The fairy excused herself from the dining table and headed to her office on the second floor. Although Madame Weatherberry had said there wasn't a problem, Brystal knew their instructor wasn't being honest with them. Madame Weatherberry left with the same intensity she had expressed after Brystal mentioned the Northern Kingdom the day before.

"I'm glad you asked her that," Skylene told Brystal. "I've always wondered who sends Madame Weatherberry those letters, but I never wanted to pry."

"You mean, they're sent frequently?" Brystal asked.

"Almost every day," Skylene said. "But if you ask me, I don't think they're actually updates on her sick friend."

"What do you think they are?" Brystal asked.

Skylene grinned. "I think Madame Weatherberry has a *secret admirer.*"

Everyone around the dining table laughed at Skylene's theory except for Brystal. She didn't think

Madame Weatherberry had an *admirer*, but the fairy definitely had a *secret*.

"The last time I had a secret admirer, dragons roamed the earth! *HA-HA!*" Mrs. Vee quipped. "Get it? Because I'm old."

Even with an explanation, her young audience didn't crack a smile.

"Sorry, if all my jokes were good I certainly wouldn't have this job! *HA-HA!*"

The housekeeper cleared the dining table and stepped into the kitchen. Once she was gone, Emerelda turned to Tangerina and Skylene with a sharp look.

"Are *any* of her jokes good?" she asked.

Tangerina and Skylene slowly shook their heads in agony, like they had been victims of Mrs. Vee's insufferable humor for too long.

"No…" Tangerina groaned. "Not a single one…"

After they finished breakfast, the children waited for Madame Weatherberry outside on the castle's front steps. It was taking their instructor much longer to respond to the letter than she had estimated, and Brystal became even more suspicious.

Just when they were about to check on their teacher, the students and apprentices heard a peculiar noise coming from a distance. It was a compilation of horns, drums, and cymbals that played the same quirky tune over and over again. They all looked toward the edge of the property, and a colorful caravan emerged from the hedge barrier. It was bright blue with red wheels and a yellow roof. Instead of the caravan being pulled by horses, a man and a woman sitting in the driver's seat propelled the contraption forward by moving pedals with their feet.

The strangers wore makeup and flamboyant clothing. The man had a mustache, a gold earring in his right ear, and a tall top hat with a large red feather. The woman wore a scarf over her head, several beaded necklaces, and a long flowing dress. As they pedaled toward the castle, the gears triggered instruments attached to the vehicle, and the repetitive tune was played. Identical signs on both sides of the caravan said:

THE GOOSE TROUPE

The couple steered their vehicle to the front steps of the castle and then pulled the brakes. When the caravan came to a complete stop, the music finally stopped as well. The visitors seemed relieved to see the children outside, but the students stared at the extravagant wagon with wide, curious eyes.

"Hello there," the man said, and tipped his top hat. "Is this Madame Weatherberry's School for the Magically Inclined?"

"It's just Madame Weatherberry's Academy of Magic now," Tangerina said.

"She decided less was more," Skylene added.

"Oh, that's terrific," the woman said, and then called into the caravan behind her. *"Lucy, get your things! We're here!"*

The vehicle's back door was aggressively kicked open and a girl about thirteen years old jumped down from inside. She was small and plump, her hair was short and curly, and she had a round rosy face. The girl wore a black bowler hat, an oversize black jumpsuit, big black boots, and a bottle-cap necklace. She carried a small suitcase made from a taxidermy porcupine, and a canteen made from a beaver skull was draped over her shoulder. The odd girl scowled at the majestic castle in front of her, like she was greatly underwhelmed by it.

"Well, this place is obnoxiously cheerful," she said.

"Excuse me, but who are you?" Tangerina asked.

The girl turned to the students on the front steps. She glared at them with a raised eyebrow, like they were just as disappointing as the castle.

"The name's Lucy," she said. "You don't recognize me?"

"Recognize you from what?" Skylene asked.

"I happen to be a famous tambourine player," Lucy said, and pointed to the sign on the caravan. "Perhaps you've heard of my family's band?"

"Wait a second," Tangerina said with a patronizing laugh. "Your name is *Lucy Goose*?"

The young tambourine player turned bright red and sent Tangerina a scathing look.

"It's pronounced *Goo-say*," Lucy said. "But you would know that *if* you had any class. So why don't you just shut your mouth and mind all that beeswax?

Someone wearing honeycomb has no right to be that high-and-mighty. *Ever.*"

Brystal, Xanthous, and Emerelda laughed at Lucy's remarks before they could stop themselves. Tangerina was agitated and her bumblebees buzzed aggressively.

"Don't listen to her, Tangerina," Skylene whispered. *"She's dressed like she just came from a funeral."*

"I'm sorry, did the *walking puddle* just insult my clothes?" Lucy asked. "I'll have you know I won this hat after arm-wrestling a goblin! And I removed the caps on my necklace from bottles with my bare teeth! And then I drank them with a tribe of trolls! What's the coolest thing you've done lately? *Evaporate?*"

The children were floored by Lucy's comments. The girl's parents shook their heads and sighed at their daughter's rudeness.

"Please forgive Lucy, she's just a little nervous," Mrs. Goose said. *"Lucy, you promised us you were going to be nice! This is no way to make friends at your new school!"*

"They started it," Lucy mumbled.

"Hold on," Tangerina exclaimed. "She's *staying* here?"

Mr. and Mrs. Goose glanced at each other with uncertainty.

"Actually, that's what we're here to speak with Madame Weatherberry about," Mr. Goose said. "Is she around?"

"She's in her office on the second floor," Brystal said. "I can take you there if you'd like."

"That would be wonderful, thank you," Mr. Goose said.

Brystal escorted the Goose family up the front steps of the castle. Lucy shot Tangerina one last dirty look before stepping inside.

"Don't worry, *honeypot*," she said. "Madame Weatherberry doesn't want someone like *me* at her school. I'll be out of your sticky hair before you know it."

The Gooses followed Brystal into the entrance hall and up the floating stairs to the second floor. As they went, Lucy winced at everything she saw, like the castle was so ugly it hurt her eyes. Brystal knocked on Madame Weatherberry's door and peeked inside. The fairy was pacing in front of her bubbling fireplace, obviously troubled by something.

"Madame Weatherberry?" Brystal said.

The fairy wasn't expecting company and jumped at the sound of her name.

"Yes, Brystal?" she asked.

"There are people here to see you," Brystal said. "They've brought their daughter to the castle hoping you'll take her as a student."

"Oh, really?" Madame Weatherberry was surprised to hear it. "Very well, please show them in."

Brystal ushered the Gooses into the office and then left to give the family privacy as they talked with Madame Weatherberry. She figured the conversation would delay lessons even further, so Brystal headed to her bedroom to retrieve a book to pass the time.

As she searched her shelves, Brystal heard a peculiar murmur coming from somewhere nearby. She followed the sound like a dog following a scent and realized it was coming from behind the books on a bottom shelf. Brystal moved the books off the shelf and found a small hole in the wall behind them. Curious, Brystal peeked through the hole and discovered it peered directly into Madame Weatherberry's office on the second floor below.

She saw that Mr. and Mrs. Goose were sitting across from Madame Weatherberry at her glass desk. Lucy wandered around the office and inspected the fairy's belongings while the adults chatted, but the girl didn't seem impressed by anything she found. Brystal didn't want to snoop on the family's conversation, but Mrs. Goose said something that instantly caught her attention.

"It all started with the ravens," she said. "That's when we knew Lucy was going to be *special*."

"The ravens?" Madame Weatherberry asked. "Oh my."

Mrs. Goose nodded. "While I was pregnant with Lucy, the birds started showing up outside our home. We figured they were passing by as they flew south for the winter, but even as the seasons changed, the ravens stayed. The larger Lucy grew in my womb, the more ravens flocked to our house. My husband did everything he could to get rid of them, but they never left. The night I went into labor, all the birds started screeching outside.

It was deafening and maddening to listen to! But as soon as Lucy was born, all the ravens flew away. To this day we don't know what they were doing there."

Madame Weatherberry rubbed her chin as she listened to the story. Brystal could tell the fairy knew exactly what the birds were doing at their house, but she didn't want to share that information just yet.

"How interesting," Madame Weatherberry said. "I imagine even stranger phenomena began happening shortly after she was born."

"Strange to say the least," Mr. Goose said. "And it continued through her childhood. It was all very eerie but harmless for the most part. The button eyes on her stuffed animals turned into real eyes and watched us as we moved around the house. We had to put a cover over Lucy's crib because she would levitate when she took naps. If we turned our back to her while she was taking a bath, we'd find the whole tub suddenly filled with frogs."

"The instances were inconvenient but simple enough to handle back then," Mrs. Goose said. "But lately, things have gotten completely out of hand. We're traveling musicians and have performed all over the world, but there are places we can never return to because of the things Lucy has done."

"Such as?" Madame Weatherberry asked.

"For instance, this one night we were performing at a pub in the Western Kingdom," Mr. Goose recalled. "The crowd had a lot to drink and became rowdy. They started booing us and Lucy got upset. She shook her fist at them and all the alcohol turned into *dog urine*! People were gagging and vomiting all over the pub."

"Another time, we were performing a private show for aristocrats in the Northern Kingdom," Mrs. Goose recalled. "Lucy was in the middle of a tambourine solo when a duchess in the front row began to yawn. It hurt Lucy's feelings and the duchess's braids suddenly turned into snakes!"

"A few months ago, we were performing in a small theater in the Southern Kingdom," Mr. Goose said. "At the end of the night, the owner of the theater refused to pay us. He claimed our instruments were out of tune and hurt the audience's ears. As we drove off, the whole theater imploded behind us, as if it had been flattened by an earthquake! But all the buildings nearby stayed perfectly intact."

"My word," Madame Weatherberry said.

"For the record, I'm proud of that last one," Lucy said. "That jerk had it coming."

"Luckily, no one has suspected any of these things were Lucy's fault," Mrs. Goose said. "Nonetheless, our act is gaining a reputation for tragedy. We're worried people are going to realize what Lucy is and try to hurt her."

"That's why we've brought her here," Mr. Goose explained. "We love our Lucy more than anything, but we can't take care of her anymore. It's just too much for us."

Brystal knew this must be heartbreaking for Lucy

to hear. The girl stopped searching through Madame Weatherberry's things and went very still. She turned and gazed at the bubbles in the fireplace, so the adults wouldn't see the tears forming in her eyes.

"How did you learn about my academy?" Madame Weatherberry inquired.

"My brother is a minstrel for royalty in the Eastern Kingdom," Mrs. Goose said. "He was hiding in the next room when you recently visited Queen Endustria. He heard you discussing plans for your academy of magic and how you asked the queen for permission to recruit students in her kingdom. He knows about our troubles with Lucy and wrote to us immediately to tell us about your school. We've spent the last three days in the In-Between looking for it."

"I see," Madame Weatherberry said. "Well, Mr. and Mrs. Goose, forgive me, but I have to be very frank with you. My academy isn't designed for students like your daughter. The gathering of macabre animals at her birth, the unsettling phenomena that occurred when she was younger, and the problems she's been causing lately are not expressions of *magic*."

Mr. and Mrs. Goose looked to each other and both let out a long, exasperated breath.

"We're painfully aware of that, Madame Weatherberry," Mr. Goose said. "There are two sides to the magical community, and it's very clear which side our daughter belongs to. But we were hoping you might make an exception for Lucy?"

"Please, Madame Weatherberry," Mrs. Goose pleaded. "She's a good kid who needs a good home that understands her. My husband and I just can't do it anymore. We're desperate for someone to help us."

The Gooses' request wasn't a simple matter. Madame Weatherberry went quiet and leaned back in her glass chair as she considered. Tears ran down Lucy's round face after hearing her parents' plea to get rid of her. Brystal's heart ached as she watched Lucy wipe her tears away before anyone noticed them.

After a few moments of careful consideration, Madame Weatherberry got to her feet and approached Lucy. She leaned down to the girl with a kind smile and placed a comforting hand on her shoulder.

"It may be a challenge, but challenges are what life is all about," Madame Weatherberry said. "I would love for you to join our academy, Lucy. I can't promise I'll always know *how* to assist you like I will the other students, but I promise I'll always do my best."

Lucy was shocked. Obviously, acceptance to Madame Weatherberry's academy was the last thing she had expected—and the very last thing she wanted. Lucy's parents, on the other hand, sighed with relief and embraced each other in celebration.

"Wait!" Lucy exclaimed. "I can't stay. I don't belong here."

"Lucy, this is a wonderful thing," Mrs. Goose said. "Madame Weatherberry will provide a much better home for you than your father and I ever could."

"But I don't *want* to live at the academy!" Lucy professed. "I want to live with you! We're not just a family, we're *the Goose Troupe*! You can't have a band without its star tambourine player!"

"Actually, your uncle is going to join us on the road," Mr. Goose said. "He's going to take over all your solos with his fiddle."

"His *fiddle*?" She was outraged.

Lucy pulled her parents to the side of the office to have a private word, but Brystal was still perfectly in earshot.

"But, Mom? Dad? Today is my birthday," Lucy whispered to them. *"You can't abandon me on my birthday!"*

"This is for your own good, Lucy," Mrs. Goose said. "One day you'll understand."

Mr. and Mrs. Goose kissed their daughter good-bye and profusely shook Mrs. Weatherberry's hand. From her bedroom window, Brystal saw the couple return to their colorful caravan outside. They pedaled the vehicle into the distance and disappeared through the hedge barrier without a hint of remorse for leaving their daughter behind. Madame Weatherberry escorted Lucy to the third floor and Brystal peered into the corridor as they walked by. The castle had already created a new room for Lucy, and a sixth door had appeared next to Brystal's bedroom.

"This will be your room, Lucy," Madame Weatherberry said. "I hope you'll be comfortable inside. The castle grows bedrooms based on the number of occupants, and the space is usually furnished for the specific needs of—"

"Yeah, yeah, yeah," Lucy said. "Thanks a million, Madame Whateverberry. If you don't mind, I'd like to be alone now."

Lucy entered her bedroom and slammed the door behind her. As soon as it was shut, Brystal and Madame Weatherberry could hear the girl sobbing on the other side.

"Do you think she'll be all right?" Brystal asked.

"It isn't going to be an easy adjustment for her," Madame Weatherberry said. "I think we should postpone today's lessons to after lunch so Lucy has time to get settled. I'll let the others know."

Madame Weatherberry left the corridor to tell the other students about the change of plans. Brystal stayed in her doorway and listened to Lucy cry in her bedroom. She knew exactly what it felt like to be rejected by a parent and she tried to think of a way to make her new floormate feel better. Brystal realized there was very little she could *say* to ease Lucy's troubles, but perhaps there was something she could *make*.

Brystal hurried down the spiral steps to the first level of the castle, down the hall, through the dining room, and into the kitchen. Brystal hadn't seen the castle's kitchen yet and was surprised to find it was four times the size of the kitchen at the Evergreen house. Mrs. Vee was in the middle of cooking lunch, and Brystal was taken aback by all the magic that was going into the meal's preparation.

Fruit, vegetables, spices, and utensils floated through the air. There were bowls that stirred ingredients on their own, food was chopped and diced by hovering knives, oven doors opened and closed without assistance, and trays of baked goods removed themselves from the oven's heat. Mrs. Vee stood in the center of the kitchen and conducted the magic around her like it was a symphony of invisible chefs.

"Well, hello there, dear," Mrs. Vee said when she noticed Brystal. "What brings you to my neck of the woods? Did you need a snack?"

"No, I'm still full from breakfast, thank you," Brystal said. "Mrs. Vee, I was hoping I could use your kitchen to make something by myself?"

"You mean, on your own?" Mrs. Vee asked. "You're not trying to take my job, are you? Because I'm warning you, it's not as glamorous as I make it look! *HA-HA!*"

"Oh no, it's just a family recipe," she said. "I could make it in my sleep. I'd hate to interrupt you while you're in the middle of cooking lunch, though. I promise I'll stay out of your way."

"It's no problem at all," Mrs. Vee said. "Family recipes are always welcome unless a family is *in* the recipe! *HA-HA!* Go ahead and help yourself to whatever you need."

A little more than an hour later, Brystal carried two forks and a freshly baked chocolate cake to the third floor. Mrs. Vee didn't have any birthday candles, so Brystal had to borrow thirteen candles from different candelabras and lanterns throughout the castle. Each candle was a different shape and color, but it did the trick. Brystal took a deep breath as she stood outside Lucy's bedroom door and knocked on it with her elbow.

"Lucy?" she said. "It's Brystal Evergreen, the girl who showed you and your parents to Madame Weatherberry's office."

"What do you want?" Lucy groaned from inside.

"I have a surprise for you if you'll just open the door," Brystal said.

A couple of moments later Lucy reluctantly opened her bedroom door. Her eyes were bloodshot from crying and she was very surprised to see the lit-up birthday cake in Brystal's hands.

"Happy Birthday!" Brystal cheered. "I hope you like chocolate."

Unfortunately, her floormate's reaction was not what Brystal was expecting.

"How did you know it was my birthday?" Lucy asked suspiciously.

Brystal opened her mouth to respond, but she didn't have any words to explain herself. She was so focused on cheering up Lucy, she had completely forgotten she only knew it was her birthday because she had been eavesdropping.

"Didn't you mention it when you arrived?" Brystal asked.

"No," Lucy said, and folded her arms.

"Oh...then it must have been a lucky *hunch*,"

Brystal said with a nervous laugh. "Forgive the candles. I assumed you were about thirteen, is that right?"

Lucy wasn't buying it. "You were *eavesdropping* on our meeting with Madame Weatherberry, weren't you?" she said, and raised an accusatory finger.

Brystal frantically shook her head, but it only made her seem guiltier.

"Okay, okay, yes," she confessed. "I admit, I was eavesdropping! I didn't mean to pry, but I heard your mother talking about the ravens and I couldn't look away."

"If we were in a goblin colony I could have your *ears cut off* for snooping!" Lucy said.

"Look, I'm sorry for invading your privacy!" Brystal said. "I know what it's like to be dumped in a strange place by a parent. I heard you say it was your birthday, so I thought if I baked you a cake, it might cheer you up. It was a mistake, so I'll leave you alone now."

Brystal was furious with herself for handling the situation so poorly. She hurried down the corridor before Lucy had any more reasons to dislike her. Just as Brystal reached the stairs, Lucy stopped her.

"Lucky for you, I'm not a girl who turns down sweets," she called. "That cake smells delicious, so I'll forgive your treachery just this once."

Lucy opened her bedroom and gestured for Brystal to come inside. Brystal was thrilled for a second chance and rushed inside the bedroom before Lucy changed her mind.

As she stepped inside, Brystal had to remind herself she was entering a thirteen-year-old girl's bedroom, because Lucy's chambers looked like a tavern. There was a large billiard table in the center of the floor, a row of dartboards hung on the wall, and just above that was a big sign that said: PLAY HARD. WORK HARDLY. Another wall was covered in musical instruments and dozens of posters that advertised the Goose Troupe's past performances. Every corner was filled with a massive taxidermy animal that was a morbid hybrid of different species. Last, Brystal noticed that instead of chairs or a bed, the room had beanbags and a hammock.

"Wow," Brystal said. "This is quite a room."

"I've got eclectic tastes," Lucy said. "That's what happens when you grow up in show business. You get exposed to more than your average child."

Lucy pushed two beanbags together and the girls had a seat. Brystal held up the cake and Lucy closed her eyes and blew out the candles.

"Do you see a barrel of peppermint cider anywhere?" Lucy asked.

"Um . . . no," Brystal said.

"*Dang.* My wish didn't come true."

Lucy leaned back in her beanbag and shoveled the chocolate cake into her mouth. Brystal couldn't take her eyes off all the Goose Troupe posters on the wall behind her. She was fascinated by all the locations Lucy's family had been to.

"Have you really performed in all those places?" she asked.

"Oh yeah," Lucy bragged. "And those don't include the underground circuit."

"What's the underground circuit?" Brystal asked.

"You know, the places they don't always include on the map," she explained. "Goblin colonies, troll camps, elf compounds, ogre conventions—you name it, the Gooses have played it! *Gosh, this cake is good.*"

"And the creatures in the In-Between didn't *hurt* you?"

"Not at all," Lucy said. "Creatures in the In-Between are so desperate for entertainment they wouldn't dare. They're also the best audiences a performer could ask for. Subjugated species always know how to have a good time."

"Oh, look!" Brystal said, and pointed to one of the posters. "You performed in Chariot Hills! That's where I'm from!"

Lucy clenched her teeth. "Yikes," she said. "The Southern Kingdom is the *worst* place to perform. They've got all these rules about what artists are allowed to do. We can't sing profanity, we can't play loudly, we can't dance crudely, everyone has to be clothed—it takes all the fun out of it! I can't even bang my tambourine on my hip without being fined! Like, if *that's* the kind of show you're looking for—*just go to church*! Am I right?"

"I'm not surprised," Brystal said. "I can't tell you

how glad I am to be away from it. I would have given anything for a childhood like yours."

"Yeah, I've had some good times," Lucy said. "I guess all my adventures are over now that I'm stuck in this place."

Lucy stopped eating and looked sadly at the floor.

"I wouldn't say that," Brystal said. "You should give this place a chance. It might surprise you."

"Easy for you to say—you belong here," Lucy said. "But you heard what Madame Weatherberry told my parents. The academy isn't meant for children like me!"

Brystal sighed—she understood how Lucy felt more than the girl realized.

"To be honest, I'm not sure I belong here, either," she said. "All of Madame Weatherberry's students have been doing magic their whole lives. I just recently found out I had magical abilities and I needed the help of an old spell to conjure anything. To make matters worse, I'm apparently the only fairy in the entire world who doesn't have a specialty. Xanthous has his fire, Emerelda has her jewels, Skylene has her water, and Tangerina has her—"

"Charm?" Lucy asked sarcastically.

"Don't worry about Tangerina," Brystal said. "She grows on you after a while."

"So does fungus."

"Back to my point," Brystal continued. "You're not the only person who feels like they shouldn't be here. I know it seems like Madame Weatherberry made a mistake, but I doubt she would open her doors for us if she didn't genuinely think she could help us."

"But at least you're a fairy," Lucy said. "I'm a *witch*, Brystal! That means my heart is full of darkness and all my powers are fueled by evil that's growing inside me! You have no idea what it's like to know that one day, no matter what I do, I'm going to become an ugly and mean old hag! I'm going to spend my adulthood cursing people and collecting cats! *And I don't even like cats!*"

The thought made Lucy burst into tears. She rapidly scooped the cake into her mouth to drown her sadness, and within a couple more bites, she had finished the whole plate. Brystal dried Lucy's tears with the corner of her gray-and-black-striped dress.

"If it makes you feel better, I don't think you're a witch," Brystal said.

"Are you crazy?" Lucy asked. "Madame Weatherberry specifically said—"

"Madame Weatherberry never said you were a witch," Brystal said. "She just said her academy isn't meant for students like you, and that could mean a number of things! Besides, if you had evil and darkness in your heart, there's no way you would enjoy performing as much as you do. It takes way too much joy and excitement to make audiences happy."

Lucy nodded along. "And exceptional talent." She sniffled. "Don't forget exceptional talent."

"Exactly," Brystal said. "A wicked old witch would never have that in her."

Lucy wiped her nose on Brystal's sleeve and shrugged. "I suppose so," she said. "If you don't think I'm a witch, then what the heck am I? What's causing all the creepy stuff that happens around me?"

Brystal tried her best to think of something to put the troubled girl at ease.

"Maybe you're just a fairy with a specialty for trouble," she said.

Lucy thought the suggestion was so ridiculous the corner of her mouth curled into a tiny grin. Brystal was glad to give Lucy her first smile at the academy.

"That's the dumbest thing I've heard," Lucy said. "But I appreciate the effort."

"Personally, I think life is way too complicated for anyone's fate to be set in stone," Brystal said. "Take it from me. In the last month I've gone from being a schoolgirl to a maid to a prisoner to a correctional facility inmate, and now I'm studying to become a fairy!"

"Whoa," Lucy said. "And I thought *my* life was eventful."

"I'm just saying nothing is certain until it's certain," Brystal said. "In fact, whether you become an ugly and mean old witch or not, there's only one thing we know for sure."

"What's that?" Lucy asked.

"Tangerina and Skylene won't think any differently of you."

Without missing a beat, Brystal and Lucy both erupted in laughter. They chuckled so hard their stomachs hurt and happy tears ran down their faces.

"Boy, they must hate my guts," Lucy said. "Well, despite my intentions, I'm glad I made at least *one* friend today. Thanks for being so nice to me, Brystal. Something tells me we're going to be partners in crime for a very, very long time."

"Me too, Lucy," Brystal said. "Me too."

CHAPTER ELEVEN

MAGICLEXIA

L unch was uncomfortably quiet at the academy. Lucy
sat by herself at the far end of the table to keep her
distance from the others and didn't say a word for
the entire meal. She picked at her food and occasionally looked up at her new classmates with a suspicious
glance, almost daring them to provoke her. Tangerina
and Skylene had received enough of Lucy's insults for one
day, so the girls remained silent and purposely avoided
making eye contact with her.

Brystal tried to defuse the tension with harmless

conversation topics, but no one was interested in what she had to say. Her efforts were distracted when Mrs. Vee entered the dining room and presented Madame Weatherberry with a second scaly black envelope.

"Another letter has arrived for you, Madame," she said.

The new message made Madame Weatherberry more anxious than the first. Before anyone could ask about her alleged "sick friend," their teacher got to her feet and headed out of the room with the mysterious letter in hand.

"We'll begin our very first lesson in just a few minutes," Madame Weatherberry called behind her as she hurried out of the dining room. "I'll meet you outside."

After lunch, the students and apprentices followed Madame Weatherberry's instructions and gathered around the castle's front steps. However, just like earlier, their teacher was taking her time before joining them. The students became more impatient the longer they waited.

"I'm starting to think we're *never* going to learn anything at this academy," Emerelda said.

"What's taking her so long?" Xanthous asked. "You don't think she's reconsidering the academy, do you? I wouldn't have anywhere to go if she shut it down!"

"Will you both calm down," Tangerina said. "Madame Weatherberry is probably keeping us waiting for a reason. It's like the classic phrase goes: *When the student is ready, the teacher appears.*"

"I was *ready* forty-five minutes ago," Emerelda said. "This is getting rude."

"*The patient bird gets the worm,*" Skylene said with a confident nod. "That's another classic phrase."

Tangerina rolled her eyes and pulled her friend aside.

"Skylene, the phrase is *The early bird gets the worm,*" she said. "It's supposed to encourage people to wake up early."

"Oh," Skylene said. "But that's not very encouraging for an *early worm.*"

As they waited, Brystal kept her attention on the windows of Madame Weatherberry's office. She stood on her tiptoes, hoping to catch a glimpse of what their teacher was up to, but she couldn't see anything. When she eventually gave up, Brystal noticed that Lucy was still keeping her distance from the others. The musicians' daughter sat on a boulder a few yards away from the castle's front steps and watched her classmates like they were infected with a plague. Brystal felt sorry for Lucy and sat beside her on the boulder to keep her company.

"They aren't going to bite you, you know," Brystal teased her.

"Oh, I know," Lucy said. "I just don't want any of them to get too attached, you know, in case this academy doesn't work out for me. People form quick bonds with celebrities."

Brystal laughed. "That's very considerate of you," she said. "I was worried you were being anti-social."

"Not at all," Lucy said. "So tell me more about these clowns we're working with. What's the dynamic I'm stepping into?"

"To be honest, I'm not sure," Brystal said. "I just met everyone yesterday. Tangerina and Skylene have been at the academy the longest. Technically, they're Madame Weatherberry's *apprentices* because they're more advanced than *students*—it was the first thing they mentioned to us. Madame Weatherberry found them when they were both very young, after they had been abandoned."

"Can't say I blame their families," Lucy said. "What about Emerelda? What's her story?"

"Emerelda was also abandoned when she was just an infant," Brystal said. "She was raised by dwarfs in a coal mine. Emerelda didn't want to come to the academy but her father made her go."

"Raised by dwarfs, huh? I guess that explains her short fuse and tunnel vision. What about the little paranoid guy? Why does he wear a medal? Did he win something?"

"It's called a Muter Medal," Brystal explained. "It's supposed to mute Xanthous's magical abilities until he's able to control them. The poor boy has been through the wringer! A few nights ago, Xanthous got caught doing something he wasn't supposed to be doing, and his father started beating him. It ignited his powers and Xanthous accidentally started a huge fire that burned down their house, killed his father, and set most of the Northwest

Foothills ablaze. When Madame Weatherberry and I found him, he was on his way to drown himself in a lake. He thought that was the only way to stop himself from harming people."

Lucy sighed with relief. "Oh, thank God," she muttered.

"Excuse me?"

"Sorry, I mean *how terrible*," Lucy corrected herself. "I'm just happy to hear there's some *drama* and *depth* to these people. I was afraid I was stuck with a stone-cold pack of losers. What did Xanthous's father catch him doing?"

"I don't know," Brystal said. "He wouldn't say, but I could tell it was something he was *really* ashamed about."

"I love a good mystery," Lucy said, and grinned at Xanthous with intrigued eyes. "Give me a week and I'll pry it out of him. I'm good at solving cases. My parents and I used to perform at murder mystery parties."

Brystal looked up at Madame Weatherberry's office and let out a long sigh.

"Xanthous isn't the only mystery around here," she said.

Before Lucy could inquire any further, the students and apprentices suddenly screamed and ran away from the castle. Sparkling lights had appeared around the front steps and they grew brighter and brighter, glimmering faster and faster.

"What the heck is *that*?" Emerelda asked.

"It isn't me, I swear!" Xanthous said. "Look, I still have my Muter Medal on!"

"Skylene, extinguish it with your water!" Tangerina ordered.

"I'm not your *early worm*!" Skylene exclaimed. "Use your honey!"

The sparkling lights were followed by a blinding flash of violet light, and all the children shielded their eyes. When they looked back, Madame Weatherberry had appeared, out of thin air, on the castle's front steps, and she struck a theatrical pose with both hands raised in the air. Her gown was made entirely from clocks of all shapes and sizes. She wore a cuckoo clock as a fascinator, her gloved arm was wrapped in watches, and a pendulum swung from her belt.

"Now *that's* what I call an entrance," Lucy whispered to Brystal. "And I've worked with a lot of divas."

Madame Weatherberry was delighted by all the amazed and alarmed expressions on her students' and apprentices' faces.

"Welcome to your very first lesson," she was happy to announce. "Before we begin, I have one question to ask you. Can anyone tell me what the difference is between a wound and a scar? Between weakness and strength? And between hatred and love?"

Emerelda raised her hand. "Is it *time*?" she asked.

"Correct!" Madame Weatherberry cheered.

"How did *you* know that?" Tangerina asked.

"She's an hour late and she's dressed in clocks,"

Emerelda said. "I figured it was a safe bet."

"Time is the most complex device in the universe," Madame Weatherberry went on. "It is both the problem and the solution to most of life's dilemmas. It heals all wounds, but in the end, it takes us all. Unfortunately, time is rarely in anyone's favor. We have too little or too much but never the time we want or need. Sometimes we're born into a time that doesn't value us, and too often, we let those times determine how we value ourselves. So for your first assignment, you are going to get rid of any unfavorable opinions, insecurities, or self-hatred that the times have instilled within you. If we are going to successfully change the world's perspective of us, we must start by changing our perspective of ourselves. Follow me."

Madame Weatherberry led her students to the lake on the academy grounds. She placed Brystal, Lucy, Xanthous, and Emerelda at the edge of the water, spacing them a few feet apart from one another.

"Take a look at your reflections in the water," she instructed. "Now ask yourselves, is this the reflection of *who you are* or the reflection of the person *the world wants you to be*? If you could change your appearance to match the person inside you, what changes would you make? What would you need for your personality and your physicality to be one and the same? I want you to each close your eyes and search your soul for the answers. Find the qualities you value the most about yourself and the qualities that make you unique. Then imagine wrapping your hands around your *true self* and pull your true self to the surface with all your might. Emerelda, let's start with you."

Being called on first made Emerelda feel vulnerable. She closed her eyes, let out a deep breath, and tried her best to follow Madame Weatherberry's instructions. She smiled and grunted to herself as she mentally sorted through her good and bad qualities like a pile of laundry. After a minute or two of total silence, Emerelda suddenly gasped for air like she was coming up from a deep dive underwater. Her burlap dress stretched into a robe and the rough material turned into beaded strands of bright emeralds, and a diamond headband appeared on her forehead.

Emerelda looked at her reflection in the lake and couldn't believe her eyes.

"This is incredible!" she said, and caressed her new clothes. "I had no idea my inner self looked so expensive!"

"Well done, Emerelda," Madame Weatherberry said. "Xanthous, why don't you take off your medal and give it a try?"

"I can't take off my Muter Medal!" Xanthous objected. "There's too many flammable objects around us!"

"Don't worry, I'm standing right beside you," Madame Weatherberry said. "Go on."

Xanthous nervously removed the medal from around his neck and set it on the ground. Flames instantly appeared on his head and shoulders. He closed his eyes

and took a few deep breaths to calm himself. His classmates could tell he was having more difficulty finding
his inner self than Emerelda had, because Xanthous's
brow scrunched tighter and tighter as he searched
deeper and deeper. Then, without warning, his whole
body was engulfed in powerful flames. The fire burned
for a couple moments, then slowly died down. When it
finally diminished entirely, the others noticed Xanthous
wasn't wearing his patchy vest and brown pants anymore. The boy's clothes had turned into a golden suit
that was ablaze with a thin layer of fire. A trail of smoke
hung off his jacket like suit tails and he wore an iron bow
tie that was so hot it glowed.

Xanthous stared at his reflection in the water like he
was looking at a stranger.

"I can't believe it," he said. "My whole outfit is fire-
proof!"

"And *very* dapper," Madame Weatherberry said with
a proud smile.

After admiring his new reflection, Xanthous quickly
put the Muter Medal back around his neck. All the
flames throughout his body disappeared, his bow tie
cooled to a normal color, and his smoky suit tails blew
away.

"Way to go, Sparky," Lucy said. "That's a tough act
to follow."

"Lucy, would you like to go next?" Madame
Weatherberry asked.

"No thanks, MW," she said. "I'm actually really

content with the way I look. It took me a long time to develop my trademark style."

"Well, that's wonderful, dear," Madame Weatherberry said. "Then that just leaves you, Brystal."

As Brystal gazed down at the Bootstrap Correctional Facility uniform in her reflection, it wasn't difficult to imagine a more authentic version of herself. On the contrary, after a lifetime of being oppressed in the Southern Kingdom, Brystal was very in touch with the intelligent, respectable, and influential girl she had always wanted to be. She closed her eyes and pictured her inner self perfectly, but for whatever reason, she couldn't bring her to the surface.

"I can't do it," Brystal said.

"Yes, you can," Madame Weatherberry said to encourage her. "Just focus and visualize the person inside your heart."

"I can see the person inside my heart, but I've never done magic by myself," Brystal said. "Is there a spell or an incantation I could recite to help me?"

"Not all magic can be accomplished with spells and incantations," Madame Weatherberry said. "If you want to be a successful fairy, you'll have to learn to produce it on your own. But just this once, I'll help you find the magic inside."

Madame Weatherberry twirled her finger, and suddenly, Brystal felt a warm and joyful sensation growing in the pit of her stomach. The feeling reminded Brystal of the excitement she had when reading a particularly good book. It grew stronger and stronger, sending chills up and down her limbs, and it spread through her body until she was so full she thought it might burst out of her skin. To Brystal's surprise, Madame Weatherberry and all her classmates gasped.

"Well, well," Madame Weatherberry said. "It looks like Miss Evergreen has finally arrived."

Brystal opened her eyes and glanced down at her reflection in the lake. Her faded gray-and-black-striped uniform had turned into a sleek and sleeveless pantsuit with a long train that flowed down from her waist. The fabric was the color of the sky and sparkled like a starry galaxy, and she wore a pair of matching formal gloves. Her long hair was curly, covered in white flowers, and styled over her right shoulder. Brystal covered her mouth and tears welled in her eyes at the beautiful and dignified young woman she had become.

"Are you all right, sweetheart?" Madame Weatherberry asked.

"Yes," Brystal said, and wiped away her tears. "It just feels like I'm seeing myself for the first time."

· · ★ · ·

The following morning after breakfast, Madame Weatherberry took her students and apprentices to a large maple tree in the middle of the academy's property. She snapped five twigs off the tree's branches and placed them on the ground, then positioned her students behind them.

"All magic can be divided into four categories: *Improvement, Rehabilitation, Manifestation, and Imagination*," Madame Weatherberry explained. "From now on, each lesson will focus on developing our skills in these four areas. Today's lesson will be an introduction to *magical improvement*. Over your careers as fairies, you'll encounter many people, places, and objects that you'll improve with magic—the greater the improvement, the more magic it will require. To begin, we'll start with something very small and simple. I want each of you to transform the twig in front of you into something you believe is an improvement. Skylene, will you please give us a demonstration?"

Skylene nodded eagerly and stepped forward. She held her right hand over the twig, and the students watched in amazement as it slowly morphed into a colorful piece of coral.

"Good work," Madame Weatherberry said. "By focusing on the twig, and simultaneously visualizing another object in her mind, Skylene has changed it into something she believes is an improvement. Xanthous, would you like to start?"

The boy cautiously removed his Muter Medal and flames immediately returned to his head, shoulders, and golden suit. Xanthous hovered over the twig and tried his best to concentrate on how to improve it. As he concentrated, the twig began to swell and turn bright red. It became a cylinder, and a small string grew out from its top.

"Great job, Xanthous!" Madame Weatherberry said. "You've transformed the twig into a firecracker!"

"I did it!" he said. "I actually did it!"

Xanthous was so proud of himself he jumped up and down in celebration, but he stepped too close to the firecracker, and his blazing pant leg accidentally ignited it. The explosion made a piercing whistle that echoed through the property and it shot colorful sparks in all directions.

"Hit the deck!" Lucy yelled.

Madame Weatherberry and her students dived to the ground and covered their ears. Skylene splashed the firecracker with water and it eventually fizzled out. Xanthous blushed and flames appeared on his cheeks.

"Sorry about that!" the boy peeped.

His classmates glared at him with expressions that were far more scorching than his flames. Xanthous swiftly put the Muter Medal back on before he caused any more damage and helped the others to their feet.

"We're off to a decent start," Madame Weatherberry said. "Emerelda, you did so well in yesterday's assignment. Would you like to go next?"

"Oh, this is going to be a piece of cake for me," Emerelda said.

She reached for the twig but Madame Weatherberry stopped Emerelda before she made contact.

"We all know you can turn objects into jewels with your touch, but today, I'd like you to try improving the twig with your mind," the fairy said.

"With my *mind*?" Emerelda asked.

"Yes," Madame Weatherberry said. "Not everything

we want in life will be within our physical reach. Sometimes we must use our *imagination* to grasp what we seek. Go on."

Emerelda shrugged and gave it her best try. She reached for the twig and, following Madame Weatherberry's advice, imagined herself touching it with invisible fingertips. A few moments later, the twig began to twist and curl. It coiled like a snake and grew shiny, and soon the twig had become a beautiful diamond bracelet. Emerelda was thrilled she had managed to pull it off, and slid the bracelet over her wrist.

"Well done, Emerelda," Madame Weatherberry said. "Lucy, you didn't get a chance to practice your magic yesterday. Would you like to try now?"

"I think I'll pass," Lucy said. "Trust me, if I could transform a stick into something as nice as a diamond necklace, I wouldn't have so much gambling debt."

"Miss Goose, your talents may be *different* from the others', but you're here to perfect them just the same," Madame Weatherberry reminded her. "Now give it your best and we'll see what you come up with."

Lucy groaned and reluctantly stepped forward. She placed a hand over the twig and tried to magically enhance it. The twig became limber, it started to wiggle, and was coated in a sticky liquid. When she was finished, the twig had turned into a fat and slimy slug. Lucy was very impressed by her creation—clearly, she had expected something much worse to appear—but her classmates weren't as enthusiastic.

"You call that an improvement?" Tangerina asked.

Before Lucy could respond, a gryphon suddenly swooped down from the sky and snatched the slug off the ground with its beak.

"At least I made *him* happy," Lucy said with a shrug.

"That was excellent, Lucy," Madame Weatherberry said. "A slug is an *interesting* improvement, but as I always say, beauty is in the eye of the beholder. Now that just leaves you, Brystal."

Brystal took a step toward the twig and prayed she could find her own magic without Madame Weatherberry's assistance. She closed her eyes and desperately tried to re-create the joyful sensation she had experienced the day before. After several moments of careful concentration, Brystal felt a hint of magic growing in the pit of her stomach. She focused on the feeling with all her might and willed it to grow stronger, all the while deciding which object she wanted the twig to become. She tried to think of something that would please Madame Weatherberry but also make Lucy feel better about her slug.

Think of a caterpillar... Brystal told herself. *Think of a caterpillar.... Think of a caterpillar.... Think of a caterpillar....*

Instead of the twig turning into the adorable and plump caterpillar she was imagining, all the leaves on the maple tree above her suddenly transformed into large butterflies. The insects flew away from the branches, leaving the tree completely bare, and then moved through the property like a big fluttering cloud. Brystal, Madame Weatherberry, the other students, and the apprentices watched the butterflies in complete shock.

"My word," Madame Weatherberry said. "That was *quite* the transformation."

The fairy's astonished gaze moved to Brystal and stayed there. She couldn't tell what her teacher was thinking, but Brystal knew Madame Weatherberry was concerned and confused by the magic she had just witnessed.

"Class dismissed," Madame Weatherberry said.

· • ★ • ·

Brystal had trouble sleeping that night—not just because Lucy was snoring like a grizzly bear next door, but because she felt like a complete failure. Usually, Brystal looked forward to any opportunity to learn something new and productive, but since each lesson turned into another embarrassment, Brystal was starting to dread her time with Madame Weatherberry. If her magical incompetence continued, she worried her days at the academy would be numbered.

The next morning after breakfast, Madame Weatherberry led the children to a small horse stable at the side of the castle. However, instead of horses, the stable's pens were occupied by magical creatures. In the first pen, there was a shoebox placed on a stool. The students peered into the box and saw a male pixie resting inside.

Unfortunately, the pixie's colorful wings had been torn off and lay in pieces beside him.

The second pen held two injured unicorns. The first unicorn sat on the floor with cracked and chipped hooves. The second unicorn's horn was bent at the end like a crowbar. Both creatures looked horribly depressed, as if their egos were damaged along with their bodies.

In the third pen, a gryphon the size of a large dog lay on a pile of hay. His front claw was mangled and wrapped in a white bandage. He was hunched over and trembling from the pain the broken limb was causing him. Brystal didn't know how long gryphons lived, but she assumed he was rather old for his species because most of his feathers had turned gray.

"Poor things," Brystal said. "What happened to them?"

"The pixie flew too far from his flock and was attacked by an owl," Madame Weatherberry said. "Pixies stay in large numbers to protect themselves. Without his wings, he'll never be able to join his family and he'll be much more susceptible to predators. The unicorns hurt themselves after they slid down a rocky cliff. Thankfully, their injuries aren't critical, but unicorns are a prideful species and quite vain when it comes to their appearance. These two have been too ashamed to rejoin their herds ever since their incident. Sadly, the gryphon is in the third act of his life and his bones aren't what they used to be. His front claw shattered after a rough landing. Just like birds, gryphon bones are hollow and become fragile as they get older."

"Is this an animal hospital, then?" Xanthous asked.

"Indeed," Madame Weatherberry said.

"Then where are the animal doctors?" Emerelda asked.

"*We're* the animal doctors," Madame Weatherberry said with a twinkle in her eye. "Today's lesson will be your first foray into *magical rehabilitation*. The most profound ability the magical community possesses is the ability to heal those in pain. So this morning, you'll each choose a wounded animal and use your magic to help relieve or heal their injuries. Tangerina, would you please give us an example?"

Tangerina approached the first pen with a cocky bounce in her step. She stood in a meditative pose with open palms, and closed her eyes to concentrate. A dozen bumblebees flew out of her hair and zoomed toward the injured pixie. The oncoming swarm terrified the pixie and he frantically tried to climb out of the shoebox. The bumblebees landed on top of the pixie and held him down as they used their stingers and honey to stitch and seal his wings back together.

In a matter of minutes, the pixie's wings were as good as new and he blissfully fluttered into the air. The pixie hugged Tangerina's face and expressed his gratitude in a high-pitched pixie language that sounded like gibberish to the students. Even more surprising, Tangerina apparently understood what the pixie was saying and replied,

"You're welcome," in the strange tongue. The pixie flew out of the barn to reunite with his family, as the other students stared at Tangerina dumbfounded.

"What are you looking at?" she asked defensively.

"How did you know what to say to him?" Emerelda asked.

"Pixien is very close to Beenglish," Tangerina said. "Everyone knows that."

"Thank you, Tangerina," Madame Weatherberry said. "Would anyone like to go next?"

"Umm, Madame Weatherberry? May I have a word?" Lucy said, and pulled the fairy aside. "Look, I really appreciate your intentions to teach me—you're a swan among swine—but I don't think I should participate in this lesson given my track record. These animals have been through enough already."

"That's a wise choice, Lucy," Madame Weatherberry said. "I must confess, I had the same concern. That's why there are only four creatures in the stable. You can be an observer for today's lesson. Now that that's settled, why don't we have Emerelda go next?"

"Can I use my hands this time?" Emerelda asked.

"Absolutely," Madame Weatherberry said. "There is no wrong way to heal."

Emerelda inspected the animals and chose the unicorn with broken hooves. Leg by leg, she placed a hand on the steed's damaged hooves and filled the cracks and chips with ruby. Once the hooves were fixed, Emerelda gave the creature diamond horseshoes to prevent the injuries from happening again. The unicorn happily trotted in circles around the stable and gave Emerelda a thankful neigh. He then raced outside to show off his glittery new feet to his herd.

"Outstanding, Emerelda!" Madame Weatherberry said. "And very clever!"

"I don't get it," Skylene said. "Why would you give a unicorn *diamond* shoes?"

"Because diamonds are one of the hardest materials in the world," Emerelda said. "They'll protect his feet if he slides down another cliff."

"They're tough and beautiful, just like you," Madame Weatherberry said with a smile. "Xanthous, would you like to go next?"

Xanthous removed his Muter Medal with a little more confidence than he had in the previous days. He looked back and forth between the second unicorn and the gryphon as he decided which creature to help. Eventually, he selected the unicorn, who became alarmed by the fiery boy approaching her.

"It's okay," he whispered. "I think I know how to help you."

By soothing the unicorn, Xanthous also soothed himself, and the flames covering his body diminished on their own. Once he gained the unicorn's trust, Xanthous rubbed his hands together until they glowed with heat. He gently touched the unicorn's horn and it softened in his warm grip. As if it was clay, Xanthous shaped the horn back into its natural position and then blew on it until it cooled down. The unicorn licked the side of Xanthous's face and then she galloped out of the stable and rejoined the herd nearby.

"That was marvelous, Xanthous!" Madame Weatherberry exclaimed.

Xanthous was so proud he almost forgot to put his Muter Medal back on. Now that he was finished, all the attention was on Brystal. Her whole body went tense as she worried about how her magic might betray her during the assignment.

"Brystal, you're always last but never least," Madame Weatherberry said. "Can you assist the gryphon with his broken claw?"

"I'll try my best," Brystal said through a nervous smile.

She stepped into the third pen and knelt beside the injured gryphon. Brystal closed her eyes and willed the magical sensation to return to her core. Just like before, she summoned the feeling to grow stronger, but this time, she carefully kept it from getting *too* strong. Once her magic was bubbling at what she considered a steady level, she took the gryphon's claw into her hand. Brystal imagined his bones healing, his pain fading, and his energy returning. She pictured the gryphon in the first act of his life, freely flying and landing wherever he wanted without the consequences of old age.

Just then, the gryphon stopped trembling and sat up much taller than before. He confidently puffed out his chest, looked around the stable with wide, vibrant eyes, and his feathers returned to their original auburn color. The gryphon chewed off his bandages and revealed a claw that was just as straight and strong as his other limbs. For the first time in a long while, the creature triumphantly stood on all fours.

"Oh my gosh," Brystal said in amazement. "I healed him! My magic did what I wanted it to for once!"

"Congratulations, Brystal!" Madame Weatherberry said, and led her students into a round of applause. "I knew you had it in you. All you needed was a little practice, a little patience, a little perseverance, and everything would—"

Everyone went silent, because *Brystal's magic wasn't over yet*! After his claw was healed, the gryphon's whole body started to shrink. The creature squawked in horror and tried to run and fly out of the stable, but its legs and wings became too small to carry him. The gryphon shrank to the size of an apple, and then an orange eggshell with black spots appeared around him. For a few seconds, the egg stayed perfectly still on the ground, but then it started to shake. The gryphon hatched from the egg and emerged as a featherless, gooey, and very confused newborn.

"You reversed his *aging process*?" Tangerina asked in astonishment.

"Can we even do that?" Skylene whispered to her friend.

Brystal's classmates watched her like she was a magical creature herself, but one they were discovering for the very first time. She looked to Madame Weatherberry for reassurance, but only found the same troubled expression her teacher had worn the last time she conjured magic.

"That's all for today, children," Madame Weatherberry said. "Tangerina? Skylene? Please find the baby gryphon a safe home somewhere on the property. Brystal? Will you please join me in my office? I'd like to have a private word with you."

Madame Weatherberry hurried out of the stable and Brystal followed. She couldn't tell if she was in trouble or not, and as Brystal glanced back at her classmates' long faces, she knew *they* couldn't tell, either. Madame Weatherberry didn't say a word to Brystal until they arrived in her office. She had a seat behind her glass desk and gestured for Brystal to sit across from her. Brystal was in the chair for less than five seconds when she abruptly burst into tears.

"I'm so sorry, Madame Weatherberry!" she cried. "I'm trying so hard to follow your directions, but my magic doesn't work like everyone else's! Please don't expel me from your academy!"

Madame Weatherberry did a double take at Brystal's emotional display.

"Expel you?" she asked. "Good heavens! Why would I want to expel you?"

"Because my magic is obviously broken!" Brystal said. "I don't have a specialty, I never complete your assignments correctly, and my magic always results in something I didn't intend! If you're going to change the world's perspective on magic, you're going to need students you can depend on, and you can't depend on me!"

According to Madame Weatherberry's puzzled expression, there was a lot she wanted to discuss with Brystal, but expulsion was not on the agenda.

"Brystal, it's only your third day at the academy," Madame Weatherberry said with a laugh. "No one is expecting you to be perfect except yourself. And seeking perfection is a side effect of the oppression you've endured. So let's start our conversation by addressing that."

"I don't understand," she said. "Are you saying the Southern Kingdom turned me into a perfectionist?"

"Just like many members of the magical community, at some point, society made you believe that *your* flaws were worse than anyone else's flaws," the fairy explained. "And now, consequently, you've convinced yourself that being *flawless* is the only way to gain approval. Having such impossible standards is no way to live life, and it's certainly not the way to get an education. On the contrary, if you're going to be successful at this academy, you need to embrace your flaws and learn from your mistakes, or you'll never know what challenges you're here to overcome."

Brystal dried her tears. "So you haven't called me into your office to expel me?"

"Absolutely not," Madame Weatherberry said. "I have to admit, I've been very concerned about you—not because I've lost any faith in your magic, but because I've been trying to understand how to help you. What you've done in the last few days has been extraordinary—your clothing, the butterflies, the gryphon—it all points to remarkable power and potential. And after this morning, I think I've finally figured out why you're having trouble controlling and guiding your abilities."

"Why?" Brystal asked from the edge of her seat.

"You have *magiclexia*," Madame Weatherberry said.

"Magiclexia?" she asked. "Am I sick?"

"No, no, no—it's nothing like that," Madame Weatherberry explained. "Magiclexia is a harmless but frustrating disorder that runs in the magical community—it's a sort of *block* that prevents fairies from accessing their abilities. Sometimes as a survival method, fairies suppress their magic so deep within themselves that it becomes extremely difficult to reach it. I have no doubt that while living in the Southern Kingdom, you developed a few subconscious blocks that are now debilitating you."

"Can magiclexia be cured?" Brystal asked.

"It usually takes someone a lifetime to identify and destroy all the barriers holding them back," Madame Weatherberry said. "Luckily, just like the glasses you wear to read, the magical community has tools to help us work around our ailments."

Madame Weatherberry opened the top drawer of her glass desk and removed a shimmering scepter. The object was made of pure crystal and was easily the most beautiful thing Brystal had ever laid eyes on. Although she had never seen it before, Brystal felt a strong connection to the scepter, like they had been waiting to meet each other.

"This is a *magic wand*," Madame Weatherberry said. "It's very, very old and belonged to the fairy who mentored me. The wand will put you in touch with your magic and help you manage it more efficiently."

"Will it help me find my specialty?" Brystal asked.

"Perhaps," Madame Weatherberry said. "Although I don't want you to feel inferior to the other students while you wait for it to appear. Not all specialties are as easy to spot as Tangerina's and Skylene's. Sometimes, although it's rare, a fairy's specialty manifests itself *emotionally* rather than physically. It's very possible that what you're looking for is already part of who you are. Whatever it is, I'm sure this wand will help you discover it when the time is right."

Madame Weatherberry presented the wand to Brystal like it was a sword. As soon as Brystal wrapped her fingers around the crystal handle, the magical sensation returned to her core. However, unlike the other times, it felt like the magic was completely in her control. She waved the wand toward Madame Weatherberry's rack of fascinators, and suddenly, all the hats turned into colorful birds. The transformation startled Brystal and she quickly turned them back.

"Oh, I'm sorry! I didn't mean to—" Then Brystal had an epiphany and stopped herself mid-apology. "Wait a second—that's *exactly* what I meant to do! As I waved the wand, your hats reminded me of birds, and *that's* what they became! I didn't even have to concentrate that hard! *The wand works!*"

Madame Weatherberry didn't reciprocate Brystal's excitement. The fairy's eyes were glued to the enlarged Map of Magic on the wall above her fireplace. Something on the map had captivated the teacher's attention and made her mouth drop open.

"What's wrong?" Brystal asked her. "You look distraught."

Instead of answering, Madame Weatherberry jumped to her feet and moved closer to the map. After studying it for a few moments, the fairy touched a large star on the map near the location of the academy. The name *Brystal Evergreen* appeared beside it.

"Incredible," Madame Weatherberry whispered to herself.

"What's incredible?"

"As soon as that wand touched your hand, your star on the Map of Magic grew nearly twice in size," she said. "It's the same size as my star—maybe even a little bigger."

Brystal gulped. "But what does that mean?"

Madame Weatherberry turned to her and couldn't hide the astonishment growing in her eyes.

"It means we can expect great things from you, Miss Evergreen."

CHAPTER TWELVE

THE UNWANTED

Everything changed for Brystal after Madame Weatherberry gave her the magic wand. By the end of her
second week at the academy, Brystal wasn't only
catching up to Emerelda and Xanthous; her abilities
were surpassing Tangerina's and Skylene's. She was
completing all of Madame Weatherberry's magical
assignments with much more ease and efficiency than
her classmates. In fact, Madame Weatherberry started
asking Brystal to give demonstrations for the others
instead of asking the apprentices.

Although Brystal did everything she could to keep the peace with Tangerina and Skylene, her rapid progress earned their resentment.

"*It's not fair,*" Skylene whispered to Tangerina. "*Why does Brystal get a wand?*"

"*Apparently she has a* disorder," her friend whispered back.

Skylene grunted. "Lucky," she said. "I want a disorder."

Despite their occasional remarks and dirty looks, Brystal was too excited to let the girls' jealousy dampen her spirits. Now that she was in touch with her magic, she became infatuated with it, and used magic for everything she possibly could. Brystal waved her wand to open doors and drawers, to put on her shoes and clothes, and at night before bed, she would dance about her room and make her books magically twirl around her. At meals, Brystal even used magic to feed herself, levitating food directly into her mouth. However, she quickly stopped this practice as it seemed to annoy *everyone* at the dining table.

"Okay, now you're just showing off," Emerelda said.

Once the students had all mastered their early improvement and rehabilitation exercises, Madame Weatherberry moved on to the next subject in her curriculum. She led her students to a tower in the castle that was completely empty except for dust and cobwebs.

"Perhaps the most miraculous part of magic is the ability to create *something* from *nothing*," Madame Weatherberry said. "So for your first manifestation lesson, I want you to fill this room with pieces of furniture. Keep in mind that manifestation is similar to improvement, except there are no existing materials to work with. Summoning elements to appear out of thin air requires even greater concentration and visualization. Try to imagine every inch of the object you wish to create, focus on its dimensions and weight, picture exactly where you want it to be and how it would change your surroundings. Brystal, would you like to begin?"

Without looking, Brystal could feel Tangerina's and Skylene's cold stares on the back of her head.

"Actually, why don't we have Tangerina and Skylene start today?" Brystal suggested. "I'm sure they have much more experience with manifestation than I do."

The girls were surprised by Brystal's recognition. They pretended to be annoyed by the opportunity, but deep down, Brystal could tell they were eager for the attention. Tangerina stood in the center of the tower and manifested an orange armchair with honeycomb tufts. Skylene made a bathtub appear beside Tangerina's chair, and it was overflowing with soap bubbles. After the apprentices were finished, Emerelda summoned a quaint vanity with several jewelry boxes, and Xanthous conjured a brick oven. Brystal didn't want to outshine the others, so she waved her wand and made a modest but elegant wardrobe appear.

"Well done, everyone," Madame Weatherberry said. "That just leaves Lucy—wait, where did Lucy go?"

No one had realized Lucy was missing until now and they looked around the room for her.

"She's hiding behind Tangerina's chair," Emerelda said. "I can see her boots peeking out from behind it."

Lucy groaned after her classmates found her. Clearly, she was hiding to avoid Madame Weatherberry's lesson, but Lucy pretended she was innocently searching for something on the ground.

"Sorry, I thought I saw my lucky shamrock," Lucy said.

"When did you lose it?" Xanthous asked.

"About four years ago," she said. "But you never know when or where things will turn up."

Lucy begrudgingly got to her feet and moved to the center of the tower. She thought long and hard about the object she wanted to manifest and smiled as her head filled with pleasant images of it. Unfortunately, Lucy was greatly disappointed when a stack of wooden coffins appeared in the corner of the tower.

"In my defense, I was trying to make a bunk bed," she said.

Madame Weatherberry gave Lucy a comforting pat on the back.

"A for effort, dear," she said.

Regardless of how much Madame Weatherberry encouraged her, Lucy left every lesson feeling worse than she had after the one before. And now that Brystal was armed with a magic wand, Lucy didn't have someone to commiserate with. Brystal sympathized with her friend, but she couldn't imagine the mental torment she was going through. With each passing day, Lucy's worst fears about *who* and *what* she was became more and more probable.

· · ★ · ·

The next morning, Madame Weatherberry's lesson started immediately after they finished breakfast. It was the first day since Brystal had arrived that Madame Weatherberry hadn't received a strange letter in the mail. Brystal couldn't tell if she was just imagining it, but the fairy seemed even cheerier than usual, and she wondered if not receiving a letter had something to do with that. Perhaps no news was good news.

Madame Weatherberry escorted her students and apprentices through the academy's picturesque property and halted the procession in the middle of two steep hills. Mrs. Vee was joining their lesson that day, and the students were curious about why the housekeeper was there.

"Now that you've been introduced to *improvement*, *rehabilitation*, and *manifestation*, today's lesson will focus on the fourth and final category of magic, *imagination*," Madame Weatherberry announced. "Always remember, a fairy's limitations are only defined by the limits of their imagination. Over the course of your careers, you'll encounter problems and obstacles without obvious solutions. It'll be up to you, and you alone, to create remedies for those particular predicaments. Mrs. Vee has kindly volunteered to help us with today's exercise."

"I have absolutely no idea what I've signed up for and am genuinely terrified! *HA-HA!*" Mrs. Vee said.

The housekeeper climbed to the top of the first hill and anxiously waited for the activities to begin.

"For this morning's assignment, each of you will use your *imagination* to magically transport Mrs. Vee from one hill to the other," Madame Weatherberry instructed. "Try to make your method as original as possible. Use what you learned in our *improvement, rehabilitation,* and *manifestation* exercises to bring your imagination to life. Lucy, we'll start with you."

"Ah, geez," Lucy said in despair. "Mrs. Vee, I'm really sorry for however this turns out."

The musicians' daughter cracked her knuckles and focused all her energy on the housekeeper. Suddenly, a massive sinkhole appeared underneath Mrs. Vee and swallowed her whole. A few tense moments later, another sinkhole appeared on the second hill and spat the housekeeper out like a piece of rotten fruit.

"Oh, thank God!" Lucy said with a deep sigh of relief. "To be honest, I wasn't sure we'd ever see her again!"

Mrs. Vee was anything but relieved. She got to her feet and wiped the dirt off her clothes with shaky hands.

"Madame Weatherberry?" the housekeeper asked. "Could we please add a clause about *safety* to your instructions? So today's lesson doesn't kill me? *HA-HA!*"

"Of course we can," Madame Weatherberry obliged. "Children, I don't think this will be a problem for the rest of you, but try transporting Mrs. Vee without the use of natural disasters. Brystal, you're up next."

To Mrs. Vee's delight, Brystal's approach was much gentler than Lucy's. She waved her wand and a giant bubble appeared around the housekeeper. The bubble floated through the air and calmly carried Mrs. Vee to the opposite hill.

"Well, that was just lovely," Mrs. Vee said. "Thank you, Brystal."

One by one, the students and apprentices stepped forward and applied their own solutions to the task. Tangerina sent hundreds of bumblebees buzzing toward Mrs. Vee, and the insects raised her into the air and plopped her down on the other hill. Skylene summoned water from a nearby stream, and it transported Mrs. Vee like a moving waterslide. Emerelda moved her hand through the air, like she was slowly waving good-bye, and a bridge made of golden topaz appeared between the hills.

"Wonderful work, ladies," Madame Weatherberry said. "Xanthous, that just leaves you."

Everyone turned to the boy—but he wasn't paying any attention to the lesson. Xanthous was staring into the distance with a disturbed expression, as if he had seen a ghost.

"Madame Weatherberry, who are *they*?" he asked.

Xanthous pointed, and the others looked in the

direction he faced. At the edge of the property, just inside the hedge barrier, were four people in matching black cloaks. The mysterious figures stood perfectly still and watched the fairy and her students in complete silence. The visitors instantly made everyone uncomfortable— no one had noticed them arrive, so no one knew how long they had been standing there. However, none of the children was more unsettled by the unexpected guests than their teacher was.

"Madame Weatherberry, do you know those people?" Emerelda asked.

The fairy nodded, and a complicated mix of anger and fear surfaced on her face.

"Unfortunately, I do," she said. "I'm sorry, children, but we need to postpone the rest of today's lesson."

Once their presence was known, the cloaked figures crept toward Madame Weatherberry and her students. Their bodies were completely covered except for their faces, and although they were shaped like women, the closer they got, the less human they appeared. The first woman had round yellow eyes and a pointed nose like a beak. The second woman's eyes were red with thin pupils like a reptile's, and a forked tongue slipped in and out of her mouth. The third woman had oily skin, enormous lips, and bulging black eyes like a fish. The fourth woman had green eyes like a cat, her face was covered in whiskers, and a sharp underbite poked out of her mouth.

"Hello, Celessste," the woman with the forked tongue hissed.

There was so much tension between Madame Weatherberry and the cloaked women, the students could have sworn the air became thicker.

"Children, this is Crowbeth Clawdale, Newtalia Vipes, Squidelle Inkerson, and Feliena Scratchworth," the fairy announced. "They're old acquaintances of mine."

Lucy crossed her arms and gave the visitors a distrusting glare.

"I'm guessing those are *chosen* names?" she said.

Feliena jerked her head in Lucy's direction. "You wouldn't *believe* some of the choices we've made," she growled.

The whiskered woman gave the children a creepy grin, exposing her piercing teeth. The students and apprentices took a fearful step backward and hid behind their teacher.

"All right, that's enough," Madame Weatherberry ordered. "Obviously, you've made the journey to speak with me, but I will not do it in front of my students. We will continue this conversation in the privacy of my office or not at all."

The women didn't object to Madame Weatherberry's demand. The fairy turned on her heel and escorted her unwelcome guests toward the castle. Brystal and her classmates had so many questions about the visitors, but as they looked to one another for answers, everyone was equally confused. Even Tangerina and Skylene were puzzled about what was happening.

"Mrs. Vee?" Tangerina asked. "Who are those women?"

Mrs. Vee watched the visitors move across the property with disgust. "Those aren't women," she said. "Those are *witches*."

The students and apprentices collectively gasped.

"Witches?" Skylene asked in shock. "But how do you know?"

"You can always spot a witch by her appearance," Mrs. Vee told them. "Witchcraft leaves a mark on those who practice it. The more a witch partakes, the more it changes her into a monster. And if my eyes aren't deceiving me, *those four* have had an awful lot of practice."

As the witches climbed the front steps, Crowbeth spun her head all the way around like an owl to send the children one final scowl before she entered the castle.

"But why are they at an academy of magic?" Emerelda asked. "What do they want with Madame Weatherberry?"

"I don't know," Mrs. Vee said. "But we'd all be wise to keep our distance from them."

The housekeeper's advice was reasonable, but keeping a distance was the last thing Brystal wanted. The witches only added to the ongoing mystery of Madame Weatherberry, and Brystal craved answers more desperately than ever before. As soon as she remembered the hole in her bookshelf, Brystal took off running as fast as her feet would carry her. She just hoped she could reach her bedroom before missing a single word of the fairy's conversation with the witches.

"Brystal, where are you going?" Lucy called after her.

"Bathroom!" Brystal yelled over her shoulder.

"When nature calls, nature calls," Mrs. Vee said. "That reminds me, I need to stop adding so many prunes to the oatmeal. *HA-HA!*"

Brystal hurried inside the castle and sprinted up the floating staircase to her bedroom on the third floor. When she peeked into Madame Weatherberry's office, she saw her teacher furiously pacing in front of the bubbling fireplace. The four witches stood around her, eyeing the fairy like vultures waiting for their prey to die.

"How dare you come here unannounced!" Madame Weatherberry said. "You have no right to barge into my academy like this!"

"You left us no choice," Crowbeth screeched. "You stopped responding to our letters."

"I told you I was *finished*," Madame Weatherberry exclaimed. "We're not working together anymore!"

"Now is not the time for reluctance," Squidelle grumbled. "The Northern Conflict is nearing the point of no return. The enemy is gaining ground and growing stronger every day. If we don't act soon, we'll be defeated."

"Then find someone else to help you," Madame Weatherberry snapped. "I can't do it anymore."

"Celessste, we ssstill want the sssame thing," Newtalia hissed. "We're all ssseeking a sssafer world and acceptance for our kind. Helping us end the Northern Conflict will move us one ssstep closer to that goal."

"Don't imply that you and I are the same!" Madame Weatherberry said. "If it weren't for people like you, people like me wouldn't have to fight for acceptance in the first place!"

"Celeste, don't act superior," Feliena growled. "Before you got the bright idea to start this academy, we all agreed the Northern Conflict was the best way to change the world's opinion about the magical community. We put our differences aside and created the plan together. None of us predicted it would last this long, none of us expected it would be this grueling, but like it or not, the conflict continues. Victory is still possible, but if we don't finish what we started, everything we've worked for will be lost."

Madame Weatherberry had a seat behind her desk and covered her face with her gloved hand. Brystal had never seen the fairy look so overwhelmed.

"You don't understand," she said. "I still believe in our plan—I can't help you because I can't face *her* again."

Brystal had no idea who Madame Weatherberry was talking about, but the way the fairy referenced the person gave Brystal chills. She hadn't thought her teacher was scared of anything or anyone, but obviously Madame Weatherberry was *deathly* afraid of whoever they spoke of.

"Celeste, you're the only one who *can* face her,"

Crowbeth screeched. "No one has the power to stand up to her but you—*no one.*"

"Each time I face her, she grows stronger and I become weaker," Madame Weatherberry said. "I barely survived our last encounter. If I fight her again I may never return."

"Yes, but last time we nearly won," Squidelle grumbled. "And you were more than willing to make sacrifices back then."

"Things are different now," Madame Weatherberry said. "I have an entire academy depending on me—I can't put myself in that kind of jeopardy again. Even if we resolve the Northern Conflict, there's no guarantee that the hate and hostility toward the magical community will stop. But once my students have finished their training, *they'll* accomplish what we've always wanted."

"You're putting an awful lot of faith in this academy," Feliena growled. "But do you honestly believe a world that burns people at the stake for sport is going to be persuaded by the *good deeds* of fairies? No! If we want to change the world, we must earn the world's respect. And bringing the Northern Conflict to an end is the best opportunity we've had in centuries."

"But General White has made great progress," Madame Weatherberry said. "I'm sure he's found a way to destroy her by now!"

"General White has done a brilliant job keeping the Northern Kingdom from extinction," Crowbeth screeched. "But we all know his army is no match for *her.* There's only one way to finish the Northern Conflict once and for all—and that's *you*, Celeste."

Newtalia leaned toward Madame Weatherberry and took her hand.

"Join usss," she hissed. "Together we can make a brighter future, not just for ourselvessss, but for your ssstudents asss well."

Madame Weatherberry went very silent as she considered the witches' request. Tears came to her eyes and she slowly shook her head, not because she disagreed with her visitors, but because she knew they were right.

"Fine," the fairy said with a heavy heart. "I will help you end the Northern Conflict. But afterward, I never want to see the four of you ever again."

"You'll find no objection from us," Feliena growled. "End the Northern Conflict, and we'll never need you for anything again."

"Good," Madame Weatherberry said. "Then God have mercy if I don't succeed."

The witches were pleased they had convinced her. Madame Weatherberry put a few of her belongings into a glass suitcase and left her office. Brystal hurried out of her bedroom and caught up to her teacher and the witches in the entrance hall.

"Madame Weatherberry?" she called to her. "Are you going somewhere?"

It was difficult for Brystal to pretend she didn't know what was happening, but not nearly as difficult as it was for Madame Weatherberry to pretend everything was all right.

"I'm afraid I have to leave the academy for a couple days," the fairy informed her. "The ill friend I was telling you about has taken a turn for the worse."

"Will you—I mean, will *she* be all right?" Brystal asked.

"I certainly hope so," Madame Weatherberry said. "Can you let Mrs. Vee and your classmates know I'm gone?"

"Of course," Brystal said.

The fairy gave her a bittersweet smile and led the witches out of the castle. Brystal ran after them and stopped her teacher on the castle's front steps.

"Madame Weatherberry!" she called. *"Wait!"*

"Yes, dear? What is it?"

To the fairy's surprise, Brystal threw her arms around her and gave her teacher a hug good-bye. Madame Weatherberry eyed the girl's curious behavior, not knowing what to make of it.

"Please be safe," Brystal said. "Illnesses can be contagious, you know."

"Don't worry, I'll be fine," the fairy said. "Please look after the others while I'm away."

Brystal nodded and released Madame Weatherberry from her tight embrace. The fairy tossed her brooch on the ground, and the golden carriage grew to its full size. She whistled to a field nearby, and four unicorns excitedly galloped toward the carriage and its reins magically fastened around them. The fairy and the witches climbed aboard the golden carriage, and it raced through the property, eventually disappearing into the hedge barrier.

Brystal waved as they left, but as soon as they were out of sight, she froze and looked into the distance with fear. She couldn't fight the terrible feeling that she'd never see Madame Weatherberry again.

CHAPTER THIRTEEN

THE WATCHER IN THE WOODS

W hile Madame Weatherberry was away, Brystal
spent the days practicing magic and the evenings reading *The Tales of Tidbit Twitch* to
her classmates. Although the exercises and reading were
productive, she mainly used them as a distraction from
her troubling thoughts. After eavesdropping on Madame
Weatherberry and the witches, Brystal finally had answers
to some of the questions haunting her, but the more she
had learned, the more elaborate the mystery had become.

Now she understood why Madame Weatherberry

had reacted so strongly to the mention of the Northern Kingdom. Something known as the Northern Conflict was destroying the country, and someone the fairy feared was at the center of it. The scaly black letters had been coming from the witches, not to update Madame Weatherberry about a *sick friend*, but to ask for the fairy's assistance with the conflict. And apparently, if Madame Weatherberry helped the witches end the Northern Conflict, it would ensure worldwide acceptance for the magical community.

But what was the Northern Conflict? How would Madame Weatherberry's involvement bring peace to witches and fairies? Who was the woman that Madame Weatherberry was afraid of facing? And the most disturbing question of all: Would Madame Weatherberry *survive* another encounter with her?

Brystal's mind never took a full break from the harrowing questions. She desperately wanted to talk to someone else about it, but she didn't know who to turn to. Emerelda and Xanthous wouldn't know any more than she did, Lucy had enough of her own troubles already, and Brystal doubted Mrs. Vee would be any help. She considered talking to Tangerina and Skylene, but if the girls heard that Brystal was spying on their teacher, Brystal was certain they would tattle on her.

So Brystal thought it was best to keep her worries to herself. The concerns weighed heavily on her heart, and the longer Madame Weatherberry stayed away, the more fearful and lonely Brystal felt.

On the third evening after Madame Weatherberry's departure, Brystal was a couple of minutes late to dinner. She was in the middle of a very exciting chapter of *The Tales of Tidbit Twitch, Volume 3* and quickly finished it before joining her classmates downstairs. As soon as she walked into the dining room, Brystal could tell something was wrong. Tangerina was sitting at the table with her arms crossed, and her cheeks were flushed. Skylene stood behind her friend and rubbed her shoulders. Emerelda and Xanthous sat back in their seats wide-eyed, like they had just witnessed a spectacle.

"What's going on?" Brystal asked the room.

"Ask *them*," Tangerina said, and pointed to the others.

"Lucy and Tangerina just got into a fight," Emerelda informed her. "It was intense."

"A fight about what?" Brystal asked.

"Lucy walked in and asked Tangerina to stop clogging the bathroom sink with her honey," Xanthous recalled. "Tangerina said she was surprised Lucy knew what a bathroom was. Then Lucy suggested Tangerina's personality, not her magic, is the real reason her family abandoned her. And finally Tangerina told Lucy she doesn't belong at the academy and said she wished the witches had taken her with them."

"That's when Lucy burst into tears and ran upstairs," Emerelda said. "Personally, I thought it was all really entertaining until she got upset. It reminded me of the dwarf boxing matches we used to have in the coal mine."

Brystal sighed. "Tangerina, why would you say something like that? You know Lucy has been having a difficult time with her magic."

"Don't blame *me*!" Tangerina exclaimed. "Lucy started it!"

"But you didn't have to join her," Brystal reprimanded. "You're an *apprentice*, remember? You should be more mature than that! I'm going upstairs to check on Lucy. Someone tell Mrs. Vee I'll be right back."

Brystal left the dining room and headed up the floating staircase. She prepared a list of positive and encouraging things to say to Lucy, but in case kind words weren't enough, Brystal waved her wand and made a tray of chocolate cupcakes appear. However, as she reached the third-floor corridor, something very strange caught her eye. The door to Lucy's bedroom had disappeared and a note had been pinned to the wall in its place:

Dear Madame Weatherberry,
   Thank you for believing in me, but the academy isn't working out. I'm leaving the school and returning to show business. I know my parents' tour dates so it won't be hard to find them. I wish you and the others the best of luck.

            XO, Lucy
            PS—Tangerina sucks.

Brystal was so alarmed by Lucy's note she dropped the tray of cupcakes and it shattered on the floor. Without wasting a minute, she waved her wand and made a coat appear over her shoulders and then hurried down the floating staircase. Her classmates had heard the tray drop and peeked into the entrance hall to inspect the shatter. They were surprised to see Brystal heading for the front door in such a panic.

"Where's the fire?" Emerelda asked.

"It's Lucy!" Brystal said. "She's run away!"

"Oh no!" Xanthous exclaimed. "What do we do?"

"You aren't going to do anything," Brystal said. "Madame Weatherberry specifically asked me to look after you guys while she was gone, so *I'm* going to get Lucy. You stay here in case Lucy or Madame Weatherberry returns."

"You mean, you're going into the *In-Between*? At *night*?" Skylene asked.

"You can't leave the academy!" Tangerina said. "It's against the rules!"

"I've got to find Lucy before a horrible monster in the forest does," Brystal said. "She hasn't been gone very long so it shouldn't be difficult to track her down. I'll be back as soon as I can!"

Despite her classmates' fearful and frantic pleas to stay, Brystal raced out the door, ran down the castle's front steps, and sprinted across the academy grounds. She reached the edge of the property and waited impatiently while an archway formed in the hedge barrier.

Once it finished, Brystal ran through the barrier's leafy tunnel and emerged into the creepy forest beyond it.

"Lucy?" she called into the dark woods. "Lucy, it's Brystal! Where are you?"

Brystal looked in every direction for her friend, but she could barely see anything. Eventually her eyes adjusted to the darkness, but still, she saw nothing except crooked trees and jagged boulders. She cautiously moved down the dirt path that snaked through the In-Between, jumping at every sound she heard.

"Lucy, are you there?" she whispered. *"Can you hear me?"*

With each step, Brystal became more and more frightened of her surroundings. Soon the dirt path split into two different directions, and Brystal had to choose which path to take. Both directions looked almost identical and Brystal worried she might get lost. To help herself navigate, Brystal waved her wand and made the rocks beside the path glow in the dark, marking the parts of the forest she had already searched.

Just as Brystal started to fear she was too late to save her friend, she heard the sound of sniffling in the distance. Brystal followed the sound through the woods and sighed with relief when she finally found Lucy sitting under a tree. Lucy's head was buried in her arms as she cried, and her porcupine suitcase and beaver-skull canteen sat on the ground beside her.

"Lucy!" Brystal exclaimed. "There you are! I've been looking everywhere—"

Brystal's voice startled her friend. Lucy jumped to her feet and swung a large stick at her. Brystal dropped to the ground and barely missed getting hit.

"Lucy, relax! It's just me! It's Brystal!" she said.

"What the heck is wrong with you?" Lucy said. "You can't just sneak up on someone like that in a dangerous forest!"

"Sorry, I didn't realize there was an etiquette to this place," Brystal said.

"What are you doing here?" Lucy asked.

"I'm looking for you," Brystal said, and got to her feet. "I found the note you left and I've come to talk some sense into you."

"Well, good luck," Lucy grumbled, and threw her stick aside. "I've made up my mind, Brystal. I'm not spending another day in that academy. I knew I didn't belong from the moment I laid eyes on the castle. Madame Weatherberry's lessons have only proved that."

"But that's not true," Brystal said. "Our training has just started! You just need more time and practice. Don't let what Tangerina said make you give up on yourself."

"Stop trying to make me something I'm not!" Lucy yelled. "Face it, Brystal—*I'm a witch*! I'll never be a fairy like you and the others! And if I keep using my abilities, I'll turn into a monster like Madame Weatherberry's friends. I'd prefer to keep whiskers and scales off my face, so I'm going to stay as far away from magic and witchcraft as possible. I'm leaving and there's nothing you can do to stop me."

Lucy picked up her porcupine suitcase, swung her beaver-skull canteen over her shoulder, and proceeded down the path. As Brystal watched Lucy walk away, something inside her changed. All the sympathy she felt for Lucy drained away and was replaced with irritation. She couldn't believe she had risked entering a dangerous forest only to have Lucy turn her back on her.

"Lucy Goose, you listen to me!" Brystal ordered. "You're the best friend I have at that academy, and I'm not about to lose you! I've lost too many people in my life to let you wander off like this! Whether you believe it or not, Madame Weatherberry has given us the opportunity of a lifetime, and I *will not* let you throw it away to play a *stupid tambourine* with your parents!"

Lucy was shocked by her remarks. *"Stupid tambourine?"*

"IT'S STUPID AND YOU KNOW IT!" Brystal yelled. "You have so much more to offer the world than that! You may not believe in yourself, but *I believe in you enough for the both of us*! So we are going to march back to that academy *right now* and continue our training! You're going to stop feeling sorry for yourself, you're going to stop making excuses, and you're going to work as hard as you possibly can to be the fairy I know you can be! And if we find out you're a witch along the way, *so what*? If you're a witch, then you'll be the *best witch* there's ever been! You're going to *out-witch* all the *witchiest witches* in the world! But I promise you, you will *never* become a monster on my watch! I'll always

be there to keep you in line and stop you from making mistakes, *JUST LIKE I AM RIGHT NOW*!"

Lucy was stunned by Brystal's emotional rant and stared at her as if Brystal was the scariest creature in the woods.

"Do you honestly believe everything you just said?" she asked.

"I risked my life following you into the In-Between! What do you think?"

Lucy went quiet as she realized how significant Brystal's gesture was.

"Wow," she said. "I don't think anyone's ever believed in me that much. And I have *thousands* of adoring fans."

"So have I convinced you to come back to the academy?" Brystal asked.

A sweet grin came to Lucy's face. Apparently, Brystal's tough love was much more effective than any words of encouragement.

"Yeah," Lucy said. "I think you have."

"Good." Brystal laughed. "Because if my rant didn't work, I was about to drag you by the—"

FWITT! FWITT! Suddenly, they heard a strange sound coming from nearby. *FWITT! FWITT!* Brystal and Lucy looked around the forest but couldn't find where the noise was coming from. *FWITT! FWITT!* Something was flying through the air, but it moved too fast for them to catch a clear glimpse of what it was. *FWITT! FWITT!* Brystal felt a light breeze across her cheek, and two arrows hit the tree directly behind her. *FWITT! FWITT!* Lucy looked down and saw a pair of arrows sticking into her porcupine suitcase.

"We're being shot at!" Lucy cried.

"By who?" Brystal asked in a panic.

In the distance, the girls saw three men step out from the darkness. The first man wore a yellow vest and had a rope tied around his waist, the second man wore a red cape and an axe swung from his belt, and the third man wore a green cloak and held a pitchfork. All three were dirty and scruffy, like they had been in the forest for days, and each of them carried a crossbow that was pointed in Brystal and Lucy's direction.

"Well, well, well," the man in yellow said. "It seems to be our lucky day! The Lord has led us to *two witches* in the same spot!"

"What did I tell you, boys?" the man in red bragged. "The rumors must be true! There's a whole *coven of witches* somewhere around here!"

"Sinful scum," the man in green sneered. "Did they really think they could live in the woods without anyone noticing? They're practically begging to be hunted down!"

Brystal and Lucy exchanged a glance of terror and slowly backed away from the men.

"They're witch hunters!" Brystal whispered. *"And they think we're witches!"*

"What should we do?" Lucy whispered back.

Brystal's mind went completely blank. Although her wand was securely in her hand, all of Madame

Weatherberry's training abandoned her, and there was only one thing she could think of doing.

"RUN!"

Without a moment to lose, Brystal and Lucy bolted into the forest and ran away from the men as fast as they could. The witch hunters whistled and cheered, excited for a chase, and charged after the girls. The men shot arrows at Brystal and Lucy, but fortunately the thick forest made it difficult to aim. The ground was covered in so many overgrown roots and rocks it was almost impossible to run without tripping, but Brystal and Lucy moved as swiftly as possible, knowing one misstep could cost them their lives.

As they ran, the girls looked back and forth between the men chasing them and the ground ahead. Their escape came to a dead end when they slammed into the flat side of a hill they hadn't seen in the dark. The witch hunters surrounded them, beaming with sinister glee. Obviously, watching their prey tremble in fear was their favorite part of the hunt.

"You're awfully young and pretty to be witches," the man in yellow sneered.

"That's because we're not witches!" Brystal cried. "We're *fairies*! You're making a terrible mistake!"

The men howled with laughter, like wolves howling at the moon.

"Did you hear that, boys?" The man in yellow laughed. "The girl in the sparkling garb says she's not a witch!"

"Who cares what they are?" the man in red said. "No one in the village will know the difference. We'll be heroes when they see the bodies!"

"Make sure to aim below their necks," the man in green instructed. "I want to mount their heads to my wall."

The witch hunters reloaded their crossbows and raised them at Brystal and Lucy. The girls closed their eyes and held each other in horror, expecting to be pelted with arrows at any moment.

Just as the men were about to pull their triggers, they were distracted by something rustling in the trees nearby. Suddenly, a massive creature emerged from the woods and plowed into the witch hunters. The men were knocked to the ground and dropped their weapons. Before they could get to their feet, the mysterious beast plowed into them again, crushing the men's crossbows under its feet. Brystal and Lucy didn't know if they were in more or less danger now that the creature had joined them. It was so large and moved so quickly in the moonlight that Brystal and Lucy could only see one piece of it at a time. They saw horns and hooves, nostrils and teeth, fur and metal, but not enough to determine what they were looking at.

"Let's get out of here before we're killed!" the man in red shouted.

The witch hunters fled into the dark forest, screaming like small children as they went. However, the creature stayed with Brystal and Lucy. It became very still and all three of them studied one another in total silence. Once her heart rate slowed down and her senses returned, Brystal remembered the magic wand in her hand. She waved it through the air, and dozens of twinkling lights illuminated the forest, and finally the girls saw what kind of creature was standing before them.

"Oh my gosh," Brystal gasped.

"You don't see that every day," Lucy said.

It wasn't just one creature, but two. An enormous knight dressed from head to toe in silver armor sat on the back of a giant horse. A pair of antlers grew out of the knight's helmet, and he wore a long fur cape. The horse had a pitch-black hide and a long ebony mane, and to the girls' amazement, the steed had three heads instead of one. Everything about the strange knight and his horse was incredibly frightening, but there was an otherworldly quality about them, too. Brystal couldn't explain why, but she trusted the knight, like he was some kind of sacred being.

The knight extended an open hand toward the girls. Brystal stepped forward and reached for his hand, but Lucy quickly pulled her back.

"Are you nuts?" Lucy said. "Don't go near that thing!"

"No, it's okay," Brystal assured her. "I think he wants to help us."

"How do you know that?" Lucy asked.

"He just saved our lives," Brystal said with a shrug. "If he wanted to hurt us, he would have already done it by now."

Brystal took the knight's hand, and he pulled her aboard his three-headed horse. He reached toward Lucy next, and after some coaxing, Brystal convinced Lucy to join them. The knight tugged on his horse's reins, and together, he and the girls traveled through the dark forest. Soon they returned to the dirt path and Brystal spotted the academy's hedge barrier in the distance.

"How did he know where to take us?" Lucy whispered.

"I have no idea," Brystal whispered back.

The girls climbed down from the three-headed horse and looked up at the knight in awe.

"Thank you for saving us," Brystal said.

"Yeah, and thanks for the lift home," Lucy said. "I'd give you a tip but I'm out of cash."

"What's your name, sir?" Brystal asked.

The knight didn't reply, but Brystal didn't take it personally. She had a sneaking suspicion the knight was quiet because he *couldn't* speak.

"Well, whoever you are, we're very grateful to you," she said.

Just then, a familiar galloping noise sounded through the forest. Brystal and Lucy turned toward the sound and saw Madame Weatherberry's golden carriage traveling toward them. The knight and his horse were so large they blocked the path, and the unicorns came to an abrupt stop behind them. The carriage door flew open and Madame Weatherberry stepped outside to address the knight.

"Horence?" the fairy asked. "What are you doing here? Is everything all right?"

Clearly the fairy and the knight knew each other. He steered his horse to the side of the path, revealing Brystal and Lucy standing behind him.

"Madame Weatherberry!" Brystal cheered. "You're back!"

She was overjoyed to see her teacher, but as Brystal walked closer to greet her, Madame Weatherberry seemed very different. The fairy was so exhausted she looked ten years older than when she'd left. There were bags under her eyes, her dark hair was gray at the temples, and *both* of her arms were now covered in gloves. Despite Brystal's warm welcome, the fairy was absolutely infuriated to see her students.

"What are you two doing outside of the academy?" she yelled.

"We—we—we—" Brystal struggled to respond.

"It's my fault, Madame Weatherberry," Lucy confessed. "I went outside the property because I thought it would be fun to explore the In-Between. Brystal knew it was dangerous and came to find me. We were attacked by witch hunters, but luckily, this weird knight guy saved us."

"How dare you disrespect me by breaking the rules!" Madame Weatherberry roared. "Both of you get inside the carriage! Now!"

Brystal and Lucy followed her instructions and hopped inside the golden carriage.

"Horence, thank you for your assistance tonight, but I'll take it from here," Madame Weatherberry told the knight.

The knight bowed to the fairy like she was royalty, and then slowly steered his three-headed horse into the forest and disappeared from sight. Madame Weatherberry joined her students in the carriage and slammed the door behind her.

"How could you do this to me, Brystal?" she snapped.

"Madame Weatherberry, I told you it was my fault," Lucy said.

"But Brystal let it happen!" she said. "I trusted you, Brystal! I asked you to look after the others, and you failed me! You have no idea how disappointed I am!"

Hearing this brought tears to Brystal's eyes. "I'm—I'm—I'm so sorry."

"I don't want to hear another word from either of you," the fairy said. "As soon as we get to the castle, you will both go straight to your rooms and stay there until I say so! Is that understood?"

Brystal and Lucy nodded and stayed silent. Neither of them had seen their teacher so livid before—they didn't even know the fairy was *capable* of such anger. It was like Madame Weatherberry had returned to the academy as a completely different person.

CHAPTER FOURTEEN

ANGER

Brystal barely slept after her and Lucy's night in the In-Between. Not only was she heartbroken about breaking Madame Weatherberry's trust, but every time she closed her eyes, she saw the faces of the witch hunters who had tried to kill them. Brystal had nightmares all night about dodging the men's crossbows. Every twenty minutes or so, she awoke in a panic and had to remind herself she was out of the forest and safe in her bed at the academy.

Although terrifying, the encounter wasn't a complete

surprise. Brystal knew the world was filled with people who despised magic and wanted to harm members of the magical community—but until last night, she had never seen the hatred with her own eyes. It was her first exposure to a very ugly side of humanity, and now that she had witnessed it, Brystal would never think of humankind in the same way again.

The morning after her restless night, there was a knock on Brystal's bedroom door and Tangerina poked her head inside.

"Brystal?" she said. "Madame Weatherberry wants to see you in her office."

Facing another wave of the fairy's extreme disappointment was the last thing Brystal wanted to do, but she climbed down the floating staircase to her teacher's office anyway. When she arrived, Madame Weatherberry's wooden door was opened a crack and she could see her teacher standing behind her glass desk, gazing through the window at the sparkling ocean. Brystal took a deep breath, braced herself for whatever was about to happen, and lightly tapped on the door.

"Madame Weatherberry?" she asked. "Tangerina said you wanted to see me."

As soon as the fairy turned around, Brystal could tell she was in a much better mood than the night before. She could still see that Madame Weatherberry's journey had taken an obvious toll on her—there were still bags under eyes, her hair was still gray at the temples, and gloves still covered both of her arms—but the teacher's cheerful spirits had returned.

"Hello, dear," she said. "Please come in and have a seat."

Brystal stepped into the office, closed the wooden doors behind her, and sat down across from Madame Weatherberry at the desk.

"I owe you a very big apology," the fairy said. "I was utterly exhausted when I arrived last night and I completely overreacted when I saw you and Lucy outside the academy. Tangerina spoke to me this morning and said the entire ordeal was her fault. She said Lucy tried to run away after they exchanged some hurtful comments and that you went into the forest to find Lucy. What you did was brave and selfless, and you didn't deserve such a harsh scolding. I hope you can forgive me."

Brystal sighed with relief and sank into her chair.

"You have no idea how glad I am to hear that," she said. "Of course I forgive you, Madame Weatherberry. I imagine the last couple of days have been grueling for you. It must have been very difficult, you know, *visiting your sick friend*. How is she doing?"

Brystal purposely brought up the topic in hopes of learning more about the Northern Conflict. Now that Madame Weatherberry had returned, Brystal wondered if her teacher and the witches had succeeded in bringing the conflict to an end. Unfortunately, Madame Weatherberry only elaborated on her original story.

"She's not well, I'm afraid," Madame Weatherberry said. "But she's a fighter."

"What's her name?" Brystal asked.

Madame Weatherberry went quiet and Brystal assumed she needed time to make up a name for her fake friend.

"It's Queenie," the fairy said. "We've known each other our entire lives. She's battling a terrible disease that grows stronger every day and it won't be long until it consumes her. Although it doesn't excuse my behavior, I hope that explains why I was so distressed last night. It's very hard watching someone you love in so much pain."

Even though Brystal knew the real reason Madame Weatherberry had left the academy, the fairy was very convincing as she spoke about her "sick friend." Brystal questioned if there was more honesty to her teacher's words than she realized. Perhaps "Queenie" and the woman Madame Weatherberry was afraid to face in the Northern Conflict were the same person? Or perhaps the disease her friend was battling was the conflict itself?

As Brystal searched for the truth in her teacher's eyes, she noticed a dark mark peeking out from under her new glove.

"Is that a bruise on your arm?" Brystal asked. "Did something hurt you?"

Madame Weatherberry glanced at her right arm and quickly pulled the glove over the exposed injury.

"Oh, that's nothing." The fairy deflected the question.

"Just a little mark I received while caring for Queenie. Poor dear hates being mothered and doesn't know her own strength. I didn't want anyone to worry so I covered it with a glove. But that's enough about all that."

Brystal could tell Madame Weatherberry was eager to change the subject so she didn't inquire any further into the matter.

"Now, moving on," the fairy said. "The main reason I called you here was to see how you're feeling. I wanted to speak with you and Lucy individually to assure you both that, regardless of what lurks in the In-Between, you're very safe within the perimeters of this academy. Still, I'm sure last night's events were traumatic for you."

"It was a brutal dose of reality," Brystal said. "I've always known the world hated people like us, but I never thought someone would actually want to hurt *me*. It all feels so personal now."

"Everyone thinks they're immune to discrimination until it happens to them," Madame Weatherberry said. "It only takes one tragic event to change your perspective forever."

Brystal nodded. "Last night, those men spoke to us like we were objects without feelings or souls. We pleaded for our lives and told them they were making a mistake, but they didn't even flinch. And although we did nothing wrong, they acted like we . . . like we . . . well, I don't know how to say it."

"Like you deserved to be punished simply for existing," Madame Weatherberry said.

"Exactly," Brystal said. "Thank God that knight showed up when he did, otherwise we would have been killed."

"His name is Horence," Madame Weatherberry said. "And believe me, my gratitude to him knows no bounds. He's rescued me from countless episodes of peril."

"Who is he?" Brystal asked. "Is he even human?"

"Not anymore," Madame Weatherberry said. "Many years ago, Horence was a commander in the Northern Kingdom's army. Along his travels, Horence had the misfortune of falling in love with a witch. The witch used to own a great deal of land in this area, including the grounds that our academy was built on. Naturally, such a relationship was forbidden, so for over a decade, Horence and the witch carried on a secret affair. When Horence's soldiers discovered the relationship, the men betrayed their commander. They burned Horence at the stake and forced the witch to watch it happen."

"That's terrible," Brystal said.

"As you can imagine, the witch was devastated," Madame Weatherberry continued. "To ease her broken heart, the witch conjured one of the darkest spells in witchcraft to bring Horence back to life. However, there are certain spells that are so ghastly they should *never* be performed, and the witch died in the process. Horence returned to life as a dark and unnatural being, a shell of the man he once was. Now he's doomed to roam the witch's property for eternity, and he spends his time saving others from suffering an untimely demise like his own."

The tragic story made Brystal so angry her eyes welled.

"They just wanted to be together," she said. "Why did humankind have to tear them apart? I'll never understand why the world hates a community that just wants to be loved and accepted. I'll never understand why people are so cruel to us."

"It's not about the *prey*, it's about the *hunt*," Madame Weatherberry said. "Humankind has always needed something to hate and fear to unite them. After all, if they had nothing to conquer and triumph over, they'd have nothing to fuel their sense of superiority. And some men would destroy the world for an ounce of self-worth. But that doesn't mean humanity is a lost cause. As I told Emerelda in the coal mine, this academy could produce the examples that inspire humankind to change their hateful ways."

Brystal shook her head and stared at her teacher in disbelief.

"I don't get it," she said. "After everything you've been through, how do you manage to stay so optimistic? Why aren't you angry all the time?"

Madame Weatherberry went quiet as she thought about Brystal's question, and then a confident smile grew on her face.

"Because *we're* the lucky ones," she said. "To fight for love and acceptance is to *know* love and acceptance. And anyone who actively tries to steal these qualities from others is admitting they've never known love at all. The people who want to hate and hurt us are so deprived of compassion they believe the only way to fill the voids in their hearts is to create voids in the hearts of others. So I render them powerless by refusing to accept their voids."

Brystal let out a deep sigh and looked hopelessly to the floor.

"It's a nice philosophy," she said. "It just seems easier said than done."

Madame Weatherberry reached across her desk and squeezed Brystal's hand.

"We *must* pity the people who choose to hate, Brystal," she said. "Their lives will never be as meaningful as the lives filled with love."

· • ★ • ·

Tensions between Lucy and Tangerina were at a record high. The girls spent all morning exchanging dirty looks without saying a word to each other, as if they were playing a vindictive game of catch. Their childish feud carried on into the early afternoon and frustrated everyone to no end. Finally, Brystal decided enough was enough and devised a plan to end the dispute. After lunch, she invited all her classmates to her bedroom.

"Is this an intervention?" Emerelda asked.

"Sort of," Brystal said. "I've asked you all here so we can settle things between Lucy and Tangerina once and for all."

"Good luck," Skylene said. "You're more likely to settle things between a squid and a whale."

Brystal ignored the remark and stuck to her plan.

"As everyone knows, Lucy has been struggling with her magic," she said. "Due to the strange and peculiar ways her abilities manifest, there is a possibility that Lucy is a witch. Because of this, Lucy has lost all self-confidence, and Tangerina has gone out of her way to make Lucy feel like she doesn't belong at our academy. It appears there will be no peace for anyone until we have an answer, so we're going to prove whether Lucy is a fairy or a witch *right now.*"

Everyone went stiff and nervously glanced at Lucy.

"How are we going to prove that?" Xanthous asked.

"The same way I discovered my own magical abilities," Brystal said. "We're going to have Lucy recite an incantation for witchcraft and an incantation for magic and see which one her powers respond to."

Brystal searched her bookshelves and retrieved her copy of Madame Weatherberry's *The Truth About Magic*. She opened the book to the page with the first incantation and handed it to Lucy, but her friend didn't accept it. Lucy looked down at the text and gulped in fear, like it contained the results of a serious medical examination.

"I don't think I should do this," she said. "Maybe *not knowing* is the better option."

"Lucy, you're going to find out eventually," Brystal said. "The sooner we know, the sooner we can plan for it. Now read the text aloud so the rest of us can go on with our lives."

With shaky hands, Lucy took the book from Brystal, set it on the floor, and knelt beside it. She paused for a couple of seconds to build up courage, then let out a deep breath, and reluctantly recited the ancient incantation for witchcraft. All her classmates stepped closer and hovered over her while she read.

"*'Ahkune awknoon ahkelle-enama, telmune talmoon ahktelle-awknamon.'*"

As soon as she was finished, Lucy covered her eyes with both hands in anticipation of something dreadful occurring. The others were also convinced the incantation would work, and they anxiously looked around the room, but nothing happened. They waited for five whole minutes, but Brystal's bedroom remained exactly the same.

"It must be *terrible* if you're all being this quiet!" Lucy exclaimed. "Did all of Brystal's books turn into killer crabs? Did Skylene turn into steam? Did Xanthous turn inside out? Did Emerelda disappear? Did Tangerina multiply? *Just tell me already!*"

"Lucy, everything is fine," Brystal said. "Nothing happened."

Lucy didn't believe her and peeked through her fingers to see for herself. She was shocked to find that nothing foul or grotesque had appeared or taken place.

"This can't be right," she said. "Are you sure this incantation works? Maybe there's a typo."

"Read the next one to be sure," Brystal said.

Lucy turned the book to the next page and read the ancient incantation for magic.

"'*Elsune elknoon ahkelle-enama, delmune dalmoon ahktelle-awknamon.*'"

When nothing happened for a second time, Brystal could feel her classmates starting to doubt the incantations in *The Truth About Magic*. However, after a few moments, everyone looked around the bedroom in amazement. Slowly but surely, thousands and thousands of weeds started growing out of Brystal's bookshelves and then quickly spread across the floor and ceiling.

"Holy plot twist," Lucy said to herself. *"I'm a friggin' fairy?"*

Everyone was floored by the discovery, but no one was more astonished than Lucy herself. She kept rubbing her eyes to make sure they weren't playing tricks on her, but the weeds did not disappear. Brystal beamed at her friend with a proud smile.

"Congratulations, Lucy and Tangerina, you're both *wrong*," Brystal said. "Now that we have confirmation that we're all on the same team, do the two of you have anything you'd like to say to each other?"

To everyone's surprise, Tangerina swallowed her pride and approached Lucy to make amends.

"Lucy, although all evidence pointed to you being a witch, I'm sorry for making you feel like one," she said. "I hope you'll forgive me, and I'll try my best to make you feel welcome at this academy."

"That was very nice, Tangerina," Brystal said. "Lucy? Is there something you would like to say to Tangerina?"

"Sure is," Lucy said. "For someone with so much honey, you sure spread a lot of vinegar!"

"Lucy!"

"Annnnnd," Lucy continued, "I'm sorry for all the hurtful yet witty things I said to you. From now on, I'll treat you like a member of my family, and all my insults will be meant with love."

Tangerina shrugged. "That works for me," she said.

The girls shook hands and everyone felt the tension lift between them.

"You see, this is how it should be," Brystal told the room. "As Lucy and I were reminded last night, there are enough people in this world who hate us and want to harm us—we shouldn't be fighting with each other, too. Before we leave, I want the six of us to make a pact. Let's promise to always encourage, support, and protect one another, no matter *who* or *what* tries to tear us apart."

According to the smiles on her classmates' faces, Brystal could tell there were no objections to her idea, only enthusiasm for it. Lucy reached into her jumpsuit, pulled out a pocketknife, and started cutting the palm of her hand with its small blade. The sight of her blood made the others scream.

"Oh my God, Lucy!" Tangerina yelled. *"What the heck are you doing!"*

"What?" Lucy asked innocently. "We're not making a blood pact?"

"A *verbal* pact is good enough for me," Brystal said.

"Oh, sorry," Lucy said. "I misinterpreted that one. Back to you, Brystal."

Lucy put her pocketknife away and wiped the blood onto her pants.

"So we're all in agreement?" Brystal asked. "We promise to look out for one another, to help one another succeed, and to inspire one another along the way?"

She put her hand in the center of their group, and one by one, her classmates placed their hands on top of hers.

"I promise," Emerelda said.

"Me too," Xanthous said.

"Me three," Skylene said.

"I promise, too," Tangerina said.

"So do I," Lucy said.

"Great," Brystal said. "Now everyone, help me get rid of all these weeds."

CHAPTER FIFTEEN

CIRCLE OF SECRETS

The following morning, Mrs. Vee rang the chimes to announce breakfast, and Brystal climbed down the floating steps to the dining hall. She and her classmates took their seats around the table, but strangely, Madame Weatherberry was absent. They all assumed their teacher was just running late until Mrs. Vee entered from the kitchen and started serving the meal without her.

"Who's hungry?" Mrs. Vee asked. "Today I'm trying a little recipe I invented called *egg-white surprise*. Last one to guess what the surprise is has to do the dishes! *HA-HA!*"

"Shouldn't we wait for Madame Weatherberry to join us?" Brystal asked.

"Oh, Madame Weatherberry isn't here," Mrs. Vee said. "She received a letter late last night and left the castle early this morning."

"Did she say where she was going or when she would be back?" Brystal asked.

The housekeeper scrunched her brow as she tried to remember.

"Now that you mention it, I don't believe she did," Mrs. Vee said. "She's probably making a quick trip to visit her sick friend again. She *did* say she wanted all of you to keep practicing your improvement, rehabilitation, manifestation, and imagination exercises while she's gone. Although you'll have to find another volunteer because I'm officially retired from *that* position! *HA-HA!*"

Hearing that Madame Weatherberry had snuck off without saying good-bye was troubling. The teacher's odd behavior must have meant the Northern Conflict was still going on, and Brystal felt foolish for having hoped it was already resolved. All her fears and concerns about Madame Weatherberry's safety immediately returned, depleting her appetite. Brystal sank in her seat and barely touched Mrs. Vee's egg-white surprise.

· • ★ • ·

The students and apprentices spent the rest of the morning outside practicing their magic. Brystal acted like a substitute teacher and encouraged her classmates as they conducted the exercises. She even gave them little assignments to boost their improvement, rehabilitation, manifestation, and imagination skills. With the truth finally revealed about what she was, Lucy practiced her magic with much more confidence than she had before, and she didn't cower from the challenges like she used to.

"Great job, Lucy!" Brystal praised her. "I asked you to manifest a hot spring, and that's *exactly* what you did!"

"Yeah, but it's filled with boiling manure," Lucy said.

"You're *still* making progress, and that's all that matters," Brystal said. "Now don't take this personally, but I have to do something about that smell before we all pass out."

Later that afternoon, the students and apprentices were forced inside the castle when a powerful rainstorm blew in from the north and drenched the academy grounds. As they waited for the storm to pass, the students and apprentices gathered in the sitting room and listened to Brystal read *The Tales of Tidbit Twitch* aloud. Unfortunately, the rain didn't stop, so Brystal continued reading into the evening. The evening turned into night and Mrs. Vee headed to bed, but the students and apprentices were enthralled with the story and begged Brystal to keep reading. Even the deer and elk heads mounted to the wall seemed interested.

"'Tidbit splashed through the mushy plains of Swamp Valley for three days and four nights,'" Brystal read aloud. "'Everywhere he turned, the flooded swampland looked exactly the same in all directions, and the mouse feared he had been wandering in circles. He began worrying he would never see his beloved Mouse Kingdom again, but then the hazy air began to clear and he saw a fiery volcano glowing in the distance. Tidbit's heart raced because he knew he had finally arrived at the dragon's secret lair.'"

Her audience cheered at the exciting passage, but not everyone was as enchanted by Tidbit's adventure.

"I'm *boooooooored*," Lucy moaned.

"What do you mean you're bored?" Emerelda said. "This is the part we've been waiting for! Tidbit is finally going to fight the dragon!"

Lucy rolled her eyes. "Look, I mean no disrespect to Mr. Tidbit—he's a peacock among penguins—but all we ever do is sit around and listen to Brystal read! Don't you guys want to do something *different* for a change?"

"But we're almost finished with the story!" Xanthous said. "Don't you want to hear the ending?"

"Oh please, everything in children's fantasy is the same," Lucy complained. "Let me guess, our lovable but unlikely hero, Tidbit, eventually arrives at the volcano and confronts the evil dragon. After a nail-biting fight, all seems lost for Tidbit, but then by a lucky twist of fate, the little rat manages to defeat the dragon and Tidbit learns he was much braver than he ever gave himself credit for. Am I close?"

Everyone turned to Brystal to see if Lucy was correct. Brystal was shocked by the accuracy of Lucy's guess, and her mouth dropped open.

"Spoiler alert," Skylene groaned.

"See, I told you!" Lucy said. "Now let's do something *fun!*"

"Well, you've already ruined our night," Tangerina said. "What else do you want to do?"

"I don't know, something crazy and spontaneous," Lucy said, and excitedly thought of different options. "Oh! Let's go *unicorn tipping!*"

"I am *not* going outside in this rain," Emerelda said. "If I catch a cold, I'll be coughing up emeralds for weeks."

"All right, fair enough," Lucy said. "Then maybe we could play a prank on Mrs. Vee? We can sneak into her bedroom while she's asleep and put her hand in a bowl of water! That's a classic!"

"Classically *cruel*," Brystal said. "Do you have any ideas that *don't* involve harming innocent people or animals?"

Lucy couldn't think of any off the top of her head. She went quiet and scratched her neck while she brainstormed the perfect activity.

"I've got it!" she exclaimed. "Let's break into Madame Weatherberry's office while she's gone! I'm sure we'll find *something* worth doing in there!"

Tangerina and Skylene were appalled by Lucy's proposition.

"We can't go into Madame Weatherberry's office!" Tangerina said. "It's against the rules! And we don't have many rules to begin with!"

"And you've already broken like half of them!" Skylene added.

"We'll only get into trouble if we get caught," Lucy said. "Madame Weatherberry will never know we were in there. We'll just pop in for a quick second, take a look, and if we don't find anything entertaining, I promise we'll turn around and leave. What do you say?"

Normally Brystal would never have endorsed such an activity, but she was intrigued by Lucy's idea. Since Madame Weatherberry had left the academy in such a hurry that morning, it was possible she might have left something behind that would reveal where she had gone. Perhaps Brystal would find a letter from the witches that Madame Weatherberry had left out? Perhaps she'd find a clue that offered insight into what the Northern Conflict was? If nothing else, Brystal could probably determine Madame Weatherberry's location on the enlarged Map of Magic hanging on the office wall.

"Come on, guys!" Lucy pleaded. "I feel like I'm in solitary confinement! Can we *please* do something stimulating just this once? I'm begging you!"

"You know, even though it's against the rules, sneaking into Madame Weatherberry's office is practically harmless," Brystal told the others. "And if it gets Lucy to shut up about being bored..."

"Fine, we'll give it a try," Tangerina said. "But I

sincerely doubt we'll get inside. Madame Weatherberry's office is probably protected by a powerful enchantment."

A sly grin came to Lucy's face. "Challenge accepted!" she said.

Lucy hopped off the sofa and proceeded into the entrance hall. The others followed her into the hall and up the floating staircase to the second floor. The children gathered around Madame Weatherberry's office and Lucy tried opening the doors the traditional way, but they didn't budge. Lucy then removed a hairpin from her pocket and sat on her knees while she examined the doorknobs and peeked through the keyhole.

Tangerina and Skylene nervously looked back and forth between the unicorn and gryphon carvings on Madame Weatherberry's doors—as if the magical creatures were judging their mischievous behavior.

"This is a mistake," Tangerina said. "We should go back downstairs and find something else to do. Maybe we could play a board game? Or hide-and-seek? Or we could dress up the mounted heads in the—"

"Door's open!" Lucy announced.

"What?" Tangerina asked in shock. "How did you get past the enchantment?"

"I just picked the lock," Lucy said with a shrug. "Come on! Let's go in!"

Lucy pushed open the doors and led her timid classmates inside. Madame Weatherberry's office was always a welcoming and cheerful place, but since it was strictly off-limits during their teacher's absence, the charming room felt eerie. The pouring rain and thunderstorm outside didn't help matters. With every flash of lightning, Madame Weatherberry's glass furniture lit up like chandeliers.

As soon as they were inside, Lucy started searching through all the fairy's cabinets and shelves. She pushed the potions and spell books aside, as if she was looking for something in particular. Her classmates stayed in a close huddle by the door, afraid to touch anything. Brystal stayed with the others but looked around the room thoroughly. She tried to spot something out of the ordinary, but unfortunately the office was impeccably organized and Brystal didn't see a single thing that seemed out of place.

"Aha!" Lucy exclaimed. "She still has it!"

"Still has what?" Skylene asked.

Lucy removed a beautiful crystal bottle from a cabinet and held it up for her classmates to see. As she presented the bottle, a devious smile spread across her face.

"Have you guys ever tried Fabubblous Fizz before?" Lucy asked.

"Fabubblous Fizz?" Xanthous asked. "I've never heard of it."

"It's a magical beverage," Lucy eagerly explained. "It's a celebratory drink the magical community serves on very special occasions. When my family was on tour a couple years ago, a member of the Goblin Tenors gave me a bottle for my eleventh birthday. Believe me, it's unlike anything you've ever tasted! When my parents brought me to the academy, I saw Madame Weatherberry had a bottle stashed in here. *We should have some!*"

"You can't drink that!" Tangerina said. "She'll know we were in here!"

"Put it back before you incriminate us!" Skylene said.

"Will you two lighten up?" Lucy said. "The whole cabinet is covered in dust. Madame Weatherberry won't even notice it's missing. *I'm going to take the first sip!*"

Before they could convince her otherwise, Lucy used her teeth to pull the cork out of the bottle and took a satisfying swig. After her first gulp, Lucy burst into a fit of giggles and held her stomach like the Fabubblous Fizz was tickling her from the inside out. She started hiccupping, and large pink bubbles floated out of her mouth.

"Now *that's* some good stuff." Lucy laughed. "Who wants a taste?"

"Not me!" Tangerina said.

"Me neither!" Skylene said.

"I'll have some!" Emerelda said.

Tangerina and Skylene were visibly disappointed in Emerelda's willingness, but it didn't stop her. Lucy passed the bottle to Emerelda and she took a sip. She swirled the Fabubblous Fizz in her mouth for a couple of moments in a sophisticated manner. After she swallowed, Emerelda started chuckling just like Lucy, and she blew bubbles out of her mouth one at a time.

"She's right—that's delicious," Emerelda said. "It reminds me of the Coal Brew the dwarfs used to drink in the mine, except it doesn't have the charcoal aftertaste. You guys are missing out if you don't give it a try."

Emerelda handed the Fabubblous Fizz to Xanthous, and he peered inside the bottle as if it contained poison.

"There isn't any *alcohol* in this, is there?" Xanthous asked.

Lucy had to think about it and Brystal could tell she didn't know the answer.

"Of course not," Lucy decided. "Go on, Sparky! Give it a try!"

Xanthous was overwhelmed by the peer pressure and took a quick drink. The sensation was much more amusing than he had predicted, and he laughed so hard bubbles erupted from his nose. After watching Xanthous's pleasant reaction, Tangerina and Skylene didn't want to be left out, so they tried the Fabubblous Fizz next. The girls giggled at each other and popped their bubbles as they burped them up. Brystal had the very last sip of Fabubblous Fizz, and just like the others, she chuckled as the fizzy beverage filled her stomach, and the bubbles tickled her tongue as they floated out of her mouth.

"All right, we've had our fun," Tangerina said. "Now let's get out of here before we wake Mrs. Vee."

"What are you talking about?" Lucy said. "We're just getting started!" She snatched the empty bottle of Fabubblous Fizz from Brystal. "I know what we should do next! *Let's play circle of secrets!*"

"What's circle of secrets?" Skylene asked.

"It's a version of spin the bottle that you play with unattractive people," Lucy explained. "No offense—I'd just rather have lemon juice in my eye than kiss any of you. The game is simple. We all sit in a circle and spin a bottle. Whoever it lands on has to share a secret they've never told anyone."

Before her classmates could object to playing the game, Lucy positioned everyone in a circle and sat them on the floor. She placed the bottle in the center and gave it a strong spin. As it came to a stop, Lucy blew on the bottle until it pointed to herself.

"Oh great! I get to start us off," she said. "Okay, I've got a good one! A few years ago, my family was performing in a variety show in the Western Kingdom. Well, it just so happened that Vinny Von Vic—the most famous tambourine player in the whole world—was performing in that same show. Naturally, I was jealous and I worried he would outshine me. So I locked him in his dressing room and he missed the performance. To this day, I still feel guilty whenever I think of old Vinny Von Vic, and sometimes when it's quiet, I can still hear him banging on that dressing room door."

"I *doubt* that's the worst thing you've ever done," Tangerina said.

"He was in there for three weeks and missed the birth of his first child," Lucy added. "All right, let's keep this pheasant flying! Who's next?"

Lucy gave the bottle another spin and it landed on Brystal.

"Oh gosh, this is a tough one," she said. "Actually, now that I think about it, I don't really have any secrets—not anymore, at least. When I was living in the Southern Kingdom, everything I did was a secret. I had a secret collection of books, I had a secret job at the library, and of course, being a fairy was the ultimate secret. I guess none of that matters now that I'm here. It's funny how a change of scenery can completely change someone."

Lucy groaned and rolled her eyes. "Yeah, it's *hysterical*," she said. "Moving on!"

She spun the bottle with gusto, and when it finally stopped, the bottle was pointing directly at Xanthous.

"I don't really have any secrets, either," he said.

"Are you *sure*?" Lucy asked.

When the others weren't looking, Lucy winked at Brystal. It suddenly dawned on her why Lucy wanted to play circle of secrets—she was trying to figure out what Xanthous's big secret was about the night his father perished in the fire.

"I'm positive," the boy said. "I spent so much effort hiding my powers I didn't have time for any other secrets."

"Come on, Xanny, I'm sure you've got one in you," Lucy said. "You've never done something you knew you weren't supposed to? You've never been caught in the middle of misbehaving? You've never committed a forbidden act that resulted in an accidental but horrific event?"

"Those are *very* specific questions," Emerelda noted.

Xanthous was confused by Lucy's interrogation, but it didn't take long for him to remember the event she was fishing for. The memory made the color drain from his cheeks. He looked to the floor with a devastated gaze, and he gripped his Muter Medal with both hands.

"Oh yeah," he said softly. "I suppose something like that *did* happen to me once."

"And?" Lucy pressed.

"I don't want to talk about it," Xanthous said. "It happened on the night my father died."

"I'm afraid you have to tell us," Lucy said. "Otherwise it's seven years' bad luck."

"Seven years?" Xanthous asked in a panic.

"I don't make the rules, I just play the game," she said.

Brystal covered Lucy's mouth and took over the conversation before Xanthous was traumatized any further.

"Xanthous, this game isn't going to give you bad luck," she said. "This is just Lucy's unique way of trying to help you. We all know how terrible keeping a secret can feel. Secrets are like parasites—the longer you keep them inside you, the more damage they cause. So if you ever want to talk about the night your father passed away, we'll be ready to listen."

The troubled boy thought about it and slowly nodded.

"You're right," Xanthous said. "It doesn't do me any good keeping it to myself. I just hope it doesn't change your opinion of me."

"Of course it won't," Brystal said. "We made a pact, remember? You couldn't get rid of us if you tried."

Her smile gave Xanthous the courage he needed. The boy sat straight up and let out a deep breath.

"A few nights before Madame Weatherberry recruited me into her academy, I was at home by myself," he told the others. "That night, my father came home from the pub earlier than he normally did. He walked into the house and caught me doing something I knew I shouldn't have been doing—it was something he'd repeatedly told me not to do. My father began beating me and I accidentally started a fire that burned down our house and took his life."

"What did he catch you doing?" Emerelda asked.

Recalling that night made Xanthous's eyes water and his jaw quiver. Everyone in the room was on pins and needles as they waited for him to answer.

"He...he...he...," Xanthous said with difficulty. *"He caught me playing with dolls!"*

After the confession was made, tears streamed down his cheeks and he covered his face in shame. His classmates were shocked, not because of what he had confessed, but because it was nothing even close to what they were expecting.

"Dolls?" Lucy exclaimed. *"That's* your big secret?"

Xanthous lowered his hands and peeked at his classmates.

"You don't think that's wrong?" he asked.

"Wrong?" Lucy blurted out. "Xanthous, do you

know how many men play with dolls in show business? Let me put it this way—if they all disappeared overnight, there *would be no show business!*"

"Really?" Xanthous asked. "You're not just saying that to make me feel better?"

"I never say things to make people feel better!" Lucy said. "Gosh, I'm so disappointed right now. I was hoping you were making weapons, or hosting rooster fights, or writing radical manifestos! Not in a million years would I have guessed it was something as simple as *playing with dolls.* If your father was cruel enough to beat his own son for *that,* then he deserves to be dead!"

The whole room gasped at Lucy's extreme statement, but in many ways, it was exactly what Xanthous needed to hear. Brystal knew what he was thinking without having to ask him. Xanthous had been raised to believe his interests and preferences were shameful and despicable—to finally have someone dismiss them as *simple* and *shameless* was the greatest gift he could have been given. The boy sighed with relief like an invisible weight had been lifted off his shoulders.

"I understand how you feel," Brystal told him. "It's ironic, but when I was growing up in the Southern Kingdom, I was *forced* to play with dolls. I was always furious about the expectations they placed on girls, but I never realized it was just as unfair for the boys."

Xanthous nodded. "Maybe it was for the best," he said. "If we had had everything we wanted, then we might never have found what we need now."

Brystal and Xanthous shared a warm smile, knowing how grateful they both were to put the Southern Kingdom behind them.

"That's it, we're done with this game!" Lucy announced. "Playing circle of secrets with you guys is like playing I spy with blind mole rats. Let's find something else to do."

"Oh, I have an idea," Tangerina said. "Why don't we play Leave the Office While We Still Can?"

"That sounds terrible," Lucy said. "Instead of playing a game, why don't we tell *ghost stories*? The weather is perfect for it."

"That sounds like fun!" Xanthous said. "Who wants to go first?"

"I know a good story," Emerelda said. "Back in the coal mine, the dwarfs used to talk about a phantom mine cart that moved through the caverns all by itself."

"Ooooooh, creepy!" Lucy said. "Go on."

A blank expression came to Emerelda's face. "Well, there was a phantom mine cart that moved through the caverns all by itself," she repeated. "What more do you want?"

"That can't be the best story you've got," Lucy said.

Emerelda bit her lip and squinted at the ceiling while she thought about it.

"Actually, there is another story I could tell," she said. "And the scariest part is that it's about someone who's still living. Have any of you guys heard of the *Snow Queen*?"

All her classmates shook their heads, excited to learn more.

"She's a real person causing a really big problem right now," Emerelda explained. "The Northern Kingdom has tried to keep her a secret to prevent mass hysteria, but when you live in the In-Between like I did, you tend to get the unabridged version of bad news."

"Wait a second," Brystal said, and leaned forward. "Did you just say she's causing trouble in the *Northern Kingdom*?"

"Trouble is an understatement," Emerelda said. "The Snow Queen is causing destruction like the world has never seen. Many years ago, the Snow Queen was just a simple witch with a specialty for controlling the weather. One night, an angry mob found her home and killed her family! The loss devastated the witch. Her rage made her powers grow stronger than ever before, and she became the Snow Queen we know today. Right now, as we speak, the Snow Queen is attacking the Northern Kingdom as part of her revenge against humankind. And according to what I heard, she has more than half the kingdom in her frosty clutches!"

"Oh, I *have* heard about this woman," Lucy said. "She's the reason the North has been so cold lately! My family had to cancel the northern leg of our last tour because all the roads were frozen!"

Skylene leaned close to Tangerina and whispered in her friend's ear: *"I wonder if the Snow Queen has anything to do with the Northern Conflict."*

The girls' conversation caught Brystal's attention and she jerked her head in their direction. She couldn't believe her ears—Skylene had said exactly what Brystal was thinking.

"Did you just say the *Northern Conflict*?" Brystal asked.

"Yeah," Skylene said. "Have you heard of it?"

"Once or twice," Brystal said. "Do you know what it is?"

"We wish," Tangerina said. "Me and Skylene heard Madame Weatherberry bring it up when she met with the sovereigns to talk about the academy, but we could barely make out what they were saying. She always asked us to leave the room before they started talking about it."

"In that case, I bet the Snow Queen *is* the Northern Conflict," Lucy said. "Every show worth talking about has a strong leading lady."

"But how can we be sure the Snow Queen actually exists?" Brystal asked. "How do we know it's not just a story?"

"My papa has customers who have seen her with their own eyes," Emerelda said. "They say the Snow Queen can summon a blizzard in seconds. They say she wears a giant snowflake as a crown and a fur coat made from the hair of her enemies. They say she abducts children from their homes and feasts on their innocent flesh. They say it doesn't matter how hard the Northern Kingdom's army fights her, she only becomes stronger and stronger. And most terrifying of all, they say the

Snow Queen won't stop until the whole world is covered in her icy wrath!"

As if Emerelda had planned it, the conclusion of the story was followed by a flash of lightning that made everyone scream.

"Well, *I* say it's time for bed," Tangerina said. "I've had as much mischief and horror as I can stand for one night."

"I agree." Skylene yawned. "I'm going to have nightmares enough as it is."

"We don't have to be *worried* about the Snow Queen, though, do we?" Xanthous asked. "I mean, there isn't a chance she might come to the academy, is there?"

"Probably not," Emerelda said. "The Northern Kingdom is so far away from here, I bet someone stops her before she gets close to us."

The classmates called it a night and headed for the door, but Brystal stayed seated on the floor. Her heart was racing after listening to Emerelda's story, not because the tale frightened her, but because of how frighteningly familiar it all sounded.

"Brystal, are you coming?" Lucy called from the doors. "I've got to lock up on our way out so it doesn't look suspicious."

"Just a moment," she said. "I want to check something before we go."

Brystal moved a chair under the enlarged Map of Magic that hung over the fireplace. She climbed onto the chair and took a close look at all the glittering stars that represented the different fairies and witches living around the world. However, when Brystal's eyes moved past the Northern Kingdom, the majority of the country was blank. Even the areas surrounding the major cities and the kingdom's capital were completely vacant of magical life. Brystal wondered if it was just a coincidence, or if the magical community had evacuated to save themselves from the Snow Queen's destruction.

Only a small cluster of five stars remained in the dark area of the Northern Kingdom, and among them was one of the brightest stars on the map. One by one, Brystal touched the stars with her finger and the names Feliena Scratchworth, Crowbeth Clawdale, Squidelle Inkerson, and Newtalia Vipes appeared next to them. Then Brystal touched the largest star in the group and gasped when the name *Celeste Weatherberry* appeared beside it.

"So *that's* Madame Weatherberry's secret," Brystal said to herself. "She hasn't been leaving the academy to visit a sick friend—*she's been in the Northern Kingdom fighting the Snow Queen!*"

CHAPTER SIXTEEN

PROMISES

B rystal tossed and turned all night with nightmares of Madame Weatherberry battling the Snow Queen. She dreamed the fairy was repeatedly knocked to the ground by a ferocious monster in a fur coat and snow-flake crown. Madame Weatherberry reached for Brystal and begged for help, but there was nothing Brystal could do because she was frozen inside a large cube of ice. Even as she woke up in a cold sweat, the images in her dream were so lifelike Brystal was convinced it was actually happening. And for all she knew, it *was*.

Between the nightmares of Madame Weatherberry in peril, and the dreams of witch hunters chasing her through the In-Between, Brystal was starting to think she'd feel more rested if she just stayed awake. She stepped out of bed and decided to take a walk through the castle to clear her head.

As Brystal walked down the third-floor corridor, she could hear a couple of her classmates snoring in their bedrooms. She passed Xanthous's door and remembered his painful confession from circle of secrets. Brystal's heart filled with sympathy for the boy. She decided to check on him and quietly pulled open his heavy steel door. When she peeked into his room, Xanthous was sound asleep on his metal bed, wrapped up in his foil sheets. He had set his Muter Medal on his iron nightstand, and while Xanthous slept, the flames on his body increased and decreased as he inhaled and exhaled.

Brystal felt strange watching him sleep, but it was nice to see Xanthous resting so peacefully. With his secret finally off his chest, she figured he was sleeping better than he had since arriving at the academy. Before leaving, Brystal waved her wand, and a collection of aluminum dolls appeared in the corner of Xanthous's room, so he would have a fun surprise to wake up to in the morning.

The castle was dark and quiet as Brystal moved through it, but she found the solitude comforting. She stepped outside and stood on the castle's front steps and was happy to see that the rain had finally stopped. The night sky was starting to lighten as dawn approached, and the gryphons were already awake, hunting for breakfast. Watching the majestic creatures flying through the air reminded Brystal of how lucky she was to live in such a wonderful place. She had been at the academy for less than a month, but already Brystal couldn't imagine living anywhere else in the world—and she hoped she'd never have to.

As she gazed around the property, admiring all the colorful trees and flowers, Brystal spotted something shiny moving toward her in the distance. Madame Weatherberry's golden carriage had returned to the academy, and Brystal was so thankful to see it she jumped up and down with excitement. Eventually the carriage pulled up to the castle's front steps and Brystal ran to it to greet her teacher.

"Madame Weatherberry!" she cried. "I'm so glad you're back! I was worried you—"

The carriage door swung open and Brystal stopped in her tracks—she hardly recognized the woman inside. Madame Weatherberry had aged another decade, she wore a thick violet coat that covered her whole body from the neck down, and there was a large black bruise on the left side of her face. She looked at Brystal and the castle in a daze like she was confused about where she was. Madame Weatherberry tried to climb down from the carriage, but she was so weak she could barely stand, and the fairy collapsed on the ground.

"Madame Weatherberry!" Brystal screamed.

· • ★ • ·

Madame Weatherberry spent the whole day resting in her office. The only person she allowed inside was Mrs. Vee, and that was to deliver bandages and rubbing alcohol. Brystal paced outside the doors and waited for the housekeeper to emerge with an update. When Mrs. Vee finally stepped out, the concern in her eyes told Brystal everything she needed to know.

"How is she?" Brystal asked.

"Better, but not by much," Mrs. Vee said. "I cleaned the wound on her face, but it was the only injury she would let me look at. A few of her bones might be broken, but she wouldn't let me get near them."

"Can't she heal herself with magic?" Brystal asked.

"Usually," Mrs. Vee said. "Unless the injuries were *caused* by magic."

"Did she tell you what happened?" Brystal asked.

"She said she slipped and fell while she was visiting her friend," Mrs. Vee said.

"A *fall*?" Brystal said. "She said a *fall* caused this?"

Mrs. Vee sighed. "I don't want to start rumors, but if I'm honest with you, I'm starting to get a little suspicious. With all the strange letters, the unexpected trips, the witches, and now *this*—I think something is going on that Madame Weatherberry isn't telling us."

Clearly, the housekeeper thought her suspicion was a brand-new discovery.

"I'm glad you found me this morning," Mrs. Vee said. "Lord knows Madame Weatherberry would rather have crawled into the castle than call for help. She wants to save the world, but heaven forbid if someone cares for *her*. What did you tell your classmates?"

"I just told them Madame Weatherberry returned early this morning and wasn't feeling well," Brystal said. "I tried to be as vague as possible so they wouldn't worry."

"Well, I hope it works," Mrs. Vee said. "Madame Weatherberry said she would like to speak to you now. Maybe you'll have better luck finding out the truth than I did. But I have to warn you, she's not in her normal spirits."

The housekeeper headed down the floating staircase to put the unused bandages away. Brystal knocked on Madame Weatherberry's door and peered inside the office.

"Madame Weatherberry?" Brystal asked. "Mrs. Vee said you wanted to see me."

The fairy was seated behind her glass desk and looked so exhausted Brystal thought she might fall asleep at any moment. She had popped the collar of her violet coat to conceal the bruise on her face. The veil on her fascinator was lowered to cover her weary, bloodshot eyes. Besides being tired and injured, Madame Weatherberry was completely drained of her cheerful disposition, and she stared at the floor with a melancholy longing.

"Close the door behind you," she said softly.

Brystal followed her instructions and then sat at Madame Weatherberry's desk.

"How are you feeling?" Brystal asked. "I heard you had a bad fall while you were visiting your—"

"You can stop pretending, Brystal," Madame Weatherberry said sharply. "I know you're aware of much more than you're letting on."

Brystal's initial instinct was to act like she didn't know what the fairy was talking about, but as Madame Weatherberry looked deeply into her eyes, Brystal realized a performance was useless.

"How did you know?" she asked.

"Sometimes magic has a mind of its own," Madame Weatherberry said. "On your first day at the academy, I suspected the castle put you in a bedroom directly above my office for a reason. It wasn't until I was leaving with the witches, and you hugged me good-bye, that I realized *why*. The castle put you in that room because it *wanted* you to spy on me. It knew we would be having this conversation long before I did."

"Madame Weatherberry, I don't understand," Brystal said. "What conversation are we having?"

"Before we get into that, I want to make sure we're on the same page," the fairy said. "I'm sure you've developed a few theories to explain my questionable behavior. So tell me what you think is going on, and I'll fill in the blanks."

Brystal was thrilled for an opportunity to finally learn the truth, but she worried that Madame Weatherberry wasn't in the right state of mind to be handing out information.

"Are you sure you want to do this now?" she asked. "I don't want you to regret it later."

"I insist," Madame Weatherberry said.

"All right, then," Brystal said. "From the information I've gathered so far, I know you haven't been leaving the academy to visit a sick friend—you've been traveling to the Northern Kingdom to help solve something called the Northern Conflict."

"And what do you suspect the Northern Conflict is?" Madame Weatherberry asked.

Brystal hesitated to respond. "As ridiculous as it sounds, I believe the Northern Conflict is just a code name for a woman known as the Snow Queen."

"Go on," the fairy said.

"Well, the Snow Queen is a very powerful witch who's been attacking the Northern Kingdom," Brystal continued. "She's covered the kingdom in icy blizzards and caused massive amounts of destruction. No matter what the Northern Kingdom's army does, they haven't been able to defeat her yet. Before you had the idea to start our academy, you saw defeating the Snow Queen as an opportunity to gain worldwide acceptance for the magical community. You thought if someone *like you* saved the world, then the world would finally have a rea-son to respect people *like us*. So you teamed up with the witches and created a plan to stop her, but it's been more difficult than you predicted."

Brystal felt silly after hearing herself say it all out loud. She half expected Madame Weatherberry to laugh at the outlandish theory, but the fairy never flinched.

"You're only wrong about one thing," Madame Weatherberry said.

"Which part?" Brystal asked.

"The Snow Queen *is* the sick friend that I've been visiting," she said. "I haven't been lying about that. After a very tragic loss, my dear friend Queenie became infected with *hate*—and hate is the most powerful disease on the planet. For years, I watched the illness consume her and change her into a monster, and regrettably, I did nothing to help her. By the time she was wreaking havoc on the Northern Kingdom, it was too late to reason with her. Queenie has been blinded by vengeance, and now violence is the only language she speaks."

"But how could you be friends with a witch in the first place?" Brystal asked. "Wasn't she full of evil and darkness to begin with?"

"It's possible to love a person beyond their demons, Brystal," Madame Weatherberry said. "After all, there was a chance that Lucy was a witch, but it didn't stop you from following her into the In-Between. You chose to love Lucy for *who* she was instead of *what* she was, and I made the same choice with Queenie. But unlike you, I failed Queenie as a friend. The angrier and more hateful she became, the more distance I put between us. I abandoned her when she needed me most, and now I'm partially to blame for what she's become."

"Then she's still alive, isn't she?" Brystal asked. "If you had already defeated her, you wouldn't be referring to her in present tense."

"My friend has been dead for years," she said. "But unfortunately, the Snow Queen is still very much alive, and stronger than ever."

Brystal glanced up at the enlarged Map of Magic above the fireplace. "If she's so strong, why doesn't she appear on the map?" she asked.

"I'm afraid you won't find the Snow Queen on any Map of Magic," Madame Weatherberry said. "She's made herself untraceable so she can attack without warning. I've managed to stop her destruction from spreading beyond the Northern Kingdom, but each encounter is more taxing than the last."

"You aren't going to face her again, are you?" Brystal asked.

Madame Weatherberry closed her eyes and nodded in despair.

"I'm afraid I have no choice," she said. "No one else *can* face the Snow Queen. Right now I'm the only thing standing in the way of her attempts at global obliteration."

"But, Madame Weatherberry, you can't!" Brystal objected. "Fighting her in your condition would be suicide!"

Madame Weatherberry raised a hand to silence Brystal, and her eyes beamed with a grave urgency.

"Now we must have the conversation I was referring

to earlier," Madame Weatherberry said. "Please don't share this with the others, but there is a very strong possibility I won't survive defeating the Snow Queen. I remain optimistic, but one must never let positivity outweigh practicality. It's only a matter of time before I'm called back to the Northern Kingdom, and if I should perish, I want *you* to take over the academy."

"Me?" Brystal asked in shock. "But what about Mrs. Vee? Or Tangerina? Or Skylene?"

"Mrs. Vee and the girls aren't as strong as you are, Brystal," the fairy said. "From the moment I placed the magic wand in your hand, and watched your star on the Map of Magic grow, I knew you were the only person who could replace me. So please, if I don't live to see another year, promise me you'll continue my work, promise me you'll help your classmates reach their full potential, and promise me you'll use your magic to help and heal people, and change the world's perspective of the magical community."

Tears ran down Brystal's face as she imagined a world without Madame Weatherberry. She couldn't believe the responsibility her teacher was asking her to accept, but Brystal knew in her heart there was nothing she *wouldn't* do for the fairy.

"No one could ever replace you, Madame Weatherberry," she said. "I could never repay you for the life you've given me, but I promise to continue your legacy in your absence, whether that day comes soon, or decades from now."

A faint grin grew on the fairy's face, but it quickly faded. Brystal could tell there was something else that Madame Weatherberry needed to discuss with her and it was a topic the fairy dreaded with all her might.

"And now I'm afraid I have an even greater request to ask of you," Madame Weatherberry said. "It brings me great pain to place such a heavy burden on your shoulders, but there is no way around it."

Brystal was confused. She couldn't imagine a bigger task than the one she had already accepted.

"What is it?" she asked.

Madame Weatherberry took a deep breath before making the difficult request.

"In the event that I perish *without* defeating the Snow Queen," she said with difficulty, "then *you* must kill her, Brystal."

Brystal felt like she had been kicked in the stomach. Her heart began racing, her palms became sweaty, and the office started spinning around her.

"Madame Weatherberry, I can't *kill the Snow Queen*!" she exclaimed. "I've never hurt anyone before! I couldn't even defend myself against the witch hunters— I panicked under the pressure!"

"That wasn't your fault—it was *mine*," Madame Weatherberry said. "I've made a grave mistake as your teacher. My lessons have been preparing you and your classmates for the world I *wanted* you to live in, but I have *not* prepared you for the world that actually exists. Starting tomorrow, I'm going to begin instructing you and the others in how to use magic to defend yourselves. You may not be ready to face the Snow Queen today, but one day you will be."

"But, Madame Weatherberry, I'm only fourteen years old!" Brystal reminded her. "I'm just a child! You can't ask me to do this!"

"Brystal, you may be young, but you've never had the luxury of being a *child*," Madame Weatherberry said. "You've been a fighter since the day you were born. You looked beyond the limits the world placed upon you and strove for a better life, and now you must look beyond the limits you're placing upon yourself and strive for a better world. If neither of us can successfully defeat the Snow Queen, then everything—the world, the academy, and life as we know it—will be destroyed."

Madame Weatherberry was putting Brystal in an impossible position. She had never killed anything before, but now she was being asked to kill the most powerful witch in the world. Brystal wanted to refuse her request with every fiber of her being, but Madame Weatherberry gazed at her with such desperation in her eyes, Brystal didn't have the heart to disappoint the fairy. She looked to the floor and reluctantly nodded in agreement.

"Okay," Brystal said. "I hope and pray it never comes to that, but if you can't kill the Snow Queen . . . I will."

After Brystal made her second promise, Madame Weatherberry closed her eyes, leaned back in her chair, and sighed with relief.

"Thank you, Brystal," the fairy said. "You have no idea how comforting it is to hear you say that. Now if you'll please excuse me, I should rest. We'll both need all our strength for the days ahead."

· • ★ • ·

The next morning, Madame Weatherberry met her students and apprentices on the castle's front lawn to begin their first lesson in magical self-defense. The fairy hadn't joined them for breakfast, and when she finally appeared, the children were shocked to see their teacher in such a fragile state. Besides her bruised face, Madame Weatherberry walked with a glass cane and needed Mrs. Vee's assistance to climb down the castle's front steps. She was completely drained of her usual charm and energy, and had to conduct the lesson while sitting on a glass stool.

"Please forgive my delicate appearance," Madame Weatherberry told her concerned pupils. "I'm recovering from a nasty fall I had while visiting my friend."

"Did you fall off a *cliff*?" Lucy asked.

"It looks worse than it feels," Madame Weatherberry said, and swiftly changed the subject. "Now for today's lesson, we'll be using our magic for a purpose we haven't explored yet. It doesn't matter how much joy and comfort we spread; because of the challenging times we live in, it's very likely that we'll cross paths with people and creatures who wish to harm us. And when the situation is justified, we can use our magic to protect ourselves and others from danger. Your assignment this morning is to use your magic to defend yourself from the forces trying to hurt you. Xanthous, we'll start with you."

Xanthous gulped nervously. "And what *kind* of forces will I be defending myself from?" he asked.

Instead of responding, Madame Weatherberry tapped her cane on the ground six times, and six scarecrows appeared in the nearby field. The fairy tapped her cane again, and the first scarecrow came to life and detached itself from its wooden post. As soon as its feet touched the ground, the scarecrow charged toward Xanthous with arms flailing in all directions. The boy screamed and the scarecrow chased him in circles around the property.

"I'm not ready for this!" Xanthous yelled. "I think someone else should go first!"

"These situations can be alarming, but it's important to remain calm and keep a clear head," Madame Weatherberry said. "Take a deep breath and imagine the quickest way to disarm your attacker."

Despite the fairy's recommendations, Xanthous couldn't summon tranquility to save his life. The scarecrow eventually caught up to the boy and wrestled him to the ground. His classmates desperately wanted to help him, but Madame Weatherberry wouldn't let them intervene. Xanthous removed his Muter Medal and, thanks to his anxiety, his body was instantly engulfed in flames. The scarecrow was burned to a crisp and crumbled into a pile of ashes. Xanthous's classmates cheered for him, and the boy stayed on the ground until he caught his breath.

"Well done, Xanthous," Madame Weatherberry said. "Tangerina, you're up next."

For the rest of the morning, Madame Weatherberry's students took turns magically defending themselves from the enchanted scarecrows. Tangerina splashed her scarecrow's feet with honey, and it became stuck to the ground. Emerelda trapped her scarecrow inside an emerald cage before it even climbed down from its wooden post. Skylene pointed her finger at her scarecrow, and a powerful geyser erupted from her fingertip and ripped it to shreds. Brystal waved her wand, and a flock of white doves raised her scarecrow into the air and dropped it into the sparkling ocean behind the castle. Lucy clapped her hands, and her scarecrow was crushed by a massive piano that fell from the sky.

"Finally, something I'm good at!" Lucy said.

Madame Weatherberry's self-defense lesson was by far the most enjoyable lesson the students and apprentices had participated in. They laughed and applauded one another as they defeated the scarecrows one by one. Brystal was envious of the fun her classmates were having with the assignment. Unbeknownst to the others, Madame Weatherberry's lesson was designed specifically for *her*, and the exercises were preparing Brystal for a potential confrontation with the Snow Queen. It was hard for her to enjoy herself when the fate of the world depended on how well she perfected her skills.

"Terrific work, everyone," Madame Weatherberry said, and clapped with the little energy she could muster. "You've done a wonderful job defending yourself from *one* attacker, but let's see how you manage when you're outnumbered by the—"

"Madame Weatherberry!" Skylene suddenly shouted. *"The witches are back!"*

Everyone jerked in the direction Skylene pointed to, and sure enough, they saw four cloaked figures standing at the edge of the property. Just as on their previous visit, the witches instantly made the children uneasy, but no one was more fearful than Brystal. She knew there was only *one* reason why the witches had traveled to the academy.

As soon as their presence was known, Crowbeth, Newtalia, Feliena, and Squidelle crept toward the fairy and her students. Madame Weatherberry was already so fatigued it was hard to gauge her reaction to the unexpected guests. The fairy slowly got to her feet and stared at the approaching witches with a stoic gaze. Before they exchanged a single word in front of the children, Madame Weatherberry headed for the castle, and the witches followed her.

"I suppose this means the rest of our lesson is postponed," Brystal told the others. "I think I'll take a quick nap before lunch."

Brystal hurried into the castle and ran up the floating staircase to her bedroom. By the time she looked through the hole in her bookshelf and peered into Madame

Weatherberry's office, her teacher was already seated behind her glass desk. The witches hovered over the fairy like looming predators. Madame Weatherberry rested her head on her hand and didn't even look up at her visitors.

"Well? Get on with it," the fairy said in a faint voice. "What news have you brought this time?"

"King Nobleton is dead," Crowbeth screeched.

Madame Weatherberry sat straight up in her chair.

"What?" she gasped. "He didn't evacuate Tinzel Heights before she attacked?"

"No," Squidelle grumbled. "General White warned him she was approaching and told him to leave the capital, but the king was stubborn and ignored his advice. He and the royal family were in the middle of dinner at the palace when she struck. No one survived."

"That foolish, foolish man," Madame Weatherberry said, and angrily shook her head. "I always knew his pride would be the death of him."

"Only one city remains in the Northern Kingdom," Feliena growled. "The entire population has fled to Appleton Village—and it's only a few miles away from Tinzel Heights. General White is days away from surrendering, and when he does, the kingdom will face extinction!"

"What about the other sovereigns?" Madame Weatherberry asked. "Why haven't King Champion or Queen Endustria or King Warworth sent reinforcements? Don't they realize their kingdoms are in just as much danger as the North?"

"The sovereigns are in denial," Crowbeth screeched. "Nobleton assured them he had the situation under control, so *that* is what the monarchs choose to believe. General White has sent word of Nobleton's death, but they've *still* denied his requests for help!"

"The sovereigns believe the conflict can be contained by closing the borders," Feliena growled. "They've shut down the Protected Paths, and now the Northern refugees are trapped. The truth is, Champion, Endustria, and Warworth will not recognize the threat until the destruction crosses into their kingdoms."

"Those selfish idiots!" Madame Weatherberry yelled, and hit her desk with a clenched fist. "I met with the monarchs and warned them of the danger! All of this could have been avoided if they had granted General White's first request for help!"

Madame Weatherberry closed her weary eyes and massaged her graying temples while she contemplated what to do next.

"I thought I would have more time to rest...," she said weakly. "I wanted to be stronger before I faced her again.... I didn't think it would be so soon...."

"Celessste, we mussst ssstrike!" Newtalia hissed. "Thisss could be our lasst chance to sssecure the ressspect we dessserve!"

To Brystal's surprise, Madame Weatherberry looked toward the ceiling at the exact spot where she was watching from. She knew the next thing out of Madame Weatherberry's mouth was meant for her ears.

"You're wrong, Newtalia," the fairy said. "If we don't succeed, *someone else* will secure acceptance for our community in the future. And I have absolute confidence in them."

The message was so intimate and direct Brystal had to remind herself she wasn't actually in the room with Madame Weatherberry. The witches weren't sure *who* the fairy was talking to and looked around the office in confusion. Madame Weatherberry stood with difficulty and collected her suitcase.

"If it must be done, it must be done," she told the witches. "We can leave as soon as I say good-bye to my students."

Madame Weatherberry hobbled out of her office and the witches followed. Brystal couldn't believe the fairy's courage—she could barely stand, and yet she was willing to stand up to the Snow Queen in spite of her failing condition. Brystal's stomach was in knots as she worried about losing her teacher and fulfilling the promises she had made her.

By the time she and the others regrouped, everyone was standing outside the castle and Madame Weatherberry had already broken the news of her departure.

"You're leaving *again*?" Tangerina said. "Already?"

"Unfortunately so," Madame Weatherberry said. "My friend has become very ill and doesn't have much time left. I need to say good-bye while I still have the chance."

"When will you be back?" Skylene asked.

"I don't know," Madame Weatherberry said. "I may be gone for a long time, so I want you to continue your training while I'm away. Brystal will be in charge until I return, so please listen to her and show her the respect you'd normally give me."

Madame Weatherberry became teary-eyed as she said farewell.

"I'm going to miss you all very, very much," the fairy said. "Being your teacher has been the greatest privilege of my life, and watching you all blossom into fairies has been my greatest joy. Be good to one another, children."

They were puzzled by their teacher's touching remarks. Madame Weatherberry hugged each of her students, her apprentices, and Mrs. Vee good-bye. When it was Brystal's turn, Brystal pulled her teacher into a tight embrace so she could whisper into Madame Weatherberry's ear without the others hearing it.

"Please don't go," Brystal whispered. *"We aren't ready to lose you."*

"I wish I could stay," Madame Weatherberry whispered back. *"But the universe has other plans for me."*

"Then take me with you," Brystal pleaded. "Let's face the Snow Queen together. You don't have to do this on your own."

"The others need you more than I do," the fairy said. "Take care of them, Brystal. And please, remember what you promised me."

Madame Weatherberry tossed her brooch on the ground, and the golden carriage grew to its full size.

Four unicorns emerged from a nearby field, and the carriage's reins magically fastened around them. The witches helped Madame Weatherberry into the carriage and took their seats beside her. As they traveled through the property, Madame Weatherberry looked out the window at the grounds, the castle, and the students of her beloved academy, and with one final bittersweet smile, the fairy said a thousand good-byes.

"That was odd," Emerelda said. "She's coming back? Right?"

Mrs. Vee and the children turned to Brystal for an answer. Even after Madame Weatherberry's carriage disappeared into the hedge barrier, Brystal continued staring into the distance so the others didn't detect the dishonesty in her eyes.

"Of course she's coming back," Brystal said. "Madame Weatherberry would never abandon us. *Never.*"

· • ★ • ·

Two whole weeks passed without any word whatsoever from Madame Weatherberry. Brystal didn't think it was humanly possible to worry more than she already was, but her concerns multiplied the longer she waited. She practically lived on the castle's front steps while the fairy was gone, and she spent the majority of each day eyeing the edge of the property, hoping her teacher's golden carriage would reappear in the distance.

Every few hours, Brystal snuck into Madame Weatherberry's office to check the fairy's whereabouts on the Map of Magic. Thankfully, her teacher and the witches' stars were still shining in the Northern Kingdom, so Brystal knew Madame Weatherberry was alive.

By the end of Madame Weatherberry's second week away from the academy, Brystal was so distraught she couldn't hide her anguish anymore. She kept to herself and avoided her classmates whenever possible. She barely spoke, but when she did, it was only to bark out orders or make passive-aggressive comments while she supervised the self-defense lessons. The students became so good at the exercises, they could each battle a dozen scarecrows on their own, but Brystal still forced them to practice harder and longer each day.

"Tangerina, that honey needs to be deeper! Xanthous, those flames need to be higher! Skylene, that water won't be enough to stop a man in armor! Emerelda, that cage needs to be stronger! And, Lucy, self-defense is about more than just dropping heavy instruments on your enemies— think of something else! Everyone do it again!"

Her classmates were getting tired of Brystal's attitude, but no one was more irritated than Lucy. Brystal's constant commanding and criticizing flustered Lucy to no end and she eventually lost her patience.

"That's it!" Lucy shouted. "We're not practicing anymore!"

Before Brystal could enchant a new batch of scarecrows for the lesson, Lucy snatched Brystal's wand out of her hand and held it above her head.

"Lucy, give me back my wand!" Brystal ordered.

"No!" Lucy said. "I'm sick of you squawking at us!"

"Stop being so immature!" Brystal said. "Madame Weatherberry told you to respect me!"

"I'll respect you when *the real you* shows up!" Lucy said. "What's gotten into you, Brystal? You've been acting mean and moody ever since Madame Weatherberry left. I know something is wrong and I'm not giving back your wand until you tell us what's going on!"

"Nothing is going on!" Brystal lied. "Madame Weatherberry left me in charge! I'm trying to train you!"

"And *what* are you training us for?" Lucy asked. "You've been drilling us like we're going to war!"

"WELL, MAYBE WE ARE!" Brystal yelled.

As soon as the words escaped her mouth, Brystal knew there was no going back. Her outburst proved Lucy's suspicions correct, and the rest of her classmates became just as concerned. Brystal desperately wanted to explain herself, but Madame Weatherberry had specifically asked her not to share the truth with her classmates. Brystal didn't know what to do and was suddenly overwhelmed. She sat on the castle's front steps, and tears spilled down her face.

"Brystal, what's the matter?" Emerelda asked. "Why are you crying?"

"I wish I could tell you," Brystal said.

"Of course you can tell us," Tangerina said.

"We might be able to help you," Skylene said.

"No, it's between me and Madame Weatherberry," Brystal said. "I don't want you to worry about it."

"It's a little too late for that," Lucy said. "Come on, whatever's troubling you can't be as bad as you think it is. I mean, it's not like it's the end of the world."

Lucy's comment only made Brystal cry even harder. Xanthous sat on the steps beside her and placed a comforting hand on her shoulder.

"Please tell us what's wrong," he said sweetly. "Secrets are like parasites, remember?"

Her friends' curiosity made the situation even more suffocating, and Brystal buckled under the pressure. She knew admitting the truth wouldn't solve anything, but if it released just an ounce of the agony inside her, it would be worth breaking her teacher's trust.

"Madame Weatherberry hasn't been leaving the academy to visit a sick friend—at least, not in the way you think," she said. "She's been traveling to the Northern Kingdom to fight the *Snow Queen*."

"Whaaat?" Lucy blurted.

"I know it sounds crazy, but it's the truth!" Brystal said.

"How do you know this?" Emerelda asked.

"Madame Weatherberry told me herself," Brystal said. "*That's* the Northern Conflict that she's been discussing with the sovereigns and the witches in secret! The Snow Queen has become so powerful Madame Weatherberry is the only person who can stop her. So far, she's prevented the Snow Queen's destruction from spreading beyond the Northern Kingdom, but each encounter leaves Madame Weatherberry weaker than before. I begged her to let me go with her, but she was adamant about going alone."

"Are you saying Madame Weatherberry is in danger?" Tangerina asked.

"As much danger as someone can be in," Brystal said. "Madame Weatherberry said she's optimistic, but she's already made plans in case she doesn't survive. If she perishes while defeating the Snow Queen, Madame Weatherberry wants me to take over the academy—and if she perishes *before* defeating the Snow Queen, she says *I'm* the one who has to kill her!"

At first it was difficult for her classmates to believe everything Brystal said, but the more they thought about it, the more it explained Madame Weatherberry's mysterious behavior. Brystal didn't blame her friends for being skeptical—she had known the truth for weeks and it was *still* hard for her to believe it.

"Well, the chicken thickens," Lucy said, and placed her hands on her hips.

"Brystal, why didn't you tell us sooner?" Skylene asked.

Brystal sighed. "Madame Weatherberry didn't want you to know," she said. "That's why I've been acting like such a lunatic—it's been torture keeping all of this to myself! I'm not ready to lose Madame Weatherberry—and I'm certainly not ready to kill the Snow Queen! I've never felt so helpless in my entire life! And now I've only made it worse by burdening you guys with my problems!"

"*Your* problems?" Emerelda said. "Brystal, I appreciate your loyalty, but you're crazy if you think these are only *your* problems! If Madame Weatherberry is in danger, then it concerns all of us! You shouldn't have to go through all this by yourself!"

"Emerelda's right," Lucy said. "And I don't care what she asked of you, if Madame Weatherberry doesn't survive, we would *never* let you face the Snow Queen on your own!"

"Yeah!" Xanthous said. "We made a pact to help and protect each other! You'll always have us as backup!"

Brystal was touched by her friends' support. Their willingness to help her lifted some of the weight Madame Weatherberry had placed on her shoulders.

"Thank you," she said. "I just wish there was something I could do besides wait! I've been hoping and praying Madame Weatherberry defeats the Snow Queen and lives to tell the tale, but that doesn't—"

Suddenly, Brystal went quiet when she was distracted by something strange in the distance. The academy grounds were cloaked in a dark shadow that gradually consumed the entire property. The students and apprentices looked up and saw that the darkness was being caused by a thick layer of gray clouds that had rolled in from the north and covered the sun. Brystal figured it was just another rainstorm until she noticed something white and fluffy descending from the sky. She reached out her hand and watched in amazement as a single snowflake landed in her palm.

"Is that snow?" Skylene asked.

"It can't be," Tangerina said. "It's never snowed here before."

"It's not even cold out," Emerelda said.

A quiet hush fell over the classmates and they exchanged fearful expressions. The students and apprentices knew they were all thinking the same exact thing—there was only *one* explanation.

"It's the Snow Queen!" Lucy declared. "Her powers must be growing if her storms are reaching us!"

"And Madame Weatherberry must be in trouble!" Xanthous exclaimed.

The others began to panic, but as Brystal watched the snowflake melt in her hand, she had a significant change of heart: She wasn't going to waste any more time living in *fear*. She wasn't going to spend another ounce of energy *worrying*. She was done with *waiting* and *hoping* for Madame Weatherberry's safe return. And after weeks of feeling helpless, Brystal knew exactly what she needed to do.

"I don't know about you guys, but I refuse to sit back and let a frosty old witch take Madame Weatherberry away from us," she said.

"What should we do?" Xanthous asked.

Brystal turned to her classmates and beamed with determination.

"Everyone, get your coats," she said. "We're going to save her."

CHAPTER SEVENTEEN

THE IN-BETWEEN

Shortly before cooking dinner, Mrs. Vee entered the dining room to set the table and was surprised to find the students and apprentices gathered there. The children had already set the table with bowls and silverware, and a steaming pot of stew had already been prepared.

"Surprise!" the children told the housekeeper in unison.

"What's all this?" Mrs. Vee asked. "It can't be my birthday because I stopped having those after fifty. *HA-HA!*"

"We wanted to do something special for you, Mrs. Vee," Brystal said. "You work so hard cooking and cleaning for us every day, so as a token of our appreciation, we thought it'd be nice to make *you* dinner for once."

Mrs. Vee placed a hand over her heart.

"Well, that is just so thoughtful of you!" the housekeeper said. "You know, I don't care what my generation says about young people—you are *not* a bunch of lazy, selfish, and entitled attention-seekers. Some of you are just downright pleasant! *HA-HA!*"

Xanthous pulled out a chair for Mrs. Vee, Emerelda tucked a napkin into her shirt, Skylene filled her glass with water, and Tangerina handed her a spoon. Lucy opened the lid of the pot, letting a scrumptious aroma fill the air, and Brystal poured a generous serving of stew into the housekeeper's bowl.

"That smells heavenly," Mrs. Vee said. "What did you make?"

"My mother's creamy-mushroom-and-potato stew," Brystal said. "It's an old Evergreen family recipe. I hope you like it."

The housekeeper excitedly moved her spoon like it was a swimming fish, and eagerly took her first bite.

"It's absolutely delicious!" Mrs. Vee said. "*A little salty*, but delicious nonetheless! Thank you so much for treating me to such a special meal. I can't tell you how wonderful it feels to be so loved and appreciated by you. I don't want to get too mushy, but sometimes I think of you as my own children. *Boy, that's salty*—I'll be so bloated I won't fit into my shoes tomorrow! *HA-HA!* But all jokes aside, this is honestly the nicest thing anyone's ever—"

BAM! Mrs. Vee's head fell into her bowl and splashed the whole room with stew.

"That was quick," Lucy said. "I thought it would take longer than that."

Tangerina carefully raised the housekeeper's head out of the bowl and gently set it down on the table. She held a clean spoon under Mrs. Vee's nostrils to make sure she was still breathing, but the housekeeper didn't exhale.

"Skylene, how much Simple Slumber Sleeping Salt did you put in the stew?" she asked.

"I just followed the instructions on the back," Skylene said, and removed the bottle of Simple Slumber Sleeping Salt from her pocket. "The directions say an *inch of salt* will put someone to sleep for a week."

Tangerina snatched the bottle from her friend and took a look for herself. As she inspected it, something didn't seem right, and she wiped the bottle with a napkin.

"Skylene!" Tangerina exclaimed. "The instructions say a *pinch of salt* will put someone to sleep for a week— not an inch!"

Skylene went pale and her eyes grew wide.

"Oops," she said.

"Oh my God, we just killed Mrs. Vee!" Xanthous cried.

"Everyone, calm down!" Brystal said. "We found the Simple Slumber Sleeping Salt in Madame Weatherberry's potion cabinet. If it was lethal, I doubt she'd keep it in her office."

To everyone's extreme relief, the unconscious housekeeper let out a loud snore and started breathing normally.

"The old girl will be out for a while, but she'll be fine," Lucy said, and patted Mrs. Vee on the back.

"Did we do the right thing?" Emerelda said. "It feels weird putting her to sleep like this."

"We talked about this," Brystal said. "If Mrs. Vee woke up tomorrow morning and discovered we were all missing, it would give her a heart attack! And if she found out we were traveling to the Northern Kingdom, she would have come after us! Letting her rest while we're gone is better than letting her worry. Now let's put her in her room and leave before the Snow Queen gets any stronger."

It took all six children to lift Mrs. Vee's unconscious body from the chair and transport her out of the dining room. She was much heavier than they expected and it required all their strength. They carried her through the kitchen and into her bedroom as carefully as possible, and did their best to avoid bumping her head and limbs in the doorways. By the time they plopped her down on her bed and tucked her in, the students were all sweaty and out of breath.

"Wait a second," Lucy said. "Why didn't we just use *magic* to transport her?"

Her classmates groaned at their own collective stupidity.

"Aw, man," Xanthous said. "I keep forgetting that's an option."

Before they ventured to the Northern Kingdom, each of the students and apprentices manifested a unique coat to keep themselves warm for the journey. Brystal waved her wand, and a sparkling blue coat with fuzzy white cuffs appeared over her pantsuit. Emerelda created a beaded emerald wrap that matched her beaded emerald robe. Tangerina gave herself a thick jacket made from quilted patches of honeycomb. Skylene covered her body in a layer of warm water that wrapped around her like a transparent jumpsuit. And finally Lucy snapped her fingers and manifested a coat made from dark turkey feathers.

"Not exactly the pheasant I was hoping for, but it'll do," Lucy said.

"Xanthous? Don't you need a coat?" Skylene asked.

"I should be fine," he said. "I'm never cold."

"Then we're almost ready," Brystal said. "I just need to collect a couple things before we go."

Brystal packed a sack with food, water, and other supplies and then shrank it to the size of a coin purse so it would be easy to carry during their trip. She borrowed one of Mrs. Vee's sharp knives from the kitchen and took it to Madame Weatherberry's office. She stood on a glass chair and cut out the Northern Kingdom from the enlarged Map of Magic on the wall. Brystal was glad to see Madame Weatherberry's star was still shining on the map, and hoped they would save her before it disappeared. She rolled up the extracted piece of the map and tucked it into her coat.

Before heading downstairs, Brystal made a quick stop in her bedroom. She retrieved a large geography book from her shelves that contained detailed maps of the In-Between and the Northern Kingdom. Brystal waved her wand and shrunk the book to the dimensions of a matchbox so she could carry it in her pocket. Once the map and geography book were collected, Brystal met her classmates downstairs by the front door.

"Well, this is it," she said. "What we're about to embark on may get dangerous, it may get scary, and we may get hurt in the process."

"We call that a *Saturday* in show business," Lucy said.

"I'm being serious," Brystal said. "Once we walk out that door and leave the academy, there's no turning back. We all know what we're getting ourselves into, right?"

Brystal looked closely into each of her classmates' eyes to make sure they understood the stakes. Instead of finding any hesitation, she saw the students and apprentices nodding at her with confidence, knowing exactly what they had signed up for.

"I'm willing to throw a few punches for Madame Weatherberry," Emerelda said.

"So am I," Xanthous said.

"Me too," Tangerina said.

"Me three," Skylene said.

"Sounds *exactly* like the thrill I've been looking for," Lucy said.

Brystal was energized by her classmates' enthusiasm, but she still let out an anxious sigh before opening the front door.

"All right, then," she said. "Here goes nothing."

The children left the castle and hurried through the property to the hedge barrier. As the barrier opened for them, Brystal and her classmates all took a deep breath and squeezed one another's hands for courage. They walked through the barrier's leafy tunnel and took their first steps into the In-Between, and their journey began.

It was only dusk when Brystal and her friends departed the academy, but it was as dark as midnight in the thick forest. Regardless of their new self-defense skills, the students and apprentices were intimidated by the creepy woods. Every screeching raven and hooting owl seemed like a warning to turn around, but the classmates persisted, and traveled down the winding path. Brystal waved her wand and illuminated the forest with twinkling lights that followed them through the In-Between like a swarm of fireflies.

The classmates made it through their first mile without any trouble, but that quickly changed as they reached the end of their second mile. Suddenly, an enormous horned creature stepped out from the crooked trees and blocked the path. As it approached their twinkling lights, Brystal and Lucy were relieved to see it was

Horence and his three-headed horse, but their friends screamed at the knight and prepared themselves to fight him.

"Don't be afraid," Lucy told them. "This guy is a friend."

"Of course Lucy is friends with a demonic knight!" Tangerina exclaimed.

"Color me not surprised!" Skylene said.

"No, I mean he's not going to hurt us," Lucy said. "He's the one who saved me and Brystal from the witch hunters."

The classmates relaxed a bit after hearing this, but only slightly. Brystal stepped forward to greet the strange entity.

"Hello, Horence," she said. "What are you doing here?"

Instead of a verbal response, the knight pointed to the path behind the students. For reasons she couldn't explain, Brystal didn't need words to understand what Horence was trying to communicate.

"I know the woods are dangerous, but we can't go back," Brystal said. "Madame Weatherberry is in trouble and she needs our help. She's battling a horrible witch known as the Snow Queen. If we don't make it to the Northern Kingdom and save her, she might die."

"How does she know what he's saying?" Emerelda whispered to Lucy.

"They've got a weird thing," Lucy whispered back. *"Just go with it."*

After a few moments of silence, Horence bowed to Brystal, and gestured to the path ahead of them. Once again, the knight didn't utter a single word, but Brystal knew exactly what he was saying.

"Thank you," Brystal said. "That would be wonderful!"

"Um, Brystal?" Lucy asked. "What's happening here?"

"Horence is going to escort us through the forest," Brystal said. "He wants to protect us from the other creatures in the In-Between."

The knight steered his three-headed horse down the path and the children followed him. Brystal walked beside Horence as they traveled, but the rest of the group kept their distance. She couldn't blame her friends for being timid—she was scared the first time she saw Horence, too—but the farther they traveled, the more trusting of him they became.

"So what is Horence?" Emerelda asked. "Is he a man? A soldier? *A deer?*"

"I suppose he's more a *spirit* than anything else," Brystal explained. "Madame Weatherberry told me Horence was in love with a witch who used to own a bunch of land around here, including the academy's property. After Horence was murdered, the witch used witchcraft to bring him back to life. The spell was so dark and vile, the witch died in the process, and Horence returned to earth as an unnatural version of himself. Madame Weatherberry says he now roams the witch's former land and acts as a guardian angel for people in danger."

"If that's *Brystal's version of a guardian angel, I never want to see her version of a demon,"* Tangerina whispered to Skylene.

"Hey, Horence!" Lucy called to him. "Can we call you *Horns* for short?"

The knight slowly shook his head, and everyone understood his message that time.

Brystal and her friends followed Horence through the night and into the following morning. They could have sworn they saw wolves and bears watching them through the trees, but the animals didn't dare approach the children while they were with the knight. Eventually, the path came to a stream and the students and apprentices crossed a small stone bridge. Brystal and her classmates made it across the bridge without any trouble, but when they turned back, Horence had stayed on the other side.

"What are you doing, Horence?" Brystal asked. "Aren't you coming with us?"

The knight slowly shook his head and pointed to a tree on his side of the stream. Brystal looked closer and saw a heart with two sets of initials carved into the tree trunk:

At first, Brystal had no idea why Horence was show-ing her the carving or who HM and SW were. However, it didn't take her long to remember the knight's life story, and she quickly realized why he had stopped at the stream.

"Those are your and the witch's initials, aren't they?" Brystal said. "You must have carved them into that tree when you were both alive. And you can't travel beyond it, because it marks the end of her former property."

Horence slowly nodded. The knight then performed a series of gestures that Brystal found confusing. First he pointed in the direction she and the others were traveling, and then with the same hand, he showed Brystal two of his fingers, and then reduced them to one. He repeated the motion several times: pointing, two fingers, one finger; pointing, two fingers, one finger; pointing, two fingers, one finger; but no matter how many times he performed the gesture, Brystal couldn't figure out what Horence was trying to say.

"The distance? Two fingers? One finger?" she asked as he reenacted the movement. "The distance? Two fingers? One finger?"

For whatever reason, the connection between them had broken, and they couldn't communicate as easily as before. Brystal wondered if it was because she was standing on the other side of the stream. Before she could cross the bridge and get a clearer answer, Horence pulled on his horse's reins and disappeared into the trees.

"What was he telling you?" Lucy asked.

"Actually, I have no idea," Brystal said. "But I think it was a *warning*."

· • ★ • ·

As the morning became the afternoon, Brystal and her friends' bodies were aching from exhaustion, and their feet were swollen and pounding in their shoes. They had been traveling for almost an entire day and had rarely stopped to take a break. Without Horence's protection, Brystal was afraid if they lingered anywhere for too long, their scents and sounds would be noticed by a predator. So she made her classmates push through their fatigue, and forced their procession forward.

"How much longer until we get to the Northern Kingdom?" Xanthous asked.

"According to my geography book, we're about a quarter of the way there," Brystal said.

"Only a *quarter*?" Skylene said in shock. "I thought we were nearly there! The air has been getting so much colder."

"It's about to get a lot colder than this," Brystal said. "Trust me, you'll know when we arrive. The Northern Kingdom is covered in the Snow Queen's blizzards."

"What part of the Northern Kingdom are we headed to?" Lucy asked.

Brystal removed the Map of Magic from her coat and unrolled it for her classmates.

"The map shows Madame Weatherberry is somewhere

between Appleton Village and the kingdom's capital, Tinzel Heights," Brystal said. "The Snow Queen recently attacked Tinzel Heights, so I imagine Madame Weatherberry is trying to keep her destruction from spreading. If the Snow Queen reaches Appleton Village, the Northern Kingdom is doomed."

Their mutual fear fueled their efforts, and the classmates continued on without complaining. A few more miles down the path, Brystal and her friends passed through a pleasant clearing with sunlight, a stone bench to sit on, colorful berries to eat, and a fresh spring to drink from. It was unlike anything they had seen in the In-Between since leaving the academy, and the apprentices were tempted to stop.

"I'm sorry, but I've *got* to take a break!" Tangerina whined.

"Me too!" Skylene said. "Even I feel dehydrated."

Brystal had been pushing her classmates so hard, she figured they had earned a quick rest. She didn't object when Tangerina and Skylene left the path and headed for the stone bench. Lucy eyed the clearing suspiciously, though, and stopped the apprentices before they sat.

"Wait! Don't sit there!" she said.

"Why not?" Tangerina asked.

"Because we're not safe here," Lucy said. "It's obviously a trap."

"Lucy, you're just being paranoid," Tangerina said. "This is the most decent part of the woods we've seen!"

"Exactly!" Lucy said. "It's charming—*too charming*!

We'll be much safer if we keep walking and find some-place gloomy and uninviting."

"Great, we'll meet you there!" Tangerina said. "But if I don't sit for five minutes, my feet are going to fall off my—"

SWOOSH! Like a giant mousetrap, as soon as Tangerina and Skylene touched the stone bench, an enormous net fell on top of them. The girls screamed and struggled to free themselves, but the more they squirmed, the more entangled they became. Brystal, Lucy, Xanthous, and Emerelda ran to help their friends, but the net was so thick they couldn't get it off the girls.

The classmates heard the sound of a horn coming from nearby. Suddenly, a tribe of strange creatures jumped out from behind the trees, and soon the children found themselves surrounded by over a hundred trolls.

The trolls were short creatures with dirty orange skin and hairy bodies. They had big eyes, big noses, big feet, big teeth, and tiny horns. They wore clothing made from the fur of foxes, raccoons, and squirrels, and jewelry made from the bones of their prey. Each troll carried a heavy club and they swung their weapons through the air to incite fear. A particularly large troll wearing a headdress of exotic feathers stepped forward to observe the children, and Brystal assumed he was the chief of the tribe.

"Everyone remain calm," Lucy whispered to her frightened classmates. *"Trolls are incredibly stupid creatures—they've got sight like eyeless skunks, and hearing*

*like earless rabbits. If we stay still and silent, they won't
even know we're here."*

The students and apprentices followed Lucy's advice
and stood as still as possible.

"Actually, our vision is *perfect* and our hearing is
flawless," the chief growled.

"Dang it," Lucy muttered. "I was thinking of
gophers."

"You won't need to *think* where you're going," the
chief said, and then turned to his tribe. "What shall
we do with our prisoners? Have we captured *slaves* or
snacks?"

The trolls clanked their clubs in celebration of
catching the children, and then roared their opinions on
whether to *eat* or *enslave* them.

"Gosh, why isn't there a third option?" Xanthous
cried.

"Brystal, what do we do?" Emerelda asked.

"I'm thinking, I'm thinking!" Brystal said.

The tribe was so loud Brystal could barely hear her
own thoughts. The trolls eventually voted for *slavery*,
and then crept closer to seize the children.

"Okay, I'm going to count to three," Brystal told her
classmates. "On three, I'm going to wave my wand and
cause a distraction, we're going to grab the net, and then
run out of the clearing. Got it?"

"I don't want to be dragged out of here!" Skylene
said.

"One . . . ," Brystal started. "Two . . ."

Before she could give the final signal, the ground rumbled beneath their feet. The trolls looked down in fear and started backing out of the clearing.

"Great job, Brystal!" Lucy said. "This is one heck of a distraction!"

"It's not me!" Brystal said. "I haven't done anything yet!"

Suddenly, hundreds of green hands with sharp fingernails burst out of the dirt. A colony of goblins crawled out from underground and emerged into the clearing. The goblins were tall and lean creatures with glossy green skin. They had big pointed ears, small jagged teeth, and nostrils without noses. Their clothes were made from the skins of bats, moles, and reptiles. All the goblins carried sharp spears, and they jabbed the weapons in the trolls' direction. An older goblin wearing a sash made from dead centipedes confronted the troll chief face-to-face.

"How dare you poach on our territory!" the goblin elder yelled.

"This is *our* territory!" the troll chief yelled back. "Everything above the ground belongs to us! Go back to the holes you crawled out of!"

The chief swung his club at the elder, but the goblin blocked it with his spear.

"You've already stolen our food, our water, and our land!" the elder shouted. "We will *not* let you take slaves from us, too! Leave the forest immediately or face the consequences!"

"Trolls don't cower from anything—especially *goblin filth*!" the chief declared.

Tension between the leaders escalated and the classmates worried they were about to be caught in the middle of a full-fledged battle between the species.

"Don't worry, I'll handle this!" Lucy whispered to her friends.

"Please don't!" Tangerina pleaded.

To her classmates' terror, Lucy strutted across the clearing and placed herself between the troll chief and the goblin elder.

"Whoa, whoa, whoa," she said. "Fellas, chill out before we all get hurt!"

The interruption infuriated both leaders.

"Who do you think you are?" the troll chief growled.

"You don't recognize me?" Lucy asked. "I'm Lucy Goose of the world-renowned Goose Troupe. I'm sure you've been to one of our shows. Me and my family have performed for trolls and goblins all over the In-Between. We're kind of a big deal around here."

The goblin elder squinted at her and rubbed his chin.

"Oh, yes," he said. "I remember you. You're that little fat girl who hit the obnoxious box of chimes until I had a splitting headache."

"It's called *the tambourine*," Lucy corrected him. "Look, I understand things are tough between you guys. And you don't want to make things worse by embarrassing yourselves in front of a celebrity like me. I normally don't do this, but if you let me and my friends leave the clearing in peace, I promise to come back and give you all a free performance. Come on, what do you say? There's isn't a conflict in the world that can't be solved with some good old-fashioned entertainment."

The students and apprentices cringed at Lucy's attempt to negotiate. The goblin elder turned back to the troll chief and made an offer of his own.

"Tell you what," the goblin said. "*You* can have the tambourine player, but *we're* taking the others."

"No!" the chief yelled. "*You* can have the tambourine player, and *we'll* take the others!"

The chief blew a horn in the elder's face and a brutal battle between the trolls and goblins began. Brystal and her classmates watched the brawl in horror—they had never seen such violence in their lives. The creatures ruthlessly bludgeoned and stabbed one another, and when their weapons gave out, they resorted to twisting noses and pulling ears. Brystal was just as heartbroken as she was disturbed—if humankind hadn't expelled the trolls and goblins from their kingdoms, they wouldn't have to be fighting over resources like this. However, Brystal was glad the goblins had arrived when they did—they were the best distraction she could have asked for.

"NOW!" she yelled to her classmates.

Brystal, Emerelda, and Xanthous grabbed the net and charged out of the clearing, dragging Tangerina and Skylene behind them. Lucy led the charge, pushing the trolls and goblins out of their way. Initially, the creatures were too busy fighting one another to notice, but they quickly spotted the children fleeing the area.

"THE SLAVES ARE GETTING AWAY!" the troll chief bellowed.

"AFTER THEM!" the goblin elder commanded.

The trolls and goblins chased after the classmates, and the sparring creatures moved through the In-Between as a united force. The students and apprentices ran through the forest as fast as their tired legs could carry them, using their magic to prevent the creatures from getting too close. Brystal waved her wand and sent trolls whirling through the air in giant bubbles. Emerelda threw handfuls of rubies and diamonds on the ground to make the goblins slip. Xanthous removed his Muter Medal and lit entire trees on fire to scare them off. Despite all their magical efforts, the trolls and goblins never paused their pursuit.

Lucy was running in front of her classmates and spotted something alarming in the distance ahead of them.

"Hey, guys!" she called over her shoulder. "We're heading toward the cliff of a canyon!"

"Then do something so we're *not* heading toward the cliff of a canyon!" Emerelda said.

Just as they reached the edge of the deep and rocky canyon, Lucy snapped her fingers and a rickety rope bridge with wooden panels appeared in front of them. The classmates ran across the bridge and it started to sway like a giant swing. The movement caused Xanthous to trip and he fell flat on his face. His Muter Medal slipped out from his hand and fell into the canyon below. The boy instantly started to panic and he was engulfed in flames.

"No, no, no, no, no!" he gasped.

"Xanthous, listen to me!" Brystal said. *"You have to calm down! If you get too heated, the bridge is going to—"*

It was too late—Xanthous's fire burned through the ropes and wooden panels. The bridge snapped in half and the classmates fell into the canyon. The students and apprentices screamed as they dropped through the air and plummeted toward the rocky earth below. The fall reminded Brystal of the final chapter in *The Tales of Tidbit Twitch*, but unlike the main character's fall, there wasn't a river to break hers. Brystal tried to manifest something soft for her and the others to land on, but as she waved her wand, the velocity knocked it out of her hand.

Brystal desperately reached for her wand in mid-air.... It was falling right beside her, just a few inches out of reach.... She stretched her arm out as far as possible.... Her fingertips grazed the side of it.... She wrapped her hand around its crystal handle....

POOF! The children hit the bottom of the canyon and a cloud of dust rose into the air. As the trolls and goblins looked over the cliff, they didn't wait for the dust to clear before retreating back into the woods.

Nothing could have survived *that* fall.

CHAPTER EIGHTEEN

THE GIRL OF FLOWERS AND THE TREE OF TRUTH

Brystal was awoken by a strong flowery scent. Her eyes fluttered open to see what was causing the smell, but all she saw was the color *yellow* everywhere she looked. She waited for her eyes to adjust, expecting the color to fade or turn into something she recognized, but the yellow—and *only* the yellow—remained around her. Brystal was lying on something very soft, but she didn't know where she was or how she got there.

She remembered the sensation of *falling*....She remembered how hard it was to breathe as the air rushed past her face....She remembered reaching for something descending beside her....She remembered brushing her wand with her fingertips.... And she remembered how desperately she needed it....

Brystal gasped and sat straight up as her full memory returned. She recalled running from the trolls and goblins with her classmates, she recalled Xanthous dropping his Muter Medal as they crossed the rope bridge, and worst of all, she recalled plunging toward the canyon's rocky floor. However, she hadn't landed on the hard ground as she had feared—Brystal's fall had been broken by an enormous yellow rose.

As Brystal got to her feet and peeked over the massive petals, she discovered she was in the middle of an enchanted garden. Everywhere she turned, Brystal saw flowers, mushrooms, shrubbery, and other plants that were the size of houses. Her classmates were scattered around the garden, and thankfully their falls had been broken by giant flowers, too—and just like Brystal, the impact had knocked all of them unconscious. Emerelda was nested inside a towering purple tulip, and Lucy was draped over the side of a gigantic pink lily. Xanthous was lying in a huge red carnation that was partially singed now, thanks to the boy's flames. Tangerina and Skylene were still tangled in the trolls' net, but the girls had landed safely on a sunflower.

"Is everyone alive?" Brystal called to them.

One by one, her classmates started to groan and slowly came to. They rubbed their heads, stretched their limbs, and looked around the garden in amazement.

"Well, this isn't the *worst* place I've woken up in," Lucy said.

"Where are we?" Emerelda asked.

"A big garden of some kind," Brystal said.

"But how'd we get here?" Xanthous asked.

Everyone looked up and saw that the canyon was still above them. But strangely, the garden was *underneath* the canyon's rocky floor, and it covered them like a transparent roof.

"The bottom of the canyon must have been a magic barrier," Tangerina speculated. "It's just like the hedge around our academy! We must have fallen into another magical residence!"

The classmates carefully climbed down from their giant flowers and took in their bizarre surroundings. Xanthous found his Muter Medal dangling off a daisy and immediately put it back around his neck. Brystal searched the garden for her wand and found it at the base of a milkweed plant. She waved the wand at Tangerina and Skylene, the net around them dissolved into thin air, and the girls joined the others on the ground.

"You could have done that *before* you dragged us through the woods," Skylene said.

"Sorry," Brystal said. "I'm still getting used to these *life-and-death* situations."

The students and apprentices searched for a way out

of the garden, but they couldn't find an exit anywhere. They followed a dirt path snaking through the enchanted plants, but the property seemed endless. As they walked, Tangerina's bumblebees buzzed with excitement about all the giant flowers around them. They merrily made trips to and from the enlarged blossoms, returning to Tangerina's beehive with more nectar than they knew what to do with.

Eventually, the classmates heard someone humming in the garden nearby. They rounded the corner and found a six-year-old girl watering normal-size poppies. The girl had ringlets of bright red hair and she wore a sundress made from large red rose petals. She hummed a cheerful tune to the poppies while she watered them, and after she was finished, she set her pail aside and twirled her fingers through the air above the flowers. The poppies started to grow, stretching to the height of a tree.

"Nice trick," Lucy called to her. "Do you do parties?"

The little girl wasn't expecting the classmates, and screamed. She dashed behind the giant poppies and hid from the visitors. Brystal felt terrible for frightening the little girl and approached her with an apologetic smile.

"I'm sorry, we didn't mean to scare you," she said. "You have nothing to be afraid of—we're fairies just like you. We're a little lost and were hoping some-one could show us a way out of . . . well, *wherever* we are."

"I'm not allowed to talk to strangers," the little girl said.

"Then let's fix that," she said. "My name is Brystal

Evergreen. These are my friends Lucy Goose, Emerelda Stone, Xanthous Hayfield, Tangerina Turkin, and Skylene Lavenders. What's your name?"

Brystal's friendly charm won the little girl over and she stepped out from behind the poppies.

"My name is Rosette," she said. "Rosette Meadows."

"It's nice to meet you, Rosette," Brystal said. "Now that we're better acquainted, can you please tell us where we are?"

"You're in Greenhouse Canyon," she said. "It's the world's largest botanical garden and nursery for magically enhanced plants."

"Do you grow all the plants yourself?" Brystal asked.

"It's my family's specialty," Rosette said. "The Meadowses have the greenest thumbs in the magical community. Our thumbs aren't actually green, of course—that's just a figure of speech. Although my uncle's thumb *did* turn green once, but that was just a bad infection. *Boy, I sure miss him.* Wait. If you didn't know about Greenhouse Canyon before, how'd you end up here?"

"Me and my friends were chased off the cliff by trolls and goblins," Brystal said. "We fell into the canyon, but luckily your flowers saved our lives."

"You were chased by real trolls and goblins?" Rosette asked with large eyes. "That's amazing! I've never seen a troll or goblin in real life before. This one time, I thought I saw one, but it was just an anteater. Wait. *Did you say our flowers saved your life?* Wow, that's incredible! My family should use that for marketing. I can picture the advertisements now. *'Meadows Flowers—not only are they beautiful, they're lifesaving.'* It's tough getting new customers when your location is a secret."

"Oh, I imagine that's a tough way to sell—"

"Our usual customers are all old and smell like cheese. *Why do you think that is?* You guys are the youngest people I've ever seen in the canyon! I rarely have anyone my own age to talk to. Gosh, this is nice. Is this nice for you, too? *I spend a LOT of time with plants!* They say talking to plants helps them grow. I'm not sure it's the healthiest thing for me, though. Plants are good listeners, I guess, but it's not the same as talking to people. Sometimes you just need to hear something besides your own voice, you know what I mean? *Hey, do you guys want a tour of the gardens while you're here?*"

Obviously Rosette was very excited to have company, but she talked so fast the others were having a hard time understanding her.

"We'd love to stay, but we're in a bit of a hurry," Brystal said. "Would you mind showing us how to get back to the In-Between?"

Rosette looked around the gardens curiously and scratched her head.

"Actually, I'm not sure how to get out of here," she said. "Believe it or not, I've never been outside the canyon before. My family is very protective. *Did you know the world is full of people who want to harm us?* It was news to me. My family also says I'm a *lot* for other people to handle. They say I'm best in *small doses*—whatever that means. It doesn't hurt my feelings, though. Everyone expresses love in a different language. Do you guys know what your love languages are? Mine is *quality time*. It used to be *physical touch*—but *that* wasn't working very well, so I had to change it. People are so picky about personal space and—"

"Is there someone *else* we could talk to?" Lucy interrupted.

"You'll have to speak to the Sorceress," Rosette said. "She'll know a way out."

"Did you say the *Sorceress*?" Emerelda asked.

"Yeah, she's my aunt," Rosette said. "Come with me—I'll show you where she is."

The classmates followed the little girl through the gardens, and along the way, Rosette gave them the tour they didn't want. She spoke in great detail about every flower and plant they passed. Brystal suspected she was purposely taking the long way through the garden so she had more time to talk to them. Soon they passed a bundle of bushes with colorful berries that caught Xanthous's eye.

"I recognize those," he said. "Madame Weatherberry had them in her golden carriage."

"Those are our *Meal Berries*," Rosette said. "They're one of our bestsellers. They grow different types of food depending on what time of day it is."

"What's that over there?" Skylene asked.

"Oh, that's our *Orchard of Objects*," she said. "Come on! You'll definitely want to see it!"

406

Rosette skipped toward the orchard and gestured for the others to follow her. Lucy shot her classmates a scathing look as they went.

"Stop asking her questions!" she whispered. *"She's slow enough as it is!"*

The little girl showed them an acre of trees planted in very straight rows. All the trees in the orchard were identical, but instead of fruit or flowers, each tree grew a different household object. There were trees with bars of soap, buckets and mops, pillows and blankets, candles and candlesticks, tables and chairs, spatulas and frying pans, brushes and combs, shoes and socks, and even trees that sprouted stuffed animals.

"My family can grow just about anything on trees," Rosette boasted. "We get requests from witches and fairies all over the world. *Money* is always what people want the most. That probably isn't a surprise, though. Before you ask, the answer is *no*—we don't grow money trees. At least, not *anymore*. The last time we sold one, the Western Kingdom had an economic crisis. They still haven't recovered from the—"

"Rosette, how much farther until we reach the Sorceress?" Lucy asked. "We're in a bit of a crisis of our own."

"We're almost there," Rosette said. "Our house is just beyond the Vineyard of Vices and the Farm of Fragrances. I can't wait to show you those!"

Eventually, the tour ended at a large four-story manor. The home was constructed entirely out of vines, and it had a spiral roof of twisted thornbush. Inside, the manor had a thatched floor and walls made from colorful shrubbery. As Rosette escorted her guests through the home, the classmates heard the sounds of several different creatures coming from somewhere inside the house. When they stepped into the great room, Brystal and her friends discovered a zoo of potted plants that looked, moved, and roared like animals. There were barking dogwood blossoms, meowing catnip plants, screeching monkey-face orchids, and flapping bird-of-paradise flowers.

In the very back of the great room, an old woman was feeding a crate of live chickens to a massive bouquet of Venus flytraps. The plants caught the birds with their snapping jaws and swallowed them whole. It was an unnerving scene to walk in on, and the classmates froze halfway through the room, but Rosette happily skipped up to the old woman without hesitation.

"Auntie Floraline, we have visitors!" she announced.

Floraline Meadows was a very short woman with a wide mouth and abnormally long earlobes. She had two braids of silver hair and wore a smock made from autumn leaves. To the Venus flytraps' dismay, the old woman put a lid over the chicken crate and took a break from the feeding to meet her guests.

"Auntie Floraline, these are my new friends Brystal, Lucy, Emerelda, Xanthous, Tangerina, and Skylene," Rosette introduced. "New friends, this is my aunt, Sorceress Floraline Meadows."

The Sorceress studied the classmates with very untrusting eyes.

"Are you *customers*?" she asked them.

"No," Brystal said.

"Are you *solicitors*?"

"No."

"Then what are you doing in my canyon?"

"We're here by accident," Brystal explained. "A tribe of trolls and a colony of goblins chased us off the cliff. We don't want to disturb you, but we'd really appreciate it if you could tell us how to get out of here."

The Sorceress was still suspicious and raised an eyebrow at the classmates.

"You're awfully young to be in the In-Between by yourselves," she said. "Where are you coming from?"

"Madame Weatherberry's Academy of Magic," Skylene said.

"Huh, sounds fancy," the old woman said. "I didn't know there *were* academies for people like us."

"It's the first of its kind," Skylene said, and beamed with pride.

"Well, *la-di-da*," the Sorceress sang. "To leave the canyon, go to the northwest corner of the gardens and make a left turn at the Grove of Glassware. You'll find a ladder that leads back to the In-Between."

"Thank you," Brystal said. "We'll be on our way. It was nice meeting you."

"Thanks for dropping by," Rosette said. "No pun intended!"

The classmates headed for the door, but when Brystal turned back to wave good-bye, she noticed that Tangerina hadn't moved. The apprentice was inquisitively looking back and forth between the Sorceress and the bouquet of Venus flytraps.

"Just out of curiosity," Tangerina said, "when you said *people like us*, what were you referring to? Do Sorceresses practice magic or witchcraft?"

"Magic for the most part," the old woman said. "But I've been known to be a bit of a *witch* from time to time. It just depends on what kind of mood I'm in."

The Sorceress laughed at her own joke, but the students and apprentices didn't understand why it was funny. On the contrary, the remark only confused them.

"You're not being serious, are you?" Tangerina asked.

"Of course I'm being serious," the old woman said. "I didn't get these ears from sticking to magic over the years. I don't use it often, but occasionally a little witchcraft goes a long way."

"But that isn't possible," Tangerina said. "You're born either a fairy or a witch. No one gets to *choose*."

The Sorceress was stunned by Tangerina's assertion.

"Young lady, what on earth are you talking about?" she asked. "Having magical abilities isn't a choice, but no one in the magical community is *born* a fairy or a witch. We all get to be *whatever* we want, *whenever* we want. Personally, I've never identified as one or the other, that's why I call myself a *sorceress*."

"That…that…that's not true," Tangerina argued. "Fairies are born with goodness in their hearts, and therefore can *only* practice magic. Witches are born with wickedness in their hearts, and therefore can *only* practice witchcraft."

"And who taught you that nonsense?" the Sorceress asked.

"Our teacher did," Tangerina said.

"Well, I hate to break it to you, but your teacher is *wrong*," the old woman said. "Nothing in this universe is black-and-white. Even the darkest nights have a degree of light, and the brightest days have a pinch of darkness. The world is full of duality, and we get to *choose* where we stand in all of it."

The Sorceress was very persuasive as she stated her case, but the classmates couldn't accept it. If she was telling them the truth, then everything they knew about magic, and the very foundation of Madame Weatherberry's academy, was *all* a lie.

"No, I don't believe you!" Skylene objected. "Madame Weatherberry would never lie to us! You're clearly a *witch*, because you're trying to trick us!"

"Look, you can believe whatever you want to believe, but I'm not trying to trick anyone," the Sorceress said. "Here, I'll prove it to you."

The old woman pointed to the ground, and a large flower grew out of the thatched floor. It was the most gorgeous plant the classmates had ever seen, and its rosy petals were so vibrant the flower practically glowed.

411

After the children had a chance to admire it, and fall in love with its beauty, the Sorceress clenched her fist and the flower began to whither. Its color faded, its petals broke away, its stem weakened, and the plant decayed into a mound of dirt.

"See?" the old woman said. "Magic *and* witchcraft."

The demonstration was quick and simple, but it proved the Sorceress was correct. Brystal and her classmates were distressed as they stared at the flower's remains. Their minds were racing as they reevaluated everything Madame Weatherberry had ever said.

"But *why* did she lie about it?" Brystal asked. "Why would Madame Weatherberry act like fairies and witches were different species if it was just a *preference*?"

"You could ask our Tree of Truth," Rosette suggested.

"A Tree of Truth?" Lucy said. "Okay, now you're just yanking our tail feathers."

"No, it's real!" Rosette said. "The Tree of Truth is a magic tree that produces honesty. It may answer your questions about your teacher. There's only one left in Greenhouse Canyon. We had to stop selling them because they were driving our customers mad."

"Is it safe?" Brystal asked.

"As long as you can handle the truth," the Sorceress said. "Most people can't."

Brystal wasn't confident she could, either. Learning that Madame Weatherberry had lied about something so significant was crushing enough, but Brystal would be devastated if she discovered the fairy had lied for dishonorable reasons. However, nothing seemed more daunting than another unanswered question, so Brystal welcomed the opportunity to find the truth.

"All right," she said. "Take me to the tree."

Rosette and the Sorceress escorted their guests to the opposite side of Greenhouse Canyon. At the end of the dirt path, at the top of a tiny hill, was a small white tree. At first, the Tree of Truth looked very normal, but as the classmates walked closer, they noticed its bark was covered in carvings of human eyes. Brystal cautiously climbed the hill and stood before the tree, but she didn't know what to do next.

"How does it work?" she asked.

"Take one of its branches into the palm of your hand," the Sorceress instructed. "Then close your eyes, clear your head, and ask it the questions on your mind."

Brystal took a deep breath and held a branch. As soon as her hand closed around it, Brystal was transported far away from Greenhouse Canyon. She wasn't standing on a hill in the middle of the gardens anymore, but on a hill that floated miles above the ground. The clouds flowed beneath her like a rushing river, and the stars twinkled so clearly above her that they seemed within reach. When she looked back at the Tree of Truth, the carvings on its trunk and branches suddenly opened and became real human eyes—and every single one was staring directly at her. Brystal assumed it was all in her mind, but that didn't make it feel any less real.

"Do you have a question?" said a deep voice that echoed through the sky around her.

"That depends," Brystal said. "Do you really give honest answers?"

"I cannot predict the future, or read someone's thoughts, but I know all that is, and all that was," the voice responded.

Brystal still had doubts about the Tree of Truth, so she started with a few simple questions to test the tree's authenticity.

"Where was I born?" she asked.

"Chariot Hills," the voice answered.

"And where did I attend school?"

"The Chariot Hills School for Future Wives and Mothers."

"What does my mother do for a living?"

"Everything your father doesn't."

The last question had been a trick question, but Brystal was impressed by how the Tree of Truth had answered it. She decided not to waste any more time testing its accuracy and skipped to the questions she was there for.

"Is it true that all members of the magical community are born the same? And that being a fairy or a witch is just a preference?" Brystal asked.

"Yes," the tree said.

"Then why did Madame Weatherberry lie to us?" she asked.

"The same reason everyone lies," the tree said. "To

hide the truth."

"But why did she need to hide it? Why does Madame Weatherberry want us to believe there is a difference between fairies and witches if there isn't?"

"I cannot see her exact motivation, but I can give insight on why *others* tell similar lies," the tree offered.

"Why?" Brystal asked.

"When faced with discrimination, it is common for people to divide their communities into their oppressors' definitions of *right* and *wrong*. By categorizing fairies as *good* and witches as *bad*, it's possible that Madame Weatherberry was trying to gain *acceptance for fairies* by fueling *hatred for witches*."

The theory made sense, but if the tree was right, that meant Madame Weatherberry was encouraging humankind to *hate* and *harm* members of her own community—and Brystal couldn't imagine Madame Weatherberry wishing *hate* or *harm* on anyone.

"So is that the *real reason* she published *The Truth About Magic?* Are the incantations supposed to help humankind discover and persecute witches?"

"The incantation for witchcraft is fake," the tree said. "The incantation for magic is the only genuine spell in her book."

The revelation puzzled Brystal even more. She was starting to think the Tree of Truth should be called the Tree of Frustration, because everything it said made the situation more complicated. Her mind was spiraling into different directions, but as Brystal concentrated on the facts, it slowly dawned on her why Madame Weatherberry had done what she did.

"I think I understand now," Brystal said. "If Madame Weatherberry convinced humankind to only discriminate against *witches*, and convinced everyone in the magical community that they were *fairies*—it would save everyone! She pretended the community was divided to protect it from humankind—while *still* giving humankind something to hate and fear! Right?"

"Noble people usually lie for noble reasons," the voice said. "Sadly, you'll never know until you ask them yourself."

"How is Madame Weatherberry doing now? Is she still alive?"

"Your teacher is still alive, but she's been taken hostage by an evil energy," the Tree of Truth said. "Very little of Madame Weatherberry remains, and the life that she clings to is being drained by her captor. It won't be long until she loses the fight."

"She's been *captured*?" Brystal asked in a panic. "Where is she being kept? Do we have time to save her?"

"Madame Weatherberry is imprisoned deep within Tinzel Palace in the Northern Kingdom's capital. However, if you continue down the winding paths of the In-Between, the chances of rescuing her are unlikely."

"Is there a faster way to get there?"

"Ten miles north of Greenhouse Canyon, in the back of Black Bear Cave, you'll find the entrance to an abandoned goblin tunnel. Take the tunnel, and you'll arrive in Tinzel Heights in half the time."

"All right, we will!" Brystal said. "Thank you!"

Brystal released the Tree of Truth's branch from her grip and returned to the garden in Greenhouse Canyon. The trip back felt like she was falling to the earth all over again, and she screamed, causing all her classmates to jump.

"Did something bite you?" Xanthous asked.

"Sorry!" Brystal said. "I wasn't expecting the trip back to be so jarring."

"What do you mean *trip back*?" Emerelda asked.

"It doesn't matter—I got the answers we wanted!" Brystal said. "Madame Weatherberry *did* lie to us about magic and witchcraft—but she was only doing it to protect the magical community. I'll explain it all later because we have to go! If we don't leave Greenhouse Canyon right now, we'll never see Madame Weatherberry again!"

CHAPTER NINETEEN

THE NORTHERN FRONT

Brystal and her classmates hurried out of Greenhouse Canyon and trekked through the In-Between as quickly as possible. The closer they traveled toward the Northern Kingdom, the more the temperature dropped, and each mile felt drastically colder than the one before. The children bundled themselves tightly in their coats to endure the chilly air, but the declining weather wasn't nearly as bothersome as their sinking spirits. Brystal's conversation with the Tree of Truth was difficult for her friends to process, and hearing about it took a visible toll on them. Even though Madame Weatherberry had lied to them for honorable reasons, the students and apprentices felt betrayed by their teacher. They lowered their heads and somberly walked through the forest in silence.

When the group reached the halfway point between Greenhouse Canyon and Black Bear Cave, they took their first break since leaving the enchanted gardens. They sat on a fallen log to rest their feet, and Brystal decided to address the issue on their minds before they continued any farther.

"I understand you're all disappointed," she said. "It's never easy to find out you've been lied to by some-one you love, but if you really think about it, the truth about fairies and witches doesn't change anything. We're still the same *people* we were at the academy, and Madame Weatherberry is still the same *person* we set out to save. Everything she's ever done—writing *The Truth About Magic*, standing up to the Snow Queen, starting the academy—it's all been to protect and gain acceptance for the magical community. We can forgive her for making a few mistakes along the way, can't we?"

The students thought about Madame Weatherberry's intentions and ultimately agreed with Brystal's perspective, but the apprentices weren't convinced.

"Tangerina? Skylene?" Brystal said. "I know this is more difficult for you two because you've known Madame Weatherberry the longest. It's perfectly fine to feel whatever you're feeling right now, but one day I think you'll look back on this and—"

"It's not just about Madame Weatherberry," Tangerina confessed. "I've always thought fairies were better than witches—and I *liked* feeling better than something else. It helped me cope with all the hatred the world sent us. Believing I was born that way made me feel valuable—like the universe was on my side."

"Me too," Skylene said. "And we hated witches just like humankind hates us. But now we know we're not better than witches—and we're not any better than humankind, either."

Brystal knelt in front of her troubled friends and placed a hand on both of their knees.

"We're all just a couple of mistakes away from becoming the people we despise," she said. "So don't think *worse* of yourself, but let this change *how* you think of yourself. Start valuing *who* you are, more than *what* you are. Prove you're better than most people by showing more *acceptance* and *empathy*. And fuel your pride with what you *earn* and *create*, instead of what you're born with."

Tangerina and Skylene went quiet as they considered Brystal's encouraging proposal. The changes she suggested weren't easy, and it would take a lot of time and hard work, but her message inspired them to try.

"You're really good at pep talks," Tangerina said. "Like, sometimes it's *weird* how good you are."

Brystal laughed. "I have a good teacher," she said. "We all do."

After a short break, the classmates continued through the In-Between toward Black Bear Cave. Every few steps, Brystal compulsively checked her geography book to make sure they were going in the right direction. Within the hour, they arrived at an enormous cave at the side of a wide hill. The entrance was surrounded by several black boulders stacked to make the cave look like the mouth of a giant bear.

"I'm guessing *that's* Black Bear Cave," Emerelda said.

"Wait, do we think there are *bears* in there?" Xanthous asked.

"Probably," Lucy said. "I doubt Black Bear Cave got its name for housing flamingos."

"Doesn't that worry anyone else?" he asked. "I mean, are we actually going inside a bear cave with a girl covered in *honey*?"

Everyone turned to Tangerina and eyed her honeycomb jacket with concern.

"Oh yeah," Brystal said. "Xanthous brings up a good point."

Before they could discuss a possible precaution, the classmates were distracted by a freezing wind that blew through the forest. The wind was followed by a thunderous commotion, and suddenly, the dark woods became much darker. The group looked up and saw the gray clouds of a terrible storm rolling in from the north. As the clouds covered the sky, a powerful snowstorm surged through the In-Between like a white tsunami.

"What's going on?" Tangerina asked.

"It's a blizzard!" Brystal exclaimed. *"Everyone into the cave! NOW!"*

The classmates dashed through the forest, and the blizzard chased after them like a swirling white monster. They arrived at the cave's entrance just as the storm collided with the hillside. Brystal and her friends sprinted into the cave until the blizzard's icy winds couldn't reach them.

"That wasn't a normal blizzard, was it?" Skylene asked.

"No," Brystal said. "The Snow Queen's destruction is spreading beyond the Northern Kingdom! This isn't just about saving Madame Weatherberry anymore— we've got to get to Tinzel Heights and stop the Snow Queen before the whole world is covered in one big storm!"

The future seemed grim, and as they journeyed deeper into Black Bear Cave, their environment became just as dark. Soon the cave was pitch-black and the classmates could barely see one another. They heard another thunderous commotion coming from ahead, and they worried the blizzard had found a way inside.

"AHHHHH!" Lucy suddenly screamed.

"What happened?" Xanthous asked.

"Sorry, I just felt something hairy against my leg," Lucy said. "Tangerina, was that you?"

"Very funny," Tangerina said. "But I'm behind you."

Brystal waved her wand and illuminated the cave

with twinkling lights. All the classmates screamed when they discovered they were surrounded by over a hundred black bears. Brystal and her friends grabbed one another and looked around the cave in terror, but luckily, their panic was unnecessary because all the creatures were sound asleep on the ground. The snoring bears were even louder than the blizzard outside.

"Did someone give them Simple Slumber Sleeping Salt, too?" Skylene asked.

"No, they're hibernating," Emerelda said.

"But it's way too early for bears to hibernate," Xanthous said. "It's still spring."

"The cold weather must be confusing them," Emerelda said. "I doubt they had time to gather enough food to survive for very long."

"Nothing is going to survive a winter that lasts forever," Brystal said. "Now, everyone look for the abandoned goblin tunnel. The Tree of Truth said it's somewhere in the back of the cave."

The classmates searched every corner of the cave and finally found a tunnel flanked by two horrifying goblin statues. Brystal waved her wand, and all the twinkling lights throughout the cave flew into the tunnel to light the passageway. The classmates saw that it was perfectly round, its walls were carved with symbols from an ancient goblin language, and it seemed virtually endless as it stretched into the distance.

Before her classmates could get intimidated by the lengthy tunnel, Brystal led them inside. The students and apprentices walked for hours and hours; the passageway appeared to stretch in a perfectly straight line beneath the In-Between. Brystal tried to trace their steps in her geography book, but the tunnel wasn't recorded in any of the maps, so it was impossible to tell exactly where they were. Eventually the tunnel split into two different directions, and Brystal had the nerve-racking task of choosing which way to go.

"Well?" Emerelda asked her. "Where should we go?"

Brystal looked back and forth at the tunnels, and she glanced up and down at her geography book, but she had no idea where either branch headed.

"I think Tinzel Heights is to the right—wait, to the left—*no, it's to the right!*"

Brystal marched into the tunnel on her right, confident she was making the correct choice. Her classmates followed her, but a few yards into the new tunnel, they noticed someone was missing. Brystal looked back and saw Lucy was lingering behind them.

"Lucy, what are you doing?" Brystal asked.

"We're going the wrong way," Lucy said. "We should take the tunnel to the left."

"No, the tunnel to the right makes more sense," Brystal said. "Trust me, I've thought about this. Black Bear Cave is southeast of the Northern Kingdom, which means this tunnel is heading in a northwest direction. If the tunnel continues in a straight line, it's much more likely Tinzel Heights will be on our right than our left."

"Stop thinking logically," Lucy said. "Goblins aren't logical creatures. They didn't care how straight the tunnel was—they just dug it until they found something."

"But my gut is telling me we should go to the right," Brystal said.

"And *my* gut is telling me we should go to the left," Lucy said. "Look, we always joke that I have a specialty for trouble, and right now, I sense a *lot* of trouble coming from the left. Please, you have to trust me on this—I can feel it in my bones."

Brystal was hesitant to change directions. Her eyes darted between Lucy and the geography book, but she couldn't decide whose instincts to follow. If they made the wrong choice, they'd never make it to the Northern Kingdom in time to save Madame Weatherberry. Fortunately, Brystal didn't have to make the decision on her own.

"I think we should trust Lucy," Tangerina said.

Everyone was shocked by Tangerina's faith in Lucy.

"Really?" Brystal asked. "You do?"

"Absolutely," Tangerina said. "If there's one thing Lucy knows how to do, it's stumble into a bad situation. Her gut would never lead us to safety."

Lucy opened her mouth to argue but then went silent, because she knew Tangerina was right. None of the classmates objected to Tangerina's recommendation— they all knew Lucy had a knack for trouble. Brystal took a deep breath and prayed her friends were correct.

"All right," she said. "We're going to the left."

A couple miles into the left tunnel, Brystal was finally able to breathe easy. The passageway began curving to the right and headed in the direction Brystal had thought the other tunnel would take them. She checked the Map of Magic and was extremely relieved to see her and her classmates' stars appear in the Northern Kingdom.

"You were right, Lucy!" Brystal said. "We're almost to Tinzel Heights!"

Lucy shrugged like it wasn't a big deal.

"Don't mention it," she said. "I've got a sixth sense for danger."

"I don't mean to interrupt this warm moment of recognition," Emerelda said. "But do we have a plan for *how* we're going to save Madame Weatherberry and stop the Snow Queen once we reach Tinzel Heights?"

Brystal had been mulling over a strategy since they entered Black Bear Cave, but she was so focused on *getting* to Tinzel Heights that she hadn't told the others what to expect when they arrived.

"The Tree of Truth told me the Snow Queen is keeping Madame Weatherberry in Tinzel Palace," Brystal said. "We'll go to the palace and lure the Snow Queen out with a distraction. Once she's away, we'll go inside and find Madame Weatherberry. Then we'll wait for the Snow Queen to return, take her by surprise, and . . . and . . . and . . ."

"And *kill* her?" Skylene asked.

"Yes," Brystal said with difficulty.

"How are we going to do that?" Xanthous said. "I

suppose there are more possibilities now that we know witchcraft is an option."

Brystal knew *that* part of the plan was inevitable, but she didn't know how they were going to go through with it. Despite all the suffering and damage the Snow Queen had caused, Brystal couldn't fathom *hurting* her, let alone ending her life.

"I'm not sure yet," she told the others. "But I'll think of something."

· • ★ • ·

As they reached the outskirts of Tinzel Heights, the abandoned goblin tunnel came to a dead end at a huge pile of collapsed rocks. At the top of the pile, they could see beams of light coming from aboveground. Brystal figured this was a good place to depart the tunnel, so she transformed the rocks into a staircase, and the class-mates climbed to the surface.

As the group emerged from underground, the air was so cold the passing breeze burned their skin. Every last inch of the area, for miles and miles around them, was covered in thick snow, and even more snow fell from the gray clouds above.

They had arrived at the base of a towering mountain range with sharp peaks and steep slopes. In the distance to the north, the classmates spotted the pointed towers of Tinzel Palace peeking out from behind the moun-taintops. In the distance to the south, in the heart of a valley below the mountain range, was the small town of Appleton Village. The village was the only place in the Northern Kingdom that hadn't been destroyed, and it was obvious that the country's entire population was gathered there. The cottage homes and shops were surrounded by a sea of tents for all the refugees who had fled there.

Not only did they find themselves in the center of a wintry storm, but the classmates had also surfaced in the middle of a war zone. The base of the mountain was filled with soldiers frantically preparing for battle. A tall man with a black beard gave orders to the soldiers as they ran around him, and Brystal assumed he was the General White she had heard about.

"Get those cannons into position!" the general shouted. "As for the rest of you, I want one row behind me and two rows ahead of me! We must use whatever weapons and strength we have left! This is our last chance to save the kingdom! We cannot let her pass the mountains, I repeat, we cannot let her pass the mountains!"

Just a few dozen men were all that remained of the Northern Kingdom's army. After months of combat, every soldier was exhausted, battered and bruised, and the majority of their armor was damaged or missing. However, the men valiantly pushed through the pain and followed their general's demands.

"These guys aren't going to make it through another battle," Lucy told her classmates. "We've got to do something."

"I agree," Brystal said. "We'll help the soldiers first, and then we'll go to the palace."

The students and apprentices hiked through the snow toward General White. The general was so busy commanding his soldiers he didn't notice the classmates until they were a couple of feet away.

"What the heck are you doing here?" he shouted.

"General White, we're here to help you!" Brystal said.

"This is no place for children!" the general said. "Get to the village immediately!"

"You don't understand, we're Madame Weatherberry's students!" she explained.

"Who?" the general asked.

"Madame Weatherberry!" Brystal said. "She's the woman who's been helping you fight the—"

"I don't have time for this!" General White shouted. "Go to the village before you get yourselves killed!"

Brystal didn't want to waste any time, either—she needed much more than *words* to earn General White's trust.

With a flick of Brystal's wand, all the soldiers' damaged armor was magically repaired, and all their missing plates and pieces reappeared. General White and his men couldn't believe their eyes as Brystal's magic filled in the holes of their broken shields, popped the dents of their smashed helmets, and returned their lost gloves and footwear.

"All right, you can stay," the general told her. "But don't say I didn't warn you."

"Tell us how we can help you," Brystal said. "What do you and your men need?"

"We need a *miracle*," he said.

Just then, one of the soldiers blew a horn, and the entire army turned toward the mountains. The classmates looked up as a menacing figure appeared on the closest mountaintop. The figure wore a tall crown that was shaped like a giant snowflake and a bulky coat made from white fur, and she carried a long icicle scepter. Brystal borrowed a soldier's telescope and saw that the figure was a woman with glowing red eyes and black frostbitten skin. Her hands were so thin and bony they resembled tree branches.

Without a doubt, the students and apprentices knew they were staring at the infamous Snow Queen. Their first glimpse at the most powerful witch in the world was a chilling sight, and they shivered from much more than the cold air.

"She's here!" General White shouted. *"Prepare for battle!"*

As the soldiers hurried into position, the Snow Queen was joined on the mountaintop by four people wearing familiar black cloaks. The classmates gasped in horror when they recognized the cloaked women standing at the Snow Queen's side.

"That's Crowbeth, Newtalia, Squidelle, and Feliena!" Skylene said.

"It can't be!" Tangerina said.

"What are they doing with the Snow Queen?"

430

Xanthous asked. "They're supposed to be helping Madame Weatherberry!"

Brystal felt warmer as anger coursed through her body. There was only one reason to explain why the witches were standing at the Snow Queen's side.

"They must have tricked Madame Weatherberry!" Brystal exclaimed. "The witches are working for the Snow Queen!"

"Those *gizzard suckers!*" Lucy yelled.

Now it made sense why the witches were so desperate for Madame Weatherberry to return to the Northern Kingdom when she wasn't ready. The weaker the fairy was, the easier it would be for the Snow Queen to overpower her. There was no way of knowing how long the witches had been planning their betrayal, but Brystal had a feeling it was their plan from the very beginning.

"Load the cannons!" General White ordered.

"Sir, we have nothing to load them with!" a soldier called to him. *"We're out of ammunition!"*

"I can help you with that!" Emerelda said.

She knelt on the ground and quickly started scooping the snow into large snowballs. Once they were the size of cannonballs, Emerelda transformed the snowballs into heavy emerald spheres and passed them to the soldiers.

"Will these work?" she asked.

It didn't take long for the men to understand what Emerelda was doing. The soldiers dropped to the ground and made more snowballs for Emerelda to transform, and then loaded the emerald spheres into their cannons.

"Prepare to fire!" General White shouted. *"On three! One...two..."*

Before they could fire their first round, the Snow Queen pointed her scepter at the army, and a massive blizzard descended from the sky. There was so much snow, it was all the soldiers and classmates could see around them. The winds were so powerful that Brystal and her friends locked arms to keep from falling.

"FIRE!" General White ordered.

"Sir, we can't see anything in this snow!" a soldier called back.

"I can fix that!" Tangerina said.

The apprentice closed her eyes and concentrated with all her might. Her bumblebees vacated her hair and flew directly into the storm. Her classmates didn't understand what she was doing, but soon they realized Tangerina's concentration stretched far beyond their expectations. Thousands and thousands of bumble-bees flew into the blizzard from all over the Northern Kingdom. The swarm moved through the area like a giant buzzing net, and the insects caught the flakes of snow with their tiny legs. Soon the air was so clear the blizzard was nothing but gusts of empty wind.

General White didn't take the clear conditions for granted.

"NOW!" he ordered. *"Fire at will!"*

The soldiers lit their cannons and pelted the

mountains with Emerelda's ammunition. Each emerald sphere got closer and closer to where the Snow Queen stood. The witch roared angrily and pointed her scepter to the clouds. She summoned a bolt of lightning out of the sky, and it struck the base of the mountain. Suddenly, the ground started to rumble under the army's feet. One by one, hundreds of terrifying snowmen grew out of the snowy ground and crept toward the soldiers like a legion of icy zombies.

"ATTACK!" General White shouted.

The army charged ahead and battled the Snow Queen's frosty warriors. The soldiers courageously fought the snowmen, but they were greatly outnumbered. Brystal knew she and her classmates had to intervene before the soldiers were in trouble.

"Emerelda, keep making those cannonballs! Tangerina, keep clearing the air with your bees! Lucy, Xanthous, and Skylene—follow me! We're going to help the soldiers fight the snowmen!" she said.

"Let's kick some *ICE*!" Lucy cheered.

The classmates ran across the base of the mountain and joined the men in combat. Brystal waved her wand and sent snowmen flying through the air in large bubbles, and she used rainbows like colorful slingshots to fling them into the mountains. Lucy crushed the snowmen with falling pianos, tubas, and harps, and she made deep sinkholes appear at their feet. Xanthous and Skylene put their magic together and melted the snowmen with jets of boiling water. With the classmates' help, the Northern Kingdom's army tore through the snowmen like they were made of paper. The Snow Queen was infuriated to see her adversaries succeeding and she seethed from the mountaintop.

"This is perfect!" Brystal said.

"Really?" Lucy asked her. "Do you have other battles to compare it to?"

"No, I mean this is the perfect distraction!" Brystal said. "I'm going to sneak into Tinzel Palace and rescue Madame Weatherberry while the Snow Queen is occupied!"

"Brystal, no!" Skylene objected.

"We won't let you face the Snow Queen on your own!" Xanthous said.

"I don't plan to," she said. "If the Snow Queen heads back to the palace, then follow her and meet me there! But right now she's fixated on the Northern Kingdom's army! This might be the best opportunity we have to save Madame Weatherberry!"

Brystal's plan made her classmates nervous, but as they looked up at the Snow Queen's unwavering gaze on General White and his men, they knew Brystal was right.

"Be careful!" Lucy said. "I'm too young for you to die!"

"I will!" Brystal said. "Look out for each other while I'm gone!"

When she was certain the witches weren't looking, Brystal discreetly dashed into the mountainside and climbed toward the towers of Tinzel Palace. Brystal kept a watchful eye on the Snow Queen as she went and carefully traveled around the witch without being noticed.

Eventually, the soldiers and classmates gained the upper hand on the snowmen. The Snow Queen decided it was time to send in reinforcements, and she nodded to the witches standing beside her. Crowbeth, Newtalia, Squidelle, and Feliena descended down the mountain and entered the battle.

Although they had always stood and walked like people, the witches threw off their cloaks and revealed bodies that were more animal than human. Instead of arms, Crowbeth had large feathery wings and legs like a hawk. Newtalia had a long scaly torso that coiled like the body of a snake. Squidelle had eight flexible limbs with tentacles like an octopus. Feliena's body was covered in fur, and instead of hands and feet, she had paws with razor-sharp claws. Each of the witches set their sights on a different classmate and preyed upon the children.

Crowbeth spread her wings and swooped through the air, snatching Lucy off the ground like an eagle catching a squirrel. She raised the girl high into the sky and dangled her above the clouds. Lucy squirmed helplessly in the witch's clutches, and Crowbeth cackled as she struggled.

"I hope you enjoy your *fall* as much as you've enjoyed our winter!" Crowbeth screeched.

Lucy closed her eyes and tried to summon a mighty

force to save her. Just as Crowbeth was about to drop her, a flock of squawking geese appeared on the horizon and flew to Lucy's rescue. The geese attacked Crowbeth, using their beaks to pluck the witch's feathers and rip holes in her wings. Soon Crowbeth's wings were so damaged she couldn't keep herself in the air, and the witch plummeted into the mountains. The geese grasped Lucy with their beaks and safely lowered her back to the earth.

"Well, you're not the birds of prey that I was picturing, but you're the best gaggle a girl could ask for," Lucy told the geese.

On the ground below, Xanthous and Skylene went back to back as they were circled by Newtalia and Squidelle. They tried to hit the witches with bursts of fire and water, but Newtalia and Squidelle dodged their efforts with ease.

In one slick spinning motion, Squidelle struck Xanthous's face with all eight of her limbs. The boy fell to the ground, his eyes fluttered shut, and all the flames on his body disappeared. Squidelle lurched toward the unconscious boy; she wrapped her limbs around him and started squeezing him to death.

"It's time to put your flames out forever!" Squidelle grumbled.

However, Xanthous had other plans. When Squidelle was least expecting it, Xanthous awoke from his pretend blackout and tightly fastened his Muter Medal around the witch's neck. Squidelle frantically tried to pull the Muter Medal off, but her tentacles couldn't untie Xanthous's small knot. As her powers began to fade, Squidelle collapsed and flopped onto the ground like a fish out of water. The witch thrashed across the snow, accidentally rolled into one of Lucy's sinkholes, and never resurfaced.

"Skylene, did you see that?" Xanthous asked. "I stopped my flames all by myself! I didn't even need the Muter Medal! *Skylene?*"

His friend didn't respond because she had her hands full. Skylene was pointing at Newtalia and blasting the witch with the most powerful geyser she could muster. Unfortunately, the water wasn't enough to stop Newtalia from creeping closer. The witch dived into Skylene's geyser and swam through it like it was a stream. Newtalia slithered close enough to grab hold of Skylene, and the witch lifted the girl by her collar.

"You ssstupid girl!" Newtalia hissed. "Did you actually think a little water would ssstop me?"

"If I'm being honest," Skylene said, "I wasn't trying to *ssstop* you."

Newtalia had no clue what the girl was talking about, but suddenly, the witch became very stiff. Her drenched body started to freeze in the cold wind, and soon Newtalia was as solid as a statue. Skylene pushed her over, and the witch hit the ground and shattered into a million pieces.

"Skylene, that was brilliant!" Xanthous said. "How'd you know that was going to work?"

"Magic is no excuse to ignore science," she said with a shrug.

Across the way, Tangerina was still in deep concentration as she reduced the blizzard with her bumblebees. Feliena snuck up behind the apprentice and knocked her to the ground, leaving a bloody scratch across Tangerina's face. The girl tried to trap the witch with her honey, but Feliena jumped out of the way, avoiding each attempt.

"You and your friends will never win this fight," Feliena growled.

"I'm pretty sure we *are* winning," Tangerina said. "My friends have already defeated yours."

Feliena's green eyes glanced around the base of the mountain, and she roared angrily when she realized she and the Snow Queen were the only witches left.

"My sisters may be gone, but *I* still have all nine of my lives left!" she growled.

Feliena lunged toward Tangerina, but right as she was about to strike the girl again, she was interrupted by someone clearing their throat nearby. The witch looked over her shoulder and saw Emerelda standing right behind her.

"You may have nine lives, but *diamonds* are forever," she said.

Emerelda grabbed Feliena's paw and squeezed it as hard as she could. Inch by inch, the witch's body was slowly transformed into one large jewel, and Feliena never growled, scratched, or jumped again.

"You're a real gem, Emerelda," Tangerina said. "Thank you."

As the students and apprentices defeated the witches, General White and his soldiers conquered the last batch of snowmen. Their successful defense infuriated the Snow Queen, and the witch screamed so loudly her voice echoed through the mountain range.

"She doesn't look very happy," Tangerina said.

"What is she going to do next?" Skylene asked.

"Whatever it is, it's not going to be pretty," Emerelda said.

"General White!" Lucy called to him. "The Snow Queen is about to show us the ace up her sleeve! Go to Appleton Village and evacuate it while you can! You won't save your kingdom by sticking around here! Help your people safely across the In-Between and take them to the Southern Kingdom! We'll hold the Snow Queen off for as long as we can!"

"Thank you," General White said, and saluted the classmates. "Godspeed, children."

General White led his army toward Appleton Village, and the classmates stayed at the base of the mountain, waiting with bated breath for the Snow Queen to make a move. An eerie smile appeared on the witch's frostbitten face as she plotted her next attack. The Snow Queen slammed her scepter into the mountaintop and caused a powerful earthquake to rattle throughout the mountain range. The snow slid off all the steep mountain slopes, and soon an avalanche of catastrophic proportions was hurtling toward the classmates. If they didn't do something to stop it—*and something quick*—the classmates, the village, and the entire Northern Kingdom population would be decimated in a matter of minutes.

"Xanthous, I think this one's on you, buddy!" Lucy said.

"What?" he asked in shock. "I can't stop an avalanche!"

"You're the only one with the right skill set," she said. "You've got to create a blast of heat that's powerful enough to vaporize that thing!"

"I—I—I don't have that kind of power!" Xanthous said.

"Yes, you do!" Lucy said. "You've got to believe in yourself or the whole kingdom will be destroyed!"

The avalanche was growing, gaining speed as it raced down the mountain. It was so strong it snapped the trees in its path like twigs, and it knocked over boulders that had never been moved. The closer it got, the more frightened Xanthous was. Lucy's words of encouragement weren't helping him, so she tried a different approach.

"Think about the night your father died!" she said.

Xanthous was very confused. *"Why?"* he asked.

"Think about how your father beat you for playing with dolls!" Lucy continued. "Think about the fire that killed him and burned down your house! Think about all the shame and guilt you've had to live with ever since! Think about how you wanted to drown yourself in the lake!"

The traumatic memories made Xanthous's flames rise on his head and shoulders.

"I don't understand," he said. "What does any of this have to do with—"

"Think of all the time you spent hating yourself! Think of all the days you lived in fear of being discovered! Think of all the people who told you it was wrong to be who you are! Think of how badly you wanted to change into someone else!"

Lucy was upsetting Xanthous, and his body was soon engulfed in flames.

"Why are you bringing this up *now*?" he asked.

"Because I know part of you still hates yourself for being different! Part of you still lives in fear of the truth! Part of you still believes you don't deserve to exist! And part of you still believes you'll never be loved for who you are! I know how you feel, because we *all* feel that way!"

Fire started pouring out of Xanthous like lava flowing from a volcano.

"Stop it, Lucy!" he cried. "I don't want to do this!"

"And you don't have to anymore—none of us do! Stop carrying all that shame around! Stop wanting to change yourself! Stop worrying no one will love the real you! None of us have anything to be ashamed of! None of us have to change anything! And we'll always love and accept each other! So let go of the hate and fear that other people have instilled in you! Let it go so you never have to feel it again!"

The avalanche plowed into the base of the mountain,

and the classmates were just seconds away from being pulverized.

"Now's your chance, Xanthous!" Lucy shouted. *"Release all the pain and stop that avalanche from leaving the mountain!"*

"No!" Xanthous cried. *"I can't do it!"*

"Yes, you can!" she yelled. *"Let it out, Xanthous! Let it out!"*

"AAAAAAAHHHHHH!"

The boy fell to his knees and a massive explosion erupted from inside him. As Xanthous's fiery blast collided with the avalanche, the entire mountain range was consumed in a blinding light. Emerelda pulled Lucy, Tangerina, and Skylene into a tight huddle, and then created an emerald igloo to shield them from the heat and the snow. By the time the light faded, not only had the avalanche completely disappeared, but all the snow at the base of the mountain had melted away.

The classmates peeked out from Emerelda's igloo and looked around in amazement. Xanthous couldn't believe what he had done, either, and he stared at the land with wide, bewildered eyes. The boy turned to his friends with a bashful grin.

"That felt really good," he whispered.

"Boy, am I glad that worked," Lucy said.

The Snow Queen was so enraged that the classmates had stopped the avalanche, her frostbitten hands were shaking. The witch turned in a huff and headed back to Tinzel Palace.

"Look—she's leaving!" Skylene pointed out.

"What's she doing?" Tangerina asked.

"She's retreating!" Lucy said. "Come on! We have to get to the palace before she finds Brystal!"

CHAPTER TWENTY

THE SNOW QUEEN

Brystal climbed through the Northern Mountains as quickly and quietly as possible. She was so cold she was convinced she'd never feel warm again, and she became so tired she worried she'd collapse in the snow and never make it to Tinzel Palace. Brystal was afraid the Snow Queen would notice her sneaking through the mountains if she used any magic, so she refrained from casting any spells to assist her, and made the journey entirely on foot.

The majority of the mountain range was so steep

Brystal needed both hands to scale it, and she had to carry her wand in her mouth for most of the trip. She was making great progress until she came to a slope that was so slippery it was nearly impossible to get over. It didn't matter what she grabbed or where she placed her feet, Brystal kept sliding down the slope and having to start the climb all over again. After her fifth attempt, Brystal began to lose hope, but fortunately, something caught her eye that restored her faith.

Peeking out from the thick snow beside her was a yellow daffodil. It wasn't an exceptionally pretty flower—its color had faded and its petals had withered in the cold wind—but by some miracle, the daffodil had survived the freezing weather. Although the flower was very small, it delivered the exact message Brystal needed: *If the daffodil was strong enough to withstand the Snow Queen's storm, then so was she.*

Brystal got to her feet, climbed the slope for the sixth time, and used all her strength to pull herself over its slippery summit.

Soon Brystal was so high in the mountains that the air became thin and it was difficult to breathe. The battle between the Northern Kingdom's army and the Snow Queen was so far behind her, it was nothing but a distant murmur. Brystal knew she was getting close to Tinzel Palace because the towers stretched higher into the sky with every step she took. After an exhausting excursion, Brystal climbed over the tallest mountain peak and finally arrived in the Northern Kingdom's capital.

Tinzel Heights was a large city in the center of the Northern Mountains. Due to the limited space, all the homes and shops were stacked on top of one another, and the narrow roads wound through the capital like a giant maze. Tinzel Palace was in the very center of the town, and it soared to heights that surpassed the mountain range surrounding it. The palace was so tall and lean, and its towers so piercing, that the entire structure looked like a group of sharpened pencils. Brystal couldn't tell what color or materials the palace was constructed from because the entire city was covered in a sheet of ice. She walked slowly and carefully as she traveled through the capital so she wouldn't slip on the frosty roads.

Not only was the city physically frozen, but Tinzel Heights was also eerily frozen in time. The streets were littered with townspeople who had been frozen while going about their daily errands. Brystal peeked through windows and saw frozen butchers, bakers, and locksmiths helping frozen customers in their shops. The homes were filled with frozen fathers, mothers, and children in the middle of household chores. Obviously, the Snow Queen had struck the capital so quickly, the city's people hadn't had time to *react*, let alone run to safety.

Eventually Brystal arrived at Tinzel Palace and crossed the bridge over its icy moat. The front doors were frozen shut, so Brystal used her wand like a torch to thaw them open. As she stepped inside, her first sight of the palace made her gasp—not because of the damage the Snow Queen had caused, but because of how beautiful the palace was. Icicles hung from all the ceilings and archways like pointed chandeliers. The walls were coated with frost that sparkled like crystal. The floor was covered in crackling ice like the surface of a frozen lake. Brystal had no idea what the palace looked like before the Snow Queen attacked, but she couldn't imagine it being any more spectacular than what she was seeing.

Brystal searched through Tinzel Palace, but she couldn't find Madame Weatherberry anywhere. Occasionally, she would see someone at the end of a long corridor or spacious room. Her heart would flutter, hoping it was her teacher, but she only found frozen guards and servants at every turn.

"Madame Weatherberry?" she shouted into the cold palace. *"Madame Weatherberry, where are you?"*

Brystal entered the palace's dining hall and was startled by a gruesome sight. She found the Northern Kingdom's royal family frozen around the long dining table. King Nobleton, the queen, the two teenage princes, and the four young princesses had been enjoying a lavish meal when the Snow Queen struck. Although their skin was pale and there was no color in their eyes, the royal family seemed very much alive. The princes had died in the middle of a food fight, the queen had perished while arguing with her daughters, and the king had frozen while scoffing at all of them. Brystal half expected the family to move at any moment and continue their activities, but the royals never awoke from their icy demise.

Strangely, all the food and plates had been recently swiped off the table to make space for a collection of maps. Brystal inspected the collection and discovered a Map of Magic, a map that showed the whereabouts of the Northern Kingdom's army, and a map that showed the weather in all the kingdoms. She took a closer look at the map of weather and covered her mouth in horror— the powerful blizzard the classmates encountered in the In-Between had spread across the whole world.

Suddenly, the palace's front doors creaked open and the sound echoed through the royal residence. The temperature instantly dropped another ten degrees. Someone with heavy footsteps and rattling breath stormed inside the palace, and Brystal knew there was only one person it could be. The footsteps came closer and closer to the dining hall, and Brystal started to panic—she had thought she would have more time to find Madame Weatherberry before the Snow Queen returned. Brystal didn't know what else to do, so she hid in the cupboard at the bottom of a giant china cabinet.

The Snow Queen burst into the dining hall in a furious rage. The witch knocked over every vase and candelabra in the room and then crept toward the table. She gazed down at her map of the Northern Kingdom's army and saw General White and his soldiers evacuating the people from Appleton Village. The Snow Queen roared angrily and pounded the table with a clenched fist. She then turned to the map of weather, and as she watched her blizzard consume the world, her fury turned into delight. She let out a low raspy cackle and exposed her rotting, jagged teeth.

The Snow Queen's back was turned toward the china cabinet while she viewed the maps, and as Brystal peeked out from the cupboard, it slowly dawned on her what a profound opportunity was before her. This could be the most vulnerable position the Snow Queen had ever been in—right here and right now, with a quick flick of her wrist, Brystal could end the witch's reign of terror forever. She just needed to summon the right magic for the job. Brystal leaned out of the cupboard and pointed her wand directly at the Snow Queen's back.

However, as Brystal imagined *how* she was going to kill the Snow Queen, her train of thought shifted to the moments *after* she killed the Snow Queen. Thousands of lives would be saved, but could Brystal live with herself in the aftermath? How would it feel to slay an unsuspecting woman? Would taking another life change who she was? Would she carry any guilt or regret after it was over? She was paralyzed by her troubled conscience, and eventually, Brystal knew she couldn't go through with it.

"Well?" the Snow Queen growled. *"Do it."*

Brystal jumped at the sound of her raspy voice. She was confused about who the Snow Queen was talking to—Brystal had been so quiet, there was no way the witch could have seen or heard her hiding in the cupboard. She glanced around the dining hall to see if someone else had entered the room, but Brystal and the Snow Queen were the only ones there.

"What's the matter?" the Snow Queen growled. "Are you getting *cold feet*?"

To Brystal's absolute horror, she realized the Snow Queen *was* talking to her—*the witch could see her reflection in a mirror across the hall!*

Before Brystal had a chance to say or do anything, the Snow Queen whipped around and lunged toward the china cabinet. She grabbed Brystal by the throat and raised her into the air. Brystal dropped her wand and used both hands to pry the witch's bony fingers off her neck, but her grip was too tight. She tried to kick the Snow Queen off, but the witch was as strong as a brick wall.

"You should have killed me when you had the chance!" she roared.

As the Snow Queen choked her, Brystal was so close to the witch's face she could see every crack of her frostbitten skin, every crooked tooth of her jagged smile, and the pupils of her glowing red eyes. However, there was something about the witch's eyes that Brystal could have sworn she recognized, and once she noticed it, the rest of the Snow Queen's face became very familiar, too.

"No," Brystal wheezed. *"No, it can't be…"*

The thought was so distressing, Brystal kicked her legs even harder, and her foot knocked the icicle scepter out of the Snow Queen's other hand. The scepter fell and shattered into hundreds of pieces on the floor. As soon as the scepter slipped from her fingertips, the Snow Queen lost all her strength. The witch dropped

Brystal on the floor and collapsed beside her. The Snow Queen tried crawling away from Brystal, but the witch was so weak without her scepter, she could barely move.

Once Brystal caught her breath, she grabbed the Snow Queen's shoulder and forced the witch on her back so they could face each other. The Snow Queen's glowing red eyes slowly diminished and turned into a pair of eyes Brystal had seen many times before.

There was no denying it now—Brystal knew *exactly* who the Snow Queen really was—and the discovery made her heart feel like it had been ripped in half.

"Madame Weatherberry?" she gasped. *"It's you!"*

Brystal had never experienced such shock in her life. As the reality sank in, Brystal's whole body went numb, and she couldn't even feel the freezing air circulating the palace. Her mind was bombarded with millions of questions, but only a single word escaped her mouth.

"How?"

The exposed fairy was humiliated and covered her frostbitten face. She crawled to the dining table and used a chair to pull herself onto her feet.

"I never wanted you to find out," Madame Weatherberry said. "You were supposed to kill me before you learned the truth."

"But . . . but . . . how is this even possible? How could *you* be the Snow Queen?"

"Sometimes good people do bad things for the right reasons."

"Bad things?" Brystal asked in disbelief. "Madame

Weatherberry, nothing could possibly justify what you've done! You've been lying since the day I met you! You've covered the world in a devastating storm! You've destroyed an entire kingdom and taken thousands of lives!"

"IT'S NOTHING COMPARED TO THE LIVES THEY'VE TAKEN FROM US!"

For a split second, the Snow Queen returned to Madame Weatherberry's body. The fairy screamed in agony, as if a creature was trying to claw its way out from inside her. Brystal retrieved her wand to defend herself against the witch. As she watched Madame Weatherberry struggle, Brystal realized her teacher and the Snow Queen *weren't* the same person, but two very different beings fighting over the same body. Eventually, the fairy regained control and suppressed the witch like a growing illness.

"I never meant for any of this to happen," Madame Weatherberry said. "All I wanted was to make the world a better place for people like us—all I wanted was to secure acceptance for the magical community. But I lost myself along the way, and created *her*."

"How could someone lose themselves *that* much?"

Brystal was so befuddled she felt like she might faint. Madame Weatherberry lowered her head in shame and took a deep breath before explaining.

"Do you remember our conversation the day after you were attacked by the witch hunters? We were sitting in my office and you asked me how I managed to stay so optimistic. You asked me why I wasn't consumed with anger. I told you it was because we were *the lucky ones*. I told you that fighting for love and acceptance meant we truly *knew* love and acceptance, and how that notion gave me peace. Do you remember that?"

"Yes, I remember," Brystal said.

"Well, I lied to you," Madame Weatherberry said. "The truth is, I've been angry my entire life. When I was young, I was very sensitive to the world's cruelty, and it filled me with an unbearable fury. I ignored all the good things in my life and focused solely on the injustice around me. I became bitter, I became depressed, and I became *desperate* to get rid of my rage. But I didn't go about taking the proper steps to help myself. I was too embarrassed and prideful to seek the treatment I needed. Instead I pushed all my anger deep within myself, and I hoped if I pushed it deep enough, I'd never be able to find it. Over the years, I added more and more anger to my secret collection, and eventually, I created a monster inside me."

"You mean the Snow Queen lives inside you?" Brystal asked.

"Yes," Madame Weatherberry said. "I spent the majority of my life ignoring her, but I've always known she was there, growing stronger after every heartbreak. With time, I noticed that many people in the magical community were suffering from similar ailments. Our anger manifested itself in different ways—some drank too many potions to numb the pain, others turned to witchcraft as a way to release it—but one by one, I watched my friends lose themselves to their inner demons. I didn't want another generation of fairies or witches to experience what we were feeling, so I decided to devote my life to securing acceptance for our community, so the future would be spared from humankind's hatred."

"So you wrote and published *The Truth About Magic*," Brystal said. "You tried to convince the world there was a difference between fairies and witches—you tried to redefine the magical community to save it."

Madame Weatherberry nodded. "However, the endeavor quickly backfired. My book was banned in all the kingdoms and I became a global pariah. As punishment for my attempts, the Northern Kingdom sent a cavalcade of soldiers to my home in the In-Between. They strapped my husband to a wooden post and burned him alive while they forced me to watch."

"Horence!" Brystal gasped with large eyes. "You're the witch from his story! Horence tried to warn me before I came here. I didn't understand what he was saying at the time, but he was warning me about *you*! He was telling me that *two things* were about to become *one*! That carving in the woods—those were *your* initials!"

"Horence Marks and Snowy Weatherberry," she said. "It feels like a lifetime ago."

"Snowy is your real name?" Brystal asked. "That can't be a coincidence."

"It isn't," she said. "The fairies named me *Snowy*

Celeste Weatherberry after my specialty. They said I started causing storms from the moment I was born."

Brystal had been so focused on discovering her own specialty, she had never asked Madame Weatherberry what *her* specialty was. Now that she knew the answer, she couldn't believe she hadn't figured it out already, and not just because *weather* was in her name.

"On our first night at the academy, there was a horrible thunderstorm," she said. "You summoned that storm because you knew it would frighten us and bring us closer together, didn't you? And after Lucy and I went into the In-Between, you sent us another thunderstorm so we wouldn't leave the castle while you were gone! And two days ago, you sent that snowflake to the academy so I would come to the Northern Kingdom! You've been using the weather to manipulate us from the beginning!"

The fairy nodded again. Brystal scrunched her forehead because something about Madame Weatherberry's story still wasn't adding up.

"But why did the *fairies* name you?" she asked. "When we recruited Emerelda from the coal mine, you said you were raised by a human family. You said they tried to kill you and that's how you got the burns on your left arm."

"I lied," Madame Weatherberry said. "I only told that story to convince Emerelda to join the academy. The burns on my arm didn't come from a fire—it was *frostbite*. The same frostbite that covers me now."

"So you got those marks from using witchcraft,"

Brystal said. "That's why you started covering yourself with gloves and coats. And that's why you wouldn't let Mrs. Vee treat your wounds. The bruise I saw on your face, that was frostbite, too, wasn't it? The more damage you cause as the Snow Queen, the more the frostbite covers you."

Madame Weatherberry looked down at her bony, blackened hands and sighed with a heavy heart.

"Correct," she said. "And the more she covers me on the outside, the more she consumes me on the inside."

"But what led you to witchcraft in the first place?" Brystal asked. "How did you go from writing *The Truth About Magic* to destroying an entire kingdom?"

"After Horence was killed, I used witchcraft for the very first time to bring him back from the dead," she explained. "The spell was a complete disaster. Horence returned to earth as an unnatural being, and my left arm was changed forever—but it wasn't only my arm that changed. I told you the witch in Horence's story died after she conjured the spell—but that wasn't entirely untrue, because part of me *did* die that day."

"How so?" Brystal asked.

"My husband never committed a crime or hurt anyone in his life, but humankind murdered him simply to teach me a lesson. And indeed, I learned a very valuable lesson that day. I suddenly realized I had been foolish for believing *The Truth About Magic* was enough to change humanity's ways—they would never be persuaded by the *logic* or *empathy* of a book. The only way humankind was going to accept the magical community was to *fear* and *need* the magical community. *We* had to give them a problem, and then *we* had to be the solution. And as I laid eyes on my frostbitten skin for the very first time, I knew exactly what problem to create."

"The Snow Queen?"

"Precisely," Madame Weatherberry said. "To become the Snow Queen, I had to access all the anger that I had suppressed over the years. Just like your wand put you in touch with your magic, the scepter put me in touch with my rage. Unfortunately, there was so much fury waiting inside me, the task became overwhelming. Each time I picked up the scepter, the Snow Queen became stronger and stronger, and it became harder and harder to fight her off. I asked Feliena, Newtalia, Squidelle, and Crowbeth to join me and help me with the transitions—but the witches cared more about revenge than acceptance. They allowed the Snow Queen to control me and they used her like a weapon."

"But why didn't you stop?" Brystal asked. "If the Snow Queen was consuming you like this, why did you keep returning to the Northern Kingdom?"

"Because the world wasn't taking her seriously," Madame Weatherberry said. "My plan would only work if the *whole world* saw the Snow Queen as an unstoppable threat. It would take complete desperation for them to turn to witches and fairies for help. But King Nobleton consistently lied to the other monarchs about the destruction the Snow Queen caused. So to gain the other sovereigns' attention, I increased the attacks and made each one grander than the one before. However, it didn't matter how hard the Snow Queen struck the Northern Kingdom, the other monarchs ignored her. The only way King Champion, Queen Endustria, and King Warworth would ever acknowledge the Snow Queen was if her destruction went worldwide."

"And now you've covered all the kingdoms in a blizzard," Brystal said. "You've given humankind the ultimate problem, so how is the magical community the solution? Who are they supposed to turn to for help?"

Madame Weatherberry hesitated before responding, and Brystal could tell the answer was going to be difficult to hear.

"The academy," she confessed.

"What?" Brystal gasped.

"If the world had recognized the Snow Queen's first attack, I would have never had to involve anyone else," Madame Weatherberry said. "I could have been the problem *and* the solution to my plan. But as the attacks continued, I realized the Snow Queen would likely devour me before I completed my mission. So I recruited a coalition of fairies to finish what I had started in case I was compromised."

"So *that's* the real reason you started the academy?" Brystal asked in disbelief. "You weren't training us to help and heal people, you were training us to be your *assassins*?"

"I wasn't lying when I said teaching was the

greatest privilege of my life," Madame Weatherberry said. "Watching you and the others flourish has brought me happiness like I've never known before. I'm deeply remorseful to put you in this position now, but in order for us to succeed, I'm afraid you have to fulfill the promises you made me."

Brystal felt like her stomach had been yanked out of her body.

"Madame Weatherberry, no!" she cried. "I could *never kill you!*"

"Yes, you can," Madame Weatherberry said. "When humankind learns that *you* saved the world from global annihilation, they'll finally have a reason to respect and accept the magical community. You and your classmates will lead the world into a new era where people like us will never have to hide in the shadows, where they can live openly without fear, and they'll never be crippled by their anger again."

"No!" Brystal said. "There has to be another way!"

"This is the only way," Madame Weatherberry said. "Believe me, I wish there was an easier path to take, but this is the greatest opportunity that fairies and witches have had in centuries! If we don't do this *now*, it may be another millennium before we have a second chance!"

"No, we'll find a better solution!" Brystal said. "Come back to the academy! We'll find a way to cure you from the Snow Queen!"

"It's too late for that," Madame Weatherberry said. "Scepter or no scepter, the Snow Queen has consumed me past the point of no return. I have days—maybe *hours*—before she takes me over completely. And I don't want to spend the rest of my life imprisoned inside her."

Madame Weatherberry raised Brystal's wrist so the tip of her wand was pointing to her teacher's frostbitten forehead.

"Please, I'm begging you!" the fairy said.

"No! I can't do this!"

"We don't have a choice!"

"I'm sorry, Madame Weatherberry, but I—"

"YOU'LL NEVER BE ABLE TO DEFEAT ME, YOU STUPID INCOMPETENT GIRL!"

Suddenly, the Snow Queen resurfaced in Madame Weatherberry's body. The witch wrapped her hands around Brystal's throat and started choking her again. Brystal couldn't breathe, her vision blurred, and she started losing consciousness. If she didn't act fast, she would die in the Snow Queen's hands. Brystal raised her wand, pointed it at the witch, and made a decision that she would regret for the rest of her life.

BAM! A bright and powerful blast erupted from Brystal's wand and hit the Snow Queen directly in the chest. The witch flew across the dining hall and landed hard on the floor. Brystal kept her wand raised as she cautiously approached the Snow Queen's motionless body. The witch's eyes fluttered open, but instead of seeing the Snow Queen's glowing red gaze, Madame Weatherberry's eyes returned.

"What... what... what just happened?" she asked.

"I made my decision," Brystal said. "And I'm not killing anyone."

"You should have finished her! All of this could be over by now!"

"You might be right," Brystal said. "And later I may regret sparing you, but not nearly as much as I would regret ending your life. I'll never understand why you chose violence as a road to peace, I'll never understand why you chose fear as a remedy to hate, but I will *not* repeat your mistakes. If I'm going to continue down the path you've paved, then I'm going to walk it at my own pace."

"Brystal, humankind will need *proof* that you slayed the Snow Queen! My death is the only way you'll earn their trust!"

"You're wrong!" Brystal said. "You don't have to die for your plan to succeed—on the contrary, all the destruction you've caused, all the fear you've instilled, and all the lives you've taken will all be meaningless without you!"

"What are you talking about?" Madame Weatherberry asked.

"You said it yourself. The only way humankind will respect and accept the magical community is if they *need* the magical community," Brystal explained. "But the minute the Snow Queen is destroyed, humankind won't *need* us anymore. They'll forget she ever existed, they'll rewrite history to say *they* were the ones who conquered her, and the world will go back to hating fairies and witches just like before. But if you stay alive, and keep the world in fear of the Snow Queen striking again, the magical community will *always* have leverage over humankind."

"But I can't keep fighting her like this," Madame Weatherberry said.

"I don't believe that for a second," Brystal said. "You said you only have *days* or *hours* before the Snow Queen consumes you completely—well, I say you have *years* or *decades* left in you. You're giving up because you don't *want* to fight her anymore, but the Madame Weatherberry I know and love would never let me quit like this, and I'm not going to let you, either."

"But what do you suggest I do? Where do you suggest I go?"

"I suggest you use whatever strength and time you have left to get as far away from civilization as possible. Take yourself deep into the Northern Mountains and get lost in a cave somewhere. Find a place that's so far removed not even a Map of Magic would detect you. Send a gentle snowstorm through the kingdoms every now and then to remind humankind that you're still around, but whatever you do, keep yourself alive."

"But if she consumes me and returns?"

"Then we'll be ready for her," Brystal said. "We'll find other fairies around the world and recruit them into the academy. We'll train them using the lessons you've taught us and prepare them to face her. We'll create such a strong coalition of fairies that the Snow Queen will never stand a chance against us."

The front doors of Tinzel Palace creaked open and the sound of several sets of footsteps echoed through the corridors. Lucy, Emerelda, Xanthous, Tangerina, and Skylene entered the royal residence, and Brystal could hear their hushed voices as they searched for her.

"It's your classmates!" Madame Weatherberry said. "They can't see me like this! If they discover the truth, they'll be devastated, they'll lose faith in everything I've ever taught them!"

"Then don't let them," Brystal said. "Follow my plan! Leave the palace before they see you!"

"But what will you tell them? They can never know what I've done!"

"I'll tell them the truth," Brystal said. "I'll say that after a long battle, the Snow Queen finally overpowered you, but you managed to scare her off and send her into seclusion first. That's all they need to know."

The classmates' footsteps were growing closer in the corridor outside the dining hall. Madame Weatherberry looked back and forth between Brystal's pleading face and the open doorway, but she couldn't decide what to do.

"Please, Madame Weatherberry," Brystal said. "I know it's not what you planned, but I know *this* is what's best for all of us! And *that* is a promise I can keep forever."

There wasn't time to think of a better option. Madame Weatherberry let out a deep sigh that came from the bottom of her weary soul and accepted Brystal's proposal.

"Look for the northern lights," the fairy said.

"What do you mean?" Brystal asked.

"The lights will be my signal to you," Madame Weatherberry said. "As long as there are northern lights in the sky, you'll know I'm winning the fight. And the minute they disappear, it means the Snow Queen is coming back."

"All right," Brystal said. "I'll watch the lights."

"Good," the fairy said. "Now help me to the door in the corner. I'll sneak out the servants' corridor before the others find me."

Brystal helped Madame Weatherberry to her feet and escorted her to the door in the corner of the dining hall. Before the fairy left, she had one final thing to say. Madame Weatherberry grabbed Brystal's hand and looked into her eyes with a grave expression.

"Listen carefully, Brystal, because this is the most important lesson I will ever teach you," she said. "Don't make the same mistakes I made. No matter how cruel or unfair the world becomes, *never* forfeit your happiness. And no matter how poorly someone treats you, *never* let anyone's hate rob you of compassion. The battle of good and evil isn't fought on a battlefield—it begins in each and every one of us. Don't let your anger choose sides for you."

As Madame Weatherberry slipped into the servants' corridor, the classmates charged into the dining hall.

They were panting and frantically looked around the room in fear, but they were relieved to see Brystal was safe.

"Oh, thank God!" Lucy exclaimed. "I was afraid I'd have to perform the tambourine at your funeral!"

"I'm fine," Brystal said. "I'm glad you guys are, too."

"Where's the Snow Queen?" Xanthous asked.

"She surrendered and fled into the mountains," Brystal said.

The classmates were overjoyed to hear this and hugged one another in celebration, but Brystal looked to the floor, her face filled with sadness.

"Brystal, what's wrong?" Skylene asked.

"This is wonderful news," Tangerina said. "Isn't it?"

"Wait a second," Emerelda said. "Where's Madame Weatherberry? Did you find her?"

Brystal lowered her head and burst into tears. It wasn't until she was asked about Madame Weatherberry that the truth had finally caught up to her.

"She's gone," Brystal cried. *"She's gone. . . ."*

CHAPTER TWENTY~ONE

DEMANDS

A powerful and unexpected blizzard plowed through the Southern Kingdom for five days straight. Such a storm had never occurred in the kingdom before, and all the citizens were trapped inside their homes as they waited for the icy winds and endless snow to subside. Without any time to prepare for the catastrophic weather, the country's people found themselves in the midst of a natural disaster. Property was severely damaged, farms lost nearly all of their crops and livestock, and soon families ran out of firewood and had to burn pieces of furniture to stay warm.

As the Southern Kingdom endured its fifth day of the terrible blizzard, many began to fear the horrific storm would last forever. However, shortly before midnight, the wind began to die down, the snow started to disappear, and the clouds cleared from the sky. The weather went completely back to normal, as if nothing had ever happened.

In the eastern countryside of Chariot Hills, the storm had been gone for less than an hour when Justice Evergreen received a mysterious knock on his front door. He answered the door in his pajamas and was surprised to see a royal carriage waiting for him outside.

"What's going on?" Justice Evergreen asked.

"King Champion is holding an emergency meeting at the castle, sir," the coachman said. "He's asked for all High Justices and Justices to join him at once."

Without a doubt, Justice Evergreen knew the meeting was being called to discuss the recent storm. He quickly got dressed in his long black robe and tall square hat and climbed aboard the carriage. By the time he arrived at the castle, the King's throne room was buzzing with High Justices and Justices alike.

"How is the kingdom going to recover from this?" High Justice Mounteclair asked. "It's going to take a massive amount of money to rebuild all the damage— and the treasury is low on funding as it is!"

One by one, the other Justices gave Mounteclair their recommendations.

"Perhaps we can ask the king to sell one of his summer palaces?"

"No, His Majesty will never approve that," Mounteclair said.

"Perhaps we can start a war with the Eastern Kingdom and take their resources?"

"No, it would take too long to stage a reason for war," Mounteclair said.

"Perhaps we can reduce our salaries until the kingdom is on the mend?"

"Now *that* is out of the question!" Mounteclair said. "Come on, men! We have to come up with *one* decent suggestion before the king arrives!"

The sinister Justice Oldragaid glared at his colleagues from a corner of the room. He scratched the stone wall with his long fingernails to get the men's attention. The sound sent painful shivers through their bodies and all the Justices covered their ears.

"Yes, Oldragaid?" Mounteclair asked. "What is your suggestion?"

"I believe *now* is the best time to implement the poor tax I've been advocating," Oldragaid said.

Justice Evergreen scoffed loudly at his rival.

"That's the most absurd recommendation I've ever heard," he said. "The poor have no money to collect as tax—that's why they're called *the poor*."

"Thank you, Justice Evergreen, but I know what *poor* means," Oldragaid sneered. "But *money* isn't the only way to fix this predicament. By introducing the poor tax, the poor throughout the Southern Kingdom would immediately be charged with tax evasion. However, instead of sentencing them to prison time, we'll sentence them to community service, and we'll have a force of free labor to restore the kingdom."

The Justices nodded as they considered the tax and then cheered for Oldragaid's calculating proposition.

"That's a wonderful idea," Mounteclair said. "Now how are we going to explain the blizzard to our people? They'll want to know what caused the strange phenomenon."

"Perhaps we implore scientists to investigate the matter?"

"No, the last thing government needs is more science," Mounteclair said.

"Perhaps we frame it as an act of God?"

"Yes, that's better," Mounteclair said. "But *why* did God do it? Who should he be mad at this time?"

"Perhaps God is mad at cat lovers?"

"No, that won't work because I have a cat," Mounteclair said.

"Perhaps God is mad at vegetarians?"

"No, most of our cattle perished in the storm," Mounteclair said. "We can't have people fighting over food in the name of God—we tried that once and it led to complete chaos."

Once again, Justice Oldragaid scratched the stone wall with his long fingernails.

"Oldragaid, just raise your hand if you have a suggestion!" Mounteclair reprimanded.

"Noted for the future, sir," Oldragaid said. "I was going to recommend we tell our kingdom that God is mad at *poor people*. If we amend the Book of Faith and make poverty a sin, we'll save ourselves from any potential backlash for enforcing the poor tax."

"Another wonderful idea!" Mounteclair declared. "We'll share your proposals with His Majesty as soon as he—"

The doors leading to the sovereign's private office swung open and King Champion joined the Justices in the throne room. The men bowed to the monarch as the king crossed the room and sat on his throne. The sovereign was instantly irritated by the Justices around him and he let out a disgruntled sigh.

"Good morning, Your Majesty," Mounteclair said. "Your timing is perfect, as usual. The other Justices and I have created a plan of action to address the recent—"

"That won't be necessary," King Champion stated. "I've already made arrangements."

Nervous whispering broke out among the Justices—they didn't like it when the king made decisions without them.

"Sir, as the head of your Advisory Council, I must insist you share your arrangements with us before making them official," Mounteclair said.

"I didn't call you here to insist anything—I called you here to *listen*," King Champion stated. "There's no easy way to start this discussion, so I'll get right to the facts. For the last several months, the Northern Kingdom has been under attack by a very powerful witch known as the Snow Queen. To prevent global hysteria, King Nobleton kept the matter a secret. By the time he informed the other sovereigns about the Snow Queen, she had destroyed more than half of the Northern Kingdom, but Nobleton wasn't honest with us about the extent of her destruction. He assured us he could handle the situation, so we did nothing and left it to him. Now Nobleton is dead and all but one village in the entire kingdom has been lost. This week, the Southern Kingdom almost suffered the same fate as the north, but fortunately for us, the Snow Queen was stopped before her blizzard obliterated us."

The news made all the Justices uneasy and they gazed at one another in fear.

"Pardon me, sir," Mounteclair said. "But are you saying a *witch* caused the blizzard?"

"Oh good, you're listening," King Champion quipped. "Early last week, the Snow Queen's destruction spread beyond the Northern Kingdom. Not only did the storm seep into our kingdom, but it stretched to all four corners of the continent."

"But *what* or *who* stopped her?" Mounteclair asked.

King Champion glared at his advisers with a cocky grin.

"Technically, *I* did," he said. "Several months ago, I was paid a visit by a woman named Madame Weatherberry. She was starting an academy of magic and came to the castle, without warning, and asked for permission to recruit children from the Southern

Kingdom. Naturally, I rejected her requests, but then Madame Weatherberry informed me about the seriousness of the Snow Queen's power. She convinced me her future students could defeat the Snow Queen if the witch ever crossed into the Southern Kingdom. In a moment of what I now consider nothing short of *utter brilliance*, I decided to grant Madame Weatherberry the permission she sought. And it just so happens, those students were exactly who stopped the Snow Queen and saved us all from her icy wrath."

High Justice Mounteclair led the room into an enthusiastic round of applause for the king. The sovereign rolled his eyes and silenced the men with his hand.

"Although the Snow Queen was stopped, the witch remains at large," King Champion said. "Madame Weatherberry unfortunately passed away during the ordeal, but her students survived. They've agreed to restore our kingdom with magic and continue protecting us from the Snow Queen. However, in exchange for their services, the children had a few *demands*."

"Demands?" Mounteclair asked. "What sort of demands?"

King Champion turned toward the doorway of his private office.

"Come on out!" the king called. *"The Justices have been prepared!"*

Suddenly, the room of older men in black robes parted as a group of very colorful children emerged from the office. Brystal, Lucy, Emerelda, Xanthous,

Tangerina, and Skylene made their way through the room and stood at the king's side. The Justices were outraged to see members of the magical community in a royal residence. They shouted profanities and insults at the children, but the classmates ignored the men's outbursts and held their heads high.

It was difficult for Brystal to stand in a room with so many men who had personally tried to oppress her, but she didn't let an ounce of it show. On the contrary, Brystal made a point to look Justice Mounteclair, Justice Oldragaid, and Justice Evergreen directly in the eye so they knew she wasn't afraid of them. She had changed so much since her father last saw her it took him a few moments to recognize his daughter. Despite all Justice Evergreen's efforts, Brystal had become a calm, confident, and dignified young woman, and his mouth dropped open in shock.

"Will the young lady please inform the Justices about the demands we've been discussing?" King Champion asked.

Brystal waved her wand and a long, golden scroll appeared in her hand. Inscribed on the document were the demands they had given the king. The classmates passed the scroll around and took turns reading their demands aloud.

"'Number one,'" Brystal said. "'Magic will be officially legalized in the Southern Kingdom. All prisoners who have been convicted of non-offensive magic, or who are waiting to stand trial for non-offensive magic, will be released from the prisons and workhouses across the kingdom. This also includes privately owned detention centers such as the Bootstrap Correctional Facility. The Southern Kingdom will create social programs to diminish the discrimination directed at magic; however, if anyone in the magical community would like to develop their abilities, you'll invite them to join us at the Celeste Weatherberry Memorial Academy of Magic in the southeast In-Between. A knight named Horence will be waiting to safely escort them through the woods.'"

"'Number two,'" Emerelda read as she took the scroll from Brystal. "'The In-Between will be divided into equally proportioned territories for the people and creatures living there. The west will be given to the dwarfs, the northwest will be given to the elves, the southwest will be given to the ogres, the northeast will be given to the goblins, the southeast will be given to the magical community, and the rest will be given to the trolls. The Southern Kingdom will also send food, medical supplies, building equipment, and other provisions to those territories so they never fight over resources again.'"

"'Number three,'" Xanthous read. "'The Southern Kingdom will establish *education and employment equality*. You will abolish the law prohibiting women from reading, joining libraries, or pursing any profession they desire. Boys and girls can attend any school they wish, including the University of Law and the Chariot Hills School for Future Wives and Mothers.'"

"'Number four,'" Skylene read. "'Starting today, the

original Book of Faith will be the only Book of Faith that Southern Kingdom officials are allowed to reference. The High Justices will no longer make amendments or manipulate religion to serve their political agenda. Furthermore, attending services at the Chariot Hills Cathedral, or any other place of worship, is strictly optional and no longer a requirement.'"

"'Number five,'" Tangerina read. "'All banned books will be reprinted and made available to the public. You will also issue public apologies to the families of all the authors you "silenced" and you'll make your citizens aware of the means and methods you used to find and terminate them.'"

"'Number six,'" Lucy said. "'All rules and restrictions related to creative freedom and artistic expression will be removed from the law. Also, the tambourine will be regarded as the official instrument of the Southern Kingdom and all citizens will be required to play it for a minimum of—'"

Tangerina snatched the scroll out of Lucy's hands before she went any further.

"She's making up that last part about the tambourine," Tangerina told the men. "But the rest is in there."

Once the classmates finished reading the scroll of their demands, the throne room erupted with objections. The Justices screamed their disagreements and reservations until all the men turned bright red.

"This is outrageous!"

"They have no right to order us around!"

"How dare these *heathens* demand anything!"

"They belong in prison, not in a throne room!"

"We will never take commands from the likes of them!"

Brystal raised her hand toward the ceiling and a bright, thunderous blast erupted from the tip of her wand. All the Justices went silent and cowered away from her.

"All of this is *your* fault!" Brystal shouted. "If you had created a world where everyone was treated equally, a world that valued people's differences, and a world that recognized the potential in each citizen—*we wouldn't be having this conversation*! But you've spent your careers fueling the hate, the discrimination, and the oppression that *gave birth* to the Snow Queen! *Her frost is on your hands!* So if you expect us to clean up the mess you've made, then you *will* follow our demands—and if you don't, then I suggest you all go coat shopping, gentlemen, because you're in for a very, very long winter."

The Justices were left speechless by Brystal's remarks. It was rare for anyone to give the men an ultimatum, but a young woman had never spoken to them like that before. Lucy tried to start a slow clap for her friend, but her classmates didn't think it was an appropriate time.

"Your Majesty, you can't seriously be considering these demands?" Mounteclair asked.

"I've already agreed to them," King Champion announced.

"Without consulting us?" Mounteclair asked in shock.

"Yes, *Mounteclair*, without you," King Champion sneered. "As the current situation has proven, I tend to make my *best* decisions when the Justices aren't around. King Warworth, Queen Endustria, and King White have already signed these demands into the laws of their kingdoms, and starting tomorrow, the Southern Kingdom will do the same."

"Who's *King White*?" Oldragaid asked.

"The newly appointed sovereign of the Northern Kingdom," the king explained.

"By whose authority?" Oldragaid pressed.

"By *our* authority!" Lucy declared. "And would it kill you to take a bath and cut your dang nails? I thought you were a sloth until you opened your mouth!"

Oldragaid crossed his arms and fumed in the corner.

"And what are we supposed to call you?" Mounteclair asked the classmates. "Besides 'the six bossiest children on the planet'?"

Brystal and her friends stared at the men with blank expressions. They hadn't decided on a name for themselves yet. Before they seemed unprepared, Brystal chose the first name that came to mind.

"You can call us the *Fairy Council*," she said. "And if you'll excuse us, we have a kingdom to rebuild and a world to save."

Brystal triumphantly led her classmates through the throne room, and they headed for the door. As they went, Justice Evergreen followed his daughter and desperately tried to get her attention.

"Brystal, wait!" Justice Evergreen called to her. "Brystal, slow down!"

She had absolutely nothing to say to her father, so she ignored him and kept walking. Justice Evergreen was embarrassed to be so blatantly disrespected in front of his colleagues. He lost his temper and forcefully grabbed hold of his daughter's arm.

"Brystal Lynn Evergreen, you stop this instant!" he roared. *"I will not be ignored by my own daughter!"*

Everyone in the throne room went still and silent—even King Champion grew tense on his throne. Justice Evergreen's words got under Brystal's skin. Her father had never claimed her as family before, but now that she had saved the world, he suddenly wanted everyone to know she was his daughter. She yanked her arm out of his grip, whipped around to face him, and raised her wand threateningly toward his throat.

For the first time in his life, Justice Evergreen was afraid of his daughter, and he slowly backed away from her.

"That is the last time you will ever lay hands on me," Brystal said. "And don't you dare address me as daughter. You're no father of mine."

CHAPTER TWENTY-TWO

THE TALE OF MAGIC

A stampede of unicorns raced through the In-Between with dozens and dozens of young women on their backs. The majestic steeds retrieved all the workers from the Bootstrap Correctional Facility and transported them to the Celeste Weatherberry Memorial Academy of Magic. The exhausted and emaciated girls were completely rejuvenated by the enchanted creatures beneath them. Many of them laughed and cheered for the first time in years—some for the first time in their lives—and they looked at the thick woods around them with wide eyes and excited grins.

Within two hours of their departure, the unicorns were crossing through the hedge barrier and the young women laid eyes on the academy's picturesque property for the very first time. They were absolutely astonished by all the colorful trees and flowers, the crystal-clear streams and lakes, the sparkling ocean on the horizon, and the soaring gryphons and fluttering pixies in the bright blue sky. The unicorns unloaded their passengers at the castle's front steps, where Brystal, Lucy, Emerelda, Xanthous, Tangerina, Skylene, and Mrs. Vee were eagerly awaiting their new arrivals.

"Pip!" Brystal exclaimed.

She instantly spotted her small friend among the newcomers and ran down the front steps to give her a big welcoming hug.

"I'm so happy to see you!" Brystal said. "I've thought about you every day since I left the facility! I hope you're all right!"

"I'm doing much better now that I'm here," Pip said.

"Did those awful Edgars treat you terribly when I left?" Brystal asked.

"Nothing I wasn't used to," Pip said with a shrug. "You should have seen Mr. and Mrs. Edgar's faces when they got the command to release us from the facility! They had just accepted an order from the Eastern Kingdom for five thousand pairs of boots! Now they have to make them all by themselves!"

Brystal laughed. "I normally don't find pleasure in someone else's misfortune, but just this once, I think it's okay to relish it," she said.

Pip stared up at the castle, mesmerized by its shimmering golden walls.

"I can't believe you did it," she said.

"Did what?" Brystal asked.

"You found a house by the ocean!" Pip said. "It's even better than the one we used to dream about!"

"It's a wonderful place to live," Brystal said. "I think you'll be very happy here."

"I already am," Pip said.

Once all the girls had climbed down from the unicorns, Brystal went to the top of the castle's front steps to greet them.

"Hello, everyone, and welcome to the Celeste Weatherberry Memorial Academy of Magic," she said. "Allow me to introduce you to my friends, Mrs. Vee, Lucy Goose, Emerelda Stone, Xanthous Hayfield, Tangerina Turkin, and Skylene Lavenders."

"You may call me *Madame* Lavenders," Skylene told the girls.

"For those of you who don't remember me from the Bootstrap Correctional Facility, my name is Brystal Evergreen," she said.

"Oh, we remember *you*!" said a girl.

"How could we forget?" said another.

"Well, I'm happy we're all reunited," Brystal said. "This academy was founded by our dearly departed mentor, Madame Weatherberry, and it's thanks to her that we have a place to learn and grow. We're going to honor Madame Weatherberry's legacy by helping you improve and expand your magical abilities. And once you've mastered your skills, we'll venture beyond the academy and use our magic to help and heal the people who need us."

"Over the next few weeks, we'll be teaching you about the five categories of magic—*Improvement*, *Manifestation*, *Rehabilitation*, *Imagination*, and *Protection*," Emerelda said. "But before we give you a tour of the castle or the grounds, we wanted to share a couple of rules we'll expect you to follow while staying at the academy."

"Rule number one," Xanthous said. "Never leave the academy grounds without an instructor."

"Rule number two," Tangerina said. "Always treat everyone with respect."

"Rule number three," Skylene said. "Don't be afraid to make mistakes—that is what learning is all about."

"And rule number four," Lucy said. "Don't do anything I would do."

After the rules were announced, a loud rumbling came from above and everyone gazed up at the castle. A large tower suddenly grew out of the third-floor corridor with enough bedrooms to accommodate all the young women joining the academy.

"Looks like your rooms are ready," Mrs. Vee said. "Before you get settled, you're all going to follow me straight to the dining room for a much-needed meal. But let me warn you from personal experience, if *anyone* in the castle but me offers you food, run as fast as you can! *HA-HA!*"

The bubbly housekeeper led the young women up the front steps and into their new home. Brystal, Lucy, Emerelda, Xanthous, Tangerina, and Skylene beamed with pride as they watched their new pupils enter the academy.

"I can't believe we have *students*!" Skylene said.

"Me neither," Lucy said. "Do you think we're responsible enough for this? Maybe we should have started with a plant or a goldfish first."

"I think we'll be fine," Tangerina said. "I *love* telling people what to do."

"Wait a second," Xanthous asked. "If *we're* the teachers now, then I suppose we're not *classmates* anymore? Are we?"

"Nope, I believe this means we've officially graduated to being *fairies*," Emerelda said.

"We're not *just* fairies," Skylene teased. "We're the *Fairy Council*, remember?"

"It's a shame Brystal didn't come up with a better name," Lucy said. "I have a feeling that one is going to stick around for a while."

The fairies shared a laugh with one another, but Brystal wasn't paying attention. She was gazing across the property, watching the hedge barrier with disappointment.

"Uh-oh," Lucy said. "Brystal's doing it again."

"Doing what?" she said.

"Sadly looking off into the distance," Xanthous said. "You do it all the time."

"I do?" Brystal asked.

"Oh yeah," Tangerina said. "And now we're going to have to spend a minimum of five minutes convincing you to tell us what's on your mind."

"Well, I just don't want to—"

"Trouble us with your concerns?" Emerelda asked. "We know. But the funny thing is, you trouble us more by keeping us in suspense."

"So just spit it out already," Skylene said.

Brystal blushed at the others' playful comments and grinned against her will.

"You know, having such close friends can be a real nuisance sometimes," she said. "I was hoping more people would be here by now—that's why I looked sad. Magic has been legalized for the first time in centuries—I thought people would be rushing to join the academy! But I suppose the magical community isn't ready to come out of the shadows just yet."

"Everyone comes out in their own time," Xanthous said. "We've just got to stay patient and positive, and keep letting them know we'll be here when they're ready."

Brystal nodded. "You're right, Xanthous," she said. "You're *absolutely* right."

After the new students enjoyed a hearty meal in the dining room, the fairies helped the girls get situated in their bedrooms. Once everyone was settled, Brystal headed downstairs to continue watching the hedge barrier for any other guests who might be on their way. As she descended the floating staircase, the doors of Madame Weatherberry's office caught the corner of her eye.

Brystal had been avoiding the office since they returned to the academy. She wanted to believe Madame Weatherberry was still inside and she convinced herself a part of the fairy would always be there if they kept the doors shut. Brystal pictured the fairy sitting behind her desk, eagerly waiting for a troubled pupil to knock on her door and solicit her comforting words of wisdom. However, now that Madame Weatherberry was gone, the new students would be coming to *Brystal* for advice, and an empty office wasn't going to do anyone any good. So she forced herself to push open the wooden doors and stepped inside.

Everything in the office—the clouds drifting along the high ceiling, the bubbles floating out from the fireplace, the shelves of spell books, the cabinets of potions, the glass furniture—was exactly as Madame Weatherberry had left it. The only difference was the missing piece of the Map of Magic that Brystal had cut out. She waved her wand, and the missing chunk of the Northern Kingdom reappeared. Just as they planned, Madame Weatherberry had found someplace so secluded in the Northern Mountains that not a trace of her appeared on the map.

Brystal pointed her wand to the corner of the office, and a large globe appeared. However, unlike a regular globe, Brystal's globe showed her what the planet looked like from space. She spun the globe to inspect the Northern Kingdom and was pleased to see a small patch of northern lights glimmering through the Northern Mountains.

"Hello, Madame Weatherberry," Brystal whispered to the globe. "I hope you're well."

Brystal crossed to the window and checked the hedge barrier in the distance, but there still wasn't any sign of anyone from the magical community. She let out a long sigh and sat down behind Madame Weatherberry's glass desk. It was a subconscious decision to sit in her teacher's former seat, but once she realized where she had placed herself, Brystal quickly leaped to her feet—she wasn't ready for the significance of that just yet.

"I guess this is your office now, huh?"

The unexpected voice startled Brystal. She looked across the office and saw Lucy standing in the doorway.

"I guess it is," Brystal said. "The castle still feels so weird without her, doesn't it? I wonder if it'll always feel like something is missing."

"Probably," Lucy said. "Luckily for us, Madame Weatherberry cast herself a wonderful understudy before she left."

"Thanks," Brystal said. "I hope I can live up to the task."

"Don't worry, I've got enough faith in you for the both of us," Lucy said.

She and Brystal exchanged a sweet smile, and for a

split second, Lucy made Brystal feel like she belonged behind Madame Weatherberry's desk. Lucy, on the other hand, had no problem sitting in their teacher's seat. She made herself comfortable in the glass chair and kicked her feet up onto the desk.

"Everything is going to be different for you now," Lucy said. "Personally, I think I'm going to enjoy being best friends with the most powerful person in the world. Every world leader needs at least *one* controversial friend—I can keep the public distracted if you're ever facing a scandal."

"Oh, please," Brystal said. "I'm not the most powerful person in the world."

"Of course you are," Lucy said. "Did you hear yourself bossing those Justices around? You've got them and the sovereigns in the palm of your hand! They're so afraid of the Snow Queen, they're going to do anything you tell them to."

"Oh my gosh—*you're right*," Brystal said in disbelief. "In just a couple of months, I've gone from a schoolgirl to leader of the free world! How did that happen?"

"It's one heck of a political climb," Lucy said. "What are we going to call you now that you're so powerful? If you ask me, there's no point in having power unless it comes with a fancy title. How about *Commander of Magic*? No, that sounds like a romance novel. *Chancellor of Fairies*? No, that's the name of a terrible one-man show I saw once. *The Fairy Empress*? No, that sounds like a perfume. *Fairy Overlord*? No, too pompous. Oh,

I know! What about *the Fairy Godmother*? To me it says *Yes, I'm a nice person, but I also mean business*."

"I am not ready for a title," Brystal said. "I still can't believe I'm in charge of the academy. I'm going to need a few days before I can accept that I'm also the—"

Brystal went quiet before she finished her sentence. She suddenly realized she was much more prepared for the unexpected position than she had thought.

"Actually, maybe I did know this day was coming," she thought out loud. "Despite all those years when I was told I didn't matter, and despite all the people who told me I'd never amount to anything, I always knew I was destined for a great purpose. It makes no sense why a girl living in the Southern Kingdom would believe such things—at the time, we were only allowed to be wives and mothers—but if it hadn't been for those encouraging little voices inside me, I may never have made it this far. In a way, I feel like everything in my life has been preparing me for this moment. Perhaps that's been my specialty all along—the *faith* I had in myself?"

"Nah, that just sounds like narcissism," Lucy said. "I figured out your specialty a long time ago—I'm surprised you still haven't."

"Well?" she asked. "What is it?"

"Think about all those times you put others before yourself," Lucy said. "You helped your brother study for an examination you weren't even allowed to take. You took the fall for Pip when she got caught borrowing blankets in the facility. You spent your first night in the academy reading *The Tales of Tidbit Twitch* to the others so they wouldn't be frightened of a thunderstorm. You baked me a whole cake from scratch just so I'd feel welcome here. And then when I ran away, you went into a dangerous forest to find me! Even now, instead of letting your newfound power corrupt you, you're focusing all your efforts on making the world a better place. Obviously, you have a specialty for *compassion*."

Brystal was touched by Lucy's words.

"Do you really think I have a specialty for compassion?" she asked. "You're not just sucking up to me because I'm *the Fairy Godsomething-or-other* now, are you?"

"Nope, I mean it," Lucy said with a confident nod. "Otherwise, it would just be *weird* how much you care about helping other people."

Just then, the wooden doors swung open and Emerelda, Xanthous, Tangerina, and Skylene charged into the office. The young fairies' cheeks were bright red and they were all panting as if they had been running.

"Oh, there you are!" Emerelda said. "We've been looking all over the castle for you!"

"Brystal, you should come outside!" Xanthous said. "Like, *now!*"

"Why? What's wrong?" she asked. "Are the students okay?"

"The students are fine," Tangerina said. "People from the magical community have started showing up!"

"That's wonderful!" Brystal exclaimed. "How many have joined us so far? A dozen? Ten? At least five?"

"Umm," Skylene said with difficulty. "I'm not the best with numbers, but I'd say it's more like... *all of them*."

Brystal thought her friends were playing a practical joke on her, but the look in their overwhelmed eyes didn't waver. She turned to the enlarged Map of Magic above the fireplace and was stunned to see that the majority of the stars were moving through the southeast In-Between toward the academy. Brystal ran to the window, looked toward the hedge barrier in the distance, and gasped at what she saw.

At the edge of the property, Horence and his three-headed horse had crossed through the barrier and were followed by a line of hundreds and hundreds of people. The line kept coming and coming until there were almost a thousand members of the magical community inside the academy grounds.

The travelers were both young and old; some traveled in groups or with families, while others traveled completely alone. They had clearly journeyed from places near and far. Most had recently been released from prisons, while others had spent their entire lives on the run or in hiding. Regardless of their differences, each and every person wore the same expression of sheer amazement as they gazed around the property, and not just because of the vibrant plants and enchanted animals. For the first time in their lives, the magical community was laying eyes on a place where they would be safe from persecution, a place where they could be themselves without discrimination, and most important, a place that they could finally call home.

"We're going to need a much bigger castle," Brystal said.

"And name tags," Lucy said. "Lots and lots of name tags."

Without wasting another second, Brystal, Lucy, Emerelda, Xanthous, Tangerina, and Skylene hurried out of the office, ran down the floating staircase, and emerged on the castle's front steps to greet the newcomers. The travelers gathered around the castle and looked up to the fairies for guidance.

"Pssst, Brystal!" Lucy whispered. *"Say something."*

"What should I say?" she whispered back.

"I don't know," Lucy said. *"Something inspirational like you always do."*

Brystal's friends nudged her forward and she nervously waved to the large crowd. As she looked into all the hopeful but weary eyes of the magical community, Brystal was reminded of her final moments with Madame Weatherberry, and she knew exactly what she wanted to say.

"Hello, everyone," she said. "I can only imagine what you've all been through to get here—both in life and on the road. This historic day is possible thanks to a long history of brave men and women making tremendous sacrifices. And although the fight for acceptance and freedom may seem like it's over, our work isn't finished. The world will never be a better place for us until we make it a better place for all. And no matter what challenges await us, no matter whose favor we've yet to earn, we cannot allow anyone's hate to rob us of our compassion or dampen our ambition along the way.

"The truth is," Brystal continued, "there will always be a fight, there will always be bridges to cross and stones to turn, but we must *never* forfeit our joy to the times we live in. When we surrender our ability to be happy, we become as flawed as the battles we face. And too many lives have already been lost for us to lose sight of what we're fighting for now. So let's honor the people who gave their lives for this moment to happen—let's cherish their memory by living each and every day as freely, as proudly, and as joyfully as they would have wanted us to. Together, let's begin a new chapter for our community, so when they tell our story years in the future, *the tale of magic* has a happy and prosperous ending."

ACKNOWLEDGMENTS

I'd like to thank Rob Weisbach, Derek Kroeger, Alla Plotkin, Rachel Karten, Marcus Colen, and Heather Manzutto for all their guidance and assistance.

All the wonderful people at Little, Brown, including Alvina Ling, Megan Tingley, Nikki Garcia, Jessica Shoffel, Siena Koncsol, Stefanie Hoffman, Shawn Foster, Danielle Cantarella, Jackie Engel, Emilie Polster, Janelle DeLuise, Ruqayyah Daud, Jen Graham, Sasha Illingworth, Virginia Lawther, and Chandra Wohleber, for making *A Tale of Magic...* possible.

Also, Jerry Maybrook for directing me through the audiobooks, and of course the incredible Brandon Dorman for his breathtaking artwork.

And finally, all my friends and family for their continued love and support.

Turn the page for an excerpt from

A Tale of Witchcraft....

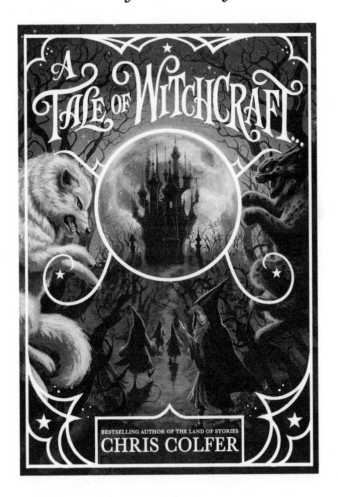

AVAILABLE OCTOBER 2020

A Righteous Return

It began in the dead of night while the world was asleep. As soon as all the streetlamps faded and the lanterns dimmed throughout the Southern Kingdom, hundreds of men across the country—three hundred and thirty-three to be exact—suddenly emerged from their homes at precisely the same moment.

The peculiar activity wasn't rehearsed. The men never discussed it with one another or even knew the identities of their fellow participants. They were from different villages, different families, and different backgrounds, but the men were secretly united by one malevolent cause. And tonight, after a long hiatus, that cause had finally called them into action.

Each man stepped into the night wearing a pristine silver robe that practically glowed in the moonlight. Matching silver cloths with two slits were draped over their heads to mask everything but their eyes, and the crest of a ferocious white wolf was proudly displayed across each of their chests. The ominous uniforms made the men seem more ghostlike than human, and in many ways, they *were* ghosts.

After all, it had been centuries since the Righteous Brotherhood's last appearance.

The men left their homes and journeyed into the darkness, all heading for the same location. They traveled entirely on foot and walked so softly their footsteps didn't make a single sound. When their towns and villages were far behind them, and they were certain they hadn't been followed, the men lit torches to illuminate the road ahead. But they weren't on the paved roads for very long. Their destination was far beyond any beaten path, and it wasn't on any surviving maps.

The Brotherhood hiked over grassy hills, stomped through muddy fields, and splashed across shallow streams as they trekked through uncharted territory. They had never been to their destination or seen it with their own eyes, but the directions were so ingrained in them that every tree and boulder they passed felt as familiar as a memory.

Some men traveled greater distances than others, some moved faster or more slowly, but at two hours past midnight, the first of the three hundred and thirty-three travelers started to arrive. And the site was exactly as they expected.

At the southernmost point of the Southern Kingdom, at the base of a rocky mountain bordering the South Sea, were the ancient ruins of a long-forgotten fortress. From afar, the fortress looked like the carcass of an enormous creature that had washed ashore. It had jagged stone walls that were horribly cracked, chipped, and stripped of all color. Five crumbling towers stretched into the sky like the fingers of a skeletal hand, and sharp rocks hung over the drawbridge like the teeth of a giant mouth.

The fortress hadn't been occupied by a single soul in over six hundred years—even the seagulls avoided it as they hovered in the night breeze—but regardless of its eerie appearance, the fortress was sacred to the Righteous Brotherhood. It was the birthplace of their clan, a temple of their beliefs, and it had served as their headquarters during the days when they imposed their "Righteous Philosophy" upon the kingdom.

There came a time when the Brotherhood was so effective at enforcing the Righteous Philosophy that such a base of operations was no longer needed. So the Brotherhood boarded up their beloved fortress, hung up their uniforms, and retreated from all activity. Over time, their existence became a rumor, the rumor became a myth, and the myth was nearly forgotten. For generations the Brotherhood sat quietly on the sidelines and relished in the profound ways they had shaped the Southern Kingdom—and, by extension, the rest of the world.

But the world was changing. And the Brotherhood's time of silence was over.

Earlier that day, a series of silver flags with white wolves were raised throughout the towns and villages in the Southern Kingdom. The flags were subtle and hardly noticed by most citizens, but to these three hundred and thirty-three men, the flags conveyed an unmistakable message: *It was time for the Righteous Brotherhood to return.* And so, later that night, once their wives and children were asleep, the men quietly retrieved their uniforms from their hiding places, wrapped the silver robes around their bodies, draped the silver masks over their faces, and promptly left their homes for the fortress in the south.

The first arrivals took position on the drawbridge and guarded the entrance. As the other clansmen trickled in, they lined up one by one and recited an ancient passphrase before entering:

"Nothing can flee the three-thirty-three."

Once they were permitted inside, the Brotherhood gathered in a vast courtyard at the heart of the fortress. The men stood in complete silence as they waited for the rest of the clan to arrive. They watched one another with extreme curiosity—none of them had ever seen a fellow clansman before. The men wondered if they recognized any of the eyes peering through the masks surrounding them, but they didn't dare ask. The first rule of the Righteous Brotherhood was never to disclose one's identity, especially to one another. As they saw it, the key to a successful secret society was keeping *everyone* a secret.

At five hours past midnight, all three hundred and thirty-three members were finally present. A silver flag bearing a white wolf was hoisted above the tallest tower to mark the Brotherhood's official return. Once the flag was raised, the High Commander of the clan revealed himself by placing a crown of sharp metal spikes on his head. The men bowed to their superior as he climbed to the top of a stone platform, where all three hundred and thirty-three pairs of eyes could see him.

"Welcome, brothers," the High Commander said with open arms. "'Tis a glorious sight to see all of you gathered here tonight. Such a meeting has not been held in over six hundred years, and our forefathers would be triumphant to know the Brotherhood has survived the test of time. For generations, the principles and responsibilities of this Brotherhood have been passed down from father to eldest son in three hundred and thirty-three of the Southern Kingdom's finest families. And on our fathers' deathbeds, we each swore an oath to devote our entire existence—this lifetime, and whatever lies beyond it—to protecting and upholding our Righteous Philosophy."

The High Commander gestured a hand to the Brotherhood, and they passionately recited the Righteous Philosophy in perfect unison.

"Mankind was meant to rule, and men to rule mankind."

"Indeed," the High Commander said. "Our philosophy is not just an opinion, it is the *natural order*. Mankind is the strongest and wisest species to ever grace this planet. We were meant to dominate, and our dominance is the key to survival itself. Without men like us, civilization would collapse and the world would return to the chaos of primitive times.

"For thousands of years, this Brotherhood has battled the dark and unnatural forces that threaten the natural order, and our ancestors have worked tirelessly to ensure mankind's rightful supremacy. They destabilized the communities of trolls, goblins, elves, dwarfs, and ogres, so the talking creatures could never organize an attack against us. They deprived women of education and opportunity to prevent the weaker sex from rising to power. And most important of all, our ancestors were the first to wage war against the blasphemy of *magic* and send its wicked practitioners into oblivion."

The clansmen raised their torches high above their heads and cheered for their ancestors' *heroic* deeds.

"Six centuries ago, this Brotherhood accomplished its greatest feat yet," the High Commander continued. "Our ancestors carried out a meticulous plan to put King Champion I on the throne of the Southern Kingdom. And then they surrounded the young king with an advisory council of High Justices, who were under the Brotherhood's control. Soon, the Righteous

Philosophy became the foundation of the mightiest kingdom on earth. The talking creatures were ostracized and stripped of rights, women were legally banned from reading books, and magic became a criminal offense punishable by death. For six hundred magnificent years, mankind ruled without opposition. With the Righteous Philosophy safely secured, our Brotherhood slowly faded into the shadows and enjoyed a prolonged period of rest.

"But nothing lasts forever. The Brotherhood has been reassembled tonight because a new threat has emerged that was unimaginable until now. And we must eliminate it *immediately*."

The High Commander snapped his fingers, and two clansmen hurried out of the courtyard. They returned a moment later carrying a large painting and set it on the stone platform beside their superior. The painting was a portrait of a beautiful young woman with bright blue eyes and light brown hair. She wore sparkling clothes, and white flowers adorned her long braid. Although she had a kind smile that could warm the coldest of hearts, something about the young woman made the Brotherhood uneasy.

"But it's just a *girl*," said a man in the back. "What's so threatening about that?"

"That's not just any girl," said a man in the front. "It's *her*—isn't it? The one that people are calling *the Fairy Godmother*!"

"Make no mistake, my brothers, this young woman is

dangerous," the High Commander warned. "Underneath the flowers and the cheerful grin lies the greatest threat the Righteous Brotherhood has ever encountered. As we speak, this monster—this *girl*—is destroying everything our ancestors created!"

A nervous murmuring swept through the courtyard, prompting a man to step forward and address the anxious clan.

"I've learned a great deal about this Fairy Godmother," he announced. "Her real name is *Brystal Evergreen*, and she's a criminal from Chariot Hills. Last year she was arrested for *female literacy* and *conjuring magic*! She should have been executed for her crimes, but Brystal Evergreen was spared because of her father, Justice Evergreen. The Justice used his connections to lessen her punishment, and instead of death, she was sentenced to hard labor at the Bootstrap Correctional Facility for Troubled Young Women. But Brystal Evergreen was only there for a couple of weeks before she escaped! She fled to the southeast In-Between and joined a devilish coven of fairies. She's lived there ever since, developing her sinful abilities with other heathens like her."

"I'd say her abilities are more than developed now," the High Commander chimed in. "Recently, Brystal Evergreen bewitched King Champion XIV into amending the laws of the Southern Kingdom. The In-Between was divided into territories so that the talking creatures *and* the fairies would have proper homes. Women were granted permission to read and seek higher education.

But worst of all, Brystal Evergreen orchestrated the worldwide *legalization of magic*. Virtually overnight, every trace of the Righteous Philosophy was stripped from the Southern Kingdom's constitution!

"But Brystal Evergreen's reign of terror doesn't end there, my brothers. She has since opened an atrocious school of magic in the Fairy Territory and invited all members of the magical community to move there and develop their own unnatural abilities. When she's not teaching, Brystal Evergreen travels across the kingdoms with a crew of colorful degenerates known as the Fairy Council. They've captured the world's attention and affection, claiming to 'help' and 'heal' those in need, but our Brotherhood will not be fooled. The magical community's objective is the same today as it was six hundred years ago: *to brainwash the world with sorcery and enslave the human races*."

The Brotherhood roared so loudly the ancient fortress shook.

"High Commander, I fear we're too late," said a man in the crowd. "Since the Fairy Council appeared, the public has grown fond of magic. I've overheard people discussing the surprising benefits the legalization has caused. Apparently, illnesses and diseases are on the decline, thanks to the new potions and elixirs that are sold in apothecaries. They say agriculture is thriving, thanks to the spells protecting crops from frosts and insects. And people are even crediting our growing economy to the popularity of enchanted products. Every man wants a self-driving carriage, every woman wants a self-sweeping mop, and every child wants a self-swinging swing set."

"Public opinion is starting to shift about the other amendments, too," said another man in the crowd. "In fact, most of the Southern Kingdom actually *likes* the changes King Champion has made to the constitution. They say allowing women to read and pursue education has elevated discussions in our schools, causing students of both genders to think outside the box. They say splitting the In-Between into territories has made the talking creatures more civilized, and now travel and trade between kingdoms is much safer than before. All in all, the people believe the legalization of magic has sparked a new age of prosperity, and they wonder why it didn't happen sooner."

"Their prosperity is a façade!" the High Commander shouted. "A hydrangea may be beautiful, its scent may be pleasurable, but it is still *poisonous* when ingested. If we don't restore the Righteous Philosophy, our world will begin to rot from the inside out. Too much diplomacy will make us *weak*, too much equality will kill *initiative*, and too much magic will make us *lazy* and *incompetent*. The magical community will dominate us, the natural order will crumble, and absolute pandemonium will ensue!"

"But how do we restore the Righteous Philosophy?" a clansman asked. "King Champion is under Brystal Evergreen's influence—and we need the king to amend the law!"

"Not necessarily," the High Commander teased. "We need *a* king, not *the* king."

From the new creases in his mask, the Brotherhood could tell their superior was smiling.

"And now for the good news," the High Commander said. "King Champion XIV is eighty-eight years old, and it won't be long until a *new* king sits on the throne of the Southern Kingdom. And as fate would have it, the *next* king is very sympathetic to our cause. He respects the natural order, he believes in the Righteous Philosophy, and like us, he has not been fooled by the Fairy Council's displays of compassion. The next king has agreed to abolish King Champion's amendments on one condition: that we appoint him as the new leader of our Brotherhood and serve him as a *Righteous King.*"

The clansmen couldn't contain their excitement. Until now, they could never imagine a world in which the sovereign of the Righteous Brotherhood and the sovereign of the Southern Kingdom would be one and the same. If they proceeded wisely, such an outcome could solidify the Righteous Philosophy for generations to come.

"What about the magical community?" a clansman asked. "They're more powerful and popular than ever before. Surely they'll revolt against the new king or bewitch him just as easily as the old king."

"Then we must terminate them *before* the next king takes the throne," the High Commander said.

"But how?" the clansman asked.

"The same way our Brotherhood nearly obliterated the magical community six hundred years ago. And believe me, brothers, our ancestors were armed with much more than a *philosophy*."

The High Commander climbed down from the stone platform and then hoisted it up like a gigantic hatch. To the Brotherhood's surprise, he exposed a massive arsenal full of cannons, swords, crossbows, spears, and chains. There were enough weapons to mobilize an army of a thousand men, but these weapons were unlike any the clansmen had ever seen. Instead of iron or steel, all the blades, arrowheads, and cannonballs were made from a red stone that glowed and flickered, as if fire were trapped inside. The crimson light flooded the colorless courtyard and mesmerized all the clansmen.

"It's time for the Righteous Brotherhood to come out of the shadows!" the High Commander declared. "We must honor the oath we made our fathers and strike before our enemies have a chance to prepare. Together, with our new Righteous King, we will preserve the natural order, restore our Righteous Philosophy, and exterminate the magical community once and for all!"

The High Commander removed a loaded crossbow from the arsenal and fired three arrows at the portrait of Brystal Evergreen—one into her head and two into her heart.

"And just like any colony of pests, first, we must *kill its queen*."

Andrew Scott

Chris Colfer

is a #1 *New York Times* bestselling author and Golden Globe–winning actor. He was honored as a member of the TIME 100, *Time* magazine's annual list of the one hundred most influential people in the world, and his books include *Struck By Lightning: The Carson Phillips Journal*; *Stranger Than Fanfiction*; the Land of Stories series: *The Wishing Spell, The Enchantress Returns, A Grimm Warning, Beyond the Kingdoms, An Author's Odyssey*, and *Worlds Collide*; and the companion series A Tale of Magic . . . .

Have you read Chris Colfer's
The Land of Stories series?